Eclipse

ECLIPSE

The Lost Book of Ascension

Dirk Strasser

Chimaera Publications

First published by Macmillan Momentum in 2013
Macmillan Momentum eBook editions published in 2013
This edition published in 2014 by Chimaera Publications

Chimaera Publications / Aurealis Books
www.aurealis.com.au
PO Box 2164, Mt Waverley Vic 3149, Australia

National Library of Australia Cataloguing-in-Publication entry: (hardback)
Creator: Strasser, Dirk, author.
Title: Eclipse: the lost book of ascension / Dirk Strasser.
ISBN: 9781922031853 (hardback)
Series: Books of ascension; 3.
Subjects: Fantasy fiction.
Dewey Number: A823.3

National Library of Australia Cataloguing-in-Publication entry; (paperback)
Creator: Strasser, Dirk, author.
Title: Eclipse: the lost book of ascension / Dirk Strasser.
ISBN: 9781922031822 (paperback)
Series: Books of ascension; 3.
Subjects: Fantasy fiction.
Dewey Number: A823.3

Praise for Eclipse and the Books of Ascension

'There is a great feeling of mythic inevitability to *Eclipse*; so much has Strasser invested into the mythos of the Mountain and its peoples one cannot help but feel, as the last acts play out, that Strasser is not so much telling a story but relating a version of a strangely familiar legend. This is, perhaps, the greatest praise that can be given to *Eclipse*. It not only provides a fitting climax to the Ascension trilogy, but one that captures the essence of the series as a whole. Imbued with the same sense of wonder and majesty that permeate *Zenith* and *Equinox*, *Eclipse* is the ending that fans have been waiting for, and one that will delight new converts for years to come. I cannot recommend this series highly enough.'
–Alex Stevenson

'An epic ending to an epic fantasy trilogy! Dirk Strasser gave an amazing ending to his series with *Eclipse*. Looking back on the first two books in the series, I feel like I was right alongside Atreu during his journey. His character arc made for an engaging reading experience. The pacing of this final book was effortless and showcased Strasser's skill as a fantasy writer... These books have shown me why I appreciate and love fantasy so much.'
–Pretty Little Pages

'All of the parts of this trilogy blend so effortlessly. And this final book is the perfect culmination. This series is one that fantasy fans will adore and fly through. If you haven't discovered Dirk Strasser's Books of Ascension series, do yourself a favor and pick them up. You'll not be disappointed.'
–Amazon review

'*Eclipse...* gathers all loose threads and plot points into an epic finale that outshines the previous parts of the series in terms of complexity and epic-ness. The scales have never been higher, the fate of the world hanging in the balance. With great writing, characters who go through such steady development readers can easily follow along on their journey, and an epic, engaging world, Dirk Strasser has weaved an intriguing fantasy series that is a must-read for all fans of epic fantasy.'

–I Heart Reading

'I must commend Dirk Strasser for his ability to deftly weave scene after scene, emotions and action into a pace that flows with ease, never too fast, but always filled with rich detail. When I finished this last book in the trilogy, I was sad to leave Atreu's world... When a reader becomes that engrossed, that connected to the tale and its people, that is the sign of masterful writing!'

–Tome Tender

'I enjoyed this book immensely and recommend it to any fan of fantasy! It grabs you and holds you from the first page of the first book to the last page of the third book as hidden secrets are revealed through tense story-telling. For those who like fantastic journeys, I say: "Buy! Buy!".'

–Amazon.de (translated from the German)

'*Eclipse* is a rarity – a final volume of a trilogy that is more than a simple conclusion. It has its own strong, internal narrative without sacrificing its duty to unite the complex themes, threads and characters of the first two books. It is a thoroughly satisfying novel, with a mature and multi-layered approach to fantasy tropes, adding a welcome freshness to the genre. Its dialogue and characterisation are first rate.'

–Michael Pryor, author of *The Laws of Magic*

'I really think it's a great achievement, because Strasser has layered so much sophistication and insight (and wisdom) into the story. It builds to a mighty crescendo – and it really proves that

Fantasy can have as much bite and guts and meaning as SF, any day.'
   –Van Ikin

'The trilogy is complete – rounded off in a very satisfying manner. And the total of the whole is bigger than any of the parts.'
   –Richard Harland, author of *Worldshaker*

'More of this please... a real story, real characters with believable backgrounds... a colossal canvas... and a good story.'
   –*Australian Realms*

'Strasser handles the elements of mysticism with insight and still keeps an entertaining flow... a mind-blowing metaphysical experience.'
   –*The Courier-Mail*

'Strasser's unique blend of adventure, esotericism, Eastern mysticism, and fantasy makes for compelling reading... Strasser has not just written down a legend, rather, he has crafted one.'
   –Amazon review

'Strasser's descriptive writing style made me feel like I was actually watching this on the big screen... I recommend this series to science-fiction and fantasy lovers. In particular those who like stories centered around epic journeys like *The Lord of the Rings*.'
   –Readers and Writers Connect

'This one will set the heart aflutter for the true fantasy reader... and with a dose of spiritualism and action tossed in the mix, it's bound to attract the attention of several genres.'
   –For the Love of Books

'The world Dirk Strasser has created is genuinely original and fascinating... with characters so engaging that I really found it hard to stop reading.'
   –Shane M Brown, author of *Plaza*

Also by Dirk Strasser

Zenith: The First Book of Ascension

Equinox: The Second Book of Ascension

Stories of the Sand

Graffiti

Aurealis Duo: Transalienation

Aurealis: The Collectors' Edition (co-editor)

The Aurealis Mega Oz SF Anthology (co-editor)

Aurealis – Australian Fantasy & Science Fiction (co-editor)

For Lucy

Acknowledgements

Some lost books are eventually found. I would like to offer my deepest thanks to the people who have helped the story to breathe: Van Ikin, Richard Harland, Michael Pryor, Stephen Higgins, Lucy Strasser, Mark Dusting, Malcolm Parsons, Eugen Strasser, Erika Strasser, Joel Naoum and Vanessa Lanaway.

When the Mountain becomes the Abyss
And what you breathe becomes what you expel
You will find what is hidden.

When the sun becomes night
And you become what you believe
You will find your heart.

When the Reader becomes the Teller
And the searcher is the one found
You will find the truth.

–The Book of Maelur

The Lost Book

Can you see them? The Teller's words are floating through the air and taking shape above your head. Clouds are whispering into half-forms as you capture the words in a place just beyond your vision. Breathe slowly. You will see them. Inhale. Exhale.

Can you see the story breathing ...

*

You are on a pre-dawn slope, and the snow is crunching under your feet as you walk. With every step, vapour clouds from your lips. Around you are boulders and sharp-toothed rocks, looming out from the white blanket. You twist and turn to avoid them.

As thin, sour tendrils of light snake into the sky, you see the still, dark waters of a giant lake in the crater below. You are about to remember why you are here when you hear a voice.

You stop dead. You had believed you were alone.

You round the next boulder slowly and see a dark, angular figure on a large, flat-topped rock to your left. The man – at least, you fervently hope it is a man – is seated with his head turned towards the paling stars. He is chanting words that sound strangely familiar, yet you cannot find meaning in them. The man's voice is sad and thin, and carries a rhythm. Its pattern escapes you just as you think you have found it.

You notice that other figures have climbed onto the rock. Again, you hope that the pre-dawn light is playing tricks and that these are also men. As the first rays of the sun pierce the Mountain peak, the chanter's voice evaporates into the still air, and the other figures break into a frenzied, yet strangely controlled, activity.

The first realisation you have makes you shudder. You can see that the men placed a body on the smooth surface of the rocky platform. You can see that they are taking various instruments out of the sacks they carry with them. You can hear a sawing sound, and your next realisation causes you to tremble to the core: they are cutting up the body. Then the pounding starts, and you know they are crushing the bones and skull to a pulp.

You cannot look away. There is something about the way the men perform their task that draws your eyes and your heart. There is no hate on the rock for the man who has died. The cutting and crushing is done with precision and it is done with reverence.

Moments later, the chanter stands and places his fingers in his mouth. A sharp whistle cuts the Mountainside. You follow the gaze of the men and see dark geyers circling in the sky above. The birds cry and screech as they swoop down on the pulped remains. Like a swarm of wasps, they descend, and then dig into the flesh and pulverised bones with their talons and beaks.

As the clear sky lightens above the surrounding cliff tops, the screeching stops and the geyers ascend again. You follow their ever-increasing circles as they fly into the heavens, and you wonder what it would be like to be buried in the sky.

When your eyes can no longer focus on the tiny black dots above you, you shift your gaze to the lake, which has now taken on a pale glow. For a moment you think you see an inverted snow-capped Mountain reflected in the waters, like an abyss. You blink, and your attention is caught by the movement of shadows on the flat-topped rock.

You turn just in time to see the last of the dark, angular figures climb down and disappear. The final realisation is one you had been keeping from yourself. These were not men.

Prologue

Whispers always travelled quickly through twilight. *The Search has come to Tsurphu. They seek the Ur.* The soft words hung like a mist over the village, soaking its inhabitants in a dense fog. *The three Tellers have come. They seek the Ur.*

A pale-skinned boy with lidless eyes huddled in his mother's arms, a circle of large boulders their only protection on the wide, flat plains outside Tsurphu. *They seek the beginning.*

'They will not have you, Lhycan.' The mother's voice was barely louder than a breath.

From where the pair crouched, the whispers appeared as a low-lying cloud, with tendrils snaking out in all directions. *The Search has come to Tsurphu.*

Lhycan reached out and swatted a tendril that was weaving its way towards his ear.

'How do we know the whispers are right, Mother?'

Tashil held her son more tightly. 'I have known since you were born that the Tellers would come for you. It has taken nine years for the Search to reach Tsurphu. As each year has passed, I have given thanks that you were still with me. The Search has almost come to an end – if only I could have kept you hidden until Zenith.'

'Let us run, Mother,' said Lhycan.

'There is nowhere to run to,' said Tashil.

Lhycan's shoulders twisted and jerked as the fog thickened around them. 'They cannot take me against my will.'

'*It is your will to come with us.*' A deep voice shot out at them from the fog, and Lhycan and Tashil froze.

Lhycan strained his lidless eyes through the gloom to see three hooded figures taking form as they passed between the boulders. When they came to a halt, he saw that they each wore a long, thick robe gathered by a clasp on the left shoulder which depicted a shattered sun.

'The Ur is found,' said the first Teller.

'We have been wrong before, Gyalsten,' said the second Teller, his voice deeper and more resonant.

'I believe this time the auspices have aligned, Gyalwa. The Ur is found.'

'No,' shouted Tashil, the word cutting a swathe through the whisper mist.

Lhycan stood, his mother making no attempt to hold him. 'How do you know I am the one you seek?' he asked.

'The auspices have led us here, to this place, after nine years of searching,' said Gyalsten.

'Auspices?'

'You are marked by your pale skin. A pale light shone on the sacred waters when the Ur was given his sky burial.'

'My skin?'

'There are other signs. You have remained hidden, as was foreseen. You have been found near the Base, an auspice we should have deciphered earlier.'

Tashil stood to face the Tellers. 'For nine years I have shuddered at the mention of Gyalsten, Gyalwa and Gedhun. Now that I see you, I feel no fear. You want to take my son from me. I despise you for what you will do to him.'

'We will do nothing,' said Gyalsten. 'It is all within him. The Nevronim will only release what he already is.'

'The Nevronim will not have my son.'

'Your son was never yours,' said Gyalsten.

'He was ... and *is*,' said Tashil. 'He will not go with you freely.'

'If he is the Ur reborn,' said Gyalwa, 'then he will come with us of his choosing.'

'You still doubt he is the one?' asked Gyalsten.

'We will only be certain with the Telling.'

'You speak as if I am not here,' said Lhycan.

'You will awaken soon, Ur,' said Gyalsten.

Lhycan's shoulders twisted against what he was being told. 'Am I not myself?'

'You are who you are,' said the third Teller, Gedhun, his voice as sonorous as a slow drum beat.

'You will change him to what you want him to be,' said Tashil.

'The change is a seed within him,' said Gedhun. 'We will bring it forth from his spirit.'

'And if I choose not to come with you?' asked Lhycan.

'You will come,' said Gyalsten, giving each word the same emphasis. 'A spirit is lost and must be found.'

The three Tellers started moving slowly, marking a circle around mother and son. Every third step they would remove a glimmerstone from beneath their robes and place it on the ground. Lhycan and Tashil watched, transfixed. When the circle was complete, the Tellers seated themselves at equal distances along the circumference of the glimmerstones.

Gyalsten was the first to breathe the words. They spilled forth from his mouth and took shape in the twilight beyond his lips. The words turned and folded in on themselves, merging in the air above Lhycan's head.

The image of the Mountain gradually came into focus. Above it shone a bright sun, and Lhycan felt its rays bore into him until a sharp pain burgeoned in the back of his head. He tried to raise his hands to shield his unprotected eyes but found he had no control over his limbs. He was paralysed as the words pulsed through him.

Then Gyalwa's deeper voice joined the first Teller's. The strange words merged with Gyalsten's, words that twisted like roiling storm clouds. As Lhycan stared at the image before him, the Mountain began burning brightly from within. As the light grew, the sun faded, until finally the Mountain shone like the brightest of glimmerstones, and the sun became as dull and opaque as a piece of granite. Just as the transformation was complete, the third Teller joined the other two voices.

As Gedhun's resonating words wafted up to merge with the others, the image shimmered through the dusk as if it was under the rippling waters of a lake. Now fine cracks appeared in the stone sun, as if it was an eggshell. As the cracks widened and the pieces fell away, a small, pale figure emerged from the remains. The figure was carrying something under its arm. Lhycan strained to look through the ripples, but could not see what it was.

Then the image began to disintegrate, until it became again a roiling cloud of words. Gradually the words ceased twisting and weaving through each other and separated, floating gently into the star-filled sky.

Tashil leant towards her son and placed her arms around him to ward off what they had just seen. 'This is what I have feared.'

The three Tellers slowly stood. 'The Telling is clear,' said Gyalwa. 'It is time for us all to prepare for Eclipse.'

'I ... I don't understand,' said Lhycan.

'You will, Ur, you will.'

Gyalwa stepped towards him, and Lhycan could see he was offering a clasp of the shattered sun. It was like the ones the Tellers wore, except the image rippled like disturbed water.

'Don't take it, Lhycan.' Tashil's eyes were on fire. 'No good will come of this. They do not know who you are.'

Lhycan looked sadly at Tashil. 'Have *you* told me who I am?'

'You are my son, Lhycan.'

'And who is my father?'

Tashil's shoulders slumped and she looked away. 'That, I cannot tell you.'

'They have told me who I am,' said Lhycan, indicating the three Tellers. 'I am the Ur reborn.'

Tashil fell silent.

'I will always be the son that you bore,' said Lhycan.

'No,' she said, facing him for a brief moment before turning away. 'I have lost you.'

'Come,' said Gyalsten, 'the time of Eclipse has begun.'

Lhycan tried to embrace his mother, but she remained unmoved. He took the clasp from Gyalwa, glanced up at the sunless sky, and then followed the Tellers into the whisper-shrouded night.

Chapter One

Nine years later ...

Cluric gritted his teeth, closing his eyes as he braced himself. There was the sickening sound of tearing sinew and muscle, and a hot wave of nausea surged up his throat and into his head.

His consciousness twisted and reformed for an instant. All the battles he had fought suddenly crowded in on him. The clash of sword on sword; the high-pitched whine of a thousand arrows shooting through the air; the burning brimstone flames; the grim, determined mouths; the frightened faces; the fleshy, half-torn skin. The eyes that could no longer see.

Then his immediate reality returned.

He looked up at the bearded man who held the bloodied arrow that had just been removed from his shoulder.

'Cluric, Cluric. Are you still with us?' The man's voice seeped through somehow.

'I ... I ...'

The man motioned to one of the other soldiers to quickly bandage Cluric's arm, stemming the blood flow.

Cluric found his voice in the back of this throat where the bile had been. 'Uncle, please don't leave me.'

The bearded man smiled. 'I'm glad you recognise me, Cluric. For a moment your eyes seemed to be somewhere else.' His smile dropped. 'I'm sorry. I had to pull it through your shoulder. It was the only way.'

'I'm all right, Uncle. I've had worse than this.'

The soldier finished bandaging Cluric and then helped him ease back onto the makeshift bed. 'There are others I need to tend to, Hrulth,' he said.

'I'll stay with Cluric,' said Hrulth. 'You go. Do what you have to do.'

Cluric lay there looking at the injured Maelir soldiers all around him. There were almost as many being tended to as attempting to give comfort. Rich tapestries that had once adorned the walls of this great house now formed blood-soaked blankets.

'We lost ground again, didn't we Uncle?' he said.

Hrulth stroked his beard. 'A little, yes, but not as much as we have in the past.'

'So our defeats are not as great as they used to be?'

'The Faemir are a formidable foe. We've known that for a long time.'

Cluric winced in pain as he tried to shift position. 'Peleusar won't go the way of Ariathe and all the others, though, will it?'

'No, Cluric. We've all become better soldiers.'

'Those of us who are left.'

'Yes, those of us who are left.'

'Did Janan and Ronan make it through?'

Hrulth nodded. 'Yes. They've each got some more wounds to add to their collection, but nothing that will keep them out of battle.'

'That's still four of us left then, Uncle.'

'Still four, yes.'

'We've been a great battalion.'

Hrulth looked at his nephew with sad eyes. 'I don't think you could say that. From the moment we left the Rimforest, the

Faemir have been whittling away at us. The instability, the Dusk-rats and the grale have all taken their toll.'

'Do you ever wonder what it would have been like if you and I had just stayed –'

'Don't say it, Cluric.'

'You have to ask yourself, though.'

Hrulth sighed. 'Is this our war, Cluric? Is there any point in asking that question now? Perhaps we could have escaped most of it if we'd stayed in the Lower Reaches. I don't know. I haven't heard news from Treyfell or Teuron in a long time.'

Cluric sighed and looked around. 'We're innkeepers, Uncle. What happened?'

Hrulth pulled at his beard. 'War happened. The Faemir attacked us, remember?'

'But –'

'You're right, Cluric. I was happy in Treyfell serving ales to the wood-smiths and providing lodgings to Rimforest travellers. I'm sure you were just as happy in Teuron – but let's not lose sight of why we're here.'

Cluric turned back to Hrulth. 'Have we made any difference?'

'It's not for one Maelir to ask that.'

'Why not? Isn't that the most important question? Did we make any difference in Ariathe?'

'You know we were too late to have any effect there. The Faemir had virtually razed the city by the time we arrived.'

'What about Walden?'

'Please, Cluric, don't torture yourself. You should be resting. We put up a good fight in Walden.'

'And lost.'

'Yes, but –'

'What about here in Peleusar? Half the city is destroyed.'

'Yes, but only half.'

Cluric waved his good arm at the scene around them. 'And the other half is like this.'

'Look, Cluric, from what the other battalion leaders tell me, while we may still be losing some ground, it will take the Faemir a long time to make any more real gains here.'

'So we have a stalemate. With the bulk of the Faemir forces focused at the Summit, the best we can achieve here is a stalemate.'

Hrulth frowned. 'Cluric, if you've had enough then we can try to get you back to the Lower Reaches. It may be possible.'

'I don't know, Uncle.' Cluric tried to shift again, but was met with a sharp pain in his shoulder. 'This wasn't what I thought war would be like. What about all the old stories? The great heroes. The legends. Where are they? I don't see any.'

'I'm looking at one.'

'Ha.'

'I think I am. You've got a fire in you. A slow burning mirwood fire – that's what true heroes have.'

A deep rumbling sound approached from the distance and the ground started shaking.

'Don't tell me the instability is starting again,' said Cluric. 'I was hoping to be able to get some sleep while the Faemir regroup.'

They watched the walls tremble, knowing that if the instability was powerful enough to bring the roof down on them, there would be no escape. Yet all they could do was wait for it to end.

The shaking eventually eased and the air was still again.

'You know, Uncle, I would have panicked at one time when the ground shook like that, yet I don't think I'm any braver than I used to be.'

'I know what you mean. We're just numb, aren't we?'

Cluric laughed. 'Not brave. Just numb.'

Suddenly he felt very tired. His eyes began to close.

'I shouldn't have kept you talking,' said Hrulth. 'I'm sorry.'

'It's all right, Uncle. I didn't want you to go. This was exactly what I needed. If you weren't here to remind me of what things used to be like, I think I would go mad.'

'Rest now, Cluric.'

Cluric could feel his breathing changing. 'I would go mad,' he whispered as his eyes closed.

As he drifted off, he was vaguely aware of the new battle sounds that had begun to emanate from the other side of the city.

*

The sunlight warmed Cluric's face, and he could almost feel his shoulder healing as he, Hrulth and four other soldiers made their way through the wide, deserted streets of Peleusar.

The last two days had been the strangest of the campaign. At night, there had been cries and screams coming from the Faemir-controlled half of the city, but the days had been silent, devoid of the familiar battle sounds. The Maelir forces had taken advantage of the inexplicable lull to strengthen their defences and barricade themselves in more securely, determined not to concede further ground. It was only on the third day that the patrols had begun venturing further afield. Cluric and the others were now well into Faemir territory, but so far there had been no sign of the Faemir warriors who had been engaging the Maelir in pitched battle.

They came to the end of a cobbled street, where it widened into a huge square that had obviously been a marketplace in better times. Upturned carts, fractured trestles and the stench of long-rotted produce greeted them as Hrulth motioned the patrol to stop.

Cluric drew his sword with his good arm and peered out into the sunlit square. Shreds of gaily coloured material danced in the light breeze, skipping across the ground in front of them. Cluric realised after a moment that the dark red that dominated the colours was blood.

'Where are they all?' he whispered.

Hrulth shrugged as he scanned the rooftops of the single-storey buildings that surrounded the marketplace. 'No sign of Faemir archers. I've got a good feel for an ambush now, and I don't think there's anyone here.' He motioned to Ronan and another soldier to start checking the rooftops.

Cluric picked up one of the shreds of material and looked at it closely. 'This blood is fairly fresh.'

Hrulth frowned. 'But this has been Faemir-held territory for weeks. As far as I know, no Maelir soldiers have set foot here in all that time.'

'It's not making much sense, is it?' said Janan.

'These battle cries at night,' said Cluric. 'Have they been coming from the Faemir half, or has the wind been carrying the sound in strange ways and playing tricks on us?'

'I think we know enough about the wind patterns in Peleusar by now to rule out sound-tricks,' said Hrulth.

'What, then?' said Janan. 'Are we being aided by reinforcements from downslope?'

'Perhaps,' said Hrulth, stroking his beard. 'Perhaps. Although we've had no reports, and as far as we know all Maelir battalions are bunkered down across the Mid-Reaches.'

'Has this been a ruse?' said Cluric. 'Have they given us Peleusar so that they can send extra forces to Crosanct and the Upper Reaches?'

There was a shout from one of the rooftops to the right. Cluric looked up and saw one of the Maelir soldiers gesturing towards him. 'Ronan's found something.'

Hrulth led the others down an alleyway and then up a narrow flight of stairs onto the flat-roofed building where Ronan stood.

'Look at this,' said Ronan.

Cluric and the others looked at the Faemir arrows strewn across the roof.

'Some of these are broken,' said Ronan, 'but most of them are intact.'

Hrulth bent down to examine the stone surface. 'There are fresh bloodstains here. The Faemir didn't go willingly, that's for sure.'

'So we *are* getting help from someone,' said Janan.

'It looks like it … but …' Hrulth's voice trailed off.

'… but how can someone have attacked the Faemir without our knowledge?' finished Cluric.

'And where are they now?' asked Hrulth.

Cluric looked down at the market square below. It was ten times the size of the square in Teuron. He tried to imagine what it would have been like on market day. The noise, the bustle, the smell of exotic spices. What a pity he had never seen it in all its glory. Instead, all he saw were torn shreds of coloured cloth fluttering across deserted cobblestones.

'All right,' said Hrulth, 'let's fan out and check all the rooftops first. Then we'll have a good look down below. I want to find out what's been happening here.'

As Cluric turned to go to the next building, he felt a sharp stab of pain from the wound in his shoulder.

*

As the day wore on, the patrol pushed further into what had been Faemir-held Peleusar. The territory was abandoned, and there was evidence of a struggle in many strategic places. It was obvious the Faemir had not gone without a fight, but there were no bodies.

The soldiers were several hours from the Maelir strongholds when they decided to rest before heading back. Cluric wiped the sweat from his brow and took a draught from his canteen.

'Do you remember the ale barrel you took with you from Treyfell, Uncle?' he asked, rays of the late noon sun warming his face.

Hrulth laughed. 'What an old fool I was. I had no idea what war was all about.'

'Who did?' Cluric took another drink of water.

They both fell silent. The other soldiers were sitting with their backs against a large stone fence. Some were staring into space; others had their eyes closed.

No one spoke for a while. It was an unexpected moment of

peace in a long campaign. Cluric absently held up his fingers and watched the shadow they made on the wall behind him.

His thoughts turned to the strange shadow puppeteer he had met on the day he left Teuron to join the war against the Faemir. What had happened to Belzalel? He had said he was bound for Ariathe too, but the funny little man never made much sense. And what of his other travelling companion, the Ascender Atreu? They could have been such good friends, had their paths taken them to the same places. Where was Atreu now? Did he make it to the Summit? Did he see Zenith? Was he still alive? With so many rumours of the slaughter of Ascenders, could he possibly have survived?

Cluric half closed his eyes. And Edric? How was his brother faring at their inn in Teuron? Was the ale still flowing there, or were they drinking only water, too? Were the farmers still grumbling about having to take their clay-caked boots off before they were allowed to come in? Was Edric still throwing out those whose tongues had been loosened by too much ale? It seemed strange, now, that Cluric had always seen Edric as the brave one. He sighed. He had long ago given up thinking about who was brave and who was cowardly. It was impossible to tell.

For the first time in a long time, Cluric felt himself relax. For once, the Faemir threat wasn't just around the corner. The loudest sound he could hear was that of his own breathing. He drifted into a state of semi-consciousness ...

A shadow play started on the wall in front of him. Two figures were battling in a furious sword fight. First one would push the other back, then the other would regain the lost ground. The thrusts and parries became increasingly frantic, but the two combatants nullified each other's efforts through their fury. In the end, they stood toe to toe, neither giving an inch.

Finally, they collapsed with exhaustion, swords falling from their hands. They lay, their chests heaving, unable to move. After a while their black shadow bodies seemed to lengthen and distort, then started to merge with the wall behind them. Everything began to shake, then a black hole suddenly appeared. As the two combatants lay paralysed, the hole grew rapidly, and finally swallowed them ...

Cluric awoke with a start, his hand instinctively reaching for his sword. He glanced at the sky and realised dusk was approaching.

'Hey!' he cried, getting to his feet. 'It doesn't take long for us to forget we are soldiers.'

The others all stirred. Hrulth was the first to stand. 'I thought I left this foolishness back in the Rimforest,' he said.

Ronan shook his head. 'It was so peaceful for once. Perhaps the war is over?'

Hrulth growled, trying to make himself sound angrier than he was. 'Don't be a fool.' Ronan had only voiced what they had all been thinking, but they couldn't afford to believe it just yet. It was a hope only – a hope that couldn't be trusted. 'Let's get back. We're a long way from Maelir-secured territory and it will be dark soon.'

The patrol quickly readied itself, regaining the battle-hardened posture that had become instinctive over the last year.

As they made their way back, Cluric felt a sense of dread rapidly overtake him. The strange half-dream of the shadow puppet play had unnerved him.

'Do you feel anything, Uncle?' he asked, as he strode alongside Hrulth.

'What do you mean?'

'Like we're being watched.'

'I don't like being in a deserted city like this, if that's what you mean.'

'No. I have a very strong sense that we are being watched by many eyes.'

'Faemir?'

'Perhaps. I'm not sure.'

'There could still be a lone Faemir Watcher around, even if all the warriors have gone.'

'That's true, Uncle, but tell me, just before we woke up, were you dreaming?'

'Dreaming? Well ... I was thinking about the inn at Treyfell, and Estla – and Audum, Silth and Fiala. I haven't thought about my family like that for a long time. I imagined I was sitting with Estla around our slow-burning mirwood fire. Silth was playing the lyre and Fiala was plaiting Audum's beautiful red hair.' Hrulth smiled. 'It was almost as if I was an innkeeper again, with a wife and three daughters. Was it a dream, or a vision, or just a thought – I couldn't say. But it was beautiful just the same.'

'Nothing else, Uncle?'

Hrulth looked at Cluric sharply. 'No. What dream did you have?'

'It was a shadow play.'

'A what?'

'A shadow play. You know, the ones puppeteers do behind screens.' Cluric proceeded to describe the sword fight he had witnessed, and the gaping hole.

Hrulth stroked his beard as Cluric finished.

'And ever since the dream ended,' added Cluric, 'I can't escape the feeling that we're being watched.'

'You know,' said Hrulth, 'that's more than a dream. Have you ever had anything like it before?'

'No,' said Cluric. 'It means something, doesn't it?'

Hrulth nodded. 'I usually am a bit dubious about claims of visions. I like to trust my own eyes and ears, but this dream of yours seems to be telling us something important.'

'It was the Maelir and Faemir fighting, wasn't it Uncle?'

Hrulth nodded. 'Both sides have fought themselves to exhaustion – that's clear.'

'Then what was the big black hole?' asked Cluric.

'I don't know.'

'And who would be watching us?'

'Cluric, let's just get back to the barricades. I feel this war is far from over.'

The roads had narrowed to alleys and were now twisting and turning. Gnarled trees crowded in on the soldiers from the cramped, deserted spaces in front of the houses on either side. Dusk had begun to fall like a cold shroud, and the chill of the autumn eve-wind gnawed at Cluric's shoulder.

'Do you remember the Ascender Atreu?' asked Cluric.

'What?' asked Hrulth as he concentrated on scanning the potholes and the side alleys.

'Atreu. Remember, in the Rimforest? The Ascender.'

'Yes, yes, of course, Cluric. Why are you thinking about him? Keep your eyes open. I don't like the feeling I'm getting here.'

'For some reason I was thinking about him. I ... I don't know why. It's tied up with the shadow play.'

'Look, Cluric –'

The sound of running feet came from one of the side alleys.

'Wait!' A voice cried out to them from the growing gloom. A female voice.

Cluric raised his sword. He strained to see the figure that was running towards them. As she got closer, he could see from her tunic that she was a Faemir Watcher.

'Grab her and bind her,' ordered Hrulth, but the Faemir simply held up her hands to show she wasn't carrying a weapon, and allowed herself to be surrounded.

'Please,' she panted between breaths. 'Please take me with you.'

Hrulth was obviously taken aback by the plea. 'You don't have to ask us,' he spluttered. 'Bind her.'

'There's no time,' cried the Faemir. 'I'm coming willingly. Let's hurry.'

'I'll give the orders –'

'Uncle,' said Cluric, seeing the fear deep in the Watcher's eyes. 'Something tells me we had better get moving.'

Hrulth nodded. 'All right. Let's go before it gets too dark for us to see.'

'Do you have torches?' asked the Faemir as they all headed off.

'No,' said Hrulth gruffly. 'We didn't expect to be out after dusk.'

'You Maelir are such fools sometimes.'

Several of the soldiers brandished their swords in her direction, but Hrulth motioned them to back away.

'What has happened?' asked Hrulth. 'Where are all the other Faemir?'

Cluric saw the Watcher swallow.

'Tell us,' said Cluric. 'We need to know.'

'The night creatures,' she said after a moment.

'You mean grale,' said Cluric.

The Watcher began to tremble.

'Where are all the Faemir warriors?' asked Hrulth again.

'Dead,' she said flatly.

'What?' Hrulth gave her a sharp look. 'But it's only been two days. We've been fighting you for months without either of us getting the upper hand.'

'It's not the days,' said the Faemir looking up at the rapidly darkening sky. 'It was the nights that did the damage.'

'So how is it that you survived and all the others died?'

'Can't you tell?' she said. 'Look – no battle armour. I'm a Watcher.'

'I've seen Faemir Watchers fight too,' said Cluric.

'Yes, well, I'm a Watcher and a coward. I hid when the night creatures came.'

The ground suddenly heaved under their feet and the cobblestones to their right broke apart to reveal a chasm.

'Run,' cried the Watcher. 'They're coming again.'

The cobblestones shifted under them and several of the soldiers lost their footing.

'Run!' cried the Faemir again, and Hrulth led the charge towards the Maelir stronghold. All around them, buildings were collapsing in the darkness. Cluric had sheathed his sword to allow himself to run more freely. Somehow he knew instinctively that if this came to a fight, he would be lost.

Horrific bellowing noises, which he knew from bitter experience were grale, filled the night sky. This time they were accompanied by a droning undercurrent that was totally unfamiliar. Cluric didn't look back. He kept his eyes on the street, watching for the potholes and chasms that opened up in his path.

The Maelir barricades were in sight now. Cluric saw the torches burning in front of him. More bellows vaulted into the sky, and he felt his shoulder aching as he ran.

Not far to go, he muttered, as he felt himself dropping behind the others. *Not far to go.*

The street under his feet buckled and he fell.

'Cluric!' Hrulth called.

'I'm all right. Go ahead.' But Hrulth was already by his side, helping him up.

'Are you hurt?' asked Hrulth.

'I think I bruised my knee,' said Cluric, 'but I can still put my weight on it. Come on.'

They dashed for the Maelir stronghold, aware that just behind them, Dusk creatures were pouring out of the ground and into the streets of Peleusar.

The rest of the patrol cheered as the pair finally reached the barricades.

'You are fools,' cried the Faemir Watcher. 'This is only the beginning. Get the fires started. It's the only thing that will stop them.'

Hrulth spoke frantically to the other battalion leaders and the orders to start fires were given.

As Cluric stared out into the blackness, he could see blood-red eyes moving like disembodied spectres through the alleys of Peleusar. The Faemir Watcher, the hated enemy, stood next to him, and he felt her fear.

'You are the first Faemir I've ever seen who was afraid,' he said.

She looked at him, shivering. 'Am I also the first Faemir you've seen without a weapon in her hand?'

Cluric nodded.

'Then I don't see why you're so surprised.'

'You said you were attacked by something worse than grale and Dusk-rats,' said Cluric. 'What is it that terrifies you so much?'

The Watcher closed her eyes as if she was trying to ward off a vision, and uttered a single word: 'Wraiths.'

Chapter Two

*T*he Watcher closed her eyes as if she was trying to ward off a vision, and uttered a single word: 'Wraiths.'

Atreu repeated the last word as he glanced up from his Book and looked at Verlinden, who was lying with her head cradled in his lap. 'Wraiths.'

'Do you know what a wraith is?' asked Verlinden.

Atreu put the Book down and shifted slightly in the bed. 'No – but they are obviously dusk-spawn of the Nazir.'

'You didn't know Cluric for long, did you?' asked Verlinden.

'Only for a short time, but he was a good friend. I almost abandoned my Ascent to go with Hrulth's battalion to Ariathe.'

'That would have been insane,' said Verlinden, 'abandoning your Ascent for battle.'

Atreu ran his fingers through her deep-red ringlets and stared out the window of their room to where the shimmering dance of the Keep lights flashed against the night sky.

'No place on the Mountain is safe,' he said. 'Not even here.'

There was an awkward silence before Verlinden spoke. 'I feel strange, lying here with you, knowing that what you are reading to me is what is actually happening. Your Book – it scares me sometimes.'

'How can you say that? It has brought Maelir and Faemir closer to peace. How can it scare you?' Verlinden had been saying some surprising things in recent days.

'I don't know, Atreu. Can we trust what we read fully?'

Atreu tensed. 'This is my Talisman. How can you say something like that? You might as well ask whether you can trust me fully.'

'Don't react that way. I'm not questioning you. Your Book, though, it doesn't always give you the answers you are seeking.'

'No – but I'm getting more control every day.' He stopped stroking Verlinden's hair. 'I've never heard you speak this way before. The Book's power has been erratic – we both know that – but I never questioned it when you were the one able to read it and I couldn't.'

'What are you saying?'

'Nothing.'

'I think you're suggesting something.'

'Well, are you sure you haven't lost trust in the power of my Talisman since you started to lose the power to read it?'

Verlinden sighed. 'Possibly, Atreu. You might be right. I don't know, I feel things have shifted slightly since we rescued the Faemir and brought them to the Keep.'

'Shifted?'

'I ... I don't know. The Book is becoming yours again when I thought it had been ours.'

'It may change again.'

'Perhaps. I know I could read it for a while when you couldn't, but I feel my grip on its words slipping every day now.'

Atreu tried to stroke her hair again, but felt self-conscious. 'It *is* my Talisman. It has defined my life since I was nine.'

Verlinden lifted her head for a moment. 'That's just it. It's your Talisman. If I can't share its power, then what is *my* Talisman? How can I be a true Ascender without one?'

Atreu leant back into the pillow. 'Should we try to get some sleep? Who knows how long it will be before the Circle is ready for us?'

'With Riell in charge, it shouldn't take as long to make decisions. I still expect us to be summoned soon.'

'Leyvin's still First Speaker, so who knows?'

'I have faith in Riell. In a time of war, the person in charge of the army should be the one in control.'

'I'm not sure if things are going to work quite the way you see them working.' Atreu fell silent, his thoughts coiled in circles. He stroked Verlinden's cheek, desperately trying to still his mind.

'You know, Verlinden,' he said finally, 'my connection with my Book *has* been growing over the last few days. I can feel my power increasing.'

'How?'

'Take what I just read you. Remember Cluric kept feeling he was being watched?'

'That was obviously the Faemir Watcher.'

'Perhaps, but I felt there was more significance to Cluric's feelings.'

'He could have had thousands of pairs of Dusk-spawn eyes watching him when he said it.'

'Yes, but why did he think of me before he had his vision? It doesn't make sense that he would think of a travelling companion from almost a year ago right at that moment. His experiences since then would have overwhelmed any memories of me, wouldn't they?'

Verlinden reached up and pressed her fingers into the base of Atreu's neck. Normally he would enjoy the massage, but for some reason it didn't feel as good this time. 'You were there when he decided to go to war, weren't you? That must have been a crucial decision in his life.'

Atreu tensed. 'Are you blaming me for Cluric being where he is?'

'No, of course not,' said Verlinden. 'It was his decision, from what you've told me. I just felt it would be reasonable for him to think about you.'

'Still ... still ...'

'What?'

'I feel my power has grown since Equinox. I can't explain it, but then, I can never explain anything to do with my Talisman.' He ran his fingers around the edge of the Book. 'I feel that I'm not just reading about events as they happen. There's something more now.'

'Perhaps your power is increasing as mine is waning,' said Verlinden. 'Most of these pages are now totally meaningless to me.'

'One thing I know for sure is that my Book is always changing. Who knows what will happen?'

'Tell me what the difference was this time, Atreu.'

Atreu struggled to find the words. 'It was as if I wasn't simply reading about what was happening ... it was as if I could *influence* the events in some way.'

Verlinden stared at him. 'You influenced what was happening?'

'Yes,' said Atreu. 'That shadow play that Cluric saw. It was as if it had been taken from my mind. The meaning of it is so obvious to me. The Truth of my Zenith was that Maelir and Faemir have to unite in the face of the Nazir attack. That's what was happening in the play. Our armies have fought each other into exhaustion, and while we lie paralysed, the Nazir are climbing out of the big black chasms to destroy both our people.'

Verlinden shook her head, and Atreu could feel the ringlets of hair tickle his skin. 'Were you thinking about your truth as you read the story?'

'No. It wasn't as simple as that. It wasn't a thought, but more like a dream I had stored away, which I had somehow given to him.'

'You're sounding very strange, Atreu.'

'But you have dreams, don't you? Strange things made of half-memories that seem real?'

'Of course I do, Atreu. But I don't pass them on to a living human being through the words in a book.'

'It's no more miraculous than what this Book has already done.'

'It's harder to prove. The evidence that we were reading real events was beyond doubt. I'm not sure about this.'

Atreu looked at her, opened-mouthed. 'You don't believe me?'

'It has nothing to do with belief. You're saying you have some power now. It has always been the Book that has had the power.'

'So that's it – you don't feel I should possess any power.'

'Don't be ridiculous, Atreu. I just don't want you to believe something that isn't true. A false sense of power – both your brother and my sister had it, and look what happened to them.'

Atreu felt a wave of nausea. He closed his eyes as the room started spinning. 'I ... I can't bear to even think of Teyth's fate at the mercy of the Dusk People.'

'And what about Valkyra? What do you think the Nazir will do to her – assuming she survived the grale and Dusk-rats?'

Atreu shrugged. 'After what she has done, I can't find any pity for her.'

'Teyth killed hundreds of Faemir, yet I feel something for his loss. But you feel nothing for Valkyra?'

'No – there would be no war if not for her.'

Verlinden jumped up from the bed in disgust.

'Hey!' shouted Atreu.

'No war?' The veins on Verlinden's neck were bulging. 'How little have you understood? There has been war from the time Maelur led his people to the Mountain. The only difference since Valkyra united us was that we were strong enough to actually challenge you.'

'I'm sorry. I'm sorry. Of course you're right. I can't change the fact that I have no pity for Valkyra, but you're right.' He held out his hand for her to return to the bed. 'Please, we're on the same side now. We both want peace.'

Just then there was a knock at the door, and Verlinden

unlatched it. Micah stood outside, his face showing the strain of a long Circle session.

'Is it time?' asked Verlinden.

'Not quite,' said the Holy Man. 'We're having a short recess first. Can I come in?'

'Of course, of course,' said Verlinden.

Micah sat down at the table and began stroking his beard awkwardly.

'What's wrong, Uncle?' asked Atreu. 'Have things not gone as we planned?'

'In most ways, yes,' said Micah. 'Perhaps I'm just not used to the intricacies of the Circle from the inside.'

'Has the Order of the Wynde been consecrated?' asked Atreu.

'Yes. It was a close vote, which I perhaps shouldn't be surprised about.'

'So the system is still working?' asked Atreu.

Micah nodded slowly, refusing to meet Atreu's glance.

'What's wrong then, Uncle? Will the Circle refuse to give me permission to find the third Book? Is that the problem?'

'We'll go anyway,' said Verlinden. 'The Circle has no power to deny us permission.'

'No, wait,' said Micah. 'I don't know how the Circle will vote on your quest. The fact that you will be enacting Praether's last words will carry considerable weight.'

'Do we care what sixty old men vote?' asked Verlinden.

'Some of us are not so old.' Micah gave a weak smile. 'Please, let's not dismiss the Circle. I want to keep it functioning – I thought we all did. In order to do that, we must accord it the power to judge as it wishes, whether we approve or not.'

'Not if it is going to go back to its old ways,' said Verlinden. 'I thought things had changed.'

'The third Book isn't the issue, is it Uncle?' said Atreu, still trying to catch Micah's eye.

'Not directly.' The Holy Man took a deep breath. 'Atreu ... I ... have not been entirely honest with you.'

Atreu's eyes narrowed. 'What do you mean?'

'I promised you that there would be no secrets between us.'

'I remember the promise clearly, Uncle. We were dangling in a basket at the end of a long rope at the time.'

'I ... I half-believed it when I made the promise, but in my heart of hearts I knew I had to keep one last Holy Order secret from you.'

Atreu could feel his body tense. 'Another secret?'

Micah looked at him. 'The final Ritual for Ascenders before they can truly complete their Ascent and enter a Holy Order.'

Verlinden's eyes suddenly blazed with the same fire as her hair. 'This secrecy is so ingrained with you people. I can't believe there's something you haven't told us. I thought you were on our side – it looks like you're still on no side but your own.'

'Look, we –'

Verlinden waved away the words. 'I don't want to hear any more of your pathetic excuses.'

'Don't dismiss me like that,' said Micah, the blood rushing to his face.

'Do you mean, don't be an impertinent Faemir?' she said, stepping back.

Atreu moved between them. 'All right, we *are* on the same side now.'

'Are we?' asked Verlinden, glaring at Micah.

'As I said, Verlinden,' said the Holy Man, 'we've consecrated the Order of the Wynde – no one would have imagined that would ever be possible. A windrider now sits in the Circle, which is unheard of. We have over two hundred Faemir warriors within the Keep, free to carry swords. You yourself have been accepted as a successful Ascender – do you understand the enormity of the change for us?'

Verlinden took a step back. 'I'm accepted as an Ascender?'

'Yes,' said Micah. 'The Circle has accepted that you fulfil all the criteria for an Ascender. You experienced Zenith, and we have accepted that the Book is your Talisman as well as Atreu's. A type of sharing of Talismans has occurred before.'

'So we've done it?' said Atreu, drawing a breath.

'Yes, we have,' said Micah.

Atreu and Verlinden looked at each other for a moment, as the lights of the Keep flickered and danced outside their window, and then they stepped towards each other and embraced.

When they drew apart, Atreu said, 'Now tell us this final secret.'

Micah frowned. 'I can't.'

'What?' said Verlinden.

'Look, both of you. We all want to reform the Circle, don't we? We don't want it, and the system that goes with it, completely destroyed.'

'If possible,' said Verlinden flatly.

'We have to leave the fundamental Rituals in place,' said Micah, 'or we'll have chaos.'

'What is this secret?' asked Verlinden.

'You will find out in your audience with the Circle. I just wanted to warn you that something further is to be revealed to you.'

'So this is for your own conscience,' said Verlinden, 'and not for our benefit.'

'In part, yes. I'll admit to that.' Micah looked at Atreu. 'But please don't feel I've betrayed you. This is the final Ritual for Ascenders to determine which Holy Order to enter. I couldn't tell you about it.'

'*The Holy Orders.*' Verlinden spat the words.

'They are changing too,' said Micah. 'You two are now the only remaining Ascenders. We have to complete what has been started.'

'Perhaps I will enter a Holy Order of my own creation,' said Verlinden, 'or perhaps I'll choose not to enter a Holy Order at all.'

'Look,' said Micah, 'anything is possible. If an apotheosis has occurred as Praether was suggesting, then everything will change again, but we need to complete the final stage.'

'And the final judgement will be at spring Equinox?' asked Atreu.

'If we're all still alive,' added Verlinden.

Micah nodded. 'Yes, if we're all still alive. Both of you, I am truly sorry, but I didn't feel I had a choice.'

'You've always had a choice,' said Atreu. 'We all have.'

'Is your conscience totally clear now, Micah?' said Verlinden.

The Liche Holy Man stared back, unable to answer.

*

'I hope you have a plan, Leyvin, because I can't see where all this will end.' Lythos gulped hurriedly from his wine goblet.

Leyvin smiled at his brother. 'How different we are. Where you see an end, I see a beginning.'

'All right, Leyvin, you tell me how having a new Holy Order made up of failed Ascenders is anything but the end of the Inner Sanctum.'

'Have you calmed down, Lythos? This is a time for clear thought.' Leyvin drank from his goblet then leaned forward with both elbows on the table.

'I have calmed down – mainly because I've given up, though.'

'Don't give up, Lythos. If all goes well, we will stay in control.'

'We have a windrider in the Circle. We have thousands of windriders who are now members of the Order of the Wynde and eligible for the Circle. Riell now commands the defence of the Keep and thereby the entire Maelir army. You said he would be paralysed with the responsibility, but the reverse has happened. I see him energised.'

'Spreading his wings, you might say?' Leyvin laughed at his own joke.

'I'm glad you have time for humour, Leyvin.'

Leyvin ran his finger slowly around the base of his goblet. 'The windriders can be tamed,' he said. 'The covenant with the Liche and the Felsen is ingrained. They have served us too long. It is part of their being. Riell is a moderate among them. He wants to maintain the Circle, and we will be able to extract concessions from him. No, Lythos, the Wynde is the least of our problems.'

'I'm glad you can dismiss it so easily. Can you dismiss the Faemir in the Keep as easily? We are healing them, feeding them, and they still carry their weapons. And now we have done the unspeakable and judged a Faemir to be an Ascender. Are you dismissing that as well, dear brother?'

Leyvin looked at his reflection in the wine. 'I never dismiss anyone. Of course I would prefer not to have the Faemir here, but they too are able to be manipulated. Once we draw them into our system, we have won. Having a Faemir Ascender forces them to play by our rules.'

'Your logic is stupid, Leyvin. Having them here has thrown all our rules over a cliff face.'

'We have a common enemy now. Don't forget that. The Nazir have taken the Summit. Things have changed, and we must adapt. I want to adapt and still be in control. Let me tell you again, if we let the Faemir take part in our Rituals then we are drawing them into our system. Let them have a small part. We have *one* Faemir Ascender. One Faemir who will complete the final Ritual and may enter a Holy Order.'

'That's one Faemir too many.' Lythos spat the words at his brother.

Leyvin laughed at him. 'Think. What have we conceded?'

'A principle.'

'Be practical, Lythos. What have we really conceded? One Faemir who may enter a Holy Order. So what! That doesn't give her any power. Any chance she would have of entering the Circle is a long way in the future. Nothing substantial has changed. The Rituals of Zenith remain intact, the Keep is still here, the Circle controls the Mountain and we control the Circle.'

'Bah!' Lythos almost knocked over his goblet in exasperation.

'Even if these concessions are small, they will add up to something in time. That's what happens when you compromise principles with practicalities.'

'We don't know what will happen in the future,' said Leyvin, smiling at his brother. 'We need the windriders and we need the Faemir at the moment. Who knows what will happen when we no longer need them?' He lifted the goblet to his lips and took a deep draught of wine.

'And what about Atreu?' asked Lythos quietly.

Leyvin choked slightly, but quickly regained his composure. 'For once you have come to the heart of the matter. He is our real concern. He is the only one who could change things – which is why I want to ensure that he gets to the Source as soon as possible. I don't want him here at the Keep causing more trouble.'

'And what of this quest to find the third Book? Why give him the Circle's blessing to undertake it? Why help him gain the power that Praether claims is in the three Books?'

'There are many unknowns with Atreu. I can see my way through all the other problems that beset us, but I don't deny there are imponderables with the Ascender.' Leyvin drank the rest of his wine. 'The quest may be meaningless. Let's not place too much store on a quest initiated by an old arch-librer on his death bed.'

'It may be meaningless ... then again, it may give him undreamed of power if an apotheosis occurs.'

'If he finds the third Book and an apotheosis occurs, then everything changes – I'll grant you that. We have no control over what happens if his quest is successful. What is within our control is doing what we can to ensure he doesn't undertake it.'

'Then suggesting he leaves for the Source as soon as possible, carried by a windrider makes no sense. Why not let him make the pilgrimage on foot, as is the correct procedure? It is far more treacherous and would delay him for weeks.'

'My strategy makes supreme sense, if you understand the subtlety. Atreu knows nothing of the final Ritual. He is currently expecting the Circle to decide whether he has its permission to undertake his quest. What would happen if the Circle insisted that he undertake the pilgrimage in the normal manner? He would find himself faced with a stark choice: quest or pilgrimage. Even if we gave him permission to complete the quest after his time at the Source, this would delay his quest inordinately, and he would still feel he had to choose. This is the beauty of my plan. Allowing him to be flown to the Source means he will feel he can do both. He will choose of his own free will to make the pilgrimage first.'

Lythos stared into his wine. 'But even if what you say is true, and he is delayed at the Source longer than he anticipates, why are you planning to offer him a windrider to carry him far into the Mid-Reaches?'

'Because Riell will offer it anyway. Never decline permission when you know you will be disobeyed. We need the Circle to appear to be in charge and sanctioning everything that happens.'

'But in doing so you may indeed give Atreu the time to complete both the pilgrimage and the quest.'

'Yes, there is some risk of that.' Leyvin smiled. 'But both of us know the way things are at the Source. Atreu could be there a long time ... who knows if he will ever leave?'

Leyvin continued to smile as he finished his wine.

Chapter Three

The dense smell of smoke filled the night air above Peleusar. Cluric and Hrulth walked with the Faemir Watcher Jenethelen along the fire line that now ran the full length of the Maelir barricade.

Cluric peered through the flames into the darkness beyond. He felt the sense of dread that had descended on the Maelir forces. A sharp pain of anticipation ran down the length of his spine. Hadn't they endured enough? Was this what was going to break the Maelir resolve? Cluric had suffered so many defeats at the hands of the Faemir. Although all his battles had resulted in a slow, inevitable retreat, his spirit had never been broken. But now, for the first time since he had left Teuron, he felt his spirit wavering.

Hrulth addressed Jenethelen. 'Is there nothing else you can suggest we do to protect us from the Dusk-wraiths?'

The Watcher shook her head. 'We had no chance. From the first attack, I could see we were doomed.'

'But your people are great warriors,' said Cluric. 'I have fought you long enough to know that. We would have had to outnumber you a hundred to one to regain control of Peleusar. How could your battalions have been decimated so quickly? I can't understand it.'

'One moment after the attack begins, you will know the answer to that question.'

As they continued walking, Cluric strained to hear past the cracking of wood in the fire to the sounds of imminent attack. He looked at the Faemir's face, which seemed to reflect the flame-light in strange ways. It no longer held the look of wild panic that had overwhelmed it earlier. In the light tunic of a Watcher, Jenethelen looked almost like the women of Teuron.

'Why aren't you as afraid as you were?' he asked.

'I don't know.'

'Do you feel safe here?'

'Safer than I have for the last few nights.'

Hrulth suddenly grabbed her by the arm. 'Is there something you're not telling us?'

Jenethelen shook her head.

'Is this some sort of trick?' asked Hrulth.

'No. I'm the only one left.' She shook herself free and looked away. 'I'm the only one who didn't stand and fight against the Dusk-wraiths. I hid, cowered in corners like a mouse. I'm not a worthy Faemir.'

'But you *are* alive,' said Cluric.

Jenethelen didn't answer.

'Tell us, then,' said Hrulth. 'How is it that you feel safer here? The Faemir are far more fearsome warriors than we are, yet these Dusk-wraiths overwhelmed you in almost no time. Why would we Maelir offer you more protection?'

Jenethelen shrugged. 'I'm a Watcher,' she said. 'I know when I can't be seen and I have an instinct for imminent danger.'

'And you don't sense it now?' asked Cluric.

'I do sense it now, but I feel you will be able to withstand the wraiths longer than we did.'

'Why?' asked Hrulth.

Jenethelen looked at him. 'We had no defences in our half of the city. No barricades. No way of lighting effective fires. Faemir warriors are not strong on defence. It's not in our nature. We can only attack. For once we met enemy where we had to defend ourselves – and we couldn't.'

'So you believe,' said Hrulth, 'that we will be able to withstand these wraiths?'

The Watcher shook her head. 'I don't *believe* anything – right now I just hope to last through the night.'

The flames, fed by a night wind, suddenly roared towards them. Cluric looked up at the sky. It could have been the smoke blotting out the lights, but the stars seemed hazy and ill-defined. He shivered. It was as if a thick icy shroud had descended upon them.

'They're coming,' said Jenethelen. 'They're coming.'

*

Atreu and Verlinden walked through the double arched doors of the Areol. The circular room was familiar to Atreu now – the giant dome and clusters of bright painted stars above his head. His footing was sure as he walked across the slightly curved floor towards the centre of the room. The sixty Holy Men sat in their Circle as they had always sat. But something had changed. There was a difference, both palpable and somehow undefined. *Of course*, thought Atreu. Riell now sat as one of them – a windrider, a failed Ascender. The balance had shifted.

'We thank you for your attendance, Ascender Atreu and Verlinden,' said Leyvin.

Atreu knew where the First Speaker sat and was looking right at him as he spoke. The subtleties of Leyvin were beyond anything he had experienced. Even with the apparent blandness of his opening remark, the First Speaker subtly lessened Verlinden's position by failing to repeat the title 'Ascender' before her name. Atreu bit his lip. He could say something, but he suspected that

Leyvin would claim innocence and somehow turn the tables to show that Atreu was the one insulting him.

'You know, of course,' said Leyvin, 'that recent events have resulted in a number of changes in the Inner Sanctum.'

Atreu scanned the faces of the Circle for Riell, and found him about a quarter turn to Leyvin's left.

'These changes, though,' continued Leyvin, 'do not affect the fundamental procedures of the Circle and the fundamental Rituals of the Holy Orders.'

'I think we all understand the changes that have been made,' said Verlinden in a measured tone. 'However, I think the changes that are still to be made are even more important.'

'Nevertheless,' said Leyvin, 'this audience is not about what you *think*. This is the audience where you, the only two remaining Ascenders, are told of the final Ritual.'

'I would hope that any audience allows communication to go both ways,' said Verlinden. 'I understand my position regardless of what you say.'

'This Faemir continues to flout the procedures of the Circle,' said Lythos.

Verlinden spun to look at him. 'It is my understanding that you should be referring to me as Ascender Verlinden. Am I right?'

Lythos scowled at her.

'The statement is correct,' said Leyvin, 'and I would like to remind everyone that all rules of debate and honorifics will be strictly adhered to.'

Lythos cleared his throat but otherwise fell silent.

'Let me begin,' said Leyvin, 'by saying that while our system may appear rigid, it has been constantly changing for centuries. From the time of Maelur's first Ascent, we have, little by little, added to our processes. Each Zenith provides new truths, which feed the changes. The system works because of this accumulation of truths, and it works because the Circle has a thorough and systematic way of assessing each new truth.'

'So, you decide what is truth?' said Verlinden.

'The Circle does, yes, but the Circle is itself subject to strict rules and its composition is constantly changing.'

'And no one has a birthright to a place here.' Atreu recognised the voice as that of Second Speaker Holthim.

'No,' said Verlinden, turning so that she was facing Holthim, 'but one can by birth be *denied* a place in the Circle.'

'Please,' said Leyvin, 'this is not the time and place for such a discussion. As we have all seen, the Circle by its very nature is mutable. Let us now concern ourselves with the future.'

Atreu cleared his throat. 'First Speaker, there are still unresolved issues greater than the immediate fate of the two Ascenders standing here.'

A flicker of annoyance crossed Leyvin's face before he recovered his mask of impartiality. Atreu knew he was referring to change that Leyvin, with all his commentary on the recent changes made, had tried to avoid.

When he responded, Leyvin's voice sounded even more controlled. 'There are always unresolved issues,' he said. 'This audience is for an explicit purpose. As you both know, the two most important Rituals for the Holy Orders are Zenith and Equinox. Zenith provides our truths with power and Equinox provides the balance. Our whole belief system is based on the assumption that ultimate truth will be attained through power and balance. There is, however, a third and final Ritual which Ascenders must experience before entry into the Holy Orders. Ascender Atreu, would you like to explain to the Circle what you know of the purpose of the spring Equinox?'

A wave of panic hit Atreu before he managed to gain control. He instinctively turned in Micah's direction, then stopped himself. This was a question he hadn't expected – Leyvin had him on the spot. Was this what Micah had been trying to warn him to expect? Atreu's thoughts spiralled in on themselves. What was this all about? Micah had told him about the importance of the second Equinox some time ago, but it was not clear what the connection between the second Equinox and the final Ritual was.

'It has been my experience,' said Lythos, with a leer on his face, 'that hesitation within the Circle is an indication of dishonesty.'

'Please, Liche Lythos,' said Leyvin, 'let us not prejudge Ascender Atreu's words before they are spoken.'

Atreu knew that a lie within the Circle was an unpardonable betrayal. He swallowed. There was no choice but to tell the truth – despite the consequences.

'First Speaker Leyvin,' he said, 'I am aware that there is a second judging at the spring Equinox, and that the decision about which Holy Order an Ascender enters is made then.'

'Why is this second judgement necessary?' asked Leyvin.

Atreu gritted his teeth. 'My understanding is that it provides the balance within a balance. One Equinox where day and night are equal in length is balanced by another Equinox.'

'How are you aware of this, Ascender Atreu?'

Atreu looked straight at Leyvin. 'My sage, Liche Micah, told me of the second Equinox soon after my arrival in the Keep.'

There was a stony silence in the Areol. Leyvin appeared to flinch slightly as he and Atreu stared at each other. Atreu sensed a trap had been set for him, but was unsure how he had fared.

'I have another question for you in relation to this,' said Leyvin finally. 'Did Liche Micah speak to you during our recess about the final Ritual?'

'Yes.' Was this about destroying Atreu's credibility or was it about discrediting Micah? Or both?

'Ascender Atreu, I would like you to think very carefully about your answer to this next question.' Leyvin enunciated the words slowly. 'Did Liche Micah warn you that you would be questioned regarding your knowledge of the final Ritual?'

'No,' said Atreu. 'He apologised for keeping information about the Ritual from me. He had assured me some time ago that he would no longer keep any secrets from me.'

Again, an unnerving silence filled the Areol.

'You have answered well,' said Second Speaker Holthim.

'Have I?'

'Yes, you have answered truthfully.'

Atreu looked at Micah and then at Leyvin. 'How do you know I've answered truthfully?'

'The Circle can sense these things,' said Leyvin.

Atreu swung around to stare at Micah again. 'Was this a test of some kind?' His uncle couldn't meet his gaze.

'The Circle has many procedures open to it,' said Leyvin.

'So I see.'

He was still staring at Micah when he heard Lythos' voice. 'Let's not forget, however, that we have an undeniable breach of our protocols. Liche Micah had no authority to speak to an Ascender about the second Equinox.'

Atreu slowly turned to look at him. 'It's not the first time,' said Atreu, reaching out to hold Verlinden's hand, 'that my Ascent has involved a breach of protocol. I suspect it won't be the last. The question is, does it matter, in light of greater issues?'

'We have been overly lenient with you, Ascender Atreu,' said Lythos.

'Nevertheless,' said Holthim, 'Ascender Atreu has answered honestly. That is of far greater weight in the Circle.' He addressed Atreu directly. 'As I said, I believe you have spoken well. There *was* a test here, and you have passed. I believe we should proceed.'

There were murmurs of assent around the Circle. Atreu felt the tension in the back of his neck relax. Leyvin's trap had been a clever one. Clearly, both he and Micah could have been irretrievably discredited.

'Liche Micah,' said Leyvin, 'I must formally condemn you for revealing unauthorised information about our Rituals to an unjudged Ascender. We will consider a naming at the next session.'

'I await the discussion, First Speaker,' said Micah, stroking his beard, but clearly relieved.

'Now, Ascender Atreu and Verlinden,' said Leyvin, 'the time has come to speak of the final Ritual.'

'If we are going to follow your rules so closely,' said Verlinden, glaring at Leyvin, 'I believe that the correct way to address me is Ascender Verlinden, or at the very least, refer to us as *Ascenders* Atreu and Verlinden.'

'Ascender Verlinden has a valid point,' said Micah.

Leyvin was clearly not pleased. 'Pardon me,' he said, 'I thought I had said *Ascenders*. I apologise.'

'A minor breach of protocol,' said Micah, smiling slightly. 'I believe we can all agree that minor breaches shouldn't interfere with the weightier matters before us.'

Atreu glanced across at Verlinden. She knew what she was doing – her comment had clearly been designed to cause Leyvin maximum embarrassment.

'As I was saying,' said Leyvin, who had lost some of his composure now, 'the final Ritual completes the entry into the Holy Orders. All Ascenders who have been judged successful at Equinox must complete the final pilgrimage to our third Holy Place.'

Atreu shuffled his feet slightly. A pilgrimage? This *was* a surprise.

'Ascenders Atreu and Verlinden,' said Leyvin, 'you have seen the Hold during your Zeniths, you have seen the Keep since then. Now it is time for you to see the most sacred of the three Holy Places – the Source of the Maelstrom.'

Atreu and Verlinden glanced at each other. 'When does this pilgrimage occur?' asked Atreu.

'It must occur as soon as possible after the first Equinox,' said Leyvin.

'That would be under normal circumstances, would it not?' said Micah.

'You wouldn't be suggesting, Liche Micah,' said Leyvin, 'that our most sacred of Rituals be abandoned?'

'There is the matter of the quest for the third Book, which the Circle is aware of,' said Micah.

'Is the ghost of Praether still influencing the Circle?' asked Lythos. 'We have discussed this issue.'

'Yes,' said Micah, 'and we decided that the final decision would be made after hearing the Ascenders' views on the matter.'

'Any pilgrimage will have to be delayed,' said Verlinden. 'We have no time. The Mountain is breaking asunder around us.'

'We have evidence of the power of the Books,' said Micah. 'Let us also not forget that we may have an apotheosis.'

'Are we truly contemplating the abandonment of a Ritual?' said a large Felsen over Atreu's right shoulder.

Several of the Holy Men began speaking at once.

'Please, please,' said Leyvin, 'we haven't heard from Ascender Atreu yet.'

Atreu took a deep breath. 'Is it possible to take a recess so that Verlinden and I can discuss this?'

'There is no scope for such a recess' said Leyvin.

'I believe, First Speaker,' said Holthim, 'that while there is no procedure for a recess of consultation, it is acceptable to ask for the Circle's permission to interrupt an address under special circumstances.'

Atreu could see Leyvin stopping himself from challenging the Second Speaker's interpretation. Leyvin had clearly grown more cautious. He only had to fail one more challenge to his ruling and he would lose the position of First Speaker.

Leyvin's voice was tense when he finally spoke. 'Who in the Circle agrees to a recess?'

Atreu turned around to see the overwhelming majority of hands go up.

*

'This pilgrimage is insane, Atreu.' Verlinden was pacing up and down.

'Please sit down, Verlinden. We haven't got much time, and I feel this is a crucial decision.'

'There's no decision to be made,' said Verlinden. 'The Books will lead us to the truth. You should be able to see that more clearly than me.'

Atreu tapped his fingers on the table, and looked at the circle patterns on the walls of the small Areol antechamber they had been led into.

'Do you know your problem?' said Verlinden, stopping in front of him. 'You can't act without a preordained path. You're still acting as if you're on your Ascent.'

'Verlinden, you don't understand.'

'I do understand. Praether was right. The solution lies in the Books. It is the Books that saved my sisters from the Dusk creatures at the Summit. It is the Books that have brought about all the change in the Circle. We both know that. How can you doubt that Praether was right? We must bring the three Books together. Only you know where the third Book is. There is no choice but to descend the Mountain to the Caves of Arach as soon as we possibly can.'

Atreu ran his fingers through his hair. 'I wish I could see all this in such a clear way.' He looked Verlinden in the eyes. 'I am what I am because of the Rituals of Zenith. My Book is a Talisman of Zenith. Praether's truth is the result of all the Rituals that have been enacted by thousands of Ascenders over thousands of years. If we deny the most sacred of Rituals, it strikes at the heart of all the other truths. We would be destroying the very thing that empowers us.'

Verlinden started pacing up and down in front of him again. 'I've told you this before. You must *act*. Ultimately, if you don't act, nothing happens.'

'Don't start with your Faemir philosophy again.'

Verlinden's eyes flashed with fury. 'I think you've spent too much time up here in the Keep,' she said. 'You've become like these Holy Men with their endless discussions. Both our peoples are under the most horrific threat and you can't act.'

'Look, Verlinden, I'm sorry. Please sit down so that we can talk this through. We're wasting time.'

'You're the one who wants to waste time going on a foolish pilgrimage to the Source of the Maelstrom.'

'You say it is foolish, yet you know nothing about it.'

'I know it will take time – time we don't have. I know that the aim of this final Ritual is entry into one of the Holy Orders. How important is that right now?'

There was a knock at the door and Micah and Riell entered the antechamber.

'Is it time?' asked Atreu.

'Almost,' said Micah, 'but we have a few moments. Riell and I have been talking to Leyvin, and we may have a solution to your dilemma.'

'I would be glad to hear it,' said Atreu, an edge of sarcasm in his voice. 'Is this another Circle-inspired test?'

'Atreu, I'm –'

'Don't say sorry, Uncle, please don't say sorry.'

'But –'

'Look, Uncle, I know now where you stand. You may feel some loyalty to me, but ultimately you put the interests of the Circle, the Inner Sanctum and the Rituals above truth to me.'

'That's not entirely fair,' said Micah. 'I believe that you will gain maximum benefit by following the Rituals.'

'I think my assessment is more than fair,' said Atreu, biting his bottom lip. 'I won't hold it against you, though, Uncle. The only problem so far has been that I have trusted you.'

Riell said, 'Now Atreu, you shouldn't doubt that Micah has your best interests at heart.'

Atreu drew a deep breath. 'How long, then, does this pilgrimage to the Source take?'

'Getting there can take weeks. Then there's the time there, which is difficult to judge,' said Micah.

'That's impossible,' said Verlinden.

'Hear us out first,' said Riell. 'I believe I will be able to arrange to get the two of you to the Source with the windriders' help. After the Ritual is complete, we may even be able to carry you as far down the Mid-Reaches as the prevailing winds allow, helping you make up the time you lose at the Source.'

'Is that allowed?' asked Atreu.

'I think, given the circumstances, it would not be a problem,' said Riell. 'We have already had far greater breaches of normal procedure than this.'

Atreu felt as if a weight had been lifted from his shoulders. 'That's the answer, then. It will be possible to complete the Rituals *and* undertake the quest.' He afforded himself a half-smile as he looked across at Verlinden.

He sensed immediately that she didn't share his joy.

'What's wrong?' he asked.

Verlinden shook her head. 'Nothing,' she said. 'I think you have the solution you wanted, haven't you? It is most convenient.'

'What do you mean?'

Verlinden eyed Micah and then Riell. 'Tell me, was this your idea or Leyvin's?'

Just then a monk appeared in the doorway and indicated that the Circle was convening again.

*

A sound like the slow, sonorous echo of a drumbeat filled the night sky. Cluric felt the vibrations pass through his body, as if every fibre was individually trembling. *What was happening?* He drew his sword but was unsure which way to face. Had the Maelir barricades already been breached? A haze now floated where the clear night sky above Peleusar once had been.

'Where are they?' he cried, grabbing Jenethelen's arm. The Watcher had frozen.

'Tell us what to expect,' said Hrulth.

Jenethelen was rigid, a look of pure terror in her eyes.

Cluric sensed the frantic activity of the Maelir soldiers behind him. They had mobilised many times before against Faemir attacks, but this was different. Everyone was taking position and bracing themselves – but for what? This was an enemy they knew nothing about.

The drum echo had now faded, replaced with a thick, sluggish silence. Cluric stared out past the flames and felt his sword trembling ever so slightly in his hand.

Nothing.

He felt his muscles tightening.

Nothing.

Sweat trickled down his temples.

Then he caught his first glimpse of them.

Out in the shadows, amid the sharp edges of Peleusar, dark, fluid forms took shape and seemed to expand out in all directions. *Were they growing? Or were they merely coming closer?* Cluric couldn't tell, but he was transfixed on the moving, pulsing figures, the shadows within a shadow heart which now emerged from the buildings and street corners of the city.

'You said the fire would stop them,' said Hrulth to Jenethelen. 'How certain are you?'

The Watcher still hadn't moved.

The dark amorphous shadows drew inexorably closer.

Cluric felt the sharp sting of raw terror surge through him. 'Jenethelen,' he cried, 'will the fires stop them?'

Maelir voices could be heard along the line of the barricade.

'We won't hold our formations,' said Hrulth. 'I can sense it.'

Cluric dropped his sword and grabbed Jenethelen by the shoulders. 'Tell us what to do!' he cried. Her body was as rigid as stone. Her eyes were open, and she was standing, but otherwise she could have been dead.

The shadows were still growing, and now towered above the flames. Cluric became aware of a bone-chilling wail, which increased in intensity as the figures drew closer.

He shook Jenethelen again, harder this time. There was a flicker of life in her eyes, but she remained paralysed.

'Grab your sword, Cluric, they are almost upon us.' Hrulth's words barely registered.

He shook the Watcher again. 'Help us!'

'What is the matter with you, Cluric?' cried Hrulth. 'Grab your sword!'

Cluric pushed Jenethelen and she hit the ground hard. Her cry of pain struck a nerve in Cluric and he realised what he had done. 'I ... I'm sorry,' he said.

He reached down, picked up his sword, and then turned to face the on-coming wraiths.

'The fires will stop them,' cried Hrulth. 'We may not know exactly what these things are, but if they are Dusk-spawn, the fires will stop them.'

Hrulth's words struck home, and Cluric sensed a semblance of discipline had been restored in the Maelir battalions. All around him stood flame-streaked soldiers, swords drawn, in battle formation.

The wail continued to increase in pitch with every passing moment. The first line of wraiths was now less than ten strides from the barricades. Sharp blood-red eyes shone from the torpid shadows, but otherwise the wraiths remained indistinct even as the flame light hit them. It was as if they absorbed the light, drinking it in.

Blind panic once again threatened Cluric's self-control. A volley of Maelir arrows whistled through the air from the rooftops behind him. As they hit their mark, disappearing into the dark shadows, a horrific groaning sound emerged from the wraiths, and they shuddered and trembled.

A half-hearted cheer erupted from some corners, but it was short-lived. The wraiths were still coming, and, if anything, still growing.

The wail now hurt Cluric's ears, and he wanted to clap his hands over them. This was far worse than any Faemir battle cry.

The flames of the barricade were now almost licking the wraith shadows. Cluric felt the ice of terror shoot along his limbs. *They are Dusk creatures. The fire will stop them.* He repeated the mantra over and over in his mind. *The fire will stop them.*

The fire will stop them.
The fire will stop them.
But it didn't.

Cries of horror rang through the air as the wraiths moved into the flames, and then through them, emerging a little less dense, but otherwise unscathed.

Soldiers rushed at them, swinging swords and battle-axes. The wraiths groaned and pulsed, enveloping the soldiers and seemingly absorbing them into their shadows.

Cluric felt something touch his leg. He looked down to see that Jenethelen had regained consciousness.

'Flee,' she said. 'Hide – it's the only way.'

Cluric scanned the battle scene and saw bedlam all around. Bolts of light flashed each time a Maelir soldier engaged a wraith. It was as if they were fighting storm clouds.

Hrulth stood grimly, watching the first wave of Maelir attack to see if he could find a weakness. He drew his second sword and threw it to the Watcher. 'Help us fight them. There is nowhere to flee to.'

Cluric helped her to her feet. 'Stand with us.'

A signal horn sounded above the tumult and a second wave of Maelir soldiers charged at the oncoming wraiths.

Cluric clenched his teeth and moved forward with Hrulth. A wraith loomed before him, bright red eyes roiling in its heart. He swung his sword into it and it groaned and spat sparks at him. A biting cold ran along the hilt of his sword and up his arm. He withdrew and saw the wraith turn and twist in on itself.

With a mighty heave, Cluric swung his sword again. This time it sank deeply into the wraith, barely missing one of the eyes, and his hand came into contact with its shadow form. He screamed in agony – his hand felt as if all the blood in it had suddenly turned to ice. He pulled back and his sword fell from his grasp.

The wraith snaked a shadowy tendril towards him and he jumped back, only to stumble and fall. The tendril went for his throat, but a sword flashed in front of him, slicing through it. The remaining stump withdrew back into the shadow.

Cluric leapt to his feet and saw that Jenethelen was brandishing the sword.

'How's your hand?'

'I … I can barely move it.'

'Come on,' cried Hrulth. 'This way.'

The three of them retreated well into the Maelir stronghold, where most of the soldiers gathered.

Cluric could still see the approaching wraiths from where he stood, but it was clear they had diminished in size and were moving far more slowly.

Hrulth had quick words with several other battalion leaders then returned to Cluric and Jenethelen.

'What's happened?' asked Cluric, moving his fingers to get the feeling back. 'Why are they getting smaller?'

'We're not sure. The wailing noise also seems to be fading a little.' He looked at Jenethelen. 'What can you tell us about them? Anything could help.'

'It must be the fire. I think they've been weakened coming through it.'

'They're still coming, though,' said Cluric. 'How do we turn them back?'

Jenethelen shook her head. 'I don't know. We were never able to drive them away. As long as it was dark, they just kept coming.'

'Do our weapons make any difference?' asked Hrulth.

'I think they do. Normally the effect is small, but in their fire-weakened state, the weapons seem to be hurting them.' She looked at Cluric's hand. 'I shouldn't have been able to cut that tendril so easily, and you shouldn't be able to move your hand again this quickly.'

Cluric shivered. Hrulth signalled to one of the other battalion leaders.

'What's the plan?' asked Cluric.

'Another all-out assault,' said Hrulth. 'You two stay here.'

Cluric lifted his sword. 'I can still hold it,' he said, but, unable to clench his fingers fully, the sword fell out of his hand.

Jenethelen, too, was reaching for her sword.

'No,' said Hrulth, 'you're the only one who has any idea how these things fight. Please stay.'

Cluric watched as Hrulth headed back towards the Dusk-wraiths. Cries of agony again filled the air as swords and battle-axes tore into the shadow-like forms. Gut-wrenching groans merged with the cries, and the wraiths quivered and flowed.

It took a moment for Cluric to realise that the forms were no longer moving forward. Tendrils arched like attacking serpents, but then collapsed back before they could strike.

Several battalions charged, carrying flaming torches. A horn sounded and the flame-carriers stopped several strides from the wraiths. The soldiers who had been engaging the shadowy creatures in combat fell back.

A thin line of torch flames now burnt in front of the wraiths, and the barricade fires still roared behind them. Cluric drew a quick breath and waited.

Then the horn sounded again, and the soldiers threw the flames into the pulsing shadows. There was a guttural scream across the length and breadth of the wraith line, and the shadows started to coil violently.

A sharp wind suddenly whipped up and swirled through the soldiers. Many lost their footing. By the time the gust hit him, Cluric had braced himself, but it still knocked him and Jenethelen over.

He got to his feet to see the Dusk-wraiths now twisting in on themselves and shrinking with ever-increasing speed. Soon, where once a line of pulsating shadows had been, there was nothing.

The Maelir erupted in a cheer, which soon stuck in their throats, as the retreating wraiths revealed the bodies of hundreds of soldiers that had been enveloped during the onslaught.

'Your people fought well,' said Jenethelen, 'but I fear this was only the beginning.'

As Cluric reached out his hand to help the Faemir to her feet, he noticed that the warmth had returned to his fingers.

Chapter Four

'You're speaking nonsense, Verlinden.' Rhea scanned the pages of the Book. 'There are no words I understand on these pages.'

'My ability comes and goes, but there is no doubt about the power of this Book,' said Verlinden. 'Why would I try to convince you of something as insane as this, if it wasn't true?'

'I don't pretend to understand your motivations. You were born a Faelen, and you will always be a Maelir woman at heart.'

'Your insults don't affect me anymore, Rhea. Listen, you think I'm making this up? Here, I'll read this last part again.

'Your people fought well,' said Jenethelen, 'but I fear this was only the beginning.

As Cluric reached out his hand to help the Faemir to her feet, he noticed that the warmth had returned to his fingers.

'Enough, Verlinden. You won't convince me that this Book you found buried in the snow gives you some strange power. It makes no sense. This Cluric, these Dusk-wraiths, are a figment of a fevered mind.'

Verlinden closed the Book and placed it on the table. She watched the lights of the Keep through her window and the play of stars above them. 'I find the Maelir frustrating to deal with at times,' she said, 'but I can see an infuriating stubbornness in my own sisters.'

'You still claim sisterhood?' asked Rhea.

'Look, Rhea, let's have no more of this. With Valkyra gone, you are now the leader of the Faemir army. Can you take nothing from what happened on the Summit, or from what's happening in Peleusar?'

'I have had no reports from Peleusar in a long time.'

'You are so stubborn and so proud.' Verlinden spat the last word at her.

Rhea slumped in her chair and looked at the table. 'You're right. I stand humiliated. I am a captured Faemir warrior. I have no right to be proud.'

'You're not captured,' said Verlinden. 'Since when do prisoners carry swords? Since when are they allowed to come and go as they please?'

'I'm finished,' said Rhea softly.

'You're still alive,' said Verlinden. 'Look, this Book, this Talisman of Zenith, has given me strange powers. Both Atreu and I can read it. I read what was happening to you at the Summit as it was happening to you.'

'What?'

'Yes – the grale attack, the Dusk-rats. That was why Atreu and I persuaded the windriders to come down and rescue you. This Book saved your life.' She tapped the leather cover.

Rhea fingered the hilt of her sword. 'Perhaps my life wasn't worth saving.'

'Don't be a fool, Rhea.'

Rhea withdrew her sword slowly and placed it on the table in front of her. 'It's a farce that I've been carrying this around up here. I'm not a warrior anymore.'

Verlinden felt a sudden surge of anger. 'You are so like Valkyra at times. Blind Faemir pride.'

'Pride is all we've had from the beginning,' said Rhea softly.

'But, of course, I'm not a true Faemir, so I wouldn't know

about pride, would I? It's not the pride I'm talking about – it's the blind part that worries me.'

'You don't understand, Verlinden. I don't think you've ever understood.'

'Look, Rhea, the battles are far from over. The time for great warriors is upon us. This Book here, the part I've just read to you, tells us what is happening. The Dusk creatures are our new enemy. We have to recognise that. We must forge an alliance between Faemir and Maelir or else the Mountain will be lost to both of us.'

Rhea looked away. 'You read stories to me as if I was a child.'

'That's just it, Rhea, they are not stories. They are real. The Dusk-wraiths, the decimation of the Faemir forces at Peleusar. Who knows where else the Dusk creatures have attacked us.'

'Exactly, Verlinden, you could be telling me anything. I'm cut-off up here. I have no news of our other battalions. How do I know the truth?'

'You have to trust me.'

'Trust you? You pass yourself off as your twin sister to try to gain control of the Faemir army, and you expect me to trust you?'

Verlinden paused for a moment, looking at the glint of Rhea's sword on the table. 'Rhea, it is just the two of us here. No one else is listening. Can you try to put aside your pride for a moment? What are Faemir lives worth?'

'They are worth nothing to the Maelir.'

'In the past, yes. But neither Maelir nor Faemir lives have any worth to the Dusk people.' The sword shone brightly. 'Rhea, you gave up the leadership to Valkyra when she was nine years old.'

'I had to.'

'Did you? I know several other coveyn leaders who wouldn't have done it. They would have fought her to the death.'

'It would have been their death.'

'Yes, but you recognised that and didn't fight her. The others would have fought anyway, knowing they would be defeated.'

'I'm a coward – obviously.'

'No, Rhea, you knew that Valkyra would be a better leader, that all Faemir, not just our coveyn, would gain from my sister's leadership.' Verlinden leant across the table and stared Rhea in the eyes. 'And you were right.'

'I didn't have the strength to stand up to her.' Rhea's voice was thin.

'It took more strength *not* to stand up to her.'

'Don't try to turn a weakness into a virtue, Verlinden. The other coveyn leaders all fell in behind her eventually too. Was I so different?'

'Yes Rhea, you were. You had shown them. You were there as second command, and you helped persuade them. Valkyra may have united the Faemir without you by her side, but only after much blood-letting. And it would have been a unity based on fear – you made it a unity which they all chose. That is true leadership.'

'Now you are trying flattery.'

'As I said, there is no one here. I would like us to speak honestly. There is no doubt Valkyra was important, but the two of you complemented each other. You balanced her blind aggression with some thoughtfulness and compassion.'

'Compassion?'

'Yes. Not weakness – compassion.'

'That's not a trait we Faemir prize very much, is it?'

Rhea and Verlinden looked at each other in silence.

'You still regret what happened to Ahrai's hand, don't you?' said Verlinden finally.

Rhea slumped into her chair and nodded. 'I ... I could have ordered Valkyra to stop all those years ago. I had the power to do it.'

'The fact that you still regret it tells me you can lead the Faemir now. There is a new enemy, and new alliances must be forged.'

'The burning smell of brimstone on bare flesh is not something you can forget.'

'Rhea, you can make amends now a thousand times over. Only you can save Faemir lives.'

Rhea was still nodding.

'Here,' said Verlinden, nudging the sword in her direction. 'Sheath your sword. There are still many battles to be won.'

Rhea fingered the sword hilt and then looked up. 'Tell me, Verlinden, how did you know I regret the damage to Ahrai's hand?'

Verlinden tapped the Book. 'These pages told me.'

'You know my thoughts?'

'Some of them. When you were down at the Summit, between grale attacks. I know that was when you regretted it most.'

Rhea reached out and touched the Book. 'To be able to read someone's thoughts – that can be a powerful weapon.'

'Yes, but weapons are not the only things that have power.'

Rhea squinted at the words on the open page. 'So both you and Atreu can read this?'

'Yes, although the ability comes and goes.'

'Tell me something,' she said, tracing a line across the page with her finger. 'Can you both read it equally well?'

'As I said, the ability is erratic, and beyond our control. Sometimes one of us can read it but the other can't.'

'But your ability matches the Ascender's?'

Verlinden hesitated for a moment. 'It's hard to judge.'

'You must have a feeling for it. All Faemir have a sense of the balance of power.'

Verlinden was acutely aware that Rhea had referred to her as a Faemir rather than a Faelen. 'The ... the balance shifts.'

'Where is it now?'

'Atreu and I are both Ascenders. The Book has been judged my Talisman as well as his. We are equal.'

'You haven't really answered my question, Verlinden. What the Maelir decide or judge is one thing, what you feel is another. Is the power you have through this Book equal to Atreu's?'

Verlinden swallowed. 'Not at the moment. But that will change again.'

'That's exactly how I feel right now about the Maelir.' Rhea slowly stood up and sheathed her sword. 'All right, Verlinden, let's do what we have to do.'

*

Cluric found the stench of burning flesh almost unbearable, even with the mask across his nose and mouth. He heaved the last body onto the barricade fires and wiped the sweat from his brow. He knew that mass burial was difficult in the city, and that the bodies provided fuel for the flames that were protecting them, but simply throwing the bodies of the dead Maelir onto the fire so soon after the battle was soul-destroying.

He fought back the nausea. There had been many dead in past battles, but none of those corpses had felt quite so cold and inhuman. The Faemir had always been formidable and often vicious fighters, but they were nothing like this new foe. The Duskwraiths left you no scope for honourable losses. They left you with no honour at all.

Cluric looked across at Jenethelen, who was also breathing heavily with exertion. Her dark hair hung in thick, tangled strands past her shoulders. How strange that they weren't at each other's throats as they would have been only a few short days ago. He followed the line of her throat down to her exposed collarbone.

'We usually bury our dead,' said Jenethelen, noticing Cluric looking at her.

Cluric felt his face flush. 'Yes, so do we.' He struggled to regain his composure. 'Tell me, why couldn't we find many Faemir bodies after the wraith attack?'

'There weren't so many of us. You lost almost as many last night alone as we had stationed in the whole of Peleusar.'

'What? I knew we had you outnumbered, but that seems difficult to believe.'

'It's true.'

'Still, we haven't found too many bodies.'

Jenethelen closed her eyes for a moment. 'I've lost count of how many Faemir warriors I've buried. That was one of my main duties in the end. I used to think the ones that the grale had mauled were horrific, but the ice cold of those killed by the wraiths was infinitely worse. You know, we used to believe that you Maelir were somehow responsible for unleashing the grale and the Dusk-rats on us. Our battalion leader thought at first that the wraiths were your doing too.' Her voice quavered. 'During the last night before your patrol found me, many of the survivors turned on each other. I've never seen anything like it. They attacked each other as if they were sworn enemies. Screaming. Screaming battle cries. Screaming in pain. It was the most frightening thing I've ever seen.'

'At least you didn't turn on the others.'

'I ... I was in hiding.' She was now almost whispering. 'I was beyond even the terror of the others. I couldn't ... do anything.'

'Come on,' said Cluric. 'I think we've finished here. Let's get some rest, and something to eat.'

Jenethelen looked surprised, as if suddenly faced with something totally unexpected. Then she nodded.

'Do you think they'll attack again before dawn?' asked Cluric, as they turned away from the stench-laden flames.

'I don't know. We were never able to repel them like this. I've got a feeling they won't be back tonight.'

They walked wearily to the large flat-roofed building that served as the quarters for Hrulth's battalion.

Once inside, they sat on a moth-ridden mattress in the corner, which functioned as Cluric's bed. Cluric passed Jenethelen a lukewarm bowl of barley stew, and they ate in silence. The other soldiers were either finishing off their meals or were lying down, attempting to get some sleep.

'This is as close to peace as it gets now,' said Cluric softly.

Jenethelen scraped the last remnants of stew out of her bowl.

'You know,' said Cluric, 'your people killed my parents and took my two baby cousins many years ago. I swore enmity to every

Faemir ever since. It's funny how things change. I feel no hatred for you.'

'How noble of you.'

'It's true. I have no urge to do you harm.'

Jenethelen grabbed a blanket and wrapped it around herself. 'I'm eternally grateful,' she said, speaking to her feet.

'What's wrong?'

'Nothing. You Maelir are very just. I'm so grateful for what you've given me.' She pulled out another blanket and put it on the floor next to the wall, then lay down on it.

'I don't understand.'

'No. No, you don't.'

Cluric shrugged his shoulders and lay down on his mattress, pulling the remaining blanket up over himself. 'You saved my life tonight,' he said. 'I … I just want to thank you.'

Jenethelen was facing the wall. She appeared to be asleep already.

Cluric sighed and turned.

'Can I now tell *you* something?' asked Jenethelen.

'Of course.'

'Your people killed my mother and two sisters. But I forgive you.'

'You forgive *me?*'

'You really don't understand, do you?'

Cluric didn't know how to answer her. He lay there until a deep weariness overwhelmed him, and sometime before dawn he fell asleep.

*

Verlinden, Rhea and Ahrai entered the healing room where the battalion leader Saretha lay. They withdrew their swords, leant them against the wall and approached the bedridden Saretha.

'I've called a conclave,' said Rhea.

'A conclave?' Saretha's tone was mocking. 'I've always thought conclaves were to discuss battle plans. Tell me, Rhea, how is it possible to discuss battle plans when we have no army?'

'Our own battalions may be all but destroyed,' said Ahrai, 'but the Faemir still have an army.'

'And a leader,' said Rhea.

Saretha snorted. 'I hear Valkyra is dead. And from what I've been told, you didn't exactly cover yourself in glory when the Dusk beasts attacked us.'

Rhea's voice was steady and calm. 'Nevertheless, with Valkyra gone, I am the leader unless successfully challenged.' She stared unflinchingly at Saretha. 'Are you going to challenge me?'

Their eyes locked, but Saretha eventually looked away.

'I may have only recently gained consciousness,' said Saretha, 'but I can't see how any of us are in a position to discuss battle plans.'

'We have reports of several Faemir battalions moving through the Upper Reaches from Crosanct,' said Ahrai. 'Things are not as bleak as they seem.'

'There is a new enemy,' said Verlinden, 'and it's time for new alliances.'

Saretha stared at her in contempt. 'If this is a conclave, then what is a Watcher doing here?'

'I have asked her,' said Rhea. 'It is my right.'

Saretha pushed herself up so that she was sitting higher in the bed. 'So are we still talking peace, or are we talking war?'

'Both,' said Rhea. 'Peace with the Maelir. War with the Nazir.'

'And what are we getting from this?'

'Victory,' said Rhea. She knew she had to argue the point carefully with Saretha. If she could persuade her, all the Faemir would follow.

'I smell the odour of defeat around me,' said Saretha. 'It's particularly strong in this room.'

'The Maelir can smell defeat too,' said Rhea. 'Why would they have rescued us? Why are they healing our injured? They could have easily left us all to die down there.'

Saretha snorted. 'It's a weakness not to allow your enemy to be destroyed.'

'But it's stupidity to allow an ally to be destroyed.' Rhea's voice remained steady.

'I ask you again,' said Saretha, 'what are we getting from this?'

'We will attain the power of Zenith,' said Verlinden.

Saretha deliberately didn't look at her. 'I am speaking to the warriors in this room, not the Faelen.'

'Listen to me,' said Verlinden. 'I have been given the title Ascender. I took part in the final Zenith. I am about to undergo the final Ritual, to see the place no Faemir has ever seen – the Source of the Maelstrom.'

'And we are here,' said Rhea, 'in the Keep. No Faemir even knew of its existence until a short time ago. And now we are free to walk wherever we wish. Isn't this what we always wanted? Isn't this what everything was for?'

'But it can be taken away from us so easily. A handful of Faemir in the Keep. One Faemir Ascender among dozens. How much is that worth?'

Verlinden grabbed Saretha's arm. 'Saretha, there are only two Ascenders left. Atreu and I. Valkyra killed all the others. Think about it. Two Ascenders. One Faemir and one Maelir. Doesn't that mean anything to you?'

Saretha pulled at the blankets, deep in thought. 'And what happens at next Zenith?'

'The Mountain is increasingly unsafe,' said Verlinden. 'Who knows whether anyone will make it through for the next Zenith. There may be nothing left for anyone but the Dusk people – but if there is, the Circle has agreed that eligible Faemir also take part in Zenith.'

Saretha continued to pull at the blankets absently.

'But none of this will happen,' said Rhea, 'unless we win some battles. We know the Maelir have poor battle strategy. They only held out so long through weight of numbers. There has never been a time like this for great warriors and great leaders.'

A sharp light seemed to suddenly shine in Saretha's eyes. Rhea knew she had her.

'There is to be a war council,' continued Rhea. 'They want us on it. Your lost battalion will be replaced by a battalion a hundred-fold in size.'

'We are to be on a War Council which commands Maelir?' said Saretha.

'Yes,' said Rhea, noting the smile that tugged at the corners of Saretha's mouth.

*

Verlinden could feel the tension rise in the war chamber as she, Rhea, Ahrai and Saretha walked through the doorway. The Faemir battalion leaders placed their unsheathed swords against the wall near the door and took their seats at the circular table. Saretha waved away an offer of assistance from Verlinden – either she had miraculously recovered from her injuries or she did not want to show any weakness.

The others were already there. Riell and Theander represented the windriders, while Leyvin, Lythos and Holthim, appointed by the Circle, made up the nine members of the War Council.

Lythos was clearly on edge. He shifted uncomfortably in his chair and his eyes darted around the room.

Riell began hesitantly. 'I ... I realise none of us are comfortable with this. As you all know, we have been given the power by the Circle to forge a new alliance between the Maelir and Faemir armies, and to coordinate our efforts to defend ourselves against the Nazir attack.'

'The Faemir army doesn't defend,' said Saretha. 'It attacks.'

'That may be something we need to change for a while,' said Riell. 'From all reports, attacking is not effective against the Nazir.'

'Then that leaves us with a serious problem,' said Rhea. 'The Faemir don't have a defence strategy. We've never needed one –

the coveyns never owned any land. And since the coveyns united under Valkyra, you Maelir have never been able to push us back.'

Riell nodded. 'Theander, could you give us news of what is happening on the Mountain?'

Theander cleared his throat. 'We are still receiving reports from regions on the Mountain where the windriders have enough updraught to fly, but we know little about the regions where we have always relied on runners for information. Even the windrider information, however, is based on the after-effects of Nazir attacks, rather than eyewitness accounts.'

'I believe,' said Verlinden, 'that the Faemir forces in Peleusar have fallen to the Nazir, and that the Maelir forces are now under siege.'

Theander looked at her. 'It is not clear what has happened in Peleusar, but I have a report which suggests that.' He cleared his throat again. 'Crosanct is currently controlled by the Faemir, but large numbers of Maelir battalions are moving upslope through the Mid-Reaches to regain Crosanct.'

'So there are no signs of the Nazir at Crosanct?' asked Ahrai.

'No,' said Theander.

'But Crosanct is of no importance to the Nazir,' said Riell.

'How can you say that?' asked Lythos. 'Our whole strategy has been focused on controlling Crosanct. It is the only major pass on this side of the Mountain through to the Upper Reaches.'

'I believe we all need to think differently,' said Riell. 'The Nazir have no need for the pass. They have already built an immense network of tunnels right up to the Summit. They took the Summit without a single Dusk creature passing through Crosanct.'

'What do you think the Nazir are trying to do?' asked Verlinden.

'Let's hear what other news Theander has for us before we try to answer that question,' said Riell.

Theander continued. 'We know of large Nazir attacks in Spa, R'in and Rathsheed, and on refugee camps like Stromspont. We have had some reports of Nazir in the Lower Reaches, but we're not sure.'

'The Lower Reaches?' asked Verlinden.

'They are unconfirmed,' said Theander.

'We don't know, of course, whether the wraiths have attacked Faemir-held territories such as Ariathe and Walden.'

'When we were still receiving news,' said Rhea, 'our battalions in Ariathe were being constantly harassed by Dusk beasts. From what I've seen of the Nazir's tactics, they always send their grale and Dusk-rats out first.'

'So there is a question over Ariathe,' said Riell. 'But there is no question over who controls the Summit. The Nazir are the only ones down there now.'

'The attacks on Peleusar are recent, aren't they?' said Rhea.

'Yes.'

'These Nazir are hard to fathom,' said Lythos. 'They have the Summit, yet it appears they may also be attacking the Lower Reaches.'

Rhea stroked her chin. 'The Faemir army started taking shape just past the Rimforest in the Mid-Reaches. We swept up towards the Summit.'

'There was no subtlety in your plan,' said Lythos.

'Did it matter?' said Saretha. 'We achieved what we set out to achieve. We had control of the Summit.'

'But it wasn't quite as easy as you first thought, was it?' said Lythos. 'You controlled the Hold, which we no longer had any use for. The real Summit is up here in the Keep.'

'We would have made it up here too,' said Saretha.

'There is no point to this,' said Verlinden quickly. 'We all know the war had reached a stalemate just before Equinox.'

'I agree,' said Riell. 'If we believe the Nazir are attacking the Lower Reaches as well, then that is an important piece of information.'

'There has been little recent movement upslope through the

Rimforest in recent times,' said Theander. 'And it has been some time since we have had any news from villages near the Base.'

'We have to be careful not to assume the wrong motivations,' said Riell. 'Yes, the Nazir have taken the false Summit below us, but why these simultaneous attacks all over the Mountain? We have been assuming they want Zenith, because we know it is the power of Zenith that drives us.'

'As it has driven us,' said Rhea.

'How many of them are there?' asked Verlinden.

'We have no idea,' said Riell. 'They only emerge at night, and even then, only for short periods. We haven't risked going close enough to have a better look.'

'So we have no idea who our enemy is,' said Ahrai. 'That's not a good start.'

Theander said, 'They took the Summit without unsheathing a single sword or shooting a single arrow. Their Dusk beasts did all the damage.'

'And from what I've read in the Book,' said Verlinden, 'there are far more fierce Dusk creatures which have not yet been unleashed in the Upper Reaches. They are using Dusk-wraiths in Peleusar.'

'It would be good to have some independent confirmation of the existence of these wraiths,' said Leyvin.

Verlinden glared at him. 'You're doubting the power of the Book again, after everything that has happened?'

Leyvin half smiled. 'Forgive me, I thought I was told the Talisman is a little erratic. Theander, do we have any firm evidence of Dusk-wraiths?'

'Nothing firm, but –'

'Let's not waste time on that question,' said Rhea impatiently. 'There are more important questions to ask. Peleusar may be a large city, but it has been all but destroyed by war. We committed only a small number of warriors there. The question to ask is, why would the Nazir have their most fearsome spawn attack a city that lies in ruins when the permanent control of the Summit and the Upper Reaches beckons?'

'As I said before,' said Riell, 'they may not be motivated by the power of Zenith.'

'Yet, they have taken possession of the Summit,' said Verlinden.

'The Keep is the true Summit,' said Lythos. 'I don't see any Dusk people here.'

'No,' said Rhea, 'but it was only a short time ago that you could have said that you don't see any Faemir here.'

Lythos glared at her.

'Is it possible,' asked Holthim, 'that the instability will decimate them down there as it did the Faemir battalions?'

'It's possible,' said Verlinden, 'but according to Atreu, the Nazir tunnelling through the Mountain for centuries is what has caused the instability, so they possibly have some control or understanding of it.'

'That's attributing considerable powers to them,' said Theander.

'Perhaps,' said Verlinden, 'but I don't think we should be underestimating them. How long have both Maelir and Faemir been at war with the Dusk people without being aware of it? This is a sinister army, and a sinister people.'

'The question of what is motivating them must be our starting point,' said Riell. 'We can only plan once we know that.'

'So, the Summit is important to them,' said Rhea, tracing invisible lines on the table in front of her, 'or else they wouldn't be here. But it is not all-important.'

'The Lower Reaches have no wealth,' said Lythos. 'Why would they attack small communities of farmers?'

'I think the answer is obvious,' said Rhea. 'Only no one wants to say it.'

'Why don't you tell us, then?' said Lythos, glaring at her.

'The Nazir are attacking all over the Mountain at once. The big cities of the Mid-Reaches, whether they are in ruin or not, the towns and villages of the Lower Reaches, the snowlands of the Upper Reaches. There is only one possible conclusion.'

Verlinden looked at the grim faces around the table as the realisation sank in.

'They want control of the whole Mountain,' said Lythos finally. 'They want to wipe us all out and replace us.'

Chapter Five

Thin rays of sunlight hit Cluric's face as he made his way down a cobbled laneway with the rest of the patrol. The sky above Peleusar was a clear blue, but it was as if the night's battle had sapped the strength out of the sun. Cluric felt no real warmth and his recent injuries had begun to ache again.

'This way,' said Jenethelen, leading the patrol into a still-smaller laneway.

It was funny, thought Cluric, that they were trusting a Faemir in such a way. Perhaps he should have been concerned that this was a trap of some kind. But he knew it wasn't. The war had changed irrevocably, and this Faemir was now an ally. He watched the way she moved with a light-footed confidence along the uneven cobblestones. There was no hint of the fear-ridden paralysis from the night before. Jenethelen was clearly convinced that the wraiths, like all creatures of the Dusk, posed no threat in broad daylight.

She motioned them through a doorway. Cluric stepped in and looked around. The room was littered with piles of arrows, and in one corner lay swords, knives and Faemir armour.

'So the Dusk-wraiths never found this,' said Hrulth.

'I don't think they search for anything that's not alive,' said Jenethelen.

'And this was command centre?' said Hrulth, stroking his beard. 'I doubt if we would have ever found it.'

'It looks quite small,' said Cluric.

Jenethelen half-smiled. 'I've told you, there weren't as many of us in Peleusar as you would think. We Faemir are very effective fighters.'

'Except against the wraiths,' said Janan.

'Dogged defence is not our natural fighting style. We wear light armour and are always prepared to move quickly. This command centre was never meant to be permanent. We were always prepared to shift it at a moment's notice.'

'All right,' said Hrulth. 'Let's take what we can carry. The arrows are going to be the most useful. Once we've got those, let's see how many swords and knives we can take as well.'

They loaded what they could and then headed back out.

Cluric watched Jenethelen as the patrol wound its way back to the other side of the city. The sun was now high in the sky, and the Dusk-wraiths seemed almost unreal. The Faemir's black hair shone as it bounced rhythmically off her shoulders. In many ways, she was similar to the girls of Teuron.

A thought like a knife's edge suddenly cut through him.

'Uncle,' he said, grabbing Hrulth by the arm. 'How do we know Teuron and Treyfell are still safe?'

Hrulth gave him a puzzled look. 'What made you think of our homes just now?'

'I ... I don't know. There seems to be no immediate danger here. My mind was wandering and ...' Cluric trailed off, not finishing the sentence.

'Let's ask the Faemir what she knows of the Lower Reaches.'

'We don't need to,' said Cluric. 'The Lower Reaches were never part of the Faemir campaign. We know that hasn't changed.' He gripped Hrulth's arm even harder. 'I'm worried about the Dusk-spawn. What is driving them?'

'Ah, I see what you're saying.' Hrulth ran his fingers through his beard. 'We have no idea, do we?'

'When was the last time we had any news of the Lower Reaches?'

'Some time,' said Hrulth. 'All the runners have come from upslope.'

'Perhaps we should send some runners downslope to the Rim-forest for once.'

'You could be right, Cluric. I will speak with the other battalion leaders.'

Cluric looked up at the sky. It was blue – for now. 'Don't leave it too late,' he said.

*

'Hey!' Atreu stepped back in surprise as an updraught of air hit him. He looked down at the hole in front of him.

Riell laughed. 'I should have warned you, but it's always fun to see the Initiate's first reaction.'

Atreu looked into the windrider's face. 'You called me an Initiate.'

'A slip of the tongue, Atreu. You can't choose a Holy Order until the final Ritual at the Source.'

'I've already said that the Order of the Wynde is the only one for me.'

'Yes, Atreu, you have. And I thanked you for your support at the time. We were all honoured, but the decision was not yours to make then.'

'So what are we doing here?'

Riell shook his head. 'You are not a normal Ascender and these are not normal times. You want to learn how to ride the wind. I know that is in your heart.'

'And you can teach me now?'

Riell laughed. 'I can begin. Windriding is a skill that takes many years to master, but I can give you a taste of what it's like.'

'But you have carried me so many places, Riell – I have felt the ground leave me.'

'Yes, you have, Atreu. And I knew from the first time at Crosanct that you were born to the wind.' He started to unfasten the harnesses on a set of wings that he had carried out of the cave entrance. 'But the true magic of windriding is the freedom to control your own flight. The greater the skill, the more intense the feeling. That's what I hope you will feel one day.'

Atreu's gaze traced the surface of the pock-marked ledge until it ended abruptly. A few cloud wisps hovered at the end, but the sky beyond was a cold blue. 'So, explain this to me again,' he said.

Riell helped Atreu into the harness. 'This ledge is the first training ground for all windriders. It is actually quite a thin wedge of rock, which juts out from the Eyries, but that doesn't bear thinking about because it would only make you nervous.'

'I think you mean *more* nervous.'

Riell smiled. 'The ledge is riddled with holes which concentrate the updraught from below. You should be able to hover just above them with these wings.'

'So I won't accidentally be blown over the edge?'

'It's always possible, but I will have a training line attached to you.' Riell indicated the rope tied onto the set of wings he was now buckling into.

There was silence as Riell checked and double checked the straps and Atreu intently watched the windrider's fingers perform the intricate task. 'You know,' said Atreu, 'it seems strange that we are out here now, doing this. Don't you feel that we are ... cheating somehow? There is a war. The Mountain hangs in balance. I have a final Ritual to complete and a quest to fulfil which could bring us the ultimate truth, and here we are ...' He trailed off.

'I know what you're saying, but I don't see it that way. Sometimes the best thing to do is to fly above something – or at least step away from it – for a moment. Windriders have always had that ability to gain a different perspective. It's what I see the Order of the Wynde offering the other Holy Orders of the Inner Sanctum. There is power in freeing yourself from tasks of gravity at times.'

'Power is something I try to avoid thinking about.'

'Why?'

'It frightens me. I sense this growing power within me every day when I read my Book.'

'It must be unnerving to read about actual events as they happen.'

'There's more to it now, though, Riell. I feel I can somehow influence a friend of mine in Peleusar through my Talisman, and this terrifies me.'

'Power is a strange thing, Atreu. I am convinced there is nothing absolute about it. It all depends on the situation you are in.'

Atreu laughed. 'Who am I talking to about power? You command the windriders and, through them, effectively the whole Maelir army.'

'Here, this way,' said Riell, indicating that Atreu should hold onto the wooden bar in front of him. 'We both know your power is greater, though – don't we?' Riell tilted his wings back slightly. 'Hold them like this,' he said. 'Not too much of an angle, or you will shoot up too high.'

Atreu tilted his wings. 'Nothing is happening,' he said after a moment.

'It will when we step over the blowholes. Follow me.'

'Riell, do you believe all this talk of an apotheosis?'

'Who am I to judge, Atreu?'

'You're my friend.'

'Hold on tight. Just a few more steps.'

Atreu felt a force under his wings and suddenly his feet were no longer touching the ground. He was vaguely aware Riell was shouting him instructions, but they weren't registering.

He looked down past his feet to the ground below. Then he lost his orientation and the sky swerved partly into view.

'Put your feet in the stirrups.' Riell's voice finally registered.

Atreu fumbled but finally got his feet in, and immediately felt more stable. He could see Riell was now hovering just above him and to his right. The training cord hung between them.

After a moment Atreu said, 'I'm not moving. Is something wrong?'

'No.' Riell's voice was partly muffled by the rush of air through the blowholes. 'I want you to try to establish a stable posture before we start moving. You're doing fine.'

Atreu swallowed. From his position, he could see over the ledge and into the blue nothingness below.

'You know,' said Riell, 'I can still remember exactly what it felt like the first time.'

Atreu felt a sudden jolt and he lost height. 'Hey, what was that?'

'Careful. The updraughts are fairly constant here, but you can never be sure.'

'Why didn't you drop, too?'

'I tilt to adjust – it's instinctive after a while. Just lean back a little.'

Atreu tilted and regained his former height.

'Now, let's try something,' said Riell.

Atreu swallowed again. 'Perhaps I can just stay here a little bit longer?'

Riell laughed. 'You look stable enough to me. Try dropping your right shoulder just a little.'

Atreu pulled on the bar with his right hand.

'No,' said Riell. 'Try to relax your shoulder muscles and use your body weight.' Atreu tried again.

'Almost.'

Suddenly he felt himself swerving to the right. He abruptly leant back and started hovering again.

'Well done, Atreu. Hold it a little bit longer this time.'

Atreu tried it again and felt his wings cut through the air.

'Again.'

Atreu looked up and saw Riell swerve with him.

'Now left.'

Again Riell moved through the air as he did.

After a while Atreu sensed the rhythm of the movements. He could always see Riell out of the corner of his eye, and with each manoeuvre, he felt the two of them become more in sync, his tilting becoming increasingly instinctive. He swerved right, then left and then right again. He hovered a few short spans above the ground, and then suddenly swooped upwards. He flew as close to the edge as he dared and peered down, imagining what it would be like to fly with no ground in sight.

Finally, Riell indicated that they should land. Atreu felt a pang of disappointment as his feet touched the ground.

'We spoke about power before, Riell,' he said. 'I sensed a great power in riding the wind.'

'Spoken like a true Initiate, Atreu. It is an art, windriding, and you either feel it or you don't.'

The two unbuckled their harnesses.

As they returned to the cave Riell patted Atreu on the back. 'Well done,' he said. 'Few pick up the rudimentary skills so easily.'

'Riell, you know you haven't answered my question. Do you believe this talk about an apotheosis?'

'I may be in the Circle now, but that doesn't mean I'm qualified to answer that question. The permanence of truth is not something for a humble windrider to decide on.'

Atreu laughed. 'A humble windrider? What about this humble Ascender from Valesend who now seems to have the fate of the Mountain in his hands?'

'Our paths are chosen for us, aren't they?'

'According to the Liche and the Felsen, yes. But what is the path of the wind? Surely it has no path, Riell?'

Riell waved his hand in a flying motion. 'There are wind currents – those are the paths of the wind.'

'But windriders can choose which current to take.'

'Yes, they can. And the more skilful they are, the greater the Freedom, but we cannot fly in places on the Mountain where there are no wind currents. Only the Upper Reaches and parts of the Mid-Reaches give us the currents to fly at will.'

Atreu looked around the cave at the broken wings that lay strewn on the ground. 'Valkyra did a great deal of damage here,' he said.

Riell shook his head. 'We have retrieved what we can, but we won't be returning to the Eyries to live. The Keep is now our home.'

Atreu sighed. 'It's strange, you know. I'm starting my descent tomorrow, but I don't feel like I'm leaving anything. What does that mean?'

'We all feel that way after Equinox. You've lost your birth-home, as we all did, and you have yet to find your new one.'

'Perhaps that's all it is,' said Atreu.

He closed his eyes, and for a moment thought he could hear the soft lapping of water on the edges of a lake on the edge of a village, on the far edge of the Mountain.

*

Rhea's eyes narrowed as she eyed Leyvin and Lythos suspiciously. 'I still don't know why the two of you are here. As I understand it, the Circle makes the major decisions, Riell commands the win-driders, and the War Council we have set up will decide the battle strategy. What do you want from me?'

Leyvin was peering at her intently, while Lythos kept looking away, as if he couldn't wait to leave the room.

'All right,' said Leyvin. 'Let me put it this way. Our system works on balances and checks. No single person can or should become too powerful.'

'You two seem to exercise a fair amount of power, from what I've been told.'

Leyvin coughed. 'The power is concentrated within the Circle, not with individuals.'

'Then why aren't you back there making your decisions?'

'Because although power is concentrated in the Circle, ideas and influence often come from outside it.'

'Which brings me to the question a third time. What do you want with me? I'm the hated Faemir leader, remember?'

Leyvin smiled. 'Hate is a strong word. I'm not sure if I hate anyone. There are only common interests and opposing interests. Right now it appears we have common interests. In answer to your question, we want to give you influence.'

Rhea's eyes narrowed further. 'Why give me anything?'

'As I said, our system works on balances. Right now there are individuals who are becoming too powerful, and threatening to upset those balances.'

Rhea snorted. 'Aren't you afraid I could become too powerful?'

Lythos spoke for the first time. 'You are not a twin and you've never been an Ascender, so you could never sit on the Circle. You could never become too powerful.'

Leyvin glared at him.

Rhea smiled. 'At last, an answer that makes some sense to me.'

Leyvin said, 'I think my brother has put it a little inelegantly.'

'At least now I'm beginning to understand why you're here. So what exactly are you offering me?'

'Our joint armies need a single decisive leader,' said Leyvin. 'I think we've learnt that lesson.'

'I thought you had one – Riell.'

'No,' said Leyvin. 'Riell has control of the windriders. The windriders are crucial for the defence of the Keep and for any battles in the Upper Reaches, but most of the battles across the Mountain will be on the ground. This requires different skills – skills that you have.'

'You are actually offering me the control of the joint Faemir and Maelir armies?'

'Effectively, yes,' said Leyvin.

'Is it yours to offer?'

'We believe we can convince the Circle. Convincing is something I'm quite good at.'

'Obviously,' said Rhea.

'Do you want time to think about our offer?'

'No, the offer is too good.'

Leyvin smiled and glanced at Lythos. 'In that case, we need to prepare our strategy for the Circle immediately.'

The two of them left the room and walked down the corridor. As soon as they were out of earshot, Lythos said, 'I really hope you know what you're doing this time, Leyvin.'

Leyvin was still smiling, and rubbing his hands together. 'We both know Riell and his windriders have used their leverage to force the consecration of the Order of the Wynde. The Order will grow too powerful too quickly. If Atreu is successful, who knows what will happen?'

'But to hand such power to a Faemir.'

'A Faemir now in our debt.'

'No, a Faemir who owes us nothing.'

'Lythos, the subtleties always escape you. Common interests – that's what it's always been about. Whether it is within the Felsen and Liche, or whether the net widens to include windriders and Faemir.'

'You're either a genius or a fool.'

'I take calculated risks,' said Leyvin.

'Remember, you were wrong when you gave control of the windriders to Riell.'

'Yes, I was wrong, and that's the reason we had to do what we've just done. We no longer had anything to bargain with. Once the windriders decided to hold us to ransom, there was no check to their power. We've just created the biggest check on the Mountain.'

'I have no choice but to accept your argument, Leyvin, but, I don't know ... a Faemir commanding Maelir forces ...'

Leyvin stopped and motioned Lythos to stop as well. 'Yes, it was inconceivable even a few short weeks ago, but we have a choice between the inconceivable and the totally unacceptable. We cannot lose control of the Circle to the Wynde, and we cannot lose control of the Mountain to the Nazir. This Rhea can help us in a way no one else can.'

'And yet ...'

Leyvin lowered his voice. 'Don't forget, above all else, nothing is permanent. The Mountain has taught us that. Who knows what is still to happen? We've forged a new alliance that is right for now. Anything can still happen if the ground shifts again.' A determined smile crossed his face. 'I just want to make sure that we are the ones left standing.'

Lythos nodded slowly, and the two brothers started walking again.

*

The Runner's chest heaved as he slumped onto the chair. He waved his hand at the Maelir battalion leaders, indicating that he was not yet able to speak.

'I think you had better get her out,' Hrulth told Cluric, indicating Jenethelen.

'No,' said the Runner between breaths. 'It's all right.'

Hrulth's brow furrowed, but he nodded his assent that Jenethelen should remain.

'I'm sorry for my impatience,' he said after he saw that the Runner was starting to breathe a little more easily, 'but we haven't had much news from outside Peleusar for some time.'

'The main report,' said the Runner, 'is that there is now a treaty between Maelir and Faemir.'

Outbursts of surprise rang around the room.

Cluric and Jenethelen looked at each other.

'What sort of treaty?' asked Hrulth.

'The two armies will be under joint command, and battle strategies against the Nazir will be coordinated.'

'So there's peace between Maelir and Faemir?' asked Cluric.

'Yes. The orders are to make immediate contact with the Faemir forces in Peleusar.'

Jenethelen took a step forward. 'I'm afraid I'm now the only Faemir force in Peleusar.'

The Runner was clearly taken aback. Recovering, he said, 'I don't have much information on Faemir casualties yet, but we have lost touch with several major Maelir battalions in recent days. We can only guess what that means.'

Hrulth said, 'And what news do you have about how wide-spread the Nazir attacks are?'

'Most of the major cities are under siege. R'in, Spa – almost all of them. Even cities that are in complete ruins, such as Ariathe.'

'And what news of the Lower Reaches?' asked Cluric.

'No clear reports,' said the Runner, 'but it appears the Nazir are attacking towns there as well, right down to the Base.'

'Besides the treaty with the Faemir,' said Hrulth, 'what is our strategy against the Nazir supposed to be?'

'Just dig in and hold ground for the moment. We need to find out what we're dealing with.'

'We've withstood two nights of attacks here,' said Hrulth. 'We may have some suggestions for you to pass on to command, but we are still doing little more than fighting blind.'

'The reports indicate that the attacks are always at night. The time for counterattacks is during the day.'

'But we haven't been able to find them during the day,' said Hrulth. 'In fact, all our battles have been with Dusk-wraiths. We haven't seen a single Nazir.'

The Runner shrugged. 'I don't think anyone has engaged the Nazir army directly as yet.'

Hrulth ran his fingers through his beard. 'We can't fight what we don't know.'

'But in the meantime, they will have an increasing advantage with the days shortening,' said Cluric.

Hrulth nodded. 'I was thinking about that. Our situation can only get worse until then. If I were them, I would try for victory by solstice. With the nights constantly getting longer and the days shorter, the length of their attacks will increase. After solstice the advantage would begin to swing back our way.'

The Runner stood up. 'I need to get moving again soon. I can't afford a night in Peleusar.'

'Of course,' said Hrulth. 'We will get you some food and water, and you can be on your way. We've sent some Runners out ourselves just this morning.'

'Are you going downslope?' asked Cluric.

'Yes, as far as Midfell. There are other Runners there who should have news from the Lower Reaches and who will take my news downslope through the Rim.'

'Tell me something,' said Jenethelen. 'Do you have news of the Faemir leader Valkyra? I cannot imagine on what terms she would accept a treaty with the Maelir.'

'Valkyra is dead,' said the Runner. 'She was taken by the Nazir at the Summit. Rhea now commands the Faemir army.'

'I see. I also heard rumours of a fearsome Maelir warrior who some believed to be a baresark like Valkyra.'

'That was the Ascender Teyth. He has been taken, too.'

'Teyth?' Cluric said the name out loud.

'Do you know the name?' asked Hrulth.

'I believe that was the Ascender Atreu's brother. A baresark warrior – how strange.' He turned to the Runner. 'Please, one more question. Do you have any news of the Ascender Atreu?'

'Yes,' said the Runner. 'Together with a Faemir, he is the only surviving Ascender. They are both undergoing the final Rituals in the Upper Reaches.'

Jenethelen opened her mouth in surprise. 'A Faemir Ascender? This sounds like a true treaty to me.'

'Please,' said the Runner. 'If I could have some food and water, I must be on my way.'

Hrulth gestured towards the table.

The Runner took a few steps, but Jenethelen went with him. 'One more question,' she said. 'Who is the Faemir Ascender?'

'It is Verlinden, Valkyra's twin.' The Runner brushed past her and sat down at the table.

Cluric pulled Jenethelen away. She was staring into space. 'What's wrong?' he said. 'Do you know this Verlinden?'

'Not personally,' she said. 'But I know Valkyra's sister was a Watcher, like me. A Watcher who has become an Ascender. I ... I find it hard to imagine.'

Cluric looked into her eyes and saw a cloudiness suddenly lift. Jenethelen was looking back at him as if seeing him for the first time.

Cluric didn't know what to say. Finally, he cleared his throat and said, 'I have to check the barricades.'

Jenethelen nodded slowly. 'I'll join you.'

Together, they headed outside.

Chapter Six

Atreu felt the air slice past him as Riell carried him along the winds of the Upper Reaches. The Keep was far behind him, and although he knew it would be bursting with activity now, somehow the image of it in his mind remained as it had been in the quiet of his pre-dawn departure. The arguments, the intrigues, and the politics already seemed a world away. Why hadn't he been sadder to leave the silver-spired city that he had seen visions of since he was a boy? Although he felt a stab of apprehension in the pit of his stomach, he was glad to be travelling again so many months after his Ascent had been completed.

In the end, it had all been so rushed. Riell had informed him that the Keep sky-watchers predicted storms within a day or two. No one wanted to delay the pilgrimage, so they made hurried preparations. Atreu looked across at Verlinden, who was being carried by another windrider, Leylan. As she shot past wisps of clouds, she had the slightly detached expression Atreu had noticed in recent days. He had tried to wave to her several times early in the journey, but she hadn't noticed. Something was wrong. He knew that. And it was not like her to keep it to herself.

What strange twists his Ascent had taken. It was as if strong winds had been blowing him in many directions. He sensed now that, although he would never be able to control the winds themselves, his aim should be to ride them along the path he wanted to go.

And how different this was from the first sunny day of his Ascent. Teyth's smiling face flashed before him. He closed his eyes to shut away the painful image, but it didn't work. Was everything worth losing his brother? The final glimpse of Teyth and Valkyra falling to the Nazir chasm cut into his vision. Atreu felt tears welling, so he opened his eyes to allow the wind to dry them. Teyth would still be alive if Atreu hadn't persuaded the windriders to rescue the besieged Faemir. Had he done the right thing? What would he tell his father if he ever saw him again – if his father was still alive?

He felt a sharp buffet that snapped his neck back.

'I should have warned you,' said Riell. 'The ride will be a little rougher from now on.'

A thought struck Atreu. 'Riell, you know I've never heard you talk about your brother.'

The wind whistled past Atreu's ears.

'Did you hear me, Riell?'

'Yes, Atreu.'

'Is he like you?'

'No, he's nothing like me.'

'You're twins. You have to be alike in some ways.'

'Twins don't have to be alike in any way. You know that.'

'Yes, but ...'

'I don't speak of my brother. He is lost.'

'He failed his Ascent?'

'Failure is an unforgiving word, Atreu. I think of him as lost. My brother is lost in many ways. To the Orders. To me. To himself. Please, don't ask me any more questions.' Riell's command of the wind seemed to falter for a moment, and the two of them swirled out of control before he regained his balance.

Atreu looked down to see that the terrain had changed. Gone was the smooth, even white surface of the Upper Reaches near the Keep. Giant, sharp-toothed crags now jutted out from the snow, hiding a myriad of narrow valleys, where shadows lurked. He imagined the sharp, angular bodies of the Nazir crowded a thousandfold into every dark crevice, just waiting for sunset, when they would swarm over the surface of the Mountain. His skin crawled at the thought. What horrific creatures these people of the Dusk were, with their pale, lidless eyes, and what bizarre warfare they were waging against the people of the Mountain. Atreu had feared the Faemir, for they were a formidable enemy, but the Nazir seemed to instil in him something beyond fear, something deeper and more soul-rending.

'I feel guilty taking you away from the War Council for my pilgrimage,' said Atreu, looking up at Riell.

'Don't feel guilty, Atreu. It is an honour. I chose to do it when I could have assigned the task to any of the other windriders. Besides, I hope to return to the Keep before the storms sweep through, so I won't be away long.'

'What are your battle plans against the Nazir?' asked Atreu.

The windrider lost some altitude briefly. 'I know I'm supposed to have all the battle plans,' he said, 'but I'm really not sure, Atreu. We need more information about them. The Faemir were our sworn enemy for thousands of years. They have been with us for as long as the Maelir have been on the Mountain. They were our enemy, yet we knew them. We have no understanding of this new enemy.'

Atreu shifted slightly, suddenly aware of the weight of the Book in his backpack. 'It's a pity I haven't been able to read anything about them in my Talisman. That could provide the key.'

'Perhaps words, rather than weapons, *will* give us victory, Atreu.'

'That's something old Praether would have said.'

A sharp gust hit them, and they were pushed in the direction of Verlinden and the other windrider.

'That was close,' called Atreu, but Verlinden didn't react.

They were now flying next to each other. Atreu tried to get her attention. 'Verlinden – are you still with us?'

Verlinden jerked her head back as if being woken suddenly. 'I'm sorry ... I think I was almost asleep. How far do we have to go?'

'With the winds prevailing,' said Riell, 'I think we will be there just after midday.'

'Will they be expecting us so soon after Equinox?' asked Atreu.

Riell laughed.

'What's the joke?'

'You'll see when you get to the Source.'

'Riddles from you, of all people, Riell. I'm surprised.'

Riell laughed again. 'I'm sorry. I wasn't playing Liche games. You'll understand when you get there. The Source is not a place where time has much meaning. You will meet some strange men there and see some of the strangest sights on the Mountain. One thing you won't see there is any appreciation of time.'

'But are they expecting us?' asked Verlinden. 'And are they expecting one of the Ascenders to be a Faemir?'

'They wouldn't be expecting *anyone*,' said Riell. 'The Holy Men there are so removed from the world that they no longer have any conception of such things. As I said, you'll see what I mean when you get there.'

'It worries me that you say there is no appreciation of time at the Source,' said Atreu. 'Time is something essential to us at the moment.'

'Yes,' said Riell, 'that will be a problem, but I don't know how you will be able to rush things once you are there.'

Atreu felt a sharp rush of wind from behind them. Turning his head, he could see dark clouds gathering in the distance. 'It looks like a storm brewing already,' he said.

'That's not good news,' said Riell, with a sudden edge in his voice. 'The sky-watchers gave us at least a full day and night before we would see anything like that. I've never known them to be wrong.'

'It's still a long way behind us.'

'Storms here move very quickly.'

'We should be able to stay ahead of it, though, shouldn't we? Aren't we riding the same winds?'

Riell was smiling grimly. 'It doesn't work that way. The winds in the heart of the storm, which are pushing those clouds, always move faster than the headwinds we're feeling now.'

Riell suddenly lost altitude and Atreu felt his stomach lurch.

'Sorry, Atreu. The headwinds are disturbing the natural thermals. The only thing we can do is ride them out.'

It took Atreu a moment to locate Verlinden and Leylan. They had lost even more altitude and were now below them.

Another strong gust hit Riell from behind, but he quickly steadied and rode with it. He signalled something to Leylan, who responded with a series of gestures.

'What's happening?' asked Atreu.

'We're trying to decide what to do. We've got three options. We can land and take our chances on the ground, or we can try to ride with the storm. We'll certainly get to the Source quickly if we ride with it, but it's very dangerous, particularly as we're both carrying passengers.'

'You've only given me two options. What's the third?'

'We can climb to an altitude above the storm clouds.'

'I hadn't thought of that. It sounds good.'

'High-altitude flying has its own dangers. Headaches, noises in your ears, breathing difficulties, mind tricks – there's a good chance that you and Verlinden will lose consciousness.'

'Wouldn't the real danger be if you and Leylan lost consciousness?'

'There's always that chance, but windriders are accustomed to high-altitude flying. It's part of our training. There are other dangers, too.'

Atreu felt another dramatic altitude drop.

Riell continued. 'Sometimes stormwinds create a suction, which draws you down into the heart of the storm.'

Atreu glanced around nervously and saw that the roiling clouds were closer now. He looked down to see the deep ravines and sharp-edged crags below. 'I'm not sure if I like any of your options.'

The two windriders continued to gesture to each other. Finally, Riell nodded and said, 'Normally I would say we should land, but with the Nazir infesting the Upper Reaches and instability everywhere, I would rather trust our skill in the air. We'll try some high-altitude flying.'

Atreu drew a breath.

'If you angle your feet down,' said Riell, 'it will help me.'

Atreu pushed back, the wings tilted up, and he and Riell started climbing. Leylan and Verlinden were almost level with them, and ascending at the same rate. The headwinds from the storm buffeted them at times, but they continued to gain altitude.

The storm clouds were approaching rapidly now, and Atreu could see flashes of lightning in the dark mass. A crack of thunder echoed through the sky.

'Hold firm, Atreu,' shouted Riell. 'This is a fast-moving storm.'

Atreu's knuckles whitened as he gripped the bar. The wings tilted even further back, and the winds were now howling around his ears.

And still they climbed.

The sky around them was darkening. 'Will we have to ride it out after all?' said Atreu.

'I hope not.' Riell's voice sounded constricted. 'We need to be at a storm's crest to ride it. If we get caught now, we're not going to have any control.'

Atreu glanced down, making sure he didn't shift his weight. The ground was now indistinct, and he could no longer make out the sharp detail of the crags.

'Look up,' shouted Riell. 'It makes a difference.'

Atreu bent his neck back and pushed back on the stirrups.

And still they climbed.

A massive wall of boiling cloud bore down on them. Lightning shot in all directions and winds screamed through the sky. Atreu felt himself being jolted left and right. He gripped the bar even more tightly.

Then suddenly it was dark, and the storm swallowed them. Atreu could see nothing beyond his outstretched hand.

And still they climbed.

The winds increased in ferocity. Atreu's face stung as splinters of ice pricked his exposed skin. Thunderclaps crashed through his head and sent tremors along the length of his body.

And still they climbed.

Atreu struggled to keep his orientation. The howls of the wind were now unbearable.

And still they climbed.

And still they climbed.

Suddenly, the sky cleared and the howls faded.

Atreu looked around the see Leylan and Verlinden emerging from the roiling mass into the clear, pale blue sky above the storm.

'We made it,' he cried.

'We're not high enough to be safe yet,' said Riell.

And still they climbed.

The howling and the thunderclaps continued to fade as the storm clouds receded below them.

'I feel a little light-headed,' said Atreu.

'That's the altitude,' said Riell. 'Keep talking to me. I want you to try to stay conscious for as long as possible. It makes flying easier.'

Atreu looked up. The sun was shining a clear light, but the air was bitterly cold. 'How high is it possible to fly?'

'I don't know,' said Riell. 'I have heard stories that some windriders in the past have tried to find out.'

'What happened?'

'According to the stories, they were never seen again. I think they would have eventually blacked out and plummeted to the ground.'

'Have you ever thought about it, Riell?'

'I don't have a death wish.'

Atreu fell silent.

'Are you all right, Atreu?'

'Yes. I just had a strange picture come into my mind.'

'Like I said, your mind often plays tricks on you at this height. Try to keep focused. It will get worse, though – we're still gaining altitude.'

'Funny. I imagined I saw a windrider tethered to several others by ropes many leagues long.'

'Your mind is toying with you.'

'No, listen, Riell. It was a flash of clarity. I saw this windrider climbing higher than anyone has ever been.'

It was Riell's turn to fall into silence. 'I see what you're saying. That windrider would be safe even if he lost consciousness. His fall would be broken by the windriders on the other end of the ropes.'

'As long as the other riders were flying further from the ground than the rope was long.'

Riell laughed. 'That is either one of the cleverest things I've ever heard, or the most stupid. I can't decide which.'

'Neither can I,' said Atreu, joining his laughter. 'But I certainly feel very strange. I've just seen another picture.'

'What is it this time?'

'It was a man and a woman coming out through the covers of a giant book, the way we just came out of the storm clouds.'

'Keep talking, Atreu. Your voice is sounding quite strange.'

'Do you think that's possible, Riell?'

'What?'

'To come out of the story you are in?'

'What are you talking about, Atreu?'

'You know – the story.'

'What?'

'It's all so clear. Of course, even if it was possible, you would probably black out. But then, if you were tethered to the story in some way ... It would work ... it could ...'

'Atreu?'

'What would you see, do you think? What ...'

'Keep talking, Atreu.'

'Outside everything ... so high ...'

Riell felt the weight on his wings shift as Atreu lost consciousness ...

*

Atreu was falling. Bright lights streaked past him as the ground approached. He reached for the crossbar but found he was no longer in a harness. Where was Riell? What had happened? The sky around him was strange, as if it was made out of shattered glass. He looked down and saw that a giant chasm had opened up in the ground, like the mouth of a monstrous beast. He screamed, but he was moving so fast the sound never reached his ears.

Then he entered the chasm.

And kept falling.

The shards of light from thousands of glimmerstones enveloped him. He was suddenly aware that he was slowing down. The myriad colours on the stone walls became sharper and more distinct. He felt his breathing slow – even his heart beat a steadier rhythm.

Finally, he came to a complete stop. He was floating in mid-air. The jade, amber and crimson lights of the countless glimmerstones winked at him, and he was weightless, suspended inside the Mountain. *This is a dream,* he thought. *This time I know it's a dream.*

He moved his arms in a swimming motion, manoeuvring himself towards the side of the chasm. As he got closer, he noticed a change in the glimmerstones. They appeared to be growing in size and intensity. To his horror, whispered voices seemed to be calling to him from within the walls.

Atreu. Come.

Atreu. You are one of us.

As he stared at the lights, the glimmerstones unfurled like flowers, each revealing a dark, throbbing heart.

His heart was racing again. Frantically, he flailed his arms and legs in an attempt to back away from the walls. The cold ice of terror gripped him. Out of each heart, a small hand was now unfurling. And each hand was reaching, fingers outstretched, towards him.

He screamed, and this time the scream filled the chasm, bouncing off the walls and back towards him in countless echoes. And each echo that sought him out brought a tiny hand, homing in on Atreu as if he was willing them towards him.

Wake up, he cried inside his head. *Wake up!*

But he didn't wake up. The arms lengthened, and the fingers twitched, as if in anticipation, as they approached. He backed away, his arms and legs pushing against the viscous chasm air ... pushing back ... pushing back – until he felt the first touch from behind.

He twisted around to see more hands reaching for him. There was no place to escape to. The fingers twitched obscenely against his skin as he tried to brush them away.

Please wake up.

The fingers now grasped at him from all sides, nails digging into his skin.

Escape.

Then the image of two figures emerging from a book came into his mind. He closed his eyes and buried himself deep in the pages of his Talisman. He could no longer feel the probing fingers. Hesitantly, he opened his eyes. All around him it was dark. This time he willed the image of the two emerging figures back into his mind, and pushed up.

As he emerged from his dream, he was aware of the harness around him and the stormwinds, which were now buffeting him.

'What's happening?' he cried.

'Atreu, can you hear me?' Riell's voice sounded strained.

'Of course.'

'We're re-entering the storm.'

Atreu felt the gale lash the exposed skin of his face. 'Why?'

'The Source is somewhere below. We don't want to overshoot it.'

'We're here?'

'Well ... it's hard to tell. The storm has moved with us, so I haven't been able to see the ground. Both Leylan and I have been guessing.'

The darkness around them grew as they continued to descend. 'Couldn't we have just hovered until the storm passed underneath us?'

'Hovering above a storm is not the easiest thing to do, Atreu. Besides, I was worried about you.'

'Me?'

'Yes, you were screaming and shouting uncontrollably.'

'It was a dream, a horrific dream. I fell from the sky into a huge chasm and –'

A violent gust blew Atreu and Riell off balance. Atreu sensed immediately that something was wrong. He had lost all sense of orientation.

'Riell!' he cried.

There was no reply, just the winds, howling around his ears. A wave of panic hit him. Was Riell still conscious?

'Riell!' he cried again, arching his neck to look at the windrider.

The first thing that caught his eye was the hole that had been ripped into the material of one of the wings.

'Left side,' came Riell's wind-blown voice. 'Pull down hard.'

It took a split second for Atreu to register that Riell was still conscious, and then he pulled down hard on the crossbar with his left hand. He felt the wings rotate wildly.

'Now right,' shouted Riell. 'Not as hard.'

Atreu pulled down with his right hand. The wings oscillated from side to side, but then stabilised.

The dark mass of clouds churned around them as they continued to descend, lashed by stinging ice-rain flurries. The wings lurched with every gust, and Atreu glanced nervously at the hole in the material, which was growing.

'We're going to have to try a vertical drop,' said Riell, straining his voice so he could be heard above the storm.

'A what?'

'A vertical drop. Our wings won't last much longer.'

'I don't like the sound of this. What do I do?'

'You shift your weight with me. Don't fight against it ...'

Atreu lost Riell's words in a violent ice-rain gust.

'... and then we pull up as close to the ground as we can.'

'I didn't hear all of that, Riell.'

'We just drop vertically. Head first. It's the quickest way down and places the least strain on the wings.'

'We just drop?'

'Yes–' They were buffeted suddenly, and Atreu saw that the hole in the wing had grown larger.

'We have to do it now,' said Riell. 'At the end of the drop, just push down as hard as you can with your feet when I tell you. We'll be close to the ground, so there's no room for error.'

'I can't even see the ground,' cried Atreu.

'Hopefully we will when we get closer.'

'Hopefully –'

'Now, Atreu! Shift your weight with me now. We have to drop.'

Atreu felt his feet lifting up above his head in a diving position, and he followed Riell's momentum. Almost immediately, he felt the air whistling past his ears and racing along the length of his body. The ice particles still hit him, but he felt less buffeting from the wind.

He stared down, desperately hoping that the ground wouldn't suddenly rear up out of nowhere, leaving them no time to pull out of the dive.

Where was Verlinden? Were she and Leylan diving too?

A thought struck him as he plummeted through the sky. *Was this his dream?* Did it seem any less real than his fall into the chasm?

'Atreu. Your feet. Now.'

Riell's voice cut into his thoughts and he pushed hard with his legs. He felt the wings arc out of the dive and swoop up slightly before they levelled out.

The winds still battered them as he looked down. Through the storm-darkened sky he could make out the wild, snow-covered terrain just below them. Jagged crags split the ground, and between them lay a desolate expanse of white.

'That was close, wasn't it?' said Atreu.

'I've pulled out of a vertical drop like that even closer to the ground,' said Riell, 'but that was as close as I want to get flying in tandem.'

'I had full faith in you. I'm sure you've done enough of these.'

'Rarely with a passenger who isn't a windrider.'

Atreu swallowed. 'At least I had some experience.' He looked up. How would Verlinden fare?

'Leylan ... is a fully trained windrider,' said Riell, as if reading his thoughts. 'I'm sure they will be coming down soon.'

As they continued to descend, Atreu scanned the sky above them. Where were they?

'Are you certain Leylan was going to do a vertical drop as well?' he asked.

'My last signal to him was that I would try it. I didn't see his reply. The clouds were too thick, and I lost sight of them.'

Atreu was becoming increasingly anxious. 'Could they have dived before us?'

'Yes, it's possible.'

'So they may be on the ground already?'

'It's possible, but the only way they could have landed already is to have dropped a lot closer to the ground than we did. I hope it wasn't too close.'

The winds still howled around them as they approached the surface of the Mountain.

'If they dropped before us,' said Atreu, 'they would be further back, wouldn't they?'

'Yes,' said Riell. 'I know what you're going to say, but we can't go back just now. The hole in the wing is now huge. Have a look. We're going to have trouble landing ourselves.'

Atreu saw that the material had torn further, and shreds were flapping furiously in the wind. Another violent gust hit them and they tilted precariously. Riell struggled to regain balance.

'Atreu, hang on, we're not out of this yet. We're going to have to land. That wing won't last much longer.'

Taking a deep breath, Atreu braced himself. The wings were now oscillating from side to side as Riell fought against the effects of the hole.

Atreu could now see the detail in the sharp-toothed edges of the thin line of rocks below.

'Pull left, Atreu,' cried Riell. 'We need to land on the flat snow.'

A crag reared up at them, but they swerved away at the last moment. Atreu heard a tearing noise from the wing, then started rotating in midair. He heard Riell start to say something, and suddenly felt himself dropping. He instinctively pulled on the harness, not having any idea if he was doing the right thing. The descent seemed to slow momentarily, then they began to fall again.

The next thing he felt was the soft crunch of fresh snow around him.

After the shock wore off he looked around to see that Riell's eyes were open. 'We made it,' said Riell.

Atreu looked at the white walls of the deep indentation they had made in the snow. The hole in the material now ran the length of the wing, and the wooden frame had snapped in two. Above his head, the storm still raged.

He half-smiled. 'Something tells me we're a long way from being safe.'

*

Rhea was aware that she, Saretha and Ahrai were all absently fingering the hilts of their swords as they sat at the table in her room. Outside, a wild storm howled, and lightning flashed through the window.

'They have no idea how to wage war,' said Saretha. 'We always suspected that, but I can see it now without a shadow of a doubt.'

'I agree,' said Rhea. 'Some of the Maelir soldiers were reasonable opponents one on one, but they have no idea of battle strategy.'

'I don't know how we didn't take control of Zenith,' said Saretha. 'We would have done it if it wasn't for those damned Nazir.'

'It doesn't matter now, though, does it?' said Ahrai. 'We all agree we have no choice but to combine our armies.'

Rhea frowned. 'The problem is, now we can be hampered by their battle decisions. Their weaknesses are now our weaknesses.'

'That Riell is a fool,' said Saretha. 'Why would the windrider commander waste time taking an Ascender on a pilgrimage? Surely any windrider would have been able to do it?'

'The Ascent is still of the highest importance to them, despite everything,' said Ahrai.

'If Riell is the best commander they have, we need to control both armies,' said Saretha. 'But how?'

Rhea drew her sword and stared at its sharp point. Outside, the wild winds screamed across the Keep. 'These Holy Orders play some very dangerous games up here in the Keep, where the rest of the Mountain is a world away.'

'What are you saying, Rhea?' Ahrai eyed her curiously.

Rhea smiled. 'The two that appear to be the ones in control – Leyvin and Lythos. They have offered me sole command of the combined armies.'

'What?' Saretha stared, open-mouthed. 'Do they have the power to do that?'

'I don't understand how everything works up here, but I believe they do.'

'So they are giving you the power to do what you wish,' said Saretha. 'To move soldiers so that Maelir battalions are most at risk and Faemir battalions are protected, if that's what you want to do?'

Rhea continued to smile. 'I don't think it would be wise to say that too loudly – but yes, command is command. Although the clever one, Leyvin, probably knows I wouldn't do that if it was a poor battle strategy.'

'And if it was a good strategy,' said Saretha, 'he probably wouldn't care about the Maelir deaths. It's not as if countless Maelir lives haven't been lost already.'

'What about Riell?' said Ahrai. 'He has a lot of influence, and the windriders are a formidable force.'

'As far as I can tell, Riell may not be an influence for some time.'

'What do you mean?' Saretha's eyes narrowed.

Rhea's smile widened. 'From what Leyvin has suggested, he encouraged Riell to carry the Ascender Atreu.'

'So?'

'He was also encouraged to leave at dawn this morning, and now look at this storm outside.'

'You think Leyvin sent them out knowing the storm was on the way?' asked Ahrai. 'Without forewarning them?'

Rhea nodded. 'He encouraged them to go as quickly as possible. Verlinden told me she hadn't expected to go for another day. I wouldn't trust this Leyvin, but he appears to be effective. If he has offered me command – it is his to give, I think.'

She waited for that to sink in and then added, 'And, of course, the commander of an army is free to choose her second and third in command.'

A bright flash of lightning suddenly lit up the room. The three Faemir looked at each other in silence, waiting for the thunder.

*

Cluric and Jenethelen returned from patrol as the sun hung low in the sky. The Maelir soldiers were busily stoking the barricade fires in preparation for the night's attack from the Dusk-wraiths.

'Any luck?' asked Hrulth.

'Same as every other time,' said Cluric. 'There is no sign of the wraiths or the Nazir during the day. Perhaps we should be reclaiming territory in daylight.'

'You don't mean that, do you?' said Hrulth.

'No. That strategy would probably mean the end of us in one night. These barricades are the only thing saving us.' His eyes were downcast. 'It's just so frustrating dealing with an enemy like this.'

'How much longer are you going to stay in Peleusar?' asked Jenethelen.

'Our instructions are to hold as much of Peleusar as possible for as long as we can,' said Hrulth.

'As a battalion leader, though, you also need to think about the safety of your soldiers, don't you? The instructions surely aren't to hold Peleusar at all costs?'

'No,' said Hrulth. 'Not at all costs. But even if we decided to abandon the city, where would we go? Do we know of any part of the Mountain that is safe at the moment?'

A chill wind suddenly whipped up around them, and Cluric looked up at the darkening sky. The sun was quickly being obscured by dark clouds at the horizon.

'This is what I feared,' said Hrulth.

Cluric stared at him. 'What?'

'I hope they aren't storm clouds brewing.'

The significance dawned on Cluric quickly. 'If there's a storm, the rain will extinguish our fires.'

Hrulth ran his fingers through his beard as he nodded.

Cluric looked at Jenethelen and could see the fear in her eyes. 'They may not be storm clouds,' he said.

'Whatever the case,' said Hrulth, 'it looks like it will be dark sooner than we expected. Let's get into battle formation.'

Cluric and Jenethelen drew their swords and headed off to their allotted position behind the barricades.

Gusts of wind soon started coming through at regular intervals, fanning the flames of the barricade into a wild frenzy. Cluric watched the fire grow. 'Perhaps this storm may help us after all,' he said hopefully.

Before Jenethelen could reply, another gust sent a burning cinder onto the rooftop of one of the buildings behind them. The roof immediately started smouldering, and several soldiers scrambled to extinguish the fire.

Jenethelen frowned. 'Do you still think the storm could help us?'

Cluric fell silent and watched the sky darken as the clouds approached.

'You know,' said Jenethelen, 'I've just thought of something.'

'What?'

'The Faemir coveyns used to use brimstones effectively when they wanted to set fire to buildings from a distance.'

'I've been on the receiving end of some of those attacks.'

'After we began our assault on the Summit under Valkyra, we used them only rarely. The brimstones are really only effective on the dry, thatched roofs of villages, and we weren't wasting time on small villages anymore.'

'What's your point?'

'If fire is the only thing we've found that has had any effect on the wraiths, perhaps we should fire some brimstones at them to see what happens.'

Cluric nodded slowly. 'It's worth a try – but where do we get brimstones from? I don't remember seeing any with the Faemir weapons we found.'

'We didn't have any,' said Jenethelen. 'The easiest thing to do would be to dig for new ones.'

'Do you know where to dig?'

'Yes, all young Faemir are taught where to look. There would be several places downslope of Peleusar that would have them.'

'I'll speak to Hrulth about it. Perhaps we could go tomorrow and find some. That may be more useful than endlessly patrolling the city, looking for an enemy who doesn't exist in daylight.'

The winds now swirled around them and the barricade fires danced a wild dance high into the prematurely dark sky.

'Of course,' said Jenethelen, 'if it rains, then we won't survive the night, and it doesn't matter if my idea works, does it?'

When the first raindrops fell, Cluric felt as if his skin had been pierced by a thousand tiny knives. He fought the feeling of despair that settled in the pit of his stomach as the barricade fires started to hiss and die.

When the full brunt of the storm hit, he stood, trembling, his sword pointing in the direction that the wraiths had come on previous nights.

When the fires finally died and night had fallen over Peleusar, Cluric still stood, alongside the other Maelir soldiers, and awaited his final battle.

Chapter Seven

Although the winds had abated a little, the storm was not yet spent as Atreu and Riell trudged through the snow, each carrying a broken wing. Atreu stared at his feet, glumly following Riell's footprints.

'Don't worry, Atreu. Leylan is an experienced windrider. I'm sure they're both safe. Perhaps they're at the Source already.'

Atreu grunted a reply.

Riell continued, 'There's no point doing a search on foot. Once we're at the Source, there's a chance I may be able to repair these wings. A search from the air is the only real option out here.'

'I know you're right, Riell. Just tell me, shouldn't someone at the Keep have known this storm was coming so soon?'

'I don't understand it. It was a fast-moving storm, and weather patterns are unpredictable in the Upper Reaches at the best of times, but there is something amiss. The sky-watchers have always been so reliable – it is a point of honour for them. They should have seen the warning signs.'

'Are the Nazir involved in some way?'

'What do you mean?'

'I don't know. I sense that they have some strange powers.'

Riell glanced back at Atreu. 'The power to control weather?

I think you're talking nonsense again. Let's not give them more powers in our own minds than they actually have.'

'You're probably right. If they can whip up a storm like that out of nothing, we are all doomed ... and yet, somehow I feel they –'

'I don't want to hear this, Atreu. The Nazir are flesh and blood. They are not some kind of sorcerers with unnatural powers. If we start believing that, we should give up the fight now. Storms are fuelled by the winds, and no one can conjure up winds out of nothing.'

Atreu looked up at the sky and saw the clouds starting to break up. In the spaces that opened up between them, he could see the heavens darkening.

'I hope there are no Nazir anywhere near this storm,' he said. 'Will we make the Source by nightfall?'

'That's hard to say,' said Riell. 'I find it hard to judge travelling time on land. I would say we will probably reach the Source sometime between nightfall and midnight.'

*

The wind dropped soon after sunset, and a bitter, gnawing cold set in. The stars had the sky to themselves now that the clouds had moved on. They clustered brightly above the jagged crags, more intense than they ever were at the Keep, where they had to compete with the lights of the towers, turrets and flying buttresses.

'We're fortunate that the moon is almost full,' said Riell, scanning the steep cliffs that reared up in front of them. 'The gaps into the Source are hard to find from the ground.'

'How many ways in are there?' asked Atreu.

'Six that I know of, but only one wide enough for us to carry these wings through.'

'That's the one you're looking for now?'

'Yes, but ... it's hard to tell. I'm still not certain of my bearings.'

Atreu followed the windrider as they walked parallel to the cliff wall.

'Ah, here's one of the gaps,' said Riell finally.

Atreu could see a break in the rock just up ahead. As they approached, Riell said, 'I'm afraid I've led us the wrong way.'

'This isn't a gap?'

'I think it is, but it's not the one I was looking for.' He glanced up at the sky, trying to orientate himself.

Atreu could see that the crevice in the rock was just wide enough for a man to walk through comfortably. 'We'll have to leave the wings here, won't we?'

Riell frowned. 'They would be like an arrow pointing to the most secret of Holy Places.' He scanned the constellations again.

'What's wrong?' asked Atreu.

'Navigating by the stars is much easier from the sky. I *have* badly miscalculated. I think we're actually half a night's walk from where I thought we were.'

'If this is a gap, I still say we go through. The night is calm and we've seen no Dusk creatures, but we don't know that things will stay that way.'

'I'm fairly certain this is one of the minor gaps, but there are several breaks in the cliffs around here and, although they look like gaps, many lead to dead ends.'

Atreu was shivering because they had been standing still for so long. 'Is there any way you can be more certain?'

'I don't think so.'

'So we'll just have to try it and see.'

'Well ...'

'Come on, Riell, we can't just stand here all night. Let's hide these broken wings as best we can and get moving.'

Riell's brow furrowed.

'What's wrong, Riell?'

'You don't understand, Atreu. A windrider's wings are his life. Once I leave them behind, I ... I have nothing.'

'But they're just a hindrance as they are at the moment. You're not making any sense.'

Riell took a deep breath. 'You're right, of course. I'm just sorry I couldn't carry you more safely.'

'I'm still alive, aren't I? Are you sure you're not the one talking nonsense now?'

'All right.' Riell pointed to a deep ravine some distance to their right. 'We'll hide the wings there.'

The sky was still clear and the air calm when they returned and entered the gap. Slivers of moonlight lit their way at first, but soon the rocks closed above them and they were plunged into darkness. They made progress by keeping one hand on each wall as they walked.

After a while, Atreu said, 'I think I may have a glimmerstone in my pack which could help.'

'How long have you had it? Don't they lose their light not long after they have been taken from the rock?'

'I've had this one since the very start of my Ascent. It seems to come to life when it's near my Book, so it may still be some help.'

They stopped for a moment and Atreu riffled through his pack, taking out his Book and then feeling for the glimmerstone.

'Ah, here it is,' he said, pulling it out.

'I can't see anything,' said Riell. 'It doesn't look like it's working.'

'No, wait. I'll open my Book.'

Atreu lifted the rich leather cover of his Talisman. Immediately, a pinprick of light appeared inside the glimmerstone.

The light grew until it illuminated the gap in the rock where they stood.

'You were right, Atreu. That will help us. Let's get going – I am not comfortable being completely enclosed like this.'

'Just a moment. I want to try something.'

Atreu reached into his pack and pulled out the Book of Maelur. 'Let's see what happens when I open this one as well.'

He opened the second Book and suddenly the stone walls

around them were alive with a faint glow. They looked around in amazement.

'Do you know what I think has happened?' said Riell examining the rock face near his right shoulder. 'There are hundreds of long-dead glimmerstones in the walls here, which have somehow been reborn.'

Atreu ran his fingers along the surface of the rock. 'Just as Praether predicted, two Books magnify the effect of one many times over.'

'There is indeed something miraculous about those Books. I don't doubt that, Atreu. They seem to have some direct connection with the Mountain.'

Atreu let his glimmerstone roll around in the palm of his hand. Its glow had also intensified now that the Book of Maelur was also open. 'I think there's enough light now. I can put this away again.'

'What happens if we close the Books?'

'Let's see.'

Atreu closed both Books and the glow around them immediately started to fade.

Riell shook his head, open-mouthed. 'So, what do we do now?'

Atreu reopened the Book of Maelur and gave it to Riell. 'Here, you carry this and I'll hold mine.' When he opened his Talisman again, the glow from the rocky walls all around them was rekindled.

'I have to say, I feel a little silly holding a book like this, Atreu.'

'You wouldn't feel silly drawing your sword here, would you?'

Riell looked at him curiously. 'You say some strange things sometimes. All right, let's get going.'

Atreu retied his backpack and they continued, progressing much more quickly now that they could see where they were going.

After a while, Riell said, 'You know, I've been thinking about this storm. The sky-watchers at the Keep *should* have seen it coming.'

'What do you think happened?'

'I don't know, but something is wrong.'

Atreu felt a tremor underneath his feet. He looked at Riell anxiously. 'This isn't exactly the best time for us to have some instability.'

'No,' said Riell. 'This passage could easily close in on us.'

'How much further is it?'

'I'm not sure. As I said before, I'm afraid I'm not the best guide on land.'

They picked up the pace as they continued along the passage under the pale glow of the reawakened glimmerstones. Atreu held his open Book in front of him. Occasionally, he seemed to recognise a familiar word on the page, but he found it impossible to walk on the uneven rocky floor and read at the same time, so he didn't bother to try to decipher it. He felt further tremors, although they didn't appear to be increasing in intensity.

Finally, the air around them seemed to freshen and Atreu sensed that they were close to the end of the gap. Soon they stepped out of the crevice in the cliff face and into the open.

Atreu watched the vapour exhale from his nose in the pre-dawn light. Everything was still, and the bitter cold stung his face.

Riell closed the Book of Maelur and handed it to Atreu. 'We won't need this anymore,' he said. He motioned for Atreu to follow him along a narrow ledge, which seemed to be descending into a mist-shrouded valley below.

Atreu put both Books into his backpack and followed the windrider, carefully watching the loose stones on the ledge.

The sky was lightening when Riell motioned him to stop. He pointed to the distance. 'Watch,' he said. 'With such a clear sky, it should be quite a sight.'

Atreu strained to see what Riell was referring to. At first all he could see was the hazy outline of the cliffs in the distance and a giant bowl of grey mist below.

Then the sun appeared over the cliffs, bringing their jagged edges into sharp focus. The rays of light spread across the rocks towards them. Miraculously, the mist below started to dissipate as it was slowly pulled skyward to be dissolved in the sunlight.

The final dispersion was as if a huge shroud had suddenly been lifted. Atreu gasped as he saw a giant crater below them, and within it, held by the circular cliff face, the still blue waters of the clearest lake he had ever seen.

Atreu's head spun. The surrounding rocks and sky were reflected by the lake so perfectly that he lost any point of reference.

He felt Riell's steadying hand on his shoulder. 'Look away,' said the windrider. 'It will take you a while to get used to it.'

Atreu drew his eyes away and stared at Riell. His legs still trembled, but the spinning started to ease.

Riell smiled. 'Welcome to the Source.'

*

Only when the sun finally rose did Cluric feel he could breathe again. He and Jenethelen were still standing in the same position, swords drawn, as they had been when the barricade fires had been extinguished by the storm. It was as if they had been frozen on the spot all night.

The weak rays of sunlight woke the realisation in him: *The wraiths hadn't come.*

He started trembling uncontrollably and felt tears of relief well up in his eyes. A moment later Jenethelen had put her arms around him and they were both weeping uncontrollably.

Cluric pulled away after a while. 'I'm sorry ... I ...'

They wiped their faces and stood back, embarrassed.

'It *is* morning, isn't it?' said Jenethelen. 'This is not some monstrous dream where we are sent a false dawn?'

'I ... I don't know. I feel ... I don't know what I feel.' Cluric looked at Jenethelen, her hair matted into thick strands by the wind and rain.

'Why didn't they come? We had no protection.'

'I don't know.' Cluric shook his head uncontrollably.

Gradually, he became aware of movement around him. The other soldiers were recovering from the shock and leaving their defensive positions.

'Come on,' said Jenethelen. 'Let's go inside. There's no use standing out here.'

'They seem to get to you even when they don't attack,' said Cluric.

'Yes – come on. We're safe for another day.'

Cluric slowly sheathed his sword. His action was deliberate and precise as he fought to regain his self-control.

'Why do you think we are still alive?' he asked.

The Faemir sheathed her sword as well. 'Sometimes the fact that you *are* alive is all that matters.'

Hrulth joined Cluric and Jenethelen as they entered the building. Offering them some steaming barley tea, he said, 'These Dusk-spawn are anything but predictable.'

Cluric warmed his hands on the cup and let the steam hit his face before he took a sip of the tea. 'I think I almost prefer it when the wraiths attack. You don't have as much time to think.'

'We haven't lost any ground since they've attacked,' said Jenethelen. 'Who knows what motivates them. Perhaps when they don't make any progress they just move on.'

'You don't really believe that, do you?' said Cluric. 'We've burned enough Maelir bodies over the last few nights for the Dusk People to realise they would wear us down eventually.'

'You're thinking like a Maelir,' said Jenethelen. 'You fight to defend, to hold on. Perhaps the Nazir have no sense of permanence. Who knows?'

Hrulth stared at the Faemir and ran his fingers through the tangle of his beard. 'We *do* have to think differently. How is it possible that we were totally exposed for a whole night and yet they did not attack?'

'Well, what was different about last night?' asked Jenethelen.

'The storm.' Hrulth shrugged.

'We know fire weakens them,' said Jenethelen. 'Perhaps storms have an even greater effect.'

'But a storm is just wind and rain,' said Cluric. 'And sometimes thunder and lightning.'

'The thunder and lightning didn't last the whole night,' said Hrulth.

'And it's been windy at other times,' said Jenethelen. 'That leaves rain.'

'It *did* rain until dawn,' said Cluric.

'But rain is just water,' said Hrulth. 'Are they afraid of water?'

'They aren't *afraid* of fire, are they?' said Jenethelen. 'Fire just weakens them. Perhaps water has an even greater effect.'

'Hmmm.' Hrulth was deep in thought.

*

As the morning wore on, the lake's surface appeared increasingly crystal-like. Atreu was mesmerised by the play of reflections as he and Riell negotiated the path down into the crater. It was as if the most exquisite lights shone from the lake's depths. He stumbled several times on the gravelly surface because he couldn't take his eyes off the water. The air was frost-still, and the only thing audible was the regular crunch-crunch of their feet on the ground. The silence clouded around them, almost as if it was hushing any sound that dared escape into the ether.

When Atreu spoke, it was only Riell's reply that convinced him that his voice had carried. 'Where do the Holy Men of the Source live?' he asked, breaking a silence that had extended through most of the morning.

'I don't want to sound elusive,' said Riell, 'but you can't think of these Holy Men as living anywhere in the way that most of us do.'

'Don't tell me we're talking about ghosts and spirits.'

Riell laughed softly. 'No, they are living Maelir, like us. But

I'm not sure if the comparison goes any further. Think of the strangest Felsen monk you have encountered.'

'The monastery at Lhorong was a strange place.'

'Well, the Holy Men at the Source would seem strange to those monks at Lhorong.'

Atreu stumbled momentarily, but quickly got his rhythm back. 'But the Holy Men here must sleep. If they don't *live* anywhere then at least tell me where they sleep.'

'They would claim they don't need sleep. The hours of meditation replace it.'

'All right, where do they eat, then? Surely they must eat.'

'Yes, but not a lot, as far as I can tell. The windriders fly in food regularly, and I know it's not a large amount. Perhaps they eat the geyers or other birds during summer as well, but I doubt it. They would claim they have trained their bodies to have minimal need for food. I think some of them may consider it a weakness to eat at all.'

A tremor shook the cliff walls, and Atreu's attention was taken by the ripples that ran across the lake and shot shards of bright colours through the water.

'The Holy Men of the Source may have removed themselves from the world,' said Atreu, smiling grimly, 'but it looks like the world is not going to let them hide away forever.'

'I've never heard of instability at the Source. But then, we all thought the Keep was immune to it.'

'Let's hope it doesn't mean the Nazir are on their way. How would the monks here protect themselves?'

'They wouldn't,' said Riell. 'There is no squadron of windriders assigned here. They've always relied on the absolute secrecy of the Source and the natural defences of this ring of cliffs.'

Atreu stared at the lake, watching the ripples gradually disperse and leaving the crystal sheen in their wake. For the first time, he became aware of dark specks floating in the water.

'What are they?' he asked.

Riell didn't answer.

'What are those things in the water, Riell? Atreu pointed to the dark specks.

'I'm sorry, Atreu. It's not good when I have too much time to think.' He followed the line of Atreu's outstretched hand. 'They are floating prayer mats. When we get a bit closer you'll see there's a monk sitting on each one.'

'What are they doing?'

'Meditating, reading the reflections in the lake, looking for auspicious signs – who knows. I don't claim to understand the ways of these Felsen.'

'So they are all Felsen monks? There are no Liche here?'

'These Holy Men are the most Felsen-like of all the Felsen monks – if you understand what I mean. While the Liche tend to dominate the Keep, and particularly the Circle, they have no place here.'

'Who would choose to stay here as a Holy Man?'

'For the Felsen the ultimate goal is spiritual stillness. What better place to achieve that end?'

'Well, I've made my choice of Holy Order.'

'I've said it before. Don't be so hasty. Some say the Felsen choose you.'

Atreu frowned. 'They can't have me against my will.'

'No, I don't mean it in that sense. The Felsen spirit somehow chooses those who have an affinity for it. It is not anything conscious. I have heard stories of Ascenders who have expressed their utter abhorrence of the Felsen way of life yet have ended up never leaving the Source.'

'They have stayed here willingly?'

'More than willingly, Atreu. They were unable to conceive of anything else.'

Atreu shivered. 'That frightens me more than anything I saw on my Ascent.'

They continued their march in silence. Atreu was beginning to feel the strain in his knees. His legs had obviously lost condition during his time in the Keep, and this constant descent was proving to be harder in many ways than walking upslope.

'Something is frightening me the more I think about it,' said Riell.

'What?'

'I can't get that storm out of my head. There is something amiss, and I think there's only one explanation for it.'

Atreu chewed his bottom lip, waiting for Riell to continue.

'No matter which way I look at it, Atreu, there's only one conclusion I can draw. And that is that those who authorised us to leave for the Source when we did must have known the storm was on its way.'

'You think Leyvin deliberately withheld the news from us?'

'I think more than that. The instruction came suddenly. I think he actively encouraged us to leave when we did, knowing full well there was a chance we wouldn't survive.'

'I've never trusted Leyvin, but that seems to be drawing a long bow.'

'There's something else.'

Atreu tensed at the windrider's tone.

'When we were in the middle of things up there, I didn't want to worry you unnecessarily, but ...' Riell trailed off.

'What is it?'

'Well, Leylan was of full rank, but no one could possibly class him as one of our strongest windriders.'

Atreu felt his throat go dry. 'Why was he chosen to carry Verlinden?'

The windrider didn't answer.

'Riell, who chose Leylan?'

'I ... it's hard to say. I suppose you could say I chose him ... it was meant to be a fairly straightforward flight. There was no need to choose a highly experienced windrider.'

'But you're probably the most important windrider, and you were carrying me. Why would you choose someone with limited experience to carry Verlinden?'

'I don't know. Leylan needed a boost to his confidence. He is young ... and he has had some problems. I had been speaking to Leyvin ... and somehow at the end of it, I had decided ... or believed I had decided ...'

Atreu was having difficulty swallowing. 'Leyvin is a subtle manipulator,' he said finally. 'I've seen him at work. He could have made you believe it was your idea.'

'How could I be so stupid?'

Atreu shook his head and closed his eyes momentarily. 'It appears Leyvin had no real intention of letting a Faemir see the Source.'

'He probably also hoped that the two of us would, at the very least, be out of the way for some time.' Riell tried to place a hand on Atreu's shoulder. 'I'm sorry, Atreu. I've been a fool.'

The stillness crowded in on them as they stopped walking and stared blankly at the lake below.

Atreu glanced at Riell, but was unable to maintain eye contact. 'Can we rest for a moment?' he said. 'I'm suddenly very tired.'

They sat down in the penetrating silence. Atreu suddenly felt as if his thoughts were being buffeted by stormwinds. The circle of cliffs whirled like a dervish. He desperately needed an anchor. Nothing was certain. He could trust no one.

Unaware of what he was doing, he instinctively opened his pack and took out his Book. Without knowing why, he began to read.

Chapter Eight

'This way,' said Jenethelen as she led Cluric through a thatch of dense bushes into flat terrain with sparse vegetation.

Cluric felt a sense of freedom as they drew away from the city. Peleusar now seemed like a prison, and the air itself felt richer and more vibrant. He was aware that he was breathing deeply as he followed Jenethelen. It occurred to him that this was the first time since he had entered the Mid-Reaches that he had been out in the open with no fear of attack. The truce with the Faemir and the new enemy only attacking at night meant that right now, at midday, he could drop his guard totally.

Jenethelen was striding purposefully in front of him. His eyes followed the line of her neck down her back and along her firm, slender legs. He had lost so many friends and family in the war against the Faemir, and yet ... the Faemir Watcher fascinated him. Was she courageous or cowardly? Capable or vulnerable? Was she on his side or only looking after herself? She seemed to be all these things. There was so much Cluric didn't understand about her. She was as confusing to him as he was to himself at times.

'There will be some down here,' she said, kneeling on the barren ground.

Cluric stared blankly at her for a moment and then knelt down beside her. 'I'm sorry, my mind was elsewhere.'

Jenethelen took two spades from her backpack and gave one to Cluric. 'Let's start digging.'

'How do you know the brimstones will be here?'

'See the pattern here – that's the most important sign.'

It took Cluric a moment to see what she meant. The spot they were digging in was surrounded by what appeared to be a series of small, concentric rocky outcrops.

'I could have walked over this place a thousand times and not noticed anything.'

'There are quite a few things you don't notice,' said Jenethelen.

Cluric tried to catch her eye, but she had turned away and seemed to be concentrating on the hole they were digging. Was that a half-smile on her face?

He continued to work, enjoying the warmth of the sun's rays on the back of his neck. The air was still, and for once he could enjoy a silence that wasn't fraught with the tension of a deserted city or expectation of an attack. He doubted the brimstones would be much help against the wraiths, but somehow it didn't matter.

'Careful now,' said Jenethelen. 'I think we may be close, and we don't want to damage any of them.'

The Faemir put her spade down and started sifting carefully through the sandy soil with her hands. Cluric copied her, burying his hands in the dirt.

'I think I felt something,' he said after a while.

Jenethelen smiled. 'That was my finger.'

'I think I know the difference between a stone and a finger,' said Cluric, deliberately grabbing at her hand this time.

Jenethelen pulled away. Her expression, like so much about her, seemed a contradiction to Cluric. 'Do you know the differ-ence between a Faemir and a Faelen?' she said.

There was an awkward pause, then Cluric said, 'I know Faelen is what your people call women who live in peace with Maelir.'

'We despise them. If it wasn't for them and their blind acceptance and obedience of your rules, there wouldn't have been a war between Maelir and Faemir.'

Cluric coughed, as some of the dust had caught in his throat. 'My mother was a Faelen. My aunt, Hrulth's wife, is a Faelen. I have three Faelen cousins.'

Jenethelen turned away and continued to sift through the soil. 'Are they the only Faelen you know?'

Cluric coughed again and put his hand back in the dirt.

'Aren't you going to answer my question?' she asked.

'Hey, I think I've found one.' Cluric pulled out a small red stone and held it out between his thumb and forefinger to show Jenethelen.

'That's one,' she said. 'Careful, don't hold it too firmly, or you'll –'

'Ah!' Cluric cried out and dropped the stone.

Jenethelen laughed. 'That's what I was going to warn you about.'

'I've burnt myself,' said Cluric, looking at his hand.

'Here, this is the best way to handle them.' The Faemir picked it up and started transferring it from one hand to the other, taking care that her touch was light and that the stone didn't remain in contact with her skin for too long.

'*Now* you tell me,' said Cluric.

'Here's another way, which can be reasonably safe for a short time.' Jenethelen placed the brimstone in her open palm. 'But if I were to close my fist around it and apply some pressure, I'd be in a lot of trouble.'

'How are we going to carry these back?' said Cluric. 'I don't want them burning a hole in my backpack.'

'That's what these are for.' Jenethelen took out a leather pouch and opened the drawstring as wide as it would go so that the pouch lay almost flat on the ground. She then took her canteen of water and poured it over the soft inner leather. 'This is the best way to carry them.'

She placed the brimstone inside the open pouch.

'They are quite powerful, aren't they?' said Cluric. 'I don't know why we have never used them.'

Jenethelen stared at him. 'You Maelir don't have the knowledge. The Faemir may not be city-builders, but there are many things we know which your people don't. These brimstones, for example, can be made much more effective if they are buried for periods of time in the right place. The ones buried during Zenith become the most potent of all.'

'I assume we want more than one – let's keep going.'

'Don't start giving me orders.'

Cluric frowned. 'I wasn't.'

'I'm not a prisoner – there's a truce, remember?'

'Have I ever treated you like a prisoner? Even before we knew there was a truce.'

Jenethelen didn't answer. Instead, she pulled out another brimstone and placed it in the pouch. 'That's one each. I believe that means we're equal right now.'

Cluric shook his head. He was no closer to understanding her. She was so very different to any woman he had ever come across.

They each found several more brimstones before Cluric spoke again. 'Have you thought about what's going to happen now that there is peace between Maelir and Faemir?'

'We're combining our armies and coordinating our battle plans. That's clear, isn't it?'

'No, I mean what happens after? Suppose we defeat the Nazir.'

'I don't know. I haven't thought about it. I don't see any signs of victory, so is it worth spending any time worrying about it?'

'If I didn't believe that all this will end up with me being able to return to my inn in Teuron, I don't think I would be able to last another night.'

Jenethelen didn't respond.

'Where will you return to?' asked Cluric, to break the silence.

'Nowhere,' she said. 'Faemir don't have homes. You know that.'

'But you must have thought about what would happen if the Faemir defeated the Maelir. You all seemed determined. You must have felt you were going to win.'

Jenethelen pulled out another brimstone and placed it in the bag. 'We used to have coveyns. They were our families, our homes, before Valkyra united us all. You live in homes made of stone and wood, we lived in homes made of people. Do you see the difference?'

'What's happened to the coveyns?'

'They're battalions now. Some coveyns have been broken up or joined with others. It's not the same anymore.'

Cluric noticed Jenethelen's face had flushed, and she was looking away.

'I miss Teuron,' said Cluric. 'It is nowhere near as grand as Peleusar, or any of the other cities of the Mid-Reaches, but I want more than anything to return there.'

'I don't understand the Maelir affection for buildings.'

'Perhaps if you lived in a town or a village for a while you would begin to understand.'

Jenethelen stopped digging and looked at Cluric. She was clearly troubled.

'I don't –' Cluric began, but he was interrupted.

'You don't see the problem, do you Cluric?'

Cluric searched for the answer in her expression.

Jenethelen's eyes seemed to bore deep. She took a deep breath. 'If there is peace between Maelir and Faemir, what is the difference between a Faemir and a Faelen?'

*

Riell tried to get Atreu to respond as they negotiated the carved steps that led down to the lake. 'I still think there's a good chance Verlinden and Leylan are alive,' he said.

Atreu felt the jarring in his knees and the quivering of his leg muscles with every step. His eyes remained fixed on where he would place his foot next. He knew Riell had been trying to speak to him since they had resumed their descent, but the words faded somewhere inside his head and never registered.

'This is not like you, Atreu. There is no point mourning for anything until you have to.'

Vivid scenes shunted into Atreu's vision. He saw the rich undergrowth of the Rimforest again, the bushes and vines shivering around him. Through the dense fronds he looked out into a firelit glade. There, he saw a tall, pale-skinned Faemir with flaming hair, her mouth open in a frozen scream ...

Then he saw a face drained pale against dark red hair staring up at him, eyes wide with fear. Below him, the waters of the Maelstrom churned with an awesome power. He reached out to grab her hand ...

Then he was digging frantically through the snow with his bare hands. He scooped up large lumps and threw them behind him in short, sharp movements. Finally, he felt something. Clearing away the snow, he could see the pale, frozen face of a beautiful Faemir. Her skin was ice and her heartbeat the faintest of whispers ...

'Verlinden,' he cried. 'Breathe!'

He exhaled, and a cloud hung before his eyes and then took shape. After a moment, the face of an old man had formed in the vapour.

'Tell me if she will live!' cried Atreu.

The old man's lips moved, but Atreu couldn't hear his voice. Gradually, a soft whisper emerged, and Atreu could make out the four words being repeated over and over again.

'The art of breathing. The art of breathing.'

As soon as Atreu deciphered the words, the image began to dissipate. He looked down at Verlinden's blood-drained face in the snow. Leaning back, he inhaled deeply and then placed his lips on hers. As he exhaled, he could see tiny wisps of steam issuing from where their lips joined.

He lifted his head and saw that the faintest pink tinge had

touched her cheeks. He inhaled again and pressed his mouth on hers. This time their lips sealed so tightly that not even the smallest sliver of steam escaped. He pulled back again and her chest began to heave.

A small cloud of vapour emerged from her mouth. As he watched the cloud ascend, it took the shape of a young girl, then billowed and reformed into a knife, and then transformed into two naked figures in a pale embrace. Finally, the cloud divided, and the two figures split apart.

Atreu looked down and saw that Verlinden's eyes were fluttering. But as he reached down to touch her face, they became still. He felt tears well up in his eyes as the faint colour in her cheeks drained away.

'Verlinden,' he cried. 'Don't leave me.'

But she could no longer hear ...

'Atreu. Atreu, please talk to me.' Riell stood on the step in front of him, blocking his path.

Atreu stopped, half-dazed, desperately trying to push away the clouds in his mind.

'Atreu,' cried Riell. 'You must throw off these demons that trouble you.'

Atreu's eyes gradually focused on the windrider's face.

'Riell ... what is happening?'

'Finally,' said Riell. 'Here – sit down.'

Atreu lowered himself down with Riell's help. 'I thought you were Verlinden,' he said. 'There is something strange happening to me.'

'I've been trying to tell you,' said Riell, 'that we don't know Verlinden's fate yet. Don't let it destroy you.'

'I tried to save her, but this time I couldn't.'

'Here, have some water.' Riell handed him a flask. 'The Source is having its effect on you already, I think. And your Book must also have something to do with it.'

'My Book? Oh yes, of course, I was reading it ...'

'That was some time ago, Atreu. We've been walking since then.'

'Have we? It feels like I've only just stopped reading.'

'You've been in a trance of some kind.'

Atreu frowned. 'I don't understand. It was like I was ... inside the story.'

'What was in there?'

Atreu shut his eyes tightly and watched the bright threads dance across the dark behind his eyelids. Slowly and deliberately, he willed the threads to cease their gyrations. Finally, he opened his eyes and saw Riell's concerned face.

'I read about my friend Cluric in my Talisman.'

'He is the one battling the Dusk-wraiths in Peleusar?'

'Yes, but I saw something this time which I haven't seen before.'

'What is it?'

Atreu shifted uncomfortably. 'I am still a fool who doesn't really understand.'

'I hardly think you're being fair to yourself.'

'I am, Riell.' He put down the flask. 'My Talisman has shown me something. I know now why Verlinden has seemed so distant in recent days. It took Cluric to show me.'

'What are you saying, Atreu?'

'Verlinden has always been lost to me. How could she ever be with me? I could never have asked it of her, and she could never have given it to me. She's a Faemir. She could never become what she is not.'

Riell drew a deep breath. 'I don't pretend to understand women, least of all Faemir, but things have changed on the Mountain. Maelir and Faemir – neither of us will be the same after all this.'

'No, I see it clearly now. Cluric has shown me. Verlinden and I have tried to build this cocoon around ourselves, to pretend that the differences don't matter – but they do. The first strong wind was always going to blow the cocoon away.'

'This is not sounding like you.'

'No, Riell, she is lost to me.' Atreu gave the flask back. 'And the sad thing is that even without the storm, we would never have been together.'

Riell tried to say something, but Atreu got up and started walking again.

*

Although it was barely mid-afternoon, the sun already threatened to disappear over the lip of the surrounding cliffs as Atreu and Riell stepped onto the shores of the lake.

Atreu stared across the vast hypnotic expanse of water, broken only by the occasional dark figure sitting on a floating prayer mat. He felt a calmness wash over him, and his dark thoughts no longer pressed against him as they had done earlier in the afternoon. He looked at the cliffs that loomed behind him. In the failing light he could see small natural openings, but none of them appeared close to ground level.

'Where do we go now?' he asked, cutting the increasingly cold air with his voice.

'We wait.'

'What do you mean? I want to get this over with. I have a quest I need to undertake.' He pointed to the openings in the cliff wall. 'Is that where we go?'

'No, Atreu, we don't *go* anywhere. The only thing we can do is wait.'

Atreu frowned. 'Are there any boats here? Can we row to one of the Holy Men out there on the water?'

'Atreu, I've tried to tell you, these are not ordinary Holy Men. They spend most of the day practising deep meditation. It is impossible to break them from it. Believe me, I speak from experience. All we can do is wait for one of them to come out of their trance and see us.'

'So we're just waiting for someone to happen to walk past. Is that it?'

'More or less.'

'At the Lhorong monastery during my Ascent, the monks wouldn't let me in until my agitation had eased. Is this the same here?'

'I don't think they are as attuned to others here at the Source as the Felsen at Lhorong. I don't pretend to understand them fully, but as far as I can tell, they are so self-absorbed that we barely exist for them.'

'It seems a strange, selfish existence.'

'Perhaps, but I think you should reserve your judgement until you've been here for a while. I wouldn't dismiss anything so easily without fully understanding it first. The windriders have been misunderstood long enough for me to be painfully aware of how wrong people's judgements – even wise people's judgements – can be.'

'There's someone coming.' Atreu saw a figure, one he had mistaken for a rock, suddenly get up and walk towards them.

'Well met,' said Atreu, when the figure was close enough to see some dark features hidden inside the cowl.

The figure simply kept walking as if they were not there. He waded into the waters in the lake and kept walking, his body gradually disappearing under the surface. When his head finally vanished from view, and the small wake left by his movement through the water had dissipated, Atreu turned to Riell, open-mouthed. 'Has he just drowned himself?' he asked, incredulous.

Riell shrugged. 'Who knows? I've seen this happen before.'

'Have I missed something? Did the Holy Man come to the surface again?' Atreu was staring out at the still lake's surface looking for any sign of the monk re-emerging.

'I don't know. Not while I was looking. I hear they walk the length of the lake along the bottom.'

'But that's impossible. How can someone go so long without breathing?'

'I've never had anyone confirm that it's true. Perhaps he's standing with his head just under the surface. As I said, the practices here at the Source are a mystery to me.'

'I'm going to swim out to see if he's still there.'

'There's no point to it, Atreu. Just leave them to it. You'll see far stranger things here.'

'But he could be drowning.'

'Somehow I don't think so.'

'But –'

He was interrupted by another figure that had emerged somewhere from the cliffs behind them and was now walking in their direction.

Atreu took several steps to cut across his path. The monk walked straight into him as if he hadn't seen him. Atreu was thrown off balance by the momentum and fell to the ground.

By the time he had got to his feet, the monk was already ankle-deep in the water.

'Hey!' he cried, but the monk didn't react. All Atreu could do was watch him continue walking, as the other monk had done, until his head disappeared under the lake's surface.

Atreu threw his hands up in exasperation. 'These men are fools.'

Riell raised his eyebrows. 'You and I climbed a huge Mountain without knowing what was at the Summit. The Keep is full of Maelir who made the Ascent blindly. Are we any less foolish?'

Atreu sighed. 'Perhaps not. I certainly feel foolish just being here. I should have ignored the Circle's exhortations to come to the Source.'

'We are all of us driven by Ritual and convention, aren't we? We do it because it gives our lives meaning.'

'You're right, Riell, but it seems to be particularly foolish to follow a Ritual that will kill you. These Holy Men are going to drown.'

'Was there no life-threatening danger on your Ascent?'

'Riell, I'm surprised at your defence of the monks here. I've always thought the windriders were men of action.'

'I don't think you have much of an understanding of the Order of the Wynde if that's all you see in us.'

Atreu noticed a slight grin at the edges of Riell's mouth. 'Are you mocking me?'

'No, no.' Riell's smile became a bit broader. 'I'm just glad that your black mood has left you. I would rather you argue with me than lose yourself in morose thoughts.'

Atreu felt a half-smile tugging at his lips. 'This is absurd, isn't it?'

'The Source is either the most absurd place I have ever been to, Atreu, or the most profound.'

Atreu looked up at the premature twilight of the crater they were in. He could see geyers flying near the distant cliff tops. 'All right,' he said, sitting down. 'Let's just wait.'

He pulled his coat tighter against the increasing cold and made himself comfortable against his pack. Riell joined him and they sat side-by-side, looking out at the glassy waters.

In the growing dusk the Source took on an increasing dream-like quality. Atreu became aware of his own breathing, and soon the air around him seemed to be pulsing in time. A soft lap-lapping of water merged with the rhythm of his breaths. After a while he realised that the dark figures on the lake were coming closer. As they approached, he could see that the cowled monks were sitting bolt upright on the floating prayer mats and paddling slowly to shore.

By the time the monks reached the edges of the lake, Atreu was mesmerised by the serene poetry of the scene. Over a hundred Source Holy Men now reached the shore and stood up from their mats in the same fluid motion. Each one remained perfectly still, facing the cliffs with their back to the lake, as the others arrived at the shore. Finally the last one arrived, and Atreu waited, expecting something to happen. He could detect no signal or sign, but as one, the monks gave out a deep sonorous tone that filled the air like honey. As he listened, the tone grew deeper and sweeter. It so enveloped him that he could not be sure that his own voice had not joined in the twilight chorus.

And when he thought no sound could be richer, he became aware that the monks by the lake had been joined by the monks in the cliffs behind him, and the chorus seemed to reach a height and depth he had never imagined. He had been moved by Felsen chanting before, but what he was hearing now was on another plane. No pictures or visions ran through his head. This was pure sound, devoid of any content or images. It was as if his head was being cleared, and filled with a single resonant note.

The cliffs, the water, the air itself, seemed to become one with the tone, adding to its depth and flavour. And then, just as Atreu lost any sense of a world that wasn't made of the sound, it faded, the last note lingering like the sweetest of aftertastes.

Atreu was suddenly aware that the Holy Men were now walking slowly towards the cliffs. He tried to gesture to them to stop, but found that his body didn't respond immediately. He resigned himself to simply watching them walk past. It was dark now; stars filled the dome of sky above his head. He had no idea how long it had been since the monks had reached the shore. They were now dark, indistinct shapes, their cowled faces hidden within an even more impenetrable darkness.

After the last monk had walked past him, Atreu was about to say something to Riell when he realised that a single Holy Man had suddenly stopped on the sandy beach. It took a moment for Atreu to register that he was gesturing to him and Riell to follow them.

He glanced at Riell and saw that he was already getting up. Atreu took a deep breath, then he too stood up. The two of them then followed the train of monks to the cliff base in silence.

Chapter Nine

A succession of screams pierced the air like a volley of arrows, each one pricking Cluric's skin. He stood with the other Maelir soldiers in a battle-ready position. Jenethelen was to his immediate right and Hrulth to his left. The barricades were aflame again, providing some sense of protection, and the clear night sky showed no threat of rain.

It was now well after sunset, and there had been no sign of the Dusk-wraiths. There had even been a slight easing of tension among the soldiers. The odd flippant remark – even some nervous laughter.

Until the screams started.

A scream was the closest human sound to the noise that pierced the air. But no man or woman made these noises – that was clear from the onset. No human lungs could produce such a gut-wrenching sound. No human voice could reach that pitch. And no human could engender such a distillation of raw fear.

Cluric felt himself swallowing convulsively until his throat ached. He couldn't stop. Each scream seemed to cut through him and then withdraw, leaving a dull ache, only to be sliced open again by the next scream.

He stared at the star-filled sky. Instinctively, he knew the screams were coming from above, but his eyes picked up no movement. He swallowed again and again. His hand twitched on the hilt of his sword as he fought for control.

A whistling sound streaked the air, and Cluric saw a dozen arrows travel in a high arc out into the darkness past the barricade walls.

'Damn fools!' cried Hrulth.

'What's happening?' said Cluric.

'Some of our archers have fired without an order. That's not a good sign.'

'How can they fire without an order?'

'Look at you, Cluric, you can barely keep still. These screams will drive us all mad if they keep going much longer.'

Cluric asked Jenethelen, 'Have you heard these screams before?'

'No, this is something new.' She was rocking backwards and forwards on the balls of her feet.

Then the screams stopped and the night air was still again. All Cluric could hear was the crackling of the barricade fires. He felt his body relaxing again and he drew several slow, steady breaths.

'Thank goodness for that,' he said.

As the words left his mouth, the screaming began anew, and because he had relaxed it now seemed to cut even deeper. His heart was beating erratically, his nerve endings twisting in pain, and the uncontrollable swallowing had started again.

Without being fully aware what he was doing, he realised he had drawn his sword and was cutting and thrusting at the empty space in front of him.

'Cluric!' cried Hrulth, not daring to get too close.

Cluric finally came to his senses. He looked around blankly and saw that many of the other Maelir soldiers had been doing exactly the same thing.

He exhaled in short, jagged gusts. 'I ... I don't understand this ... I –'

There was a shout from a group of soldiers to his far right. Cluric, Hrulth and Jenethelen rushed over.

A Maelir soldier lay on the ground with a deep wound in his stomach.

'Janan!' said Hrulth. 'What happened?'

Janan was losing blood rapidly and had a glazed look in his eyes.

Cluric saw that two soldiers had disarmed Janan's brother Ronan and were holding him firmly.

'Someone tell me what happened here,' demanded Hrulth.

'Ronan tried to kill him,' said one of the soldiers.

'What?' Hrulth walked over to Ronan and looked him in the eye. 'Is this true?'

Ronan was shaking his head convulsively, and didn't answer.

Hrulth stepped closer still. 'Ronan, talk to me. I've known you since you were a boy. Why would you try to kill your own brother?'

Ronan wouldn't look him in the eye.

'We'll have to lock him in a cell,' said one of the soldiers.

Hrulth grabbed Ronan by the shoulders and shook him. Recognition seemed to spark in his eyes for a moment, but then it was gone.

'I may be wrong,' said one of the other soldiers, 'but I think Janan attacked him first.'

Hrulth shook his head in confusion. 'What? This makes no sense at all. Take the two of them away. Do what you can for Janan and put Ronan into one of the cells. I'll have to deal with this at daybreak.'

There was another series of shouts further to their right. Cluric looked up to see four Maelir clashing swords furiously.

'Quick, stop them!' cried Hrulth.

Several soldiers intervened, and it took a while for the fighters to be subdued. Hrulth tried to get some sense out of them, but they barely recognised that he was even there.

'It's the screams, isn't it?' said Cluric as they returned to their positions.

Hrulth pulled at his beard. 'It must be. I can't see any other explanation.'

'They're going to drive us insane,' said Cluric. 'I can feel it. I'm not sure if I can take much more of this myself.'

It was then that the screams stopped again.

'Don't relax,' said Jenethelen. 'I think that's the secret. Last time they stopped we all relaxed, and when they started again our defences were down. It's a common battle technique, but I've never seen it used like this.'

'You're right,' said Hrulth.

He pointed out into the darkness past the giant flames. 'They're coming,' he cried at the top of his voice. 'They're coming.'

Cluric followed the line of Hrulth's hand. 'Are you sure you're not going mad too? I can't see anything out there.'

'There's nothing there,' said Hrulth under his breath. And then, at the top of his voice, 'Battle formation. Now. They're massing.'

There was a flurry of activity all around them as soldiers who had left their positions now returned to them.

When the screams started to pierce the night air again, the Maelir were prepared.

'It worked,' said Jenethelen. 'We didn't let down our guard this time.'

Hrulth nodded slowly. 'I still haven't worked out what's happening, but it looks like they're trying to wear us down with fear.'

'Perhaps there won't be an attack tonight,' said Cluric. 'They could be trying to drive us mad in anticipation.'

'From the sky!' cried Hrulth. 'They're coming from the sky this time!'

Cluric frowned. 'I don't think anyone's going to believe –'

'No, I'm deadly serious this time.'

Cluric gulped and followed Hrulth's gaze into the night sky.

Above them dark, amorphous shapes congealed, as one by one the stars were blanketed. In their place, countless blood-red eyes appeared, staring at them, unblinking. The screams now clearly came from the heavens, bearing down on the Maelir soldiers like a dense, living shroud.

Panic set in, and several soldiers threw their swords down in panic. Cluric's eyes darted from the oncoming mass of wraiths to the Maelir around him.

'Torches!' Cluric couldn't tell where the first call had come from, but soon battalion leaders were crying the word out as a desperate order.

'Torches!'

Cluric joined in the scramble for the alcohol-soaked torches that lined the buildings, and then raced back to the barricade fires and lit the flame.

It was then that he noticed the screams had stopped. The atmosphere now had the stillness of a tomb. Looking up, he saw nothing but a convulsing blackness, darker than the densest storm clouds, and writhing like no natural phenomenon could.

A dull, relentless drone started as the wraiths began to slowly descend. Cluric held his flaming torch high above his head and brandished his sword in his other hand. He could see the grim, fire-streaked faces of the other soldiers, all in similar stances. Only those with double-handed battle-axes stood without a torch.

'Fire!' The command was barely audible above the increasing drone.

A hundred flame-tipped arrows were shot into the Dusk-wraiths. The wraiths seemed to falter for a moment, sparks flashing in all directions, and then slivers of thick, viscous shadows rained down on the soldiers.

Human screams rang into the night air as the dark rain hit bare skin.

'Fire!' A second command was followed by another volley of arrows.

The wraith rain fell again, and Cluric cried out in agony as one of the large drops landed on the side of his face. It felt like a splinter of ice passing straight through his cheek. He reached up to feel the wound, but his face was numb. Pulling his hand away, he expected to see blood dripping from his fingers, but there was nothing.

'Jenethelen,' he cried. 'My face. What can you see?'

The Faemir, who had managed to avoid any of the drops, peered at him through the darkness. 'There's nothing,' she said. 'I can't see anything.'

Cries of pain rang out into the night. Cluric glanced around to see others who hadn't fared as well as he had lying on the ground, writhing in terrible pain.

'What do we do now, Hrulth?' said Cluric, watching the Dusk-wraiths start to regain their momentum again.

'Brace yourself,' he cried. 'We're going to fire again.'

'Fire!' The order came from behind them, and again a barrage of flame-tipped Maelir arrows hit the Dusk-wraiths.

The shadows seemed to absorb them, but again they appeared to do some damage as more wraith parts fell to the ground.

Cluric was knocked off his feet by the impact of several drops. It was as if ice spears had been driven through him, pinning him to the ground. After the initial impact, he lay stunned for a brief moment before the pain started registering.

He grabbed his torch, which had been flung from his hand, and was just starting to get to his feet when another volley of arrows created more rain. Before he could catch his breath, he was on the ground again, in excruciating agony.

'Enough,' cried Hrulth.

Cluric could see that his uncle was on his feet and running towards the archers on the rooftops, gesticulating wildly that they should stop.

By the time Cluric was upright, most of the other soldiers had also got to their feet. The Dusk-wraiths were now bearing down on them. Cluric struggled to breathe. It was as if the wraiths were keeping the air from him.

The next command filtered down the line. 'Water!' Maelir soldiers grabbed buckets that had been filled in anticipation and doused each other from head to toe.

'I hope this works,' said Cluric as he stood there, shivering, after Jenethelen had poured water all over him.

Jenethelen's expression was grim. 'This isn't something a Faemir battalion would do.'

'I don't think we have any choice but to simply defend,' said Cluric, 'or we won't survive the night.'

'Come on,' said Hrulth, who had now returned to their position. 'Get as close to the fire barricade as possible.'

Cries suddenly came from behind them, followed by the dull thuds of falling bodies. Cluric could see that the Dusk-wraiths were now level with the tallest buildings. With a sickening feeling, he realised that several of the archers on the rooftops had been swallowed up by the wraiths and had plummeted to the ground.

Cluric could feel the heat of the barricade fires. He and the other Maelir soldiers were now standing as near to the flames as they could, watching the Dusk-wraiths descend. Deep within the dark mass, blood-red eyes stared hungrily. And with every passing moment, the drone increased in volume.

Cluric looked at Jenethelen's matted, water-soaked hair. *This is insane*, he thought. *This is not a battle.*

The flames were the height of two men in places and the wraith cloud was almost touching them. Cluric felt totally enclosed. The fire in front, an impenetrable darkness behind, and the Dusk-wraiths pressing down from above.

He fought desperately against the urge to run into the fire – an urge some others couldn't resist. All around him, Maelir soldiers charged headlong into the flames, screaming in excruciating agony. Soon the stench of burning flesh assaulted his nostrils.

When the clouds touched the tips of the highest barricade flames, the wraiths hissed and writhed. For a moment the fire seemed to stem the descent, but after the wraiths coiled and convulsed, they continued, swallowing the flames as they went.

It weakens them. The thought ran through Cluric's head like a mantra. *The fire weakens them.*

He held his torch high above his head and braced himself for the onslaught. His other hand tightened on the hilt of his sword.

Still the wraiths descended. Screams came from the soldiers who had been unwilling or unable to come close to the barricades. Unhindered by fire, the shadow had already descended on them. Cluric could only guess what was happening in the darkness behind him, but the screams could not have been more horrific if they were being eaten alive.

The wraiths now licked the flames from his outstretched torch. As insubstantial as the shadows appeared, he felt a very real force suddenly push down on the torch. He looked up and saw dark coils moving down the handle towards his hand.

Without thinking, he swung his sword hard at the tendril now wrapped around the torch handle. His other hand bore the brunt of the impact and he dropped the torch. The severed tendril uncoiled once the handle had hit the ground and seemed to writhe momentarily before fading into nothing.

Cluric swung at the wraiths, who were now just above his head. The shadows drew back slightly and Cluric jumped to the side to avoid a falling wraith sliver. Now that the wraiths were in reach, the other Maelir soldiers were hacking into them furiously, creating lightning-like flashes. Cluric lashed left and right in short, sharp arcs, and all around him, the wraith-rain began to fall again.

The drone faltered under the onslaught, and while the shadows formed and reformed violently under the impact of the Maelir blades, their descent stopped, and they remained positioned just above the soldiers' heads.

A severed tendril wrapped itself around Cluric's arm, and he felt the bite of ice on his skin as he desperately shook himself free of it. Others around him weren't as fortunate. He could see many soldiers on the ground, writhing in agony as dark shadows covered their faces. Every time he moved to help, a tendril would reach down from above and threaten to encircle him.

The battle continued on into the night. There were no commands, no human voices to be heard save the screams and cries of soldiers in unimaginable pain. Slowly, as the Maelir tired and their swords flashed with less fury, the Dusk-wraiths began to descend again.

Cluric's shoulders were aching, and his sword felt as if it was made of ledstone. He was crouching down to avoid the wraiths and his thigh muscles burnt under the strain. The shadows now covered the ground behind him. It was as if the Maelir were in a giant pocket along the line of the slowly dying barricade fire. Should he run through the flames to the other side? What was waiting for him there, assuming he made it through? He heaved in ragged breaths as the air seemed to thin around him.

Soon any choice was taken from him, and he was on his knees as the Dusk-wraiths descended further, horrific red eyes staring at him from deep within the mass. He still swung his sword at the shadows, but he was tiring, and his thrusts now were nothing more than instinctive reactions.

'Help me!' He recognised Jenethelen's voice through the sense-numbing exhaustion that had overtaken him.

To his horror, he saw the wraiths coiling around her as she lay on the ground, rolling and flailing in a desperate attempt to shake them off.

He took two steps in her direction, but the moment he no longer hacked at the dark shadows above him, several tendrils shot out and sought to wrap themselves around his body. He swung at them, severing them from the main mass, and they fell to the ground.

'Help me.' Jenethelen's voice was growing fainter.

Again, Cluric tried to lunge towards her, and again the wraiths attacked. He had no choice but to concentrate all his energy on fighting them off.

The shadows now pressed even further down on him. He was

on his haunches and could no longer see any other Maelir soldiers. It was as if the air had been stripped of any sound other than the drone of the wraiths and his own ragged breaths. Jenethelen's last cry was so faint he was unsure whether he had imagined it.

He was in a cocoon now as the shadows pushed at him from all sides. His sword still thrust at the wraiths, but it was as if his arm had a will of its own. The rest of his body was crumpling, unable to carry its own weight.

He felt himself collapsing back until he was lying on the ground. His arm still moved from the elbow, and still he managed to cut into the wraiths. Finally, though, his sword disappeared into the shadows and he felt the ice-like sting pierce his hand. He lost all sensation up to his wrist, and could no longer be certain he was still gripping his weapon.

Dark tendrils were now snaking down his arm and he felt the blood in his veins freeze. He tried to lash out with his other hand, but it was one last futile action, as his arm immediately turned to ice.

In the end, he lay there, unblinking, and watched the wraiths descend towards him. Somewhere within the dark coiling shadows, he thought he saw a familiar face, but then everything was too close for him to focus.

The ice started at the tip of his nose, and he felt it progress down into his face. He lay perfectly still and waited. The battle was over.

Soon his eyes were frozen and his vision blurred ...

He was back at his inn in Teuron. It was the morning he had decided to head off to war. He grabbed Ascender Atreu by the arm. 'Listen, Atreu,' he said, 'if I could somehow get to Ariathe, I could join up with a group from another town. There are bound to be dozens there. And you're going there ... well, close enough anyway ...'

He could see his brother's shoulders slump as he spoke. 'Edric,' he said, 'we've been through this already. You know you can run the inn on your own. I have to go – you can see that, can't you?'

Edric walked over to the corner table where Cluric's pack lay. He picked it up, walked back to where Cluric sat and handed it to him. 'You'd better get going,' he said, 'before I change my mind.'

Was that a tear in Edric's eye?

Cluric wanted to say something, but suddenly everything felt very cold.

For the briefest of moments he was aware that he was no longer aware.

Then nothing.

Chapter Ten

The network of connecting passages inside the cliff face was clearly a natural formation. Glimmerstones of varying intensity encrusted the walls, helping Atreu and Riell negotiate the rough surface as they followed the train of monks. After a while Atreu realised that the number of Holy Men in front of them had reduced to a mere half dozen.

'Where have all the others gone?' he asked Riell, instinctively keeping his voice low.

'As far as I can tell, they've been disappearing into side tunnels and caverns along the way.'

'I thought we were being taken somewhere – a meeting with an important Felsen.'

'I don't think there is such a thing as an important Felsen. Least of all here at the Source.'

Atreu frowned. 'Then what are we doing here following a procession of monks? Is there any point? Do you even know which one beckoned us to follow?'

'I couldn't be sure anymore, Atreu. But don't be too worried – those Felsen who disappeared obviously didn't want us to follow them. The last one left will probably be the one who speaks to us.'

Atreu concentrated to see if he could find out how and when

the monks were disappearing. For some reason, he couldn't quite focus on when it happened. It was as if the realisation that they were gone hit him a fraction of a moment after they vanished.

Finally, there was only one monk in front of them.

'Is that the one who stopped for us?'

'I think so ...'

'If he disappears too,' said Atreu, 'would you be able to find your way back out?'

'No,' said Riell.

The Holy Man rounded several corners. Each time Atreu lost sight of him, he felt a stab of panic that this last monk would also vanish.

When the monk walked through a narrow opening, Atreu and Riell quickly followed. The cavern they stepped into was lit dimly by glimmerstones in the last throes of their ancient lives. All Atreu could see was a prayer mat in the middle of the cave and, curiously, a series of large rocks which had ropes tied around them encircling the mat.

The monk stepped through a gap in the rocks and sat cross-legged on the mat. He was facing the entrance of the cavern, where Atreu and Riell stood, but his head was bowed and he appeared to be looking at the ground.

Atreu shifted awkwardly, unsure what to do next. He glanced at Riell, but the windrider wasn't giving him any indication.

After a time span which Atreu couldn't measure, the Holy Man finally spoke, his voice cracked and strangely familiar.

'Do you wish to speak?' he asked.

'Yes,' said Atreu, after recovering from the shock. 'I am – or was – the Ascender Atreu. I am here at the Source for my final Ritual.'

He fell silent, but the monk did not respond.

Atreu coughed and spoke again. 'I have not been told what form this final Ritual will take, so I would appreciate guidance.'

'Yes,' said the monk – but added nothing to the word.

'I ... mean ... where do I go? Who do I speak to? What do I do?'

The directness of the questions provoked some sort of reaction from the Felsen. He lifted his head, and Atreu thought he could see the glint of his eyes within the darkness of his cowl.

'There is only one question we seek the answer to,' said the monk. 'These things you ask are all trivial. Do not concern yourself with them.'

Atreu was growing increasingly impatient. There was a time when he put up with the deliberate obscurities from the Holy Orders, but there was too much at stake now.

He took a step forward and peered into the Felsen's cowl. 'I have a greater journey to undertake,' he said. 'I mean no disrespect to your ways here at the Source, but I am here out of reverence for the Rituals of Zenith. I want to learn what I can, but I must depart and make a Descent as soon as possible. I am searching for the third Book, which I know to belong to Metheus.'

Was that a reaction from the monk? His head seemed to jerk slightly.

'You know the name?' asked Atreu.

'You are not an Ascender.' The monk's statement confused Atreu.

'No, I am not,' said Riell, who assumed the monk must have been talking to him. 'I am Riell of the Order of the Wynde. My duties have brought me to the Source several times in the past.'

'The Order of the Wynde?' The monk seemed to be rolling the words around in his mind. 'Does such a thing exist?'

'We have created it,' said Riell, a little defensively.

'So men now *create* Holy Orders?'

'I believe they always have,' said Riell.

'Of course. Of course.'

There was a silence, which Riell felt obliged to fill. 'I have carried Atreu here for the final Ritual. A storm has damaged my wings, and I would ask that I be given some materials to attempt to repair them.'

'You can have what is at the Source, but I am not sure you will find what you need.'

'Nevertheless, I wish to try.'

'Of course.'

'Please,' said Atreu. 'There was only one other Ascender left after the war. She was a Faemir. Her name was Verlinden. She and the windrider carrying her were also caught in the storm that brought us down. Would you be able to organise a search of some kind?'

The monk didn't respond.

'Excuse me,' said Atreu. 'Perhaps the question is not important to you, but it is to me.'

'I am sorry,' said the monk after a while. 'Breathing is all-important. All of us at the Source meditate in the way that you breathe. I must consciously stop myself.'

'I asked for help to search for the Ascender Verlinden.'

'I am aware of what you have asked. There is no need to search – all the Ascenders are here.'

'What about the windrider Leylan?' asked Riell. 'Is he here?'

'I'm sorry – these are too many questions.' The monk took the free end of a rope that was tied to one of the rocks and tied it around his leg.

'You have to answer our questions,' said Atreu. 'If Verlinden is here, please tell me where she is.'

Slowly and deliberately, the Felsen tied the other ropes to all his limbs.

Atreu made a move towards him, but Riell held him back. 'It's no use,' he said.

The monk tied the last rope tightly around his waist. Then he sat perfectly still, his head bowed.

'You can't just ignore us,' said Atreu, exasperation showing in his voice.

'He can and he will,' said Riell. 'Just stay calm. We've already got more response from him than I've heard from most Holy Men here.'

Atreu could hear the monk's deep breaths from under his cowl. 'What's going on?' he asked.

'I've heard about this,' said Riell. 'Some of the monks here practise weightless meditation.'

'What?'

'They claim to be able to reach a state where they float off the ground.'

'So that's what the rocks are for?'

'Yes – they are supposed to keep him anchored.'

Atreu stared at the monk, who now seemed like a statue. 'You mean, if we untied those ropes, he would float up to the ceiling of the cavern?'

'If the stories are true. I've never heard of anyone actually seeing a monk floating. For all I know, they may only *feel* lighter than air while meditating.'

'You mean no one's ever put it to the test? It would be easy to prove or disprove, wouldn't it?'

'You would think so, Atreu, but the Felsen of the Source would probably say they don't need to *prove* anything.'

'But this technique – if it's like the R'angkur or night vision, it can be learnt to varying degrees. This could be a most valuable skill.'

Riell laughed. 'It would make the windriders seem a little cumbersome, wouldn't it?'

'Just think, Riell, imagine what it would be like to fly without wings.'

'So why don't you untie the ropes and see what happens?'

Atreu stared at Riell. 'You're not serious are you?'

'Not really – but you could untie him if you wanted to. I wouldn't stop you, and I don't think there's anyone else at the Source who would.'

Atreu chewed on his bottom lip. 'I couldn't do it. It wouldn't seem right. But I *do* want to know if this flying without wings is possible.'

'There is another way to find out.'

'What?'

'Learn the technique yourself. That's what you really want, isn't it?'

Atreu fell silent. The glimmerstones in the cavern appeared to flicker ever so faintly. 'We're speaking as if he can't hear us,' he said. 'Can he?'

'I think what we're saying is probably registering somewhere in his mind, but he will only be able to recall it after he has finished meditating.'

'So what happens now? The Felsen at Lhorong and Crosanct gave strict guidelines. There was rarely any doubt about what I was supposed to do.'

'I told you, the Felsen here are unlike any other. This isn't a place for instruction the way Lhorong and Crosanct and the other monasteries are.'

'If it's not a place of instruction, what is it?'

'It's a place of practice,' said Riell. 'Look, I don't claim to comprehend the Source. The way I understand it, the Ascent is the time for teaching. You have achieved your insight at Zenith and your insight has been judged at Equinox. There is nothing for you to learn from the Holy Men here.'

'Then what is the purpose of the pilgrimage to the Source? If there is nothing to learn here, it seems a waste of time.'

'I didn't say there was nothing to learn here. I said there was nothing to learn from the Holy Men of the Source. You can only learn from yourself now.'

Atreu shook his head. 'Do I have to be here to do that?'

Riell sat down and leant against the cave wall. He motioned for Atreu to join him.

When Atreu had also sat down, Riell said, 'You are asking the wrong person. Someone like Micah would have a better idea of the value of the Source. My knowledge is limited.'

'I don't understand, Riell.' Atreu took off his pack. 'I know you failed your second judgement after your pilgrimage to the Source – but how were you judged?'

'That's just it, Atreu. You don't get judged again at the second Equinox. *You judge yourself.*'

Atreu felt his head jerk involuntarily. 'I judge myself?'

'Yes,' said Riell. 'This final Ritual is what you make of it, and the final judgement is your own.'

'So ... let me see if I understand this. *You* judged yourself a failure after your pilgrimage? *You* decided you weren't worthy of either of the Holy Orders?'

'Yes, Atreu. I knew I was neither Felsen nor Liche.'

'And you could have decided to be a Liche, and the decision would have been accepted?'

'It doesn't work that way. It's not that sort of decision. You can't cheat yourself.'

'So no one will tell me what I should decide?'

'That's right. Your decisions here are all yours. You decide how long you stay here. You decide what you do here. The Source is the one place on the whole Mountain where you are totally free.'

Atreu stared at the rock walls for a moment. The glimmer-stones seemed to subtly change their hue. 'What if I want to leave right now? What if I want to commence my quest?'

'Then go,' said Riell.

Atreu fell silent.

'Do you want to leave?' asked Riell.

'I ... I don't know.'

'Then perhaps now isn't the time to go.'

Atreu's head was starting to spin again. This was the first time since the start of his Ascent that no one was telling him what he should be doing. It was one thing to react against something, and do the opposite of what was expected of him, but this sudden sense of pure choice left him feeling a potent mixture of exhilaration and raw fear.

Without thinking, he reached into his pack for his Book. He pulled it out and ran his finger along the embossed A on the leather-bound cover.

'What did you do here at the Source when you first arrived after your pilgrimage?'

Riell smiled. 'I remember walking around aimlessly for who knows how long. I think all the Ascenders do that. We're used to following Rituals blindly.'

'Something must have changed at some point, though?'

'Well, I suppose it did, but I wasn't aware of it. It was gradual. I think you fall in with the rhythm of the place.'

Atreu unclasped his Book and starting flicking absently through the pages. He squinted as he searched for recognisable words. Nothing was making sense, just as during his Ascent all the words had seemed to be in some incomprehensible language. He felt himself trembling. Even his Talisman wasn't giving him any guidance this time.

'What's wrong?' asked Riell.

'This is like it was during my Ascent. It's as if I have suddenly lost the understanding I had gained. My Book is incomprehensible to me again. What can I be certain of now?'

'But you haven't unlearnt everything – you know you're not going backwards.'

Atreu was still trembling.

'Atreu ...' Riell's voice faded.

Atreu had the sensation that he was suddenly untethered, just as the glimmerstone lights flickered in a strange pattern. 'Sorry,' he said, after what he thought was just a moment. 'I couldn't quite ...'

Riell said, 'So now you're speaking to me again.'

'What do you mean?'

'You've been sitting here with a glazed look over your face for quite a while.'

'The lights seemed to go out for as long as it would take an eye to blink. Don't play games with me, Riell.'

'I'm not. I wouldn't rely fully on my own judgement of time here, but I've had a meal since you last spoke to me.'

Atreu looked at the leftover food that Riell had in front of him.

'What happened, Riell?'

'Don't ask me to explain the effect of the Source. I don't understand it. I think you fell into some sort of meditative trance.'

'That's ridiculous. You have to be aware of what you're doing when you meditate, don't you?'

'Perhaps. What was the last thing you were thinking of before the lights went out?'

'I ... I had this sense that I was cast adrift.'

'You said you felt as if you had no understanding anymore.'

Atreu nodded.

Riell continued. 'I used to get that sense each time I reached a higher level in windrider training. I was often so preoccupied with the new skill that it seemed even the old ones were deserting me.'

'You may be right, Riell. Perhaps I'm not going backwards. Although I am undertaking a Descent – that's going back in a way, isn't it?'

'It depends if the person making the Descent is the same person who made the Ascent. Are you the same person?'

'Yes and no.'

'The no part should tell you something.'

'I see what you saying, Riell. Perhaps I *am* different now, and I've reached a higher level, which I now have to understand.' He looked down at his Talisman. 'And the meaningless words here are telling me that.'

'Has anything changed?' Riell asked, indicating the Book.

Atreu turned several pages. 'No.' He sighed.

'What do you hope to see in your Talisman?'

'I ... I don't quite know,' said Atreu, as he continued to riffle through the pages. 'I suppose I hoped to read something about Verlinden.'

'The Holy Man said she was at the Source, didn't he?'

Atreu shook his head. 'He said all the Ascenders were here.

She may not be considered a true Ascender. Who knows what he meant?'

'I don't think the Felsen are known for their word-play. They leave that for the Liche.'

'Yes, but the Felsen can be economical with words. I don't believe it was an attempt at deception – but that still doesn't tell me what I want to know.'

'And there's nothing in your Talisman?'

'No – I can't even find anything about Cluric right now.' Atreu was still scanning the pages when he stopped suddenly. He flicked over the next page and then back again.

'What do you see now?' asked Riell.

'Nothing – and I mean absolutely nothing. The writing finishes here. Then the pages are blank.'

'Blank?'

'Yes,' said Atreu. 'This seems like a further step backwards. Now it's like it was when I was nine years old, when Micah first gave Teyth and I our Talismans. Blank pages. Nothing. Ignorance. Perhaps my power over my Talisman *is* disappearing.'

'The blank pages don't necessarily ...'

Atreu didn't hear the end of the sentence because he was concentrating on the last words before the pages went blank. He sensed they were important. He had to decipher their meaning. *What are they saying to me?*

His eyes started watering under the strain as he tried to force the words to form into something comprehensible. *Damn you. This time you won't escape me.*

Still they wouldn't yield.

Finally, he became aware of the monks' tone from the shores of the lake deep inside his head. His vision seemed to turn in on itself as the tone grew louder. The words spun off the page into the air and danced before his eyes. As he watched, they spiralled and cartwheeled, forming and reforming, until Atreu was aware they were on the verge of giving him meaning.

Their gyrations became increasingly sluggish until finally they were reduced to the faintest trembling. With an act of will, Atreu forced them back down onto the page. The words floated down, swaying slightly, like feathers on a still morning, until they merged again with the page and were still.

It was then that Atreu began to read.

He grabbed Ascender Atreu by the arm. 'Listen, Atreu,' he said, 'if I could somehow get to Ariathe, I could join up with a group from another town. There are bound to be dozens there. And you're going there ... well, close enough anyway ...'

What was this? His Talisman was retelling the story of his Ascent. He had been through this already. He had learnt all he could about his Ascent. This couldn't be right. Surely there was more? He looked down again.

Edric walked over to the corner table where Cluric's pack lay. He picked it up, walked back to where Cluric sat –

This was Teuron. What was there for him? Why was his Book retelling his departure with Cluric from the inn?

He focused a few lines down.

Was that a tear in Edric's eye?

Cluric wanted to say something, but suddenly everything felt very cold.

For the briefest of moments he was aware that he was no longer aware.

Then nothing.

Nothing.

Nothing.

Atreu pulled part of his mind away from the scene. As the monk's drone continued inside his head, he sensed that the scene in Teuron was an echo. The reality was the nothingness.

Cluric, what has happened to you?

He reached out slowly and turned to the previous page in a dream-like trance. He scanned the words, taking in only phrases and sentence fragments: *the shadows pushed at him from all sides ... the rest of his body was crumpling ... dark tendrils were now snaking down his arm ... watched the wraiths descend ... he thought he saw a familiar face ...*

A familiar face? Atreu started. *It's me,* he voiced silently to the page. *It's me, Cluric. I'm here with you.*

Atreu felt tears well up. *Cluric!* he cried inside his head. *Don't you leave me too. I won't let you.*

He turned back to the next page and focused on the empty space after the word *nothing.* He felt his body shudder as he stared. To his amazement, words started to form where none had been.

'Cluric,' he said out loud, 'you will not go the way of Teyth.'

When the words had fully formed, Atreu started to read again.

*

Cluric felt a sharp, clean ray of sunlight on his face. He fought the fog in his head. Where was he? In Teuron? The Rimforest? Ariathe? For some reason, the image of a cave floated into his vision. What would he be doing in a cave? And how could the sunlight reach him if he was?

He opened his eyes slowly. It was as if there were stones on his eyelids, but finally the light flooded in.

Slowly, with great effort, he started to remember. The Dusk-wraiths bearing down on him. The icy cold creeping along his body until it consumed his awareness. His brother Edric. And the Ascender Atreu.

Cloud wisps floated high in the sky above Peleusar. Where did the image of the cave fit in? Cluric couldn't remember the last time he had been in a cave.

He realised his hand was still clasped around the hilt of his sword. He released his grip and used both hands to push himself up to a sitting position. To his dismay, Maelir bodies littered the battlefield, which was ringed by the embers of a dying fire. A few were moving, but most lay motionless.

'Can anyone hear me?' he cried, his voice coming out splintered and broken.

There were a few thin, isolated replies from around him. With every sinew aching, he got to his feet. He looked across to see Jenethelen's body lying still on the ground. Rushing over as fast as his stiff limbs would allow, he bent to touch her cheek. Even to his own still-icy body, she felt to him as cold and as hard as a frozen lake.

He touched her other cheek with his left hand, cradling her face. There was no response.

He leant down and pressed his ear to her chest, but he couldn't hear a heartbeat. For a moment he thought he heard a voice call, 'Give her your breath.'

Without being fully aware of what he was doing, he took a deep breath, placed his lips on hers and exhaled. When nothing happened, he tried again.

He tried a third time, his hands still cupping her cheeks, but not even a sliver of warmth returned, and she lay motionless. Cluric closed his eyes and felt the Dusk-wraiths bearing down on him again. And something inside him died.

Opening his eyes, he placed his lips on hers once again and this time he kissed them. Only when he could no longer bear the cold did he pull away. He looked at her face, framed by her dark, tangled hair.

'What a strange place our Mountain has become,' he said softly. 'And how strange I am to myself.'

He watched Jenethelen and tried to pretend that she was asleep, until he became aware of other Maelir soldiers getting to their feet around him.

'Cluric – I am so glad that you are alive.' Cluric looked up to see Hrulth standing next to him.

'So all is not lost,' said Cluric with a bitter edge to his voice. 'Only most things.'

Hrulth ran both hands through his hair as he stared at Jenethelen. 'I'm sorry. I was almost starting to warm to her – and I never thought I'd hear myself say that about a Faemir.'

'I'm sorry too, Uncle. I'm not thinking clearly. It is good to see you alive. How did we survive?'

'I can only guess that sunrise saved us. We must have delayed the wraiths long enough for the sunlight to banish them.'

'We're finished though, aren't we?' said Cluric. 'We don't have the numbers to survive another attack. Is there any point in living through one more day?'

Hrulth's eyes looked sad. 'Are you giving up? After all the battles we've been through?'

'Sometimes giving up is the only choice left.'

'That doesn't sound like a soldier talking.' Hrulth's fingers threaded through his beard as he scanned the carnage around them, and then his body slumped, as if suddenly aware of the hollowness of his words. 'Cluric, I'm not sure if giving up is ever a solution, but sometimes walking away is.'

Cluric's eyes narrowed. 'What are you saying?'

'I'm agreeing with you. What are we doing here in Peleusar? What are we defending? The people who lived here have long been evacuated. There's nothing of value left. The city is just a collection of deserted buildings.'

'So you're saying we should just leave?'

'Let's talk to the others. I think it should be an ordered departure, but yes, we should burn the dead and then go. We're achieving nothing here, and you're right, we won't last another night.'

'The fires are out, Hrulth. Perhaps we should give these ones a decent burial.'

'You're right, Cluric. They deserve at least that. I'll give the order.'

Cluric let out a slow breath and looked down at Jenethelen, desperately trying to pretend she was asleep.

Chapter Eleven

Atreu's gaze drifted up from the Book. Had he willed Cluric back to life? The thought of such power sent a shock wave through him. It couldn't be. What if this was all some cruel self-delusion? What if Cluric had died in Peleusar after the Dusk-wraith attack? Or what if the delusion went deeper than that? What if Cluric wasn't even in Peleusar? What if he had died at the start of the war against the Faemir? Atreu had no proof of these things. All he had to hold onto was proof of the Talisman's power in the past. Was that enough? The Book had always been erratic. And now it appeared to be getting worse. He had no control over it – he could only take and use what it gave him.

And yet ... this time he had fought with the words. Had he forced the words to reveal their meaning? Or had he *created* the meaning himself? He shivered.

He became aware of Riell's breathing. The windrider hadn't moved from where he had been sitting. A calmness had settled on his face. His eyes were open, but Atreu could see there was no outward focus. The atmosphere at the Source was obviously having an effect on him, too.

Atreu realised he had no idea how much time had elapsed since he and Riell had last spoken. The monk was still motionless on his prayer mat. There was nothing in the cavern that could be used to mark time.

It occurred to him that he should be hungry. He made a half-hearted attempt to get some food from his pack, but gave up when he realised he had no desire to eat.

Am I becoming like them? he wondered. *Soon I'll be walking under the lake waters and flying through the air without wings.* He smiled to himself.

His attention was inexorably drawn back to his Book. *Verlinden, are you in there?* he voiced soundlessly. *Perhaps I can save you, too.*

He started turning the pages again. *Verlinden.* He tried to force the word onto the paper. *Verlinden.* But the words stubbornly refused to re-form for him this time. He strained, narrowing his eyes. *Verlinden.* Then he focused away from the page so that the words were in his peripheral vision.

Verlinden.

Please.

Show me where she is.

His Talisman gave him nothing.

He finally closed his eyes as they began to water under the strain. When he opened them again, tears were pouring down his cheeks.

'It always surprises me how wise and how foolish we all are.'

The voice was familiar. Atreu blinked away the tears and looked around the cave. Riell and the monk were still as they had been. Was it the monk who had spoken? The voice was similar, yet somehow far more ancient.

'The answer is right there next to you.'

Atreu wiped the last tears away. His vision cleared, and he could see an old man standing several paces to his right. 'Praether?' he said.

The old man smiled. 'Not quite.'

'The Reader?'

'That's a better name.'

'What are you doing here?'

'Seeing how wise and foolish you can be. As we all are.'

'Can you help me find Verlinden?'

'Not in the way you wish me to.'

'I don't understand what you're saying.'

'Remember, the answer is in the Books – it's always in the Books.'

'You're sounding like Praether now.'

'Talk to the part of me that is Praether, then – if that helps.'

'I've searched my Book for her.' Atreu ran his fingers across the pages. 'It's hopeless.'

'Did I say the Book?'

Atreu's brow furrowed. 'Of course you did.'

The Reader shook his head and threw an indecipherable glance in the direction of the meditating monk. 'This is more than I should be doing. I said the answer is in the *Books*.'

Atreu suddenly straightened. 'The second Book. Is Verlinden in there?'

'I've said enough.'

'Of course. I have been foolish,' said Atreu, reaching into his pack for the Book of Maelur. He placed the second Book next to his own Talisman and started scanning backwards and forwards across the pages of both Books, tracing each of the two sets of words with one hand.

He drew a sharp breath when the name *Verlinden* suddenly jumped out at him from a page in his Book.

'Thank you,' he cried to the Reader, who was now gradually becoming more insubstantial.

'It wasn't me, my young friend. There are many of us at work here. Things are not what they seem.'

'Then thank Praether.'

'He does not know the full truth, you know. He is flawed like the rest of us.'

'Thank him anyway.'

The old man smiled as he faded into the glimmerstone light. 'You already have.'

Atreu returned his attention to his Talisman, focused on the name ...

Verlinden was here – he knew it now. She was at the Source. He suddenly felt very strange, as if the air in the cave was folding in on him, again and again.

He felt himself get up, or perhaps his surroundings changed subtly, so that it appeared to him that he was getting up.

The entrance to the cave moved past his vision – had he just walked through it? He turned his head slowly, aware of the glimmerstone-encrusted walls of the tunnel as they shifted in his vision.

A fork. To the left. Another fork. The right one chose him. A third fork – this time a choice of three. The middle one drew him in.

He found himself in a dim cave. After his eyes adjusted he saw a hooded figure seated on a prayer mat. Was he back where he had started? He stepped closer. There was no sign of Riell. The cavern was different, and ...

He approached the figure and searched the darkness under the cowl. Was this who he thought it was? Drawing a deep breath, he placed his hands under the cowl and felt a tangle of long hair. Slowly, he pulled back the hood and revealed the soft features of a woman with her eyes closed.

'Verlinden,' he said softly, running his hands down her cheeks to her neck.

She opened her eyes. 'Atreu,' she said as she exhaled.

They kissed and then held each other for a time which Atreu could not measure.

'You're alive.'

Who had spoken? Atreu wasn't sure. He drew back to look at her. Her eyes shone with the most exquisite colours.

They kissed again and slowly lowered themselves to the

ground as one. They enveloped each other and Atreu lost all sense of himself ...

When Atreu became aware again, his Book lay open in front of him.

'Welcome back,' said the familiar voice of Riell.

'Where's Verlinden?' asked Atreu, looking around confused.

'I'm sure she's at the Source somewhere.'

'No, I found her. I was just with her.'

'You were in a trance, Atreu. I'm sorry, she's not here.'

'Yes, yes she was here ... or I was there ... or ...'

'Please, Atreu, I was hoping that the meditation was going to calm you.'

'I wasn't meditating. I was reading and then I went looking for Verlinden and ... and I found her ...'

Riell placed his hand on Atreu's shoulder. 'Please calm yourself. It doesn't help. I've been sitting here waiting for you to come out of your trance for quite some time.'

'Nonsense, Riell, you were in a trance yourself. I saw you.'

The windrider frowned. 'Strange things happen at the Source. We could both be right. I do remember something now.' He looked away.

'What is it?'

'I was flying – without wings.' His voice was hoarse.

'Was it real?'

'It couldn't have been, could it?'

'Perhaps you were lighter than air, as these Holy Men are.'

'These things are only going on in our heads. They're not actually happening.'

'No? I'm convinced Verlinden is alive now. She's here at the Source. I saw her.'

Riell drew a deep breath. 'Look. Atreu, this place has always been perplexing for me. I've never been back long enough for it to work its effect on me again. It sapped my confidence after my own pilgrimage, and I'm still not sure how to deal with it.'

'You haven't really told me why you judged yourself a failure while you were here.'

'I'd almost forgotten how I felt and what thoughts went through my mind until now. It's starting to come back, unfortunately.'

'Tell me, Riell. Please.'

The windrider fell silent, but finally turned to face Atreu. 'The image of me flying without wings came to me again and again when I was here, until it overwhelmed everything else.'

'What's wrong with that? It could mean many things.'

'You don't understand, Atreu. It's not the image itself that is important, it's the feeling that goes with it.'

'What was the feeling?'

'It ... it was a sense of arrogant power, of pride ... of hubris.'

'That doesn't sound like you.'

'No – I knew it had to be wrong.'

Atreu chewed his bottom lip. 'So you judged your Ascent to be a failure because you felt you had this incredible power?'

'It was false.'

'How do you know? Perhaps you really had it. Perhaps you were justified in your pride.'

'It doesn't matter now.'

'Yes it does – you obviously haven't resolved it. Your feeling, it doesn't have to be wrong. Look at you now – you have formed a new Holy Order. You have been elected to the Circle. You control the windriders in battle.'

Riell was staring at Atreu as he spoke his last words. 'Tell me, Atreu, what feeling went with this image of you finding Verlinden?'

'It wasn't an image. It was real.'

'What was the feeling?'

Atreu found it hard to meet the windrider's gaze. 'Joy at finding her.'

'Anything else?'

'I ... felt a sense of power ... that I had somehow brought her back to life through the two Books. I also felt that when I was reading about Cluric coming back from oblivion.'

'So you now feel you control life and death?'

'That sounds insane.'

'It sounds insane, but is that what you feel?'

Atreu nodded. 'Am I like you?' he asked. 'Have I failed because I believe in a power I don't have?'

'I don't know. I answered my own question years ago, and you will have to answer yours.'

Atreu heard the sound of footsteps near the entrance to the cavern. He looked up and saw a figure walk in.

'Verlinden,' he cried.

'You're alive,' she said.

*

Although Cluric was sweating under the strain of lifting so many bodies, he still felt cold inside. All these deaths. It was as if the Dusk-wraiths had taken the hearts of the hundred Maelir who had somehow survived the night. Cluric was simply going through the motions now. Hrulth, too, was as silent as stone as they carried yet another body to the mass grave.

They approached the lip of the giant hole and swung the body with just enough momentum to ensure that it landed on top of the others when they released their grip.

One, two, three. Cluric counted silently without giving it any conscious thought. By now it was as automatic as breathing. On the count of three, he and Hrulth let go, and the crumpled man who had once been a Maelir soldier flew a short distance and then fell like a rock onto the other bodies.

Cluric's shoulders slumped as he scanned the ground for the next one. Realising that Jenethelen was now one of the last bodies to be buried, he felt a further weight of despair tug at his body. He hesitated.

'We can't just leave her,' said Hrulth.

'No.' Cluric barely recognised his own voice.

'She fought well for someone who wasn't a natural soldier,' said Hrulth.

Cluric pressed his lips together. 'Like us.' He knew Hrulth could have given her no better obituary. 'Come on, Uncle. Let's get this over with.'

They trudged up to where the Faemir still lay. Cluric fought the urge to brush his hand along her cheek. Instead he grabbed her hands, just as he had with all the other bodies.

Was that the faintest of movements behind her eyelids? Impossible. His eyes were fatigued and could no longer be trusted. And yet as he and Hrulth carried her to the mass grave, he searched for other signs. A faint movement of her chest. The slightest sliver of warmth in her skin. He had almost convinced himself that there was still some hope by the time they started swinging her.

One.

Her hair streamed through the air, giving the illusion that she was moving.

Two.

Was that a tinge of red appearing in her cheeks?

Three – 'Wait!'

Hrulth had let go, but Cluric hung on to Jenethelen, and she hit the ground at his feet with a resounding thud.

'What are you doing?' said Hrulth.

Cluric stood there stunned for a moment. 'Look at her,' he said finally, pointing to the crumpled body on the ground. 'Can't you see?'

Hrulth crouched down to look more closely at Jenethelen. He felt for her pulse and then lifted one of her eyelids.

'She's dead,' he said. 'Don't fool yourself.'

Cluric reached down and placed both his hands on her cheeks and then ran them slowly down her neck and shoulders.

Hrulth looked away as Cluric continued to run his hands along her sides.

'Here,' he cried suddenly. 'I was right. I can feel some warmth.'

'What?' Hrulth's head jerked back in Jenethelen's direction. He reached down and felt where Cluric had indicated. 'You're right.'

'Wait,' said Cluric, his expression changing as he reached into the pocket of her tunic.

'What is it?' asked Hrulth.

Cluric pulled out a leather pouch and emptied its contents onto the ground. 'Brimstones,' he said. 'We never even got to try them against the wraiths.'

The dark red stones lay glowing at their feet.

Cluric stood deathly still. 'Things just come to an end, don't they?' His voice rang hollow.

'I'm afraid they do.'

They picked up Jenethelen's body again.

One.

Cluric couldn't look at her anymore.

Two.

He closed his eyes.

Three.

He heard the thud as she landed on the pile of bodies.

*

Atreu felt Verlinden's warmth against him; her breath resounded gently in his ear.

'I thought I had lost you,' he said.

'What happened?' asked Riell.

'I ... don't know,' said Verlinden, pulling away from Atreu to look at the windrider. 'I couldn't even tell you how long I've been here – wherever here is.'

'This is the Source,' said Atreu. 'You can't have been here for more than a day.'

'Really?'

'I'm not so sure about time,' said Riell. 'Strange things happen to your perception here. Are you certain you know how long *we've* been here, Atreu?'

'It's starting to come back to me now,' said Verlinden. 'There was a storm, wasn't there?'

'Yes,' said Riell. 'You were being carried by Leylan. Do you know where he is?'

Verlinden's brow furrowed. 'I ... I remember ... falling. Then there was water.'

'Could you have fallen into the lake?' asked Riell.

'Yes ... I think that's what must have happened. I remember being underwater and someone helping me with the harness. It must have been Leylan.'

'What happened then?' asked Atreu.

'I don't know. There are ... pictures inside my head, but they don't seem like memories, or even dreams. Even seeing you ... it's only now starting to feel real.'

'The Books helped me find you,' said Atreu.

Verlinden glanced at them. 'I don't understand this. I found you, didn't I? I somehow knew where you were in this maze of tunnels.'

Atreu shuddered. Strange things were happening. He was barely able to bring himself to say the next words. 'Is it possible that you were dead?'

Verlinden started. 'You're not making any sense.'

'But is it possible?'

'What sort of question is that?'

'Atreu,' Riell said, 'I think you're talking nonsense. Verlinden was obviously rescued and has fallen under the spell of the Source. Her perceptions have been warped. We know meditation here is a strange experience, but this talk of dying is foolish. We can both see she is alive.'

'Look, the powers of the Books may be unpredictable,' said Atreu, 'but my instincts about them are usually right. And one thing I am sure of is that my grasp of them *is* growing. I don't know for certain that I have somehow brought Verlinden back to life, but I'm convinced that I helped draw Cluric back from the brink of death.'

'Your friend in Peleusar?' said Verlinden.

'Yes.'

'I hope you're right, Atreu.' Riell shifted uneasily. 'Because if you're not, the only other explanation I can give is that you are going mad.'

Atreu was suddenly aware that the monk who had been meditating in the cavern had stood up.

'You have a task,' said the Holy Man, although it was unclear who he was addressing. The cracked voice coming from under the dark hood again struck Atreu as familiar.

'Yes,' said Atreu. 'I told you. I need to find the Book of Metheus.'

Again, at the mention of the Book, the monk seemed to react slightly.

'You have found what you need to find here.'

'Yes, Verlinden is here.' Atreu glanced at her and smiled.

'You have found what you need to find.'

The repetition of the statement threw Atreu into confusion. Perhaps the monk wasn't referring to Verlinden. 'Do you mean I have judged my own Truth?'

'Only you can decide that.'

Atreu drew a deep, long breath. 'Do these Books give me power over life and death?'

The Felsen Holy Man didn't reply. Instead, he got up and started walking.

'Hey,' said Atreu, 'where are you going?'

The monk just kept walking.

'Let's go,' said Riell. 'We'd better follow him or we'll never find our way back outside.'

Atreu quickly grabbed the Books and his backpack, and the three of them rushed out of the cavern after the monk.

As they made their way through the passages, more monks seemed to appear in front of them at various points. No one spoke. Only the crunch of the occasional loose stone echoed underfoot.

The procession finally filed out onto the sandy beach surrounding the lake, with Atreu ensuring that he, Riell and Verlinden were still following the Holy Man who had spoken to them. The monks immediately started to disperse, some heading for the lake, others walking along the shore.

'What now?' asked Atreu.

Riell shrugged. 'He's made it easy for us to follow him. I think we keep up with him unless he goes underwater.'

Atreu was suddenly aware that the monk was standing in the distance, facing them and gesturing.

'Don't tell me we're getting some guidance,' said Atreu.

They stepped towards him.

'Will you help us with our quest to find the third Book?' asked Atreu.

'I cannot answer your questions.'

'I need to repair my wings,' said Riell. 'Please help me.'

'There are other ways to descend.'

'We haven't got time to make the journey on foot,' said Atreu.

'There are other ways to descend. I will take you to the Maelstrom. There is a boat you can use.'

'Why are you helping us?' asked Atreu, as the monk turned and started walking along the shores.

They followed him, although he didn't respond. The day was dying and Atreu watched the sun dip towards the tops of the cliffs. He became aware of rhythmic chants echoing around him. Soon, the cliffs in front of him were afire with the sun's rays. Exquisite shadows played across the still lake waters. He reached out to hold Verlinden's hand, but she held it half-heartedly before pulling away. He tried to catch her eye, but was aware that, for some reason, there was some distance between them again.

The ground started rumbling just as the sun started to vanish behind the cliff face and the Source was plunged into darkness.

'I'm going to ask you again,' said Atreu, addressing the Holy Man. 'Why are you helping me?'

There was a long silence, and when the monk spoke, his tone was different, and it sounded even more familiar. 'All of us need to find our source. You need to find yours.'

'What do you mean? I'm already here, at the Source.'

'Your source isn't here. You must find *your* origin. You must return.'

'How do you know what I must do?'

'We all need to find our source.' What was it about the voice? Atreu quickened his step to catch up to the monk and grab his sleeve. 'Who are you? I know you, don't I?'

'Let go of him,' cried Riell.

'But I need to know who he is.'

'He has no identity, none of the monks at the Source do.'

'Yes, this one does.' Atreu's muscles tensed. 'Who are you?' He grabbed the monk's hood and pulled it back.

His knees almost buckled. 'Praether,' he cried.

The monk was clearly fighting for self-control, his ancient, lined face contorting.

'Impossible,' cried Riell. 'It's dark. Your eyes are playing tricks. Give the Holy Man back his dignity. Put the hood back on.'

Atreu shook his head. 'Look at him, Riell.' He turned to the monk. 'You're Praether. How can this be?'

The monk's shoulders seemed to slump and his expression changed. 'I'm not Praether.'

'Then you must be Metheus himself,' said Verlinden.

'Stop asking me who I am.'

'Praether is dead,' said Riell, 'and from what you've told me, Atreu, Metheus is under the Plains of Vygird. The Lower Reaches are a long way from here.'

'Please let us continue,' said the monk. 'I should not be doing this. I should have just left you to find the Maelstrom yourselves.'

Not Praether. Not Metheus. Suddenly it dawned on Atreu.

'Three. There are always three. The three Books. The three Holy Orders. The three Holy Places. The third way.'

'What nonsense are you babbling?' said Riell.

'There were three of you, weren't there?' said Atreu. 'Not just twins – *triplets.*'

The monk stared back at him silently for a moment and then drew his hood back over his head.

*

Cluric was growing increasingly dispirited as the day wore on. It was as if his limbs were dead weights which he was forced to carry with him. He and the other surviving soldiers were going through the motions of shovelling dirt onto the mass grave. It was taking most of the day to bury the dead.

'Hurry,' said Hrulth. 'We want to get out of Peleusar by night-fall, don't we?'

'How do you know the Dusk-wraiths won't find us out there?'

'We don't, but do we have any choice? We don't have the numbers to defend ourselves here for another night. Come on, Cluric, don't lose heart. We're still alive, aren't we? There's still a chance we will return to our homes.'

Cluric nodded grimly as he shovelled more dirt onto the bodies. He had left Jenethelen until last, but knew that she too had to be covered.

'What's happened to your fire?' asked Hrulth.

Cluric looked at him, confused.

'That slow-burning mirwood fire that used to be inside you,' said Hrulth. 'No Faemir or Nazir has been able to quench it yet.'

'I think I've lost more than my fire, Uncle.'

Cluric rested his shovel on the ground, suddenly unable to find the strength to lift it. He stared at the grave, barely able to focus. Hrulth's voice was registering somewhere in the back of his head, but he could no longer distinguish the words.

A flicker of movement brought things back into focus. 'What was that?' he cried.

'Don't start this again, Cluric.'

'No, look down there.' He pointed to where Jenethelen's body lay.

'Please, don't –'

'Look!'

As they both stared at the half-covered body of the Faemir Watcher, they saw a slight movement of her arm displace the soil that had been shovelled onto it.

'She's alive!' Cluric clambered over the lip of the mass grave and pushed the dirt from her.

Hrulth was now by his side and they dragged her back onto solid ground. Cluric reached down to her throat to feel her pulse. 'There's something there.' Drawing in a breath, he placed his lips on hers and exhaled. Her chest immediately responded. He gave her his breath again and again, until her chest started heaving rhythmically.

When she opened her eyes, the exchange of air turned into a kiss.

'Hey!' Hrulth's voice echoed through the camp.

Cluric's head jerked back under the shock. 'What is it?'

'Jenethelen is not the only one still alive.'

It took a moment for Cluric to realise that there were signs of movement in various parts of the grave. Then panic hit him. *What have we done?*

The surviving soldiers sprang into action, pulling body after body out of the grave. Shovelling dirt with their bare hands if necessary.

'Get them all out,' cried Hrulth. 'Every last one of them – even if they're not moving.'

Cluric carried Jenethelen away from the mass grave, made her as comfortable as he could, and then rushed back to help the others.

On and on the Maelir toiled. Bodies were carried just far enough to keep a path clear for the next body to be carried out.

It was close to dusk when the last body was exhumed. Cluric looked around. Most continued to lie deathly still, but many were showing unmistakable signs of life.

He walked over to where Hrulth was standing, bathed in sweat and dripping with exhaustion. 'What have we done?' he asked.

Hrulth closed his eyes, trying to fight back the tears.

'What about all the others we burnt?' said Cluric.

'I don't know. I don't know.'

'Hrulth, please make some sense of this.'

Hrulth forced his eyes open. 'What manner of enemy are these Nazir? They send us their wraiths instead of fighting us themselves, and now it looks like those wraiths don't even kill.'

'They've made us kill our own people,' said Cluric, a sickening pain burgeoning in his stomach.

Hrulth nodded.

'Don't tell me we burnt and buried all those others alive. Please don't tell me that, Uncle.'

Hrulth closed his eyes again.

'Please, Uncle, don't tell me that they've all suffocated under the ground or been consumed by flames because of our stupidity.'

Hrulth was shaking.

'Uncle?'

Hrulth's voice was barely a whisper. 'I gave the order.'

Cluric put his arm around his trembling uncle. 'You weren't to know. It's the Nazir. The Nazir are to blame. Not you. Not you.'

Hrulth gradually stopped trembling.

Cluric saw that Jenethelen was now sitting up and looking around her. He walked over to her.

'What happened?' she asked.

'You're alive,' said Cluric, embracing her. She seemed to resist for a moment, but then encircled him with her arms.

They only pulled apart when Hrulth's order resounded

through the camp. 'Let's get those fires started. It looks like we'll be here for one more night.'

Chapter Twelve

Saretha slammed her hand down on the table and the War Council fell silent. 'We can't go on like this.'

Theander glared at her. 'Sit down and let me finish my report – and then let's decide what can and can't go on.'

Saretha waved him away dismissively. 'I've heard enough of defeats, retreats and massacres.'

'You'd prefer not to know what is happening?' asked Theander angrily. 'How can you make any decisions without information?'

'All I'm hearing are second- and third-hand reports. I've never fought these Nazir myself. Have you? Has anyone in this room?'

'No one has,' said Leyvin. 'That's the real problem, isn't it? We've dealt with every Dusk creature they can muster, but they won't fight us directly.'

'Forget the Nazir,' said Saretha. 'These Dusk-wraiths are the enemy at the moment. The only way to fight the Nazir is to overcome them.'

'Saretha's right,' said Rhea.

'Why am I not surprised that you're agreeing with her?' said Theander.

Rhea continued. 'It's important that some of the members of this War Council have direct experience fighting these wraiths.'

'That's a good strategy for reducing the size of this Council even further,' said Theander.

'No one's suggesting that you have to endanger yourself,' said Rhea, her voice laden with sarcasm. 'I'm sure the Faemir members of this Council are prepared to do what you can't.'

'War is about tactics and understanding your enemy,' said Theander.

Saretha slammed her hand down on the table again. 'I want to face my enemy!' She leaned forward and her gaze bored into Theander's eyes.

'All right,' said Leyvin. 'I agree that we are limiting ourselves by listening to indirect reports. If the Faemir way is for its leaders to learn by engaging in battle, then let them do it.'

Theander glared at him. 'It's not our way.'

'Defeat is your way,' said Saretha. 'I've had enough of this endless talking.' She turned to go.

'Wait,' said Leyvin. 'The windriders could carry the Faemir into the thick of battle in the Mid-Reaches – if that's what we decide. Let's all hear what Theander has to say and then formulate a plan.'

Saretha remained standing, but gave no protest.

'As I was saying,' said Theander, 'I believe we have detected some sort of pattern to the attacks. Although towns and cities in both the Lower Reaches and Mid-Reaches are under siege, the Rimforest remains free, as far as we can tell.'

'And what does that mean?' asked Rhea.

'I don't know, but it must be something we can use.'

'Anything else?' asked Leyvin.

Theander said, 'It also appears that the Maelstrom itself is a safe haven. Farepont and the other smaller floating towns haven't been threatened, and no boats have ever been attacked.'

'That *is* something we can use,' said Rhea.

'The Maelstrom is large,' said Holthim, 'but how many people could we protect by getting them into boats?'

'How can we continue like this?' asked Saretha angrily.

'Can you explain what is wrong with what I said?' Holthim was clearly taken aback.

'We finally have a piece of information that can help us,' said Saretha, 'and you don't even begin to see it.'

'Tell me then what you're proposing.'

'We can use the Maelstrom for attack,' said Saretha. 'We want warriors in the boats, not children, cowards and weaklings.'

Rhea nodded. 'It will give us the mobility to attack from the Base to the Summit,' said Rhea, 'without fear of reprisal. This alone could be enough for us to turn the tide.'

'What do you think, Theander?' asked Holthim.

'We've never fought that way before, but it could work. River pirates have made their raids that way for generations.'

'All right,' said Leyvin. 'How will we organise these attacks, and how many soldiers would be involved?'

'Wait, Leyvin,' said Theander. 'I don't think we've made a decision yet.'

'Don't tell me you want to vote on it,' said Saretha in disgust.

'In the absence of Riell, we don't have a choice.'

'That's not entirely true,' said Leyvin. 'We don't have any procedures in place for the decision making of this Council. This is not the Circle.'

'Riell commands the windriders,' said Theander, 'and through them, the Maelir army. The Circle has given him that power.'

'Yes,' said Leyvin, 'but you wouldn't be claiming that command in his absence, would you?'

'Not without the sanction of the Circle.'

'We have a problem then,' said Rhea. 'I command the Faemir warriors, but who commands the Maelir army?'

'Aren't we making joint decisions here?' said Holthim. 'Why are we having all this discussion about command?'

'Because command is all-important in war,' said Rhea.

'I don't see –' Holthim began, before he was cut off.

'Of course you *don't see*,' said Saretha, mimicking Holthim's tone. 'You have no place on a War Council.'

'Wait,' said Leyvin. 'Let's examine this without so much ill-feeling. Rhea and Saretha may have a point.'

Theander looked at him, open-mouthed. 'You're agreeing with the Faemir?'

'No,' said Leyvin. 'I said they *may* have a point. Let's look at this. We created this War Council because we recognised that, while the Circle is the best body to make decisions during peace time, its ways are too cumbersome during war. We all agreed to that, didn't we?'

Theander eyed Leyvin suspiciously, but didn't contradict him.

'It follows,' said Leyvin, 'that this body has to be able to make quick decisions. Am I right?'

'What's your point, Leyvin?' asked Holthim.

'What I'm saying is that it was hard enough for decisions to be made when Riell was in command of the Maelir army. Now that we have no one in command, it has become impossible. We haven't made one change in our strategy against the Nazir since Riell left.'

'The solution is simple,' said Theander. 'The command of the Maelir should fall to me.'

'So you are claiming the command that you denied only a few moments ago?' said Leyvin.

Theander looked slightly bewildered before he regained his composure. 'The command was given to Riell because the windriders are the most important part of the Maelir army, and they are central to the defence of the Keep and the Rituals of Zenith.'

'I agree they were the reasons, Theander. But as you yourself just said, the command was *given* to Riell. It is the Circle that has the power to give the command. Do we agree on that?'

Theander frowned. 'Of course.'

'Good. Then you agree you cannot claim it?'

'Yes, but if the problem here is a lack of commander, I would argue that the Circle should appoint me in Riell's absence.'

'We could put that to the Circle,' said Holthim. 'The arguments for Theander would be the same as those put in favour of Riell.'

'No one has to remind me of those,' said Leyvin. 'I was the one who put a number of them.'

'I think we will be able to resolve the matter quickly,' said Holthim. 'Now let us consider this proposal to use the Maelstrom as our basis of attack.'

'I don't think we can continue until this is resolved,' said Rhea. 'How quickly can the Circle meet?'

'We can bring the next session forward to consider this as a matter of urgency,' said Leyvin. 'Holthim, do you agree?'

Holthim nodded.

'Then we will reconvene the War Council immediately after the Circle has completed its deliberations. Are we all agreed?'

Theander looked around at the faces in the room. He sensed there were undercurrents that he wasn't fully aware of. Everyone, including Saretha, indicated their assent. Was it going to be that easy? If only Riell was still at the Keep – he had had many more direct dealings with Leyvin and the ways of the Circle. What a tragedy that he was now lost.

As he made his way out of the War Council chamber, his concerns suddenly increased manyfold when he saw an unmistakable smile on Rhea's lips.

*

The lap-lap of oars in the still Source waters was the only sound Atreu could hear as the monk rowed them towards the large cavern that loomed ahead of them in the darkness. Atreu struggled to remain fully aware of his surroundings and keep his consciousness from drifting away. There was something about this place, something far stranger and more subtle than anything he had encountered since leaving Valesend. The awe that the Keep had inspired in him when he first saw it, the multitude of exquisite towers of light, was nothing compared to the serene calm majesty of this place. He had often been dismissive of the Felsen and their ways – many of their practices seemed absurd and meaningless – yet here, distilled to their essence, there was a purity beyond anything he could imagine.

A rumble suddenly sounded deep below them, and the serenity was disturbed by a series of ripples on the lake. Atreu felt as if his thoughts themselves had been violated.

'Is there no place these Nazir can't violate?' he said, half to himself and half to the lake.

The monk's rhythm appeared to momentarily desert him, and the lapping of the oars missed a beat.

'How long has there been instability here?' asked Atreu, not really expecting an answer from their silent guide.

'My meditations have been disturbed of late,' said the Holy Man.

'Have the tremors been the cause?'

'Perhaps.'

The monk regained his rhythm and the serene silence fell again. Atreu saw the cavern entrance immediately in front of them. He gasped as he became aware of an exquisite play of glimmerstone lights inside the cave. As they entered, he watched the bright reflections dance around the oar ripples. It took him a moment to realise that among the reflected lights were others, coming from glimmerstones shining through the crystal clear waters from the bottom of the lake.

Atreu reached out to touch Verlinden's hand. She looked at him and smiled momentarily before her expression changed, as if she had suddenly remembered something that disturbed her.

Atreu sighed. 'We're together,' he said, 'and the quest is still alive. Why –?'

Verlinden interrupted him. 'Don't ask. The problem is that you have to ask the question in the first place.'

Atreu leant back in confusion, and the boat swayed. 'Sorry,' he said to the monk, and straightened up. His truth appeared to be drifting further and further away from him. If his revelation at

Zenith was that the two twins of life, Maelir and Faemir, should be brought together, then he was failing in his personal endeavours to achieve this. Here, at the most peaceful place on the Mountain, his thoughts collided with each other. Doubts gnawed at him. Was this quest for the third Book the way to absolute truth? Was his belief in his growing powers merely arrogant self-delusion?

His thoughts were suddenly infiltrated by a rushing sound in the distance.

'What's that?' he asked.

'They are the Sheerfalls,' said the monk. 'They mark the start of the Maelstrom.'

The reality hit Atreu. He was about to embark on an irreversible Descent. The currents of the river were soon to take all his choices away from him.

A thought suddenly struck Atreu. 'Riell, you *are* coming with us, aren't you?'

The windrider jerked suddenly, as if he had been slapped in the face. 'This is not my quest, Atreu. I'm needed back at the Keep.'

'How will you get back there?'

'As I said, there must be some materials I can use here at the Source to repair my wings.'

'Do you really think there are? It sounds like a forlorn hope to me.'

'Perhaps. If not, one of the other windriders will come searching for me at some stage. I will just have to wait.'

'Can they be spared?'

'We are in a desperate war, but I'm sure one will be spared to search for Leylan and I.'

'Who will give the order to search?'

Riell's brow furrowed. 'I don't know. I hadn't thought of it. I suppose Theander will assume my responsibility in my absence.'

'Are you certain?'

'No ... Atreu ... why are you saying these things to me?'

'How do you know what is going on back at the Keep? If we

should have been warned about the storm, then there are manoeuvrings occurring that neither of us expected.'

'What do you think is happening?'

'I don't know, but if I have doubts about trusting my own uncle, then I'm not sure if I can be fully certain of anyone.'

'I have many friends among the windriders. I trust them all with my life.'

'You are the only windrider in the Circle. The Circle is making all the decisions – do you trust it?'

'I trusted Praether.'

'Praether's dead.'

Riell refused to meet Atreu's gaze. 'I could make my way back to the Keep on foot if I have no other option.'

'Listen to yourself. We have a Mountain infested by Nazir, winter is on its way, and you think you can return through the Upper Reaches on foot. You usually make so much sense.'

'Why are you doing this to me, Atreu?'

'I want you to come with us. You know the Mid-Reaches, and we need a guide. I have some remnants in my head of the maps I had to memorise for my Ascent, but most of the Mountain that the Maelstrom flows through is unknown to me.'

Riell shook his head. 'I don't know the Maelstrom and its towns very well. The winds near the river can be unpredictable, so windriders tend to avoid them. And as you have seen, I can't judge terrain as well on the ground as I can in the air. Besides, most of your Descent will be guided by the river – almost no knowledge of the places is needed. Farepont sits in a large arc where the river starts to flow parallel to the Rimforest's edge. From there you have a day's journey on foot to Treyheim, which borders the Rim, and then you travel through the forest to Treyfell in the Lower Reaches.'

'I still feel you should come. You could wait here forever before any other windriders came looking for you. Would the search start here or would they search the terrain between the Source and the Keep first?'

'I don't know.'

'Would they presume you dead?'

'I don't know, Atreu. I don't know. You're driving me insane.'

Atreu drew a breath. 'Riell, I need you because, of all the people in the Keep, you are the only one who I trust.'

'I thank you for that, Atreu, but ...'

'I just don't see what you would be achieving by staying here at the Source.'

'Atreu,' said Riell finally, 'I've told you. I'm nothing without my wings. I would be no use to you at all. My sense of direction is poor and my battle skills on the ground are adequate at best.'

'You led me here without your wings, Riell. You have helped me come to some important decisions.'

'We don't know if they're the right ones.'

Atreu expelled a loud breath in exasperation. The rushing sound of the Sheerfalls was now considerably louder. 'You doubted yourself when you first came here all those years ago, and you are doubting yourself again now. You're not a failed Ascender; you're more than a windrider. Isn't that what the consecration of the Order of the Wynde should be telling you? You've created a Holy Order. No Liche or Felsen alive today can claim that. And yet you're hanging onto a set of wings made of wood and cloth as the only way you can see yourself.'

A small tremor shook the walls around them. When it stopped, Riell was still trembling.

'Riell, we both owe a great deal to Praether. The quest has been driven by him. Please help me.'

'You know, Atreu, since I became a windrider, I have not gone a single day without riding the winds. Just now I couldn't even tell you how long I've been earthbound here at the Source.'

'You don't need your wings.'

All Atreu could hear was the increasing roar of the Falls. Finally, Riell said, 'All right, I'll come with the two of you.'

'So I'm coming as well, am I?' said Verlinden.

Atreu looked at her strangely. 'Of course. Why are you asking?'

'It looks like we're here,' said Verlinden, ignoring Atreu's question.

The monk gave the faintest of nods. Atreu could see several boats just like the one they were rowing in moored just up ahead.

'Where's the Maelstrom?' asked Atreu, peering into the pinpricks of glimmerstones ahead of them.

'I will take you there,' said the monk, guiding the boat to a rocky ledge jutting out from the cavern wall just above water level. He climbed onto the ledge and looped the rope around a rock.

After Verlinden, Riell and Atreu had also climbed out, the monk indicated that they should follow him as he stepped into a large fissure in the rock wall.

Atreu glanced back over his shoulder before he stepped into the gap. With the glimmerstones winking at him above and below, the cavern gave the illusion of a giant dome of stars. An echo of the monks' tone at dusk resounded through his head, and he couldn't help but feel he was leaving the most perfect of places.

*

Theander sensed that something unexpected had happened at the Circle sitting the moment Holthim entered the War Council chamber. He looked pale and drawn, and he couldn't meet the windrider's gaze. And when Leyvin entered with a look of satisfaction on his face, Theander knew he wasn't going to be happy with the result.

The others settled quickly when Leyvin started to speak. 'The Circle has agreed that command is an important issue for a War Council. It is concerned that we be able to make swift, firm decisions.'

'So do I now command the Maelir army?' asked Theander.

'No.'

'Then who does? You?' He looked at the First Speaker contemptuously.

'No.' Leyvin wasn't going to rush the answer.

'Please tell us of the Circle's decision,' said Rhea, her voice strangely devoid of emotion.

'The Circle felt that the issue of command was of crucial significance,' said Leyvin.

'Did it?' said Theander. 'Then no one here is in disagreement.'

Leyvin continued. 'So crucial, in fact, that it was felt that the combined armies should be under a single command.'

Theander frowned. 'A single command?' He looked at Rhea. 'Is this acceptable to you?'

'I agree with the principle,' she said.

'Then I'm back to my original question, Leyvin. Who is in command?'

'The Circle has given that power to Rhea.'

'*What?*'

'Do you want me to repeat myself?'

'You've given command of the entire Maelir army to a Faemir?'

'If Rhea will accept, yes.'

Theander sat back in his chair, stunned. 'This is madness.'

'Why?' said Leyvin. 'We have all agreed that we are now on the same side. Maelir and Faemir. It was the windriders' rescue of the remaining Faemir at the Summit which made the alliance possible. I would have thought that you of all people would applaud this decision.'

'No Faemir will command the windriders.' Theander enunciated each word slowly and precisely.

Leyvin looked shocked. 'I'm surprised you say that.'

'Don't feign surprise with me. What other reaction could you possibly expect?'

'I certainly would have expected better from Riell if he was here.'

'Riell would have thrown you out of this chamber.'

'Riell would have accepted the decision of the Circle. It has made many decisions in the windriders' favour recently. It has consecrated the Order of the Wynde, and windriders can now sit in the Circle with the Liche and the Felsen. You can't accept only those decisions that suit you.'

Theander turned to Holthim. 'You expect me to accept this?'

'I expect all the windriders to accept the will of the Circle. You cannot expect me to say anything else, can you?'

'We'll do what many of us planned to do before Equinox,' said Theander. 'We'll just leave the Keep. There is nothing keeping the windriders here. The covenant is worthless.'

Holthim tried to calm him. 'Things have changed since then, Theander. You have a Holy Order now. How can you abandon it so quickly? Does it mean so little to you?'

'As I said,' continued Leyvin, 'I believe Riell would have accepted the will of the Circle. And I think that in your heart of hearts, you know that is the wise thing to do.'

Theander buried his face in his hands.

'The sole command of the combined Maelir and Faemir armies is now with Rhea,' said Leyvin.

'I will take this decision to the windriders for them to make a judgement,' said Theander.

'You will allow those under your command to have an opinion on this?' Saretha could barely believe what she was hearing.

'I will give them more than a chance to give their view. I will give them a choice. No windrider will submit to an authority not of their choosing.'

'I always thought that the windriders were more disciplined than that,' said Rhea. 'How have you been able to function so effectively in battle?'

Theander said, 'There are many things we don't understand about each other. What you perceive as our weakness, we perceive as our true strength.' He got up. 'I can no longer participate here until I speak to the other windriders.'

'Please,' said Holthim, 'we need you here.'

'That's been the cry of the Inner Sanctum for centuries. It may be starting to fall on deaf ears.'

Slowly and deliberately, he walked out of the chamber.

'You didn't anticipate that, did you Leyvin?' said Holthim. 'Our armies are nothing without the coordination of the windriders.'

'You lost the vote, Holthim. Don't tell me you are going to question the will of the Circle now?'

Holthim appeared to be about to say something, but stopped himself.

'What will happen now?' asked Rhea.

'The windriders will elect to function under your command,' said Leyvin.

'Are you certain of this?'

'Yes. They have functioned under the control of the Circle since their inception. We have given in to all their demands. There will be some anger at first, but when they have calmed down, they will accede to your command.'

Rhea looked at Holthim. 'Do you believe this too?'

The Second Speaker sat in silence for a moment, and then said, 'Leyvin is nearly always right about these things.'

Rhea nodded. 'Then let us prepare our battle plans.'

*

Atreu made sure he had a good grip on the rocky wall of the narrow tunnel as he, Riell and Verlinden followed the monk's descent. He had already lost his footing several times on the damp surface of the roughly hewn steps. The roar of rushing water now surrounded them. Atreu guessed that the Sheerfalls must be tumbling down just on the other side of the rock.

A shot of spray hit them from below, but the monk ignored it and kept walking. Soon the spray was constant, and it seemed to Atreu as though they were descending into a storm. Riell lost his footing several times, and at one point almost took Atreu with him. After Atreu helped the windrider back up, they continued on, even more slowly.

Finally, the tunnel opened up into a huge cavern. As they continued to follow the monk through a veil of spray and a deafening roar, Atreu looked back. Behind him was a massive wall of rushing water. He opened his mouth to speak, but the spray immediately coated the back of his lungs and he started coughing.

Atreu became aware of some natural light in the distance competing with the multiflorous glint of the glimmerstones. The spray was thinning, so he could now see more clearly. The ledge they were walking on fringed a giant subterranean lake. While the waters back near the Sheerfall itself were churning, the surface was growing increasingly calm as they distanced themselves from it. Soon the roar had subsided to background noise, and the lake began to approach the glass-like quality of the Source.

The monk's destination was now clear. Just ahead were several moored boats. He led them to where a rope attached one of them to a rock.

When the monk made no effort to get in, Atreu finally asked, 'Do we take this one?'

The monk turned, as if he was about to head back to the Sheerfalls, and Atreu grabbed him. 'Where do we go from here?'

The monk pointed to the natural light, which was now more noticeable in the distance. 'There is only one way to go.'

Atreu looked dubiously at the oars that sat inside the boat. 'And when we're out of the cave?' he asked.

'This is the start of the Maelstrom. There is only one way, and it leads to Hellespont.'

'None of us are experienced on the water,' said Riell, 'and this boat looks like it's made for a still lake, not a raging river. How fast does the Maelstrom flow?'

'The river is usually calm until Hellespont.'

'And after Hellespont?' asked Atreu.

'I have brought you here. You may take the boat. I can give you no more help. I must return to my source.'

'Why can't you tell us more – you must know what happens after Hellespont?' Atreu was growing increasingly exasperated.

'Please, no more questions.'

'I can't stand this,' Atreu said, and gripped him harder. 'You must be able to give us some more advice, surely?'

'Leave him,' said Riell. 'You won't get anything else. He's already given us enough help.'

'I don't care about any vows he's taken. This quest is more important than bizarre Felsen practices.'

The monk stepped away and Atreu released his grip.

'I'm seeking Metheus, remember?' said Atreu. 'I want to find your brother.'

'I have no brother,' said the monk.

'Of course you do,' said Atreu. 'Praether is dead, but Metheus hopefully is still alive. He was perhaps the closest to Truth of any of us. His Book could bring the Mountain to peace. Please, forget all your practices for long enough to give us more help. You are still a Maelir, despite your existence at the Source. You must see the importance of this.'

Atreu could see a glint in the monk's eyes under his hood as he spoke. 'I am painfully aware that I am a Maelir,' he said, his tone distressed. 'There is much that I have forgotten, but my mortality will not leave me.'

'Please,' said Atreu. 'You're saying we should be able to row safely in this to Hellespont?'

'The current will take you even if you do not row.'

'And then?'

The monk was clearly struggling with something.

'Come on,' said Riell. 'We are wasting time now. We can find out what we need when we get there.' He started to climb into the boat and it swayed from side to side.

Atreu was about to follow him when the monk said, 'You will need a far larger vessel after Hellespont. The currents become treacherous. You will need a river captain to navigate you through to Farepont.'

'Thank you,' said Atreu.

Verlinden was already in the boat, oars in hand. Atreu unlooped the rope and then clambered in as well.

'I promise you that we will find your brother,' said Atreu, as Verlinden started rowing.

'Don't promise that which you can't,' said the Felsen. 'I wish you good fortune with your Book. Forgive me.'

As Atreu watched in confusion, the monk turned and began to walk back along the ledge. Eventually, the distance between them increased and the spray from the Sheerfalls partly shrouded him. At the point when Atreu lost sight of the hooded figure, he was unsure that the monk hadn't stepped off the ledge and into the water.

Chapter Thirteen

'Don't look so nervous, dear brother.' Leyvin filled goblets of wine from a decanter as he spoke. 'Everything has happened just as I said it would.'

'You have an unshakeable belief in yourself,' said Lythos. 'I have no doubt about that.'

'I told you that the windriders would elect to submit to the Faemir command. And that's exactly what happened.'

'I certainly don't doubt your ability to manipulate things your way, Leyvin.'

'*Our* way, dear brother.'

'Our way, then, *dear brother*.' Lythos took the goblet and nursed it in front of him on the table. 'What I'm not so sure about is whether you always anticipate all the consequences of what you do.'

'I'm not always right, Lythos. We both know that – but I've never been in a position where I've been unable to correct a mistake.'

'True, Leyvin, but your decisions are growing in scale all the time, which means the consequences are growing. Now that Rhea commands both armies, you have done what you set out to do. But do you really believe this will achieve what we want it to?'

'Do you doubt the Faemir's competence in battle?'

'Remember Valkyra was their leader ever since we've been under attack – Rhea was only second in command.'

'You have to learn to see opportunities as they arise, dear brother. We could have never dealt with Valkyra. Rhea is far more malleable.'

'People aren't clay.'

'Not all of them, no.' Leyvin smiled as he took a deep draught of wine.

'You're changing, Leyvin. With Praether dead and Riell missing, you have no real opposition in the Circle.'

'I'm not sure if either of your statements are true. Micah often speaks against what I am trying to achieve.'

'Micah is not a strong man. Everyone knows of his addiction to r'lung. He has little influence.'

'At the moment, I agree with you. I feel, though, that for someone still finding his feet in the Circle, he has presented some reasonably persuasive arguments. We must watch him. He has sentimental links with Praether in the eyes of the Circle. I also don't need to remind you that he is Atreu's sage and uncle.'

'If he is the only real opposition you have, then I repeat, you are unchallenged.'

'I'm unchallenged because I am persuasive.'

'Perhaps, but that doesn't make you right. I still have grave doubts about giving the ultimate command of the Maelir army to a Faemir.'

'You know my reasons, Lythos. With a Faemir in charge, we have the best chance of defeating the Nazir. We've achieved that while at the same time curbing the windriders' influence. What more could you ask of a strategy, given the circumstances in which we find ourselves?'

Lythos went to sip from his goblet, then put it down on the table again. 'You're growing too confident for my liking. Soon you may not need my support.'

Leyvin took a deep draught. 'You would never abandon me, would you dear brother?'

Lythos looked up to see Leyvin smiling. 'I thought that was a half-serious question for a moment.'

'Of course it wasn't.'

'Tell me, though, doesn't it concern you that Maelir soldiers can now be placed at risk by a Faemir commander?'

'We have lost so many Maelir soldiers as a result of our direct decisions – does this new risk really trouble you?'

Lythos ran his finger around the base of the goblet. 'I am troubled by some things. What is it we are trying to do here? Is all we are doing preserving our individual power?'

'I'm surprised you're asking that question, Lythos. We want to *increase* our power, not preserve it.'

Lythos looked up to see his brother smiling again. 'Strange – I don't even know if you're serious about that.'

'I'm using the word *we* differently to the way you're interpreting it.'

'Don't play your subtle word games with me, Leyvin.'

'The *we* is you and I, but it is also the Circle. We are ensuring that the Circle's power is maintained and that the Liche and Felsen thereby continue to impose order on the Mountain.'

'Aren't you forgetting the Wynde?'

'No, I hadn't forgotten them.'

'You believe your interests are those of the Mountain?'

'Of course.'

'Isn't that a dangerous belief?'

'Only if it's false.' Leyvin bent his head back and drank the rest of his wine. 'You've hardly touched yours, dear brother.'

It took a moment for Leyvin to realise that Lythos was staring at him. 'What's wrong?' he asked.

'Praether once said you always need someone to react against.'

'Praether was an old fool who placed too much store in books. Let me tell you, people are what's important.' He noticed Lythos was still staring at him. 'What *is* the matter, Lythos?'

'You've managed to get rid of just about the only three people on the Mountain who can challenge you.'

'We've had this discussion about Atreu, haven't we?'

'Not really. You've never told me how you kept the knowledge of the storm away from Riell.'

'Leave the details to me, dear brother.'

'It worries me that you only told me after the fact.'

'There was no need for you to know. Besides, sometimes opportunities just ... arise.'

'But our sky-watchers wouldn't have missed the signs. How could you have done it? I fear for what you are becoming.'

Leyvin was smiling. 'Rest assured, there was no violence involved. You know subtlety is my way. A sky-watcher who was a little confused about whether he was on duty. A roster that didn't quite match reality.'

'Is there evidence for others to find? There has been much talk about the storm. You must have heard it.'

Leyvin picked up the decanter. 'I have no time to listen to such talk. Does it matter?'

'Only if there is evidence of what you've done.'

Leyvin started pouring the wine.

'Well, is there?' asked Lythos again.

'Damn,' said Leyvin, 'you've made me spill some wine.'

*

Towards the end of their first day on the river, the air was tinged with a sharp icy edge as winter seeped into the Upper Reaches. Atreu, Verlinden and Riell had taken it in turns at the oars until mid-afternoon, but with three sets of shoulders now aching, they had decided to let the current carry them for a while.

As he ate some dried meat from his pack, Atreu watched the steep cliffs that shot up either side of the river. There was no river-bank, and at first he had worried about what would happen if the boat sank, but he decided there was little he could do about it. The almost vertical sheers were laced with chaotic patterns in every imaginable shade of brown. Occasionally, when the sunlight hit certain parts at just the right angle, a shard would glisten from the rock like a flash of lightning or a shooting star.

Atreu felt the effects of the Source still echoing somewhere inside his head. It was as if his thoughts had a wash of calm painted over them. Gradually, though, as the day had worn on, he felt the wash thinning and the sharp edge of reality outside the Source returning.

'It looks like we have no choice but to continue through the night,' said Atreu. 'Any idea how long it will take at this rate?'

Riell was rummaging in his pack for some food. He looked up. 'I've never been to Hellespont, but my guess is that with a prevailing wind, it would take me a full day and a night to fly there from the Source. At the speed we managed today, who knows? Three, four days? As I said, my estimates about travelling time when I'm not in the air are not very good.'

'Even if none of us row until morning,' said Verlinden, 'we need to take turns to watch while the others sleep. Who knows what could happen out here?' She yawned.

'It doesn't look like you'll be taking the first watch,' said Atreu.

Verlinden gave a weak smile. 'I just hope my shoulders feel a little better tomorrow. I think I'd rather walk than grapple with these oars again.'

'I'll take the first watch,' said Atreu. 'You two get some sleep.'

Atreu watched the sun disappear behind the cliffs as he finished his meal. There was a sudden transition from light to dark, and he wrapped his blanket tightly around himself as a gnawing cold set in. Verlinden had quickly fallen asleep, but Riell was still awake.

'I feel very strange, you know Riell,' said Atreu.

'Stranger than you did at the Source?'

'Nothing like that feeling. The opposite, almost. At the Source it felt like part of my Ascent – it *was* strange, but it was the strangeness of a Ritual. Many others had experienced it before me. I could accept it because I wasn't unique and what I was experiencing wasn't unique. Right now I feel ... I don't know ... as if part of me is not here.'

'Where is the rest of you then?'

'I can't explain it. It's as if part of me now is unique and part isn't – only I can't work out which is which.'

'You're talking mysteries with me, I'm afraid, Atreu.'

Verlinden shifted slightly, then started snoring softly.

'Have you noticed how Verlinden has been acting?' asked Atreu. 'She seems very distant to me.'

'I have noticed, but I don't pretend to understand any women, let alone Faemir.'

'She's changed since Equinox, and she seems to be getting worse.'

'Have you asked her?'

'Asked her what?'

'Why she's been so distant?'

'I've tried to at times, but she somehow deflects me before I can say the words.'

'It sounds to me like you haven't tried hard enough.'

Atreu stared at Verlinden's dark form as he listened to the silence of the river. 'Are windriders ...?' He let the sentence drift away.

'We take no wives,' said Riell. 'Our covenant was with the Holy Orders. We served the Inner Sanctum.'

'That wasn't quite what I wanted to ask.'

Riell laughed. 'There have been no strict rules among windriders regarding celibacy. We have aspired to being a Holy Order for so long, however, that there is almost an unvoiced assumption that we should be celibate.'

'Assumption?'

'Yes, perhaps stronger for some windriders than others.'

'I see.'

'Of course, now that the Wynde has become a Holy Order, I imagine we will make it explicit.'

'Why?'

Riell fell silent for a moment. 'I suppose because true Holy Orders are celibate.'

'The Liche and Felsen are. But surely if you are a different Order, you don't need to follow all their rules blindly?'

'It's a Ritual.'

'Sounds to me like celibacy is a non-Ritual.'

'You're playing with words now, aren't you?'

'I don't know, but if you are simply going to follow all the practices of the Felsen and the Liche, then what is the point of the Wynde?'

'Your view on things is certainly unusual at times, Atreu.'

'Do you know why Holy Men have been celibate?'

'My understanding is that it is so that they can devote their lives to their Order.'

'If women could be in the same Order, then couldn't the Holy Men be non-celibate and devote themselves to their Order?'

'I see what you're saying, Atreu, but I'm not sure the Liche or Felsen would agree.'

'Do you need their approval for the inner working of your Order?'

It took a moment for Riell to answer. 'I suppose not. Atreu, I can see why Leyvin was so keen for you to leave the Keep. You're now advocating a non-celibate Order of the Wynde which admits women.'

'I was only asking questions,' said Atreu.

'Sometimes that's the most dangerous thing you can do.' Riell settled back and wrapped his blanket more tightly. 'I'd better get some sleep before it's my turn to watch.'

Atreu leaned back and watched the bright band of stars immediately overhead. In the darkness, he reached out for Verlinden's hand.

*

It was Cluric's fourth night in the open when he decided to let the Dusk-wraiths kill him without a fight. He sat encircled by a small ring of fire with Hrulth, Jenethelen, Janan and Ronan, watching the flames cast amorphous shadows in the night sky beyond the clearing. Peleusar was now many leagues upslope, and Cluric barely gave the city he had almost laid down his life for the scantest thought. Teuron and the Lower Reaches were now uppermost in his mind. He watched Janan and Ronan nervously finger their sword hilts. How lucky the two brothers had been that Hrulth had locked them away. They had died – or at least, as close to it as was possible – like all the others under the wraith onslaught, but no one had sought to bury them, so when they came back to life, they were unharmed, save for an aching cold somewhere deep inside them.

Cluric felt it too, the gnawing ice that was now always with him. The wraiths had crossed through the fires and killed him five times now, and five times the pale sunlight of the next day had revived him. Each time, though, he had woken later in the day, and each time, the ice they had placed inside him had grown a little colder. The process was now clear to all of them. The Dusk-wraiths didn't have the strength yet to kill permanently, at least not if they came into contact with fire, but as the days grew shorter towards the winter solstice, the danger increased for Cluric and the others because their recovery time would extend further and further into the next day. Cluric refused to think about what would happen if it reached a point where he didn't recover before the next nightfall.

Finally, he let his thoughts be known to the others. 'They can have me tonight,' he said. 'I haven't got the energy to fight them for half the night and then trek for most of the next day.'

He expected a howl of outrage from Hrulth, but nothing came. 'Hrulth,' he said, 'did you hear what I said?'

Hrulth ran his hands through his beard, looking like the innkeeper he used to be. 'It doesn't matter what I think, Cluric. I have no authority over you anymore. With the others gone in search of their own towns and villages, I have no command. I'm afraid the three of you don't count as a battalion.'

'Four,' said Jenethelen.

'Well, four then.'

'So you're really not going to fight this time?' asked Janan.

'No. They always get us in the end anyway,' said Cluric. 'In fact, if we had all just laid down our weapons when they first attacked, the others would probably still be alive.'

Jenethelen gave a sour laugh. 'Perhaps being a coward like me could have saved us all.'

'So you agree with Cluric that we should just let them take us without a fight tonight?' asked Janan.

'If you asked that question of any other Faemir on the Mountain, the answer would be a laugh in your face.' Jenethelen stared at the ground. 'The answer from me is I don't know.'

The fire cracked loudly as the four Maelir looked at each other. Cluric was the first to unsheathe his sword and place it on the ground. 'Sometimes retreat is the best strategy for an army, and sometimes not fighting is the best option for a soldier. Am I right, Uncle?'

Hrulth stared blankly ahead.

Cluric made himself comfortable on the ground, using his pack as a pillow. As he stared out at the darkness crowding in past the low flames, one by one, the others joined him.

The fire cracked and hissed, and he had lost himself in half-dreams when he felt something beside him. He opened his eyes to see Jenethelen pressing herself into his body, and her warmth surged through him.

His lips searched for hers in the darkness, and his hands ran down her back and legs. As she returned his caresses, he sensed a merging of strength and softness he had never experienced before. Jenethelen's body pressed further into his, and he felt the experience of countless battles filter out through his pores and into the night sky. His eyes were closed when his need grew and he felt the naked flesh of her stomach against his. His eyes were closed when she enveloped him in a way he had never known. His eyes were closed when the sharp, urgent rhythms beat towards a crescendo. And his eyes were closed when the dark, amorphous tendril wrapped mercilessly around their throats and sucked the life from them again.

*

Micah stopped for a moment on the spiral staircase of the Sky-reach tower to catch his breath. He heaved in deep breaths as the incessant pounding in his head slowly eased. It was times like these when he most missed r'lung. He had to admit that he had cravings for it, but he knew he would never break his promise to Praether. He cursed his Talisman for the thousandth time. How could he have brought the sour weed into the Liche Order? It had given him a false sense of power when he was taking it, and with it had come a false sense of his own importance within the Inner Sanctum. He could see now that he had achieved nothing since he had joined the Liche. From now on, though, things would change.

As his breathing eased, he started climbing the stairs again. He clutched the rail in anticipation of the open section of the staircase that he knew he would soon reach. The Sky-reach tower was the tallest in the Keep. Micah knew that asking the windriders to carry him would be far easier than making the strenuous climb, but he no longer knew who to trust.

A sharp gust of wind hit his sweat-soaked face, and he gripped the handrail more tightly. As he rounded the corner, the wall disappeared and he was surrounded by the myriad lights of the Keep below and the stars of the clearest of night skies above. He felt giddy, his head throbbing as the Sky-reach tower seemed to sway from side to side. Closing his eyes, he stood still, desperately clutching the rail and trying to fight the vertigo. For a moment, the urge to turn around and go back rose from the fear in his stomach.

Perhaps the others were right – he was a weak man. He had heard the comments since he had stopped taking the r'lung. Strangely, he had been oblivious to them before, but now he was painfully aware of how he was regarded by many in the Inner Sanctum. And with Praether gone, he felt even more isolated. The urge to descend grew, but his thoughts turned to Atreu and the look on his face during his last address to the Circle, when he realised that his sage and uncle had lied to him again. And as he saw Atreu's face drop again, Micah felt tears forming under his eyelids.

With a sudden resolve, Micah opened his eyes. The wind quickly blew his tears away and the lights shone all around him with sharpened clarity. He knew he could no longer hide behind the Rituals. R'lung had been his Talisman, it had been chosen for him through the system the Order had created – yet it was wrong. Every fibre in his being now told him that. And if a Talisman could be wrong then so could other Rituals. They no longer gave him a reason to betray his nephew. With a sudden jerk, Micah started climbing the staircase again.

The tower swayed with every gust of wind, but Micah's foot-falls didn't falter. The glistening spires, turrets and buttresses of the city of light that was the Keep now lay far below him, with only a handrail between him and the night sky. Finally, he climbed through an opening onto a large platform at the very top of Sky-reach.

The sky-watcher stared at Micah open-mouthed as he clambered onto the platform and straightened himself up.

'Don't tell me the windriders are now refusing to carry Holy Men up here?'

'No,' said Micah. 'There has been tension in the past, as you would be aware, but things are functioning within the Keep.'

'I hear the occasional talk, but it doesn't interest me. I have enough here.' He waved his hand and Micah gasped at the riotous river of stars above them.

'Tell me, then,' continued the sky-watcher, 'why does a Holy

Man choose to climb the sky-stairs when far easier options are open to him?'

'I am here for a specific reason.'

'I'm sure you are.'

Micah cleared his throat. 'I'm Liche Micah, recently of the Circle.'

'Congratulations. I know how much all of that means to you down there.'

'I know you sky-watchers don't place much store in the workings of the Circle.'

'None of us have much time for the endless intrigues. I suppose that is why we choose to spend our lives up here.'

'Look – your name is Sethor, correct?'

'Well, well, you've asked some questions and delved into some logs. What pathetic little intrigue are you going to try to enmesh me in?'

'I *suspect* an intrigue, but unfortunately if my suspicions are correct, you are already hopelessly enmeshed in it.'

'Nonsense.' Sethor turned away suddenly and headed to what looked like a large pool of water near the rim of the circular platform. He appeared to have a large parchment stretched out on a low table next to the pool. Micah watched as he dipped a quill in an inkpot and started drawing on the parchment while glancing across at the pool.

'Look,' said Micah. 'I need to speak with you.'

Sethor ignored him, concentrating on the parchment.

'Please, Sethor, I've climbed the Sky-reach stairs to speak to you. At least hear what I have to say.'

'I fear you have come a long way for no gain,' said Sethor, without taking his eyes from his task.

Micah approached the sky-watcher, curious as to what he was doing. 'You don't appear to be watching the sky very much,' he said, staring at the lines and points Sethor was carefully measuring out and drawing.

'Ah, a typical low-Liche question.'

'What do you mean, "low-Liche"? I've never heard anyone called that before.'

'Perhaps you should come up here more often.'

'Why don't you tell me what you're doing here? I'm obviously ignorant. I want to be enlightened.'

'No, you don't.'

'I see – I don't.' Micah coughed. 'Why not tell me anyway? You're obviously doing masterful things here. Please give me an inkling.'

'False flattery?' Sethor jerked his head slightly, but continued. 'That may have helped you get into the Circle, but the air is too clear and thin up here for it to have any effect.'

A slight tremor shook its way up the platform, and Micah watched a series of concentric ripples emanate across the pool.

'Damn,' said Sethor. 'I hate it when that happens.'

'You're obviously not entirely immune from the goings-on below, are you?'

'A clever argument, but then, that's what you get rewarded for down there, isn't it?' The sky-watcher stopped drawing and waited for the water in the pool to reach its glass-like state again.

'You may as well talk to me,' said Micah. 'You obviously can't continue for a moment.'

Sethor looked up at Micah. 'I may have a moment, but I don't really wish to crowd my mind with your schemes.'

'Then tell me what it is you are doing. I really have no idea.'

Sethor sighed. 'I don't believe you, but I'll tell you anyway, before you twist it around to what you really came up here to ask me.' He pointed to the pool. 'You've been looking at this for long enough – what do you see?'

'Water ...' Micah hesitated. He remembered the old Liche trick of perception he had played on Atreu. Clear your mind and look through the water. He tried to see what was at the bottom of the pool.

'Ah,' said Sethor, 'you can't, can you? You're trying to see through it, aren't you?'

'Well, yes.'

'Water isn't for seeing through. I would have thought a distinguished member of the Circle would have reached that level of understanding.'

'All right,' said Micah, running his fingers through his beard, 'if you're going to treat me like a novice Ascender, then let's get it over with.'

Sethor was smiling. 'You actually have no idea, do you? You could probably present an argument that folds in on itself several times, yet you can't see what the simple purpose of this pool of water is.'

'If you're going to just stand there and gloat ...' Micah stared at the water, which was now perfectly still again. This time he saw what he was certain Sethor was referring to. 'That's a perfect reflection of the stars in the night sky.'

'Finally, young low-Liche. For a member of the Order of Light, you took a while. Congratulations, you've reached a higher plain of existence. Water isn't for seeing *through*, it's for seeing *reflections*.'

'You're copying the configurations of the night sky from the reflection in that pool.'

'Correct.'

'So that's what you sky-watchers do up here.'

Sethor frowned. 'That's like saying to one of the scribes in the librum that all they do is copy books.'

'Well, I'm sure that you use these charts to gain information.'

'Now you are really showing your ignorance. What I'm doing here is no less than *reading* the heavens.'

'And this tells you about the weather?'

Sethor spluttered out a series of words which weren't formed enough for Micah to understand.

'Excuse my ignorance,' said Micah. 'As I said, I'm asking to be enlightened.'

'Weather predictions are as important to a sky-watcher as copying a title page to a book is to a scribe. It has to be done, but there is little meaning in it. The charts we are creating here are the most important activity undertaken by any Holy Man.'

'There are hundreds of members of the Inner Sanctum who have never been up here who would make the same claim about their own activities.'

Sethor's words were now coming out in a torrent. 'Of course they would, of course they would. That's the absurdity of it all.'

'Where you see absurdity I see sincerely held beliefs.'

'Damn, look what you made me do.' Sethor had knocked over the inkwell and stained his parchment with pools of black ink.

'I'm sorry,' said Micah, 'but it seems to me that you have the luxury of sitting above everything up here and judging the rest of us without really knowing what *we* do.'

'Nonsense. I've been down there with the rest of you. I still eat and sleep in the Keep outside of my watches. The rest of the time I read the heavens, my friend. You can't even begin to comprehend what that means. The origin of everything is up here for us. The ultimate truth that we have been seeking for countless centuries? A sky-watcher will be the one to find it – not any land-crawling Liche with their clever, petty intrigues.'

'I actually don't care who finds the ultimate truth,' said Micah. 'I have a strong suspicion it won't be me, but I'm afraid you're going to be enmeshed in some less lofty matters.'

'As I suspected, you're now back to the real reason why you're here. I don't want to listen to you.' Sethor started rolling up the parchment he was working on.

Micah grabbed his arm. 'The storm that passed through the Keep seven days ago – why didn't you warn anyone about it?'

'Unhand me,' said Sethor angrily.

'The storm – why wasn't it predicted?'

'It wasn't my watch, you fool.' He tried to shake himself free, but Micah didn't let go.

'You were supposed to be up here the night before, weren't you?'

'Yes, but there was a change –'

'Why a change?'

'I don't know. Leyvin spoke to me about it. These changes sometimes occur. Why don't you speak to Aremin? He was on Sky-reach in my place.'

'No, he wasn't.'

'What?'

'I've spoken to him. He had been on the previous watch, and left early that evening.'

'No, his watch had been changed.'

'Who told you this?'

'Leyvin – but don't trust my word, just check the records.'

'I have, Sethor, and there are some anomalies.'

'I've had enough of this.' He shook himself free of Micah's hold. 'Now you're trying to accuse me of something. I will not listen to you anymore.' He put the rolled-up parchment aside and reached for another. 'If you will leave me, I must start a new chart, and I now have very little time.'

'You have to complete several of these each watch?'

'Of course. The heavens change constantly. I have to do six a night, which is why I'm getting annoyed with your stupid chatter.'

Micah placed his hands on the table so that Sethor couldn't put the fresh parchment on it. 'Do you realise that our only two remaining Ascenders, plus the leader of the windriders, were caught in that storm on their way to the Source and may now be dead?'

Sethor's expression changed suddenly. 'What? A storm that size can be predicted quite easily.'

'That's one of the things I wanted to know. It was extremely fast moving – does that matter?'

'No, the signs are clear. We would have had enough warning that night.'

'And who do the sky-watchers tell about any oncoming storms?'

'We don't *tell* anyone. We give the news to the windrider who brings up the sky-watcher for the next watch, and we record it in the weather-watch log.' He gestured that Micah should remove his hands from the table. 'Just consult our log – that will give you your answers. I don't want to get involved with this argument.'

Micah removed his hands and stood back. 'If lives aren't important to you, then I'm not sure what I can achieve here.'

'I'm glad you've finally come to that conclusion.' Sethor unrolled a second parchment and dipped his quill in the ink.

'I will check the sky-watch log as you suggest, but my investigations so far suggest there has been some tampering with your records.'

'What?' Sethor's quill was poised in mid-air. 'You're lying – that would be an unbelievable act of treachery. Everything we do relies on the accuracy of our records. It would be a crime against everything we have striven for.'

'I see what you're saying,' said Micah. 'I hadn't thought of it that way. I didn't realise the importance of your charts and records. Can I ask you to check everything over the last eight or nine days, and tell me if you notice anything strange?'

'You can ask me.'

'Well, will you do it?'

Sethor shook his head. 'I didn't become a sky-watcher to be involved with this sort of thing.'

'But you will check the records?'

'Yes, yes, I will have to, from what you've said. I just hope I don't find anything.'

Micah walked back towards the opening in the middle of the platform which signalled the start of the staircase. 'I can't say it's been a pleasure,' he said.

Sethor's head was down, and he was intent on drawing on the parchment as his head jerked backwards and forwards, moving from the parchment to the pool of water.

Micah had begun his descent when he heard the sky-watcher mumble under his breath. His head was just above the level of the platform and he could still see Sethor. 'Did you say something?' he asked.

Without looking up, Sethor said, 'If I find anything, I'll come and see you.'

'Thank you,' said Micah, receiving a grunt in return.

He glanced up at the bright star clusters and then continued down the staircase.

Chapter Fourteen

Rhea felt the sting of anticipation as she watched the windriders making their final checks on the harnesses of her sisters. For the last few days, Faemir warriors had been flown up to the Keep from Crosanct and all over the Upper Reaches to prepare for this. Now, on the flat plain past the Felsen monasts, on the very edge of the Keep, every available windrider was securing a Faemir to his wings. Over three thousand in all, they stood wing tip to wing tip in the pre-dawn light, each rider preparing to carry the once-hated enemy to battle.

Theander had barely spoken to Rhea since the windriders had begun to assemble, and now that he was securing his own harness behind her, he was determinedly silent. Rhea wondered why this windrider, who in many ways was as proud as a Faemir leader, could submit himself to someone he felt had unjustly usurped the command that was rightfully his. There was no reason why he himself had to be the one to carry her to Farepont. He had obviously chosen to do so. Although she felt she understood how the Maelir generally thought, the ways of the windriders were still a mystery to her.

The clouds swirled just beyond the Keep's edge, and Rhea tried not to think of the huge drop down to the Upper Reaches.

When they had first been flown up to the Keep, she had been too exhausted from battle to worry about it, but now, fully fit and with time to think about what was going to happen, she felt a cold tremor of fear shoot through her.

'You will have to run with me when I give the signal,' said Theander.

Rhea consciously sent a message to her legs to brace themselves.

Theander started to repeat his instructions, 'I said, you will have to –'

'Yes, yes, I understand.'

For a moment a horrific image flashed through Rhea's mind. She pictured all the Faemir soldiers running off the cliff and falling to their doom – one after the other, following each other mindlessly like a train of donkeys, seeing those in front plummeting to the ground, but continuing nonetheless. Blindly following orders.

'Now,' said Theander.

Rhea's instincts overrode her fear and she started running. The lip of the Keep loomed, and then suddenly her feet were no longer touching the ground.

'Put your feet in the stirrups now,' said Theander.

Rhea became aware that her legs were still thrashing around in mid-air, in a wild running motion. She took several deep breaths and felt for the stirrups.

It was a moment before she dared to look down. She saw clouds swirling just below them. Then she turned around and gasped at the sight behind her. The windriders, with their Faemir passengers, were unfurling into the air like a flowing tapestry. Somehow the individuals were lost in an endless, undulating human pattern, wave upon wave dipping down from the ledge only to swing up again in graceful harmony.

Rhea watched until the last Faemir was airborne behind her and all three thousand moved as one through the swirling clouds. She was determined that this was to be the Faemir's finest battle.

This time, nothing would stop their ultimate victory. She would lead her people to a place even the great Valkyra could not take them. The sun broke through briefly and the windriders' wings glinted like glimmerstones. Then the clouds gathered once again and the wings darkened.

Instinctively, Rhea's hand reached for her sword.

*

As the day wore on, Atreu watched the cliffs on both sides of the river gradually decrease in height. This, combined with a subtle increase in the current, had given him the impression that he was approaching Hellespont. Each of the four days on the Maelstrom so far had been identical. The sky had been overcast each morning, cleared around midday, and then as night approached the clouds had gathered again. He, Riell and Verlinden had fallen into a regular pattern of rowing in shifts and resting in between. At various times throughout the day and night, the three were content to leave the oars idle, allowing the current to carry them at its own pace.

Sunset was one of those times, and Atreu strained through the dusk ahead for signs of the river town that was their destination. When he saw lights winking on the banks in the distance, he felt a slight stab of panic. This would be his first contact with a Maelir town or city of any sort since Peleusar – and that seemed a lifetime ago. His dealings since then had been almost exclusively with Holy Men and windriders. How would the Maelir of Hellespont view him? Was he different now? Who was Atreu? He couldn't deny that he was no longer the naive Ascender who had followed his preordained path up the Mountain. Yet how had he changed? Was he a Holy Man now? Had the change somehow subtly occurred inside him?

'Can you see the lights?' asked Riell, pointing into the distance.

'What happens now?' asked Verlinden.

'We find a boat and a river captain to take us further down the Maelstrom,' said Atreu.

'We all know that's the plan,' said Verlinden, 'but how do we find someone who will help us?'

Atreu stared at her for a moment. 'We ask for help, of course.'

Verlinden laughed. 'Why would anyone in Hellespont help a Faemir, a windrider without wings and an Ascender who should be choosing a Holy Order instead of descending the Mountain?'

'She may have a point,' said Riell. 'This isn't an Ascent, and no one will be obliged to help you.'

Atreu frowned. This was a new sensation. 'I suppose I had thought that the people of the town would be more than willing to help me. If they don't do it for me as an Ascender, surely you could command them, Riell?'

'Perhaps, Atreu, but the fact that I command the windriders may not have any influence here. This is a frontier town, the people are far removed from the workings of the Circle. My command over the Maelir army is not a direct one – and why would they believe me anyway? I'm not known here, and I don't think my appearance is going to convince them that I'm someone important. Look at me.'

Atreu recognised for the first time how tired and gaunt Riell had become since they had left the Keep. 'I see now we might have a problem.'

'Do we have any money?' said Verlinden. 'Isn't that the way the Maelir get things to happen?'

'I always carry a little when I'm away from the Keep,' said Riell, 'but I doubt I have enough to pay someone to take us anywhere.'

'Well, this is a mess, isn't it?' said Verlinden.

'I think we all need to make some adjustments to life outside the Keep,' said Atreu, watching the lights up ahead get brighter.

'We could just take a river boat,' said Verlinden.

'What do you mean? Steal one?' asked Atreu.

'Yes, why not? If this quest is so important, then you do what has to be done.'

Atreu stared at her. 'Sometimes I don't think I know you, Verlinden.'

'Do you have a better plan?' she said. 'We're almost there.'

'It sounds like a Valkyra plan to me,' said Atreu.

Verlinden looked away.

'Look,' said Riell, 'I'm sure we will find a way.'

Atreu could now make out the rude wooden houses that lined both shores in front of them. Torches burnt at each entrance, and through many of the windows he could see roaring fires and candlelight. Riell had grabbed the oars and was now rowing. Just up ahead in the still waters of the Maelstrom were dozens of wharves jutting out from the riverbanks, with countless boats of all sizes moored at them. Several other larger ships were anchored midstream, and Riell took care to avoid running into the anchor ropes in the darkness.

The windrider steered the rowboat to a low jetty on the right bank. He climbed out onto the small ladder, clambered up and tied the rope to a post. Atreu and Verlinden grabbed their packs and followed him.

The boards creaked under their feet as they made their way onto the shore. Atreu could hear drunken shouts of merriment coming from several of the larger buildings. He could see his breath frosting under the torchlight as they walked along the row of buildings that lined the shore. A sound that Atreu had not heard in a long time reached his ears. They stopped in front of one of the largest buildings, and he listened to the minstrel music emanating through the open window. Suddenly, another time and place came to him, and he was dancing a whirling dance with a girl in a village at the other end of the Mountain. Had that ever happened? Was that the same Atreu? He shook his head.

Atreu looked through the window and watched the minstrels playing furiously. The dancers inside were throwing themselves around to match the pace of the music. He sensed a raw energy there that was a world away from his recent experiences.

'Let's go in,' he said, the words tumbling out before he knew it.

'Don't be mad,' said Riell. 'I think what we all need is a good night's sleep in a bed. There must be quieter inns than this one in Hellespont.'

'Riell, you go find a quieter inn if you wish. Verlinden and I will go in here.'

Verlinden stared at him open-mouthed. 'I can't go in there.'

'Why not? Riell, please give us some of that money of yours so that we can buy an ale or two.'

'Atreu, what has come over you?' Riell was clearly taken aback. 'This is not a time for frivolity.'

Atreu smiled. 'When is?' he said. 'Come on, Riell, you come with us too. We're back in the real world. There's nothing we can achieve tonight anyway, so let's celebrate that we are here.'

'Atreu, there's a deadly war ravaging the Mountain –'

'Please don't drag me down, Riell. Not now. Do those people in there look like they care about the war? Is anything they do tonight going to matter? No, of course not. Please, let's forget everything, just for tonight.'

Riell hesitated and then said, 'All right, Atreu. I am just pleased that the black mood that descended on you at the Source has disappeared so totally.'

'Come on,' said Atreu, grabbing Verlinden's hand.

'I can't,' she said, not moving from where she stood.

'What do you mean, you can't?'

'To walk into an inn in a Maelir town – I can't do it.'

'There's a truce now,' said Atreu. 'Besides, how would they know you are a Faemir? You're not wearing any Faemir armour.'

'I'm more concerned that *I* know what I am.'

'I don't understand.'

'I know you don't.'

Atreu grabbed her other hand as well and looked into her eyes. The music had increased its tempo and the sounds from the inn were louder and more frantic. 'Please, Verlinden, who knows what will happen tomorrow? Who knows when we will next hear minstrels playing?'

Verlinden dropped her gaze and allowed Atreu to lead her through the door, past the sign saying The Last Anchor. She expected all eyes to turn and stare, but no one seemed to even acknowledge their presence. Atreu found an empty table in one corner, and they sat down. The inn was thick with pipe smoke, and tankards of ale were being carried through the crowded dancers by several buxom server-women, including one with dark exotic looks, who placed three tankards on Atreu's table and disappeared before Riell had a chance to look for the coins he carried with him.

'I don't drink ale,' said Verlinden, shouting above the din. 'Have mine as well.'

Atreu ran his finger along the rim of the tankard and flicked off the foam the way he had seen it done in Cluric's inn.

'Why do you do that?' asked Verlinden.

Atreu shrugged. 'I don't know. It's just what you're supposed to do.' He smiled. 'Does there have to be a reason?'

Verlinden eyed him curiously. 'You are a stranger tonight.'

'Perhaps I feel like I've escaped,' said Atreu. 'Don't either of you feel it?'

'The only thing I could have escaped from is my wings,' said Riell, 'and for me that is an imprisonment, rather than an escape.'

'Don't be so morbid, Riell.' Atreu took a draught of his ale. 'When have you last heard music like this?'

'The Liche lute choir plays far more pure tones.'

'Forget the Liche,' said Atreu, 'listen to these players. Don't they beckon your feet to dance?'

'I'm afraid not, Atreu.'

'Verlinden, you will dance with me tonight, won't you?'

'Faemir don't dance.'

'Then I want to dance with the half of you that isn't Faemir.'

Verlinden was suddenly back on a Harvest Night long ago, an

awkward tall girl hoping desperately that one of the village boys would ask her to join in the merriment.

Atreu took her hand and stood up. With her mind still on another time and another place, she got up with him, and the two of them joined the whirling throng.

They bumped into many of the other couples at first, but they soon found the rhythm of the dancers. The minstrels seemed to play with even more fire, and the smoke-filled air pulsed with the twang of strings and the sharp tone of flutes. Atreu held Verlinden closer, and she didn't resist. They spun around and around until Atreu could no longer be sure that it wasn't the room spinning. He threw back his head and laughed, and when he looked up again, Verlinden's eyes were bright and a smile of joy had crept onto her lips. On and on they danced, far into the night. Only when the minstrels played their final note did they stop.

They returned to their table to find Riell was no longer there. The dark-haired server woman placed two more tankards in front of them. 'Your friend has organised lodgings upstairs for all of you,' she said. 'He retired to his room when the night was still young. Tell him he should enjoy himself a little more.' She gave a half smile. 'Here is your key.'

Atreu took it. 'Thank you,' he said, looking at it and then into Verlinden's eyes. He sensed a sadness about to return to them when he reached over and kissed her.

Verlinden closed her eyes and returned the kiss. After a moment she pulled away. 'This ... this is all so strange.'

'Why, Verlinden, we've kissed many times before. Why do you try to close yourself to me now?'

'I –'

Atreu placed his fingers on her lips. 'Please, let's not talk now. Come on.'

He held her hand as they climbed the creaking stairs to their room.

The sounds of the revellers spilling out into the night air reverberated below as Atreu opened the door. He took the burning candle from the ledge and they both stepped inside. When he shut the door, it was as if the outside world lost its reality. The shouts and laughter from below were now muffled, and he became aware of the breaths that he and Verlinden were expelling.

Slowly, he led her to the bed. He ran his fingers along her face as she looked at him, not moving. When they kissed it was with a sudden, violent urgency, as if the moment was in danger of being whisked away. They disrobed, barely feeling the cold as they embraced. Atreu pulled her down to the soft bed, and they enveloped each other with a passion and heat he hadn't experienced in a long time.

And when it was over, and the cold started to reach his nerves again as they lay entwined, he stroked her flame-red ringlets of hair and listened to her rhythmic breathing.

The candle was burning low when he finally spoke.

'This was how it was meant to be between us, Verlinden,' he said. 'What has happened since Equinox?'

Verlinden stiffened slightly in his arms.

'Please tell me. I don't understand,' he said. 'I want to do what I can to make you happy.'

'Is happiness yours to give?' Her voice was soft.

'I do what is within my power to do.'

'Not all things are within your power.' She reached for his hand and ran it down her neck, along the length of her body.

'The Talisman is yours,' she said. 'The quest is yours.'

'No, Verlinden, that's not true.'

'You carry both Books,' said Verlinden. 'You are the only one who knows where the third Book may be found.'

'Yes, but –'

'Let's not speak of these things now, Atreu.' She had now guided his hand to her stomach. 'There is something you must know.'

Atreu pulled back slightly, but Verlinden continued to hold his hand against her.

It took a moment for Verlinden's next words to sink in.

'I am with child,' she said.

*

'Are you absolutely certain of this?' said Micah, as he and Sethor pored over the charts that the sky-watcher had brought to him.

Sethor flicked through the parchments. 'There can be no mistake. There are six charts missing.'

'And they couldn't have been misplaced somehow?'

The sky-watcher glared at Micah. 'We do not lose these charts. Does a librer lose a book? Does an Ascender lose a Talisman?'

'All right. I mean no offence. It's just that the implications are so great, there shouldn't be any doubt.'

'I am not so concerned about the implications for you, but I need to find where those charts are.'

'I think you'll find that they are nowhere,' said Micah.

'What do you mean?'

'I believe no one was sky-watching during the watch we're talking about.'

'The log has been entered and signed. Look, here it is.'

Micah looked at the entry that Sethor was pointing to. 'Then the mystery can be resolved easily. Just go to this sky-watcher and find out what has happened.'

'Do you think I wouldn't have done that before I came to you?'

'Well, if you have, then you know what has happened.'

Sethor frowned. 'I'm afraid I don't.'

'I don't understand. Whose signature is this here?'

'His name is Leylan, and he is no longer in the Keep.'

'Leylan? The name is familiar to me.'

'Yes, he is the Ascender who failed three years ago and became a windrider.'

'I know barely a handful of windriders,' said Micah. 'And I'm afraid you're not making much sense. Why would a windrider's signature be on a sky-watcher's log? All sky-watchers are Liche.'

'Think a little more about what you're saying. You are answering your own question. Things have changed, remember. You should be more aware of it than I am. There is an Order of the Wynde now.'

'That still doesn't explain anything.'

'Leylan was a windrider who wasn't happy with his lot. He wanted to be a sky-watcher, but was barred from it because he wasn't a Liche.'

'So how is his signature here?'

'Over two years ago he began to seek out the sky-watchers who he was carrying to the Sky-reach tower. He wanted to learn what we did. He asked many questions.'

'As I did.'

'His were not as superficial. He wanted a deep understanding of what we did. I answered many of his persistent questions myself. He would spend my entire watch with me, examining what I did, asking question after question.'

'And you told him everything?'

'I told him everything he was able to understand at the time he was able to understand it. He was a fast learner, faster than some novice sky-watchers I have had.'

'So what happened?'

'Soon after the Order of the Wynde was consecrated, he came to me and asked if he could become a sky-watcher. He said he had never felt in his rightful place with the windriders.'

'What did you tell him?'

'That sky-watching had always been the preserve of the Order of the Liche. He asked me whether that had become a convention because no Felsen would ever show any interest in it, or if it was an immutable law.'

'And what answer did you give him?'

'I said I didn't know. I only know what has always been. Perhaps it was ultimately up to the Circle to make the decision as to whether a Wynde could become a sky-watcher.'

'I still don't see how this all fits together.'

'I'm not sure either. What I do know is that Leylan spoke to

First Speaker Leyvin, and soon afterwards he was told he could function as a novice on some watches.'

'I don't remember the issue ever being discussed within the Circle.'

'Perhaps it didn't require a Circle deliberation.'

'I don't see how Leyvin could make the decision. Was Leylan a windrider or a sky-watcher in the end?'

'His chart drawing was sufficiently accurate for him to have the technical ability for a watch. It takes many years of study to gain real understanding of what the charts are telling us, but as I said, he appeared to have a real talent for it, and he certainly had a passion for sky-watching.'

'But what did the other windriders believe he was? And what did he believe? What were his duties? How could he spend several nights studying the stars, and perform the duties required of him as a windrider during the day.'

Sethor shook his head. 'I hadn't thought about it. I just assumed Leyvin had made decisions about that.'

Micah stroked his beard. 'Then where is this Leylan who was meant to be in the Sky-reach tower when the storm was approaching?'

'I'm afraid he is missing. He may have perished.'

'What?'

'He was the windrider who carried the Faemir Ascender to the Source.'

'Of course. That's where I've heard his name. This is indeed a mystery.'

'My concern is not the mystery, Micah. I want to find the missing charts. Everything the sky-watchers do depends on accurate records.'

Micah ran his fingers along the chart open in front of him. 'Is there any reason why Leylan would take the charts he had drawn with him?'

'Not that I can see. Each chart is important as part of a greater sequence, but one night's configurations have no value in themselves.'

'Have you checked the signature?'

'What do you mean?'

'It strikes me that forging a signature may be relatively easy, but drawing a chart takes real expertise.'

'You think someone has forged Leylan's signature? Why would someone do that?'

'I have my suspicions.'

'I don't want to know. If you have an idea of what's happened, then just help me get the missing charts back.'

'As I said, they may not exist.'

Sethor frowned. 'I hope you're wrong.' He flicked back two pages in his log. 'Here is where Leylan's first signature appears.'

Micah folded the page so that the two signatures could be viewed side by side. 'They look the same to me. What do you think, Sethor?'

'Star configurations I know. I could tell the authenticity of a chart in a moment, but I make no claims to skill with signatures.' He drew a deep breath. 'What do you think has happened?'

'I'm only guessing, Sethor, but it's entirely possible that Leylan didn't go to his watch.'

'Why wouldn't he? That was the agreement.'

'Clearly Leyvin's role is central here. He seems to be the one who was controlling Leylan's transition from windrider to sky-watcher, with both windriders and sky-watchers unsure exactly what his role was.'

'So you're saying Leyvin somehow persuaded Leylan that his watch had been changed?'

'And arranged for him to carry Verlinden to the Source instead.'

'Why would he do this?'

'Because he wanted the three people who presented the greatest threat to his authority to be caught in a storm that they would be unlikely to survive.'

'I don't want to listen to any more of this. I have had some experience with the intrigues of the Inner Sanctum in the past – but you are suggesting a most horrific crime. No Holy Man could be capable of that.'

Sethor put the log book back in his satchel and began rolling up the charts when Micah grabbed his wrist to stop him. 'You cannot leave this unresolved.'

'Unhand me, Micah. I want no part of your wild speculations.'

Micah glared at him without releasing his grip. 'I may be wrong, but we need to find out the truth.'

'Don't speak to me about truth. You don't know anything about it.'

'If a monstrous act has occurred,' said Micah, 'then it must be exposed. If Leyvin has conspired in the deaths of the leader of the windriders and the only remaining two Ascenders, then he will need to be accounted for.'

'I will leave the pursuit of justice to you.'

'I need your help, Sethor.'

'I've told you what I can, Micah. Now leave me to return these charts to the archive.'

Micah released his grip. 'Go then. Their deaths will be on your conscience.'

'They won't be on my conscience. I had nothing to do with them.' Sethor started to carefully roll up the charts.

'It was your watch that should have provided the storm warning.'

Sethor swallowed. 'Don't you try to enmesh me in this. I've given you information. Now leave me alone.'

'Look, Sethor, I'm not enmeshing you. It has happened. You have to act now. It's your duty to the truth.'

'What do you know about truth?'

'I know that inaction can have as much power as action.'

Sethor pressed his lips together.

'Can you at least think about this?' said Micah. 'How would

Leyvin know there was a storm front coming if no one charted the skies that night?'

'The signs would have occurred early in Leylan's watch.'

'So Leylan could have commenced his watch but been interrupted?' asked Micah. 'That could be his signature in the log?'

'You're suggesting that Leylan was persuaded by Leyvin to leave his watch to carry the Faemir.'

'It's possible.'

'I'm not sure that you are making sense,' said Sethor. 'Why would Leylan allow himself to be persuaded to fly ahead of a storm that he had seen approaching?'

'I don't know. I was hoping you would have some answers.'

'You are doing nothing but speculating at the moment.'

'But there must be evidence somewhere if any of this has occurred.'

'I'm not so sure. The sky-watchers are usually carried up to the platform by a windrider. That would normally provide us with some evidence of who was there, but Leylan would have flown himself up there.'

'Then there must be some evidence of Leyvin flying up the platform.'

'Not necessarily. Not if Leylan was the one who carried him. Or Leyvin could have climbed the Sky-reach tower, as you did.'

'There any many questions to be answered, Sethor. Does this mean you will help me now?'

'I need to find out whether the missing charts exist somewhere.'

'You can't tell me that the possible murders are completely irrelevant to you.'

'Never mind my motivation, Micah,' The sky-watcher sighed. 'All right, I will see this through to the end with you. It will be the only way for me to get my peace and for things to return to normal.'

'Good. Now I'm going to ask some questions of a certain member of the Circle.'

'I don't think Leyvin will reveal anything to you.'

Micah smiled. 'I didn't have Leyvin in mind. I think I'll have a conversation with Lythos first.'

Sethor swung his satchel over his shoulder. 'I'll leave the intrigues to you. I will do some fact-checking.' With that, he walked out the door.

Chapter Fifteen

Atreu dangled his feet off the jetty and stared morosely into the waters of the Maelstrom. It was their third morning in Hellespont, and they were no closer to finding a river boat and captain to take them downslope than when they had first arrived. The reaction to their request had soon become predictable. They would be met with an incredulous look and a rapid shaking of the head, indicating that their request was not even worth considering. The frustration of being unable to undertake his quest coupled with Atreu's confusion regarding Verlinden's revelation. The secret she had been keeping from him since Equinox had at least explained why she had changed. But since their first night in Hellespont, Atreu had been unable to broach the subject with her. It was too far from any of his previous experiences, and his mind fought the turmoil by trying to shut it out.

'Where are your friends?'

Atreu looked up to see the dark, exotic-looking server-woman from The Last Anchor. He shielded his eyes from the sun, which hung behind her shoulder.

'They are looking for another inn,' he said. 'I'm afraid our money won't last very long staying at yours.'

The woman smiled. 'The Last Anchor is not my inn.' She

stepped up to the edge of the jetty and sat down next to Atreu. 'My name is Aeshya.'

'I'm Ascender Atreu, who used to be of Valesend in the Lower Reaches.'

'Ah, so you are an Ascender. I thought you may have stolen the garb you are wearing.'

'Stolen? Why would anyone do that?'

'It's been known to happen. Ascenders get all sorts of privileges, don't they?'

'Not the services of a river captain and the use of a boat, apparently.'

'So you swear you are a real Ascender? I heard that last Zenith's had all been killed by the Faemir, and that none of this year's Ascenders have got very far.'

'I am an Ascender. Only two of us survived last Zenith.'

'If you are, aren't you going the wrong way?'

Atreu laughed. 'How do you know where I'm going?'

'News travels fast in Hellespont. I discovered that the first day I arrived here.'

'So you're not from Hellespont?'

'No, I'm a Lower Reacher, like you.'

Atreu squinted at her in the sunlight. Her dark features were unusual. 'You don't look much like a Lower Reacher.'

'My mother was one, and I was born there – in my mind that makes me one, even if I haven't been there in a long time.'

'What are you doing here in Hellespont then?' asked Atreu. 'You couldn't be any further away from the Lower Reaches.'

'I would travel further upslope if there were any towns there.'

'Why? Are you escaping the war?'

'No. Not really. I've been travelling since long before the war started. And there are other towns downriver which are still safe.'

'Why, then?'

'You ask a lot of questions, Ascender Atreu. I was going to offer you some help, and you haven't even given me the chance.'

Atreu cocked his head. 'What sort of help can you offer us?'

'I can get you downriver through the helles.'

'The helles?'

'You don't know the Maelstrom very well, do you?'

'I crossed it near Stromspont during my Ascent, but that's it, I'm afraid.'

'The helles are the rapids which start just downslope of Hellespont. They're why Hellespont is the most isolated town on the Maelstrom. Only the most experienced navigators can steer a boat through them.'

'And you know someone who can help us?'

Aeshya stared at him. 'You haven't thought for even the slightest moment that I could take you, have you?'

Atreu hesitated. 'No. You don't look like a river captain to me.'

'How many river captains have you met?'

'Well ...'

'Exactly as I thought.' She went to get up. 'You know, sometimes I wish the Faemir had won the war, instead of us having this truce.'

'Wait,' said Atreu. 'I'm sorry. It's just that you looked too ... young to have the experience.'

Aeshya smiled at him. 'I have the experience. Don't worry about that. I may not have much else, but I have that.'

Atreu started to feel his face burn. 'Well then,' he said quickly, 'you say you could take us down the Maelstrom through the helles? I don't want to seem ungrateful, but judging by the other reactions we've had here, why would you want to do that?'

'Because I like you.' Aeshya laughed. 'And I like your tall friend.'

Atreu was at a loss as to how to reply.

'No, Ascender Atreu, I'm jesting with you. I actually have a problem that you and your friends can help me with.'

'What is it?'

'I need to return my father's riverboat to him at Farepont.'

'And why is that a problem?'

'It's a three-master, which, if you know anything about river-boats, you'll know means it needs at least two crew members.'

'I'm not sure any of us have the ability to help sail a riverboat.'

'If you can follow orders, you can crew a riverboat. It's the captain who needs all the skill.'

'Which you have, presumably.' Atreu chewed his bottom lip. There was something about this woman that he couldn't fathom. 'What I don't understand is, why would you risk going through something as dangerous as the helles with three people whose only skill on the water is with a pair of oars?'

'All right, Ascender Atreu, if you are not interested, I won't bother you any further.'

'Look, don't storm off every time you feel slighted.' Atreu pulled Aeshya back before she could get up.

She glared at him. 'Please don't touch me again without asking first.'

'I ... I'm sorry. I just don't see why you couldn't get two towns-people to come with you.'

'You've seen what their reaction is. No one wants to sail through the helles during winter if they can avoid it – and there *is* a war on down there.'

'But I've seen a few boats come and go since we've been here. There must be two people in Hellespont who would go with you?'

'You're very suspicious for an Ascender.'

'I'm not suspicious. I just ask a lot of questions. I always have – please don't take offence. I am grateful for the offer. I just can't let something be if it doesn't make any sense to me.'

Aeshya shook her thick, dark hair and it brushed across her cheeks. 'All right, Ascender Atreu, I will tell you why I'm in the situation I'm in, and why I really do need your help and that of your friends.' She pointed to a large three-masted boat moored on the other side of the river. 'That's my father's boat.'

'I see,' said Atreu. He could see several crew members unloading cargo from it.

'You're right in questioning my offer – although most Hellesponters are happy to stay here until the war is over, there are some who are willing to risk a journey downriver for potential profit. Many of them are little better than river pirates.'

'So who are those people on your father's boat?'

Aeshya's expression suddenly changed. 'They are river scum. That beautiful ship over there, the *Perisher*, was stolen from my father, and I have vowed to get it back. He was once a great river captain, the best on the Maelstrom, and now he spends all his time frequenting inns and drinking ale. When his boat was stolen from him, he lost all his dignity. I want to get it back for him.'

'I see. And how do you propose to do that?'

'That's exactly what I've been talking to you about. I am suggesting that we can help each other. You get to Farepont, and I return my father's boat to him.'

'Are you suggesting we help you steal it?'

'How can you steal something that was yours in the first place?'

'I agree, you can't, but whoever has the boat presumably won't be keen to give it up.'

'No, that's true, but someone who cannot conceive that something will be taken from them won't be too vigilant.'

'They won't expect you to try to take it?'

'No, of course not. The boat was stolen years ago. They wouldn't know who I was. Hellespont is one of the few havens in the war. The captain and crew will devote their energies to drinking and wenching while they are here. We could be a full night's sailing downriver before anyone even notices the boat is missing. And a ship with the sails of the *Perisher* is very hard to catch.'

'So you really think it is possible?'

'More than possible.'

Atreu looked at her dark eyes and saw them burning with a flame he had only ever seen in Faemir. 'This boat, here, the *Perisher*,' he said. 'If it was stolen years ago and you've been travelling for at least as long, why haven't you come across it before?'

'More questions, Ascender Atreu,' said Aeshya. 'I know this

is an offer out of the blue, but you must learn to trust me.' She looked across at the *Perisher*. 'I have seen that beautiful ship on at least a dozen occasions in various places on the Maelstrom. Each time, I have tormented myself trying to find a way to reclaim it for my father. Each time, it has sailed away from me, and I never knew if I would get another chance.'

Atreu could see tears forming in Aeshya's eyes as her voice faltered before continuing.

'When I heard that the three of you were desperately seeking passage to Farepont during the time of a most horrific war, I thought finally I would have my chance.' She looked deeply into Atreu's eyes. 'Please, give me that chance.'

'There are many risks in what you are suggesting,' he said. 'I need to speak to the other two.'

'Of course,' said Aeshya, 'but remember, the *Perisher* will only be in Hellespont for two nights, and tonight, after all the cargo has been unloaded, will be the best time to take it because there will be nothing on board for anyone to guard.'

'I see. That gives us very little time to decide.'

Aeshya got up. 'I'll be ready tonight, just in case you decide that we can help each other.' As she started to walk back along the jetty to the shore, she turned her head, and her rich black hair flicked across her shoulders. 'You know where to find me, Ascender Atreu.'

*

The sun was dipping as Atreu, Verlinden and Riell walked along the riverbank towards The Last Anchor. They kept their voices low as they spoke, and glanced around nervously.

'You know, this may be our only chance,' said Atreu. 'We could be here so long it would be quicker to descend the Mountain on foot.'

'I've given you all my reservations, Atreu,' said Riell. 'My view of our prospects is not quite as glum as yours. We've seen a boat or two leaving most days. It's not as if no one at all is going down-river. Stealing a boat, even if it is stealing a boat *back*, is not my first choice.'

'But do we have the time?' said Atreu.

'Atreu, I've already said that I agreed to the plan despite my reservations. Why do you keep asking?'

'I suppose I'm trying to convince myself. Verlinden, you haven't changed your mind, have you?'

'No, Atreu. I said before that we need to descend in whatever way we can. I know it's not how you saw us embarking on the quest, but, as we both know, chance encounters are often the most important.'

Atreu fell silent for a moment. 'All right then,' he said finally. 'Wait here and I'll get her.'

He entered the door of The Last Anchor. Inside were some ale drinkers at one table, who had obviously been there for some time. The raised area had been set for the minstrels, with the instruments ready, but the minstrels themselves were yet to be seen. There was no sign of Aeshya. One of the other server-women recognised him. 'I thought you and your friends had found other lodgings for the night,' she said.

Atreu was unsure of what to say. 'We have,' he said awkwardly.

'Come back for the ale, I see,' she said.

Atreu nodded and sat down stiffly. The server-woman brought him an ale and said, 'It looks like you need one of these tonight.'

'Is ... Aeshya here?'

The server-woman looked at him strangely. 'Ah, so that's it – the young wench has cast her spell over you.'

Atreu was about to protest, but decided to let the remark pass. Let this woman think what she wants, as long as he didn't give away what he was really doing here.

'She's busy in the kitchen at the moment,' said the woman,

'but I'll see if she wants to speak to you.' With that, she disappeared through a door.

Atreu made a half-hearted attempt at flicking the foam from his ale while he waited. This was not how he had imagined his great quest beginning, with lies and skulking in the night.

Aeshya came through the doors with a half-smile on her face and squeezed herself into the seat next to Atreu so that their thighs were touching. 'You're good at this, Ascender Atreu,' she said in a low voice. 'Jorussa won't be surprised if you and I disappear a little later.'

Atreu felt his heart racing, and he leant away from Aeshya.

'Come on, Ascender Atreu,' she said, holding his arm. 'Don't spoil the effect.'

Atreu cleared his throat. 'We've decided that your plan is probably our only chance to get out of Hellespont in the near future. From what you've said, tonight is the best time – so, what do you propose?'

Aeshya smiled again and leant so close that their faces were almost touching. 'Kiss me,' she said softly.

'What?'

'I said, "kiss me". There are several people watching. We have to make this convincing.'

Atreu had barely drawn a breath before he felt Aeshya's moist lips against his. Despite himself, he felt a sharp surge through his body.

When Aeshya pulled away, she said, 'You are good at this. That was very convincing.'

'All right – now what happens?'

'You have a rowboat, don't you?'

'Yes.'

'You and your friends row over to the left bank, where the *Perisher* is moored. All the inns are on this side, so there should be few people over there. If anyone asks what you're doing, say that you are seeking passage downstream and that one of the captains said they would speak to you.'

'Which one?'

'Does it matter?' she said irritably.

'Someone may ask.'

'Just say he didn't tell you his name, but that he had pointed to one of the two-masters moored on the left bank.'

'All right. Then what?'

'Wait for me to come. I'll tell you what to do then.'

Atreu nodded.

'Now just play with my hair a little,' she said.

Atreu glanced around. 'There's no one looking.'

Aeshya smiled. 'I know – I just like it.' She gave him a quick kiss and got up. 'Till later,' she said loudly, and headed back into the kitchen.

Atreu took a sip of his ale, then got up and walked to the door.

*

Riell negotiated his way through the anchor ropes of the moored boats. The laughter and minstrel music on the other side of the river was becoming increasingly faint. The left bank, which they were now rowing towards, had far fewer torchlights than they had become used to, and the buildings appeared more cramped.

They reached a large jetty and Verlinden tied the rope around a pole. The boards creaked underfoot as they walked ashore. Verlinden asked, 'So now we just wait for her? Here in the cold?'

'Yes, that's what she said.' Atreu watched his breath cloud in front of his face.

'Winter is almost upon us,' said Riell. 'It will be good to get as far away from the Upper Reaches as we can before it sets in.'

The three of them walked along the bank until they stood facing the *Perisher*. 'So that's her father's boat,' said Verlinden.

There were lights on board, but no movement. 'I'm not comfortable skulking about in the dark like a common thief,' said Riell.

'Do you think I am?' said Atreu. 'We can all still change our minds, if we wish.'

'I trust your judgment of people,' said Riell.

'And so you should,' said a female voice from the darkness to their right. Aeshya quickly emerged from the shadows into the moonlight.

'Do you always listen to other people's discussions?' said Verlinden.

'Only when they are loud enough to be heard. Come this way, out of the light.'

They followed her into the shadows.

'We will have to move quickly now,' said Aeshya in a low voice. 'If we are really lucky there will be no crewmen on board. At worst, one or two. If there are, the chances are they will be sleeping in the aft bunks.'

'How do you know so much about stealing boats in the middle of the night?' asked Verlinden.

'I know a lot about this boat,' she said, an edge in her voice. 'I have been waiting so long to take back what is my father's, I have planned this in my head a thousand times.'

'What do we do if crewmen are on board?' asked Riell.

'Leave them to me,' said Aeshya. 'Now, I will swim across to the *Perisher* —'

'You're going to swim?' asked Atreu. 'The water is like ice.'

'It's not very far from the jetty, and if I swim I will be almost invisible to anyone on board.'

'I thought you said they would be asleep,' said Verlinden.

'I said that the chances were that they would be asleep. I like to keep the chances in my favour. Now, when I've made sure the boat is safe, I'll signal three flashes of a lantern from starboard.'

'Starboard?' asked Atreu.

'The right side of the boat. When I flash the lantern, that will be the signal for you to row to that side. We'll hoist up your rowboat after you climb aboard so we don't leave any evidence. Then we weigh the anchors, and let the Maelstrom current take us downriver. Once we're out of sight of Hellespont, we hoist the sails.'

'Sounds too simple to me,' said Verlinden.

'The best plans are the simple ones,' said Aeshya. 'It's the timing that's the real key.'

'Won't you be missed at The Last Anchor?' asked Riell.

She touched Atreu's elbow. 'Thanks to Ascender Atreu, they won't be too surprised if they don't see me for the rest of the night.'

Atreu avoided looking at Verlinden and Aeshya. He could feel his face burning in the darkness.

*

The air was frosting around them as they waited in the shadows and watched for the three lantern flashes. Snatches of wild music and laughter and cheers wafted across from the other bank. Occasionally Atreu could hear footfalls nearby, and now and then he thought he could make out a figure in the distance, but the buildings near the water were almost deserted.

There was the sound of something heavy falling in the water near the *Perisher*.

'Could you see what that was?' asked Riell.

'My night vision is good,' said Atreu, 'but not that good.'

Verlinden was shivering. 'I don't trust her,' she said.

'I asked you several times whether you thought this was a good idea,' said Atreu. 'Don't tell me you don't want to go with her now.'

'No, I didn't say that,' said Verlinden. 'I said that I didn't trust her. It will pay us to watch our backs. As long as we are helpful to her, it's all going to be fine, but the moment we're not –'

'There's a flash,' said Riell.

They all watched as the second and third flashes appeared.

'All right,' said Atreu. 'Let's get going.'

They made their way back down to the jetty and climbed back into the rowboat. To their surprise, several sacks lay at the bottom.

'What's this?' asked Riell.

Verlinden untied one of them. 'It looks like food.'

'And a tankard of ale,' said Atreu. 'Aeshya must have put them here. She's obviously had this carefully planned for some time.'

'Why didn't she tell us?' said Verlinden. 'She's keeping too much to herself.'

Atreu grabbed the oars. 'We can get more answers later, Verlinden. I think we'd better start moving.'

As soon as they reached the *Perisher*'s hull, Atreu could see Aeshya climbing down the rope ladder that dangled over the side.

'Here, tie these around the benches and climb up,' she said, indicating two thick ropes that hung next to the ladder. Her dark hair glistened wet in the moonlight and her clothes clung to her body like skin.

They secured the ropes and then climbed up the hull. By the time he reached the deck, Atreu's arms ached – it had been a long while since he had done anything so physical.

'Are you sure there are no crewmen on board?' asked Atreu, rubbing each of his shoulders in turn.

Aeshya ignored him and beckoned them over to a large winch. 'We have to move swiftly now,' she said. 'Here, it will take two of us to move this.'

Atreu grabbed one of the large handles and started turning. His shoulders started burning anew, but the rowboat had soon been lifted out of the water and hung suspended just below the deck line.

Aeshya quickly secured it to the side of the *Perisher*, then the others followed her lead in lifting out the sacks and putting them on deck.

'Where did these come from?' asked Atreu.

'So many questions,' said Aeshya. 'Does it matter?' She moved to the front of the boat, where there was another winch. 'I will need some help with the fore anchor. Two of you go bring up the aft anchor.'

Riell stepped forward to help her while Atreu and Verlinden headed off to the back of the *Perisher*.

'I'm not used to being given orders anymore,' said Verlinden.

'Do you think I am?' said Atreu.

They unhooked the clasp on the anchor rope and started turning the handle on the winch.

Atreu was breathing heavily by the time they heard the clunk of the anchor against the hull below.

'Careful,' said Aeshya, who had joined them. 'We don't want a hole before we get started.' She secured the anchor and disappeared.

Atreu was suddenly aware that they were moving. He looked across at the right bank, where the lights were winking and music flowed into the night sky. His body was cooling down after its recent exertion, and he started shivering.

'When do you think we will dance again, Verlinden?' he asked.

Verlinden didn't reply.

Atreu half-expected to hear a tumultuous outcry from the riverbank, but the *Perisher* continued to glide silently through the water unnoticed.

'Where has Aeshya gone?' asked Riell, joining Atreu and Verlinden at the front of the boat.

'I hope she's steering this thing,' said Verlinden. It was only when the lights of Hellespont receded in the distance that Aeshya re-emerged.

'I think it's safe to up-sail now,' she said. 'I'll go up the middle mast. Two of you climb up the others and I'll show you what to do.'

Verlinden and Riell scaled the rope ladders of the outer masts while Atreu watched, massaging his shoulders and trying not to think of Verlinden with child. He saw Aeshya unfurl the centre sail. After several attempts, Verlinden and Riell managed to release their sails as well.

When they had all clambered down again, Aeshya allowed herself a smile. 'See, Ascender Atreu? I told you all that was needed was for you to follow orders. I'll make boatswains of all of you.'

'So we're safe now?' asked Atreu, watching the sails billow white in the night breeze.

'Far from it,' said Aeshya, 'but the *Perisher* is a fast boat. If its disappearance isn't noticed until morning, we will take some catching.'

'And what about these helles you spoke about?' asked Atreu.

'They are two days' sailing downriver of here in these winds. We can relax until then. Where is that tankard of ale I brought? I think we can afford to celebrate a little, can't we?'

She was already off before the others could say anything. Atreu's mouth hung open in amazement. She was so like a Faemir in many ways – her passion and energy – and yet she was also as far away as she could be from the seriousness that most Faemir had.

Aeshya appeared again, carrying the tankard, and indicated that someone should open the door to the topdeck cabin she was standing in front of. 'It will be a lot more comfortable in here,' she said.

Atreu, Verlinden and Riell followed her in, and sat down on the benches inside while Aeshya started a small fire in the hearth.

Atreu looked around. This was not what he had expected. There were large, intricately rendered paintings of riverscapes on the walls. Aeshya opened several cupboards until she found what she was looking for, then pulled out four large tankards.

'You seem at home here,' said Atreu.

Aeshya started pouring the ales. 'I told you this was my father's boat. Don't tell me you didn't believe me?'

'I believed you,' said Atreu quickly. 'Why would you lie about something like that?'

Aeshya put the tankard of foaming ale on the table in front of him. 'There are always lots of reasons for lying,' she said. 'I could have simply wanted to steal the *Perisher*.'

Atreu took a draught of his ale.

'No ale for me,' said Verlinden.

'Why not?' asked Aeshya. 'This is a time to celebrate. I've always found that if you don't take the time to celebrate something, your life ends up being marked by the bad times, rather than the good.'

'An interesting philosophy,' said Riell, 'but I'm afraid I'm not really an ale-drinker either. Tell me something, though, while we are all in here celebrating, who's steering the boat?'

Aeshya laughed as she filled her own tankard. 'I'm glad one of you finally asked me that question. The currents and wind patterns immediately downriver of Hellespont allow boats to sail through on a straight course. There's no danger of running aground.'

'What about boats coming the other way?'

'River traffic hasn't exactly been frantic, in case you hadn't noticed. The chances of any boat coming upstream at night are remote. Besides, most captains who encountered a boat the size of the *Perisher*, in full sail, heading downriver, would get their crafts out of the way as quickly as they could. First rule of the Maelstrom: anyone sailing downriver has right of way.'

'Let's just hope the crew on any boat coming upriver isn't celebrating too,' said Verlinden.

'I'm afraid I'm a little too tired for celebrating just now,' said Riell as he stood. 'Are there any beds on this ship?'

Aeshya laughed. 'You can have your choice of a dozen bunks. The stairs down to the sleeping cabins are aft.'

After Riell had gone, she said, 'Your friend makes a habit of retiring early. I might have to see if I can change that.'

'He's a windrider,' said Atreu. 'They lead a disciplined life.'

'A windrider?' Aeshya's eyes widened. 'Well, the three of you are obviously not average travellers.' She took a deep draught and addressed Verlinden. 'And are you someone as well?'

'What sort of a question is that?' said Verlinden. 'Everyone is someone.'

'I'm not,' said Aeshya. 'I have no home, no family except my father, who drowns himself in ale.'

'I have no home or family either,' said Verlinden, 'yet I know who I am.'

'Who are you then?'

She hesitated. 'I was once the Faemir Watcher Verlinden.'

'A Faemir?' Aeshya's eyes widened. 'I thought there was something about you. Remind me not to challenge you to a fight.'

'I was a Watcher, not a warrior,' said Verlinden.

'I notice you say only what you once were. What are you now?'

'I ... I'm Ascender Verlinden.'

'A Faemir Ascender?' Aeshya raised the tankard to her mouth and drank. 'Well, it's not often I'm completely surprised. My crew is two Ascenders and a windrider. Either I have the most illustrious crew on the Maelstrom or I'm a total fool for believing all of you.'

'It worries me that you even have to weigh up whether we are lying or not,' said Verlinden.

'It's in my nature, I'm afraid – I've been lied to often in my life.' She smiled. 'But never by a Faemir, I have to say.'

Verlinden suddenly stood up. 'I'm not one for all-night celebrations,' she said. 'Faemir have had little cause in the past.'

'What about Ascenders?' asked Aeshya. 'Do they ever have cause to celebrate?'

'I'll let Atreu talk to you about that.' Verlinden walked out of the room with barely a backward glance.

Aeshya poured herself another ale. 'Not much humour to those two,' she said. 'How is it that you come to be travelling with them?' She offered to refill Atreu's tankard.

Atreu shook his head. 'Now look who's asking all the questions.'

'Ah, a secret – now that's what I like to hear.'

'I would tell you the full story, but I don't think we will have enough time tonight.'

'No?' she said, looking into his eyes. 'What is it you plan to do tonight?'

'I plan to sleep after I finish this tankard,' he said.

'What a shame. There are so few moments in my life where I actually win like I have tonight. I don't want it to end.'

'It looked to me like everything went as you had planned.'

'Yes – but I had rehearsed it so often in my mind that nothing could have gone wrong.'

'You were lucky that no one was on board.'

Aeshya grunted into her ale.

'You were lucky, though, weren't you?' said Atreu.

'There was one crewman sleeping on duty, actually.' She took a quick sip of ale.

'What happened? Where is he?'

'I ... er ... threw him overboard – are you sure I can't fill your tankard?'

'You threw him overboard? I didn't hear any shouting or splashing.'

'Really?'

'No, I didn't. He must have woken up when he hit the water, surely?'

'These crewmen drink quite heavily. It takes quite a bit to wake them up sometimes. Believe me, I know.'

'But it wasn't late enough in the evening for him to have been drinking too long. The crew was hard at work carrying off cargo until close to sunset. *I know* – I was watching them. Are you going to tell me what happened?'

'Don't ever accuse me again of asking questions.'

Atreu stared at her. 'That splashing sound just before you flashed the lantern at us – that was you throwing him overboard, wasn't it?'

'Yes.'

'But it sounded more like a sack falling in the water than a man.'

'A man with his hands and feet tied and a gag around his mouth does fall like a sack,' she said.

'What? You threw him into the Maelstrom tied up?'

Aeshya nodded and put her tankard down. 'What would you expect me to do? Kiss him?'

'You killed him then. He would have sunk like a stone.'

'I imagine so. I didn't bother to look.'

Atreu fell silent and stared into his remaining ale.

'Ascender Atreu,' said Aeshya, 'don't tell me you're not going to celebrate with me now either?'

'I think I will go to bed too,' said Atreu finally.

'Go then,' she said, waving him away. 'Just think about how if it wasn't for what I did, you would still be back in Hellespont, humiliating yourself trying to gain passage downriver.'

'Good night,' said Atreu, and walked out.

The air was now frigid under the clear sky. He let out a breath and watched the steam dissipate. For a moment he thought he heard an echo of the body falling in the water.

With a sigh, he headed aft.

Chapter Sixteen

'Why are you talking to me?' Lythos grabbed a frost-apple from the bowl in front of him.

'It should be everyone's concern that our only two Ascenders may be dead,' said Micah.

Lythos shifted uncomfortably on the bench and looked around the Great Dining Hall. His agitation at being questioned in such a public place was clear, despite his attempts to mask it. 'I am concerned, of course. That's not what I meant. I just question why you are speaking specifically to me about it. This is a matter for the Circle.'

'I agree, Lythos, I agree totally – but I must bring some facts to the attention of the Circle.'

'I'm afraid I can't help you very much with any search for facts,' said Lythos, toying with the piece of fruit.

'Perhaps you're right, but I want to find out what you know about the forged signatures in the sky-watchers' log.'

Lythos went noticeably pale. 'Forged signatures? I don't know a thing about them. Why would anyone do such a thing?'

'That's what I'm trying to discover, Lythos.'

'Do you have any evidence of this forgery? Or is this just wild speculation?'

'There are ways of proving forgery,' said Micah. 'We have highly skilled scribes in our librums. That's not all, though. What do you know of the missing sky-watch charts from the night before Ascenders Atreu and Verlinden set off for the Source?'

'Missing charts? I have no understanding of sky-watch charts. I deal with Ascenders – you know that.'

'I do – which is why I'm surprised you haven't delved into the matter of the missing Ascenders more deeply. The movements of Ascenders in the Keep were your responsibility, were they not?'

'Strictly speaking, that applies only until Equinox. I have reported what information I have of their fate to the Circle.' He rolled the frost-apple from side to side.

'Yes – but there are circumstances that require investigation. Why haven't you done so?'

'What are you accusing me of here, Micah? I don't have to listen to this sort of nonsense.'

'I'm not accusing you of anything,' said Micah in a reassuring tone. If he had read Lythos correctly, this was obviously the time to back away.

'You seem to be suggesting –'

'I'm not suggesting anything, Lythos.' Micah waved his hand as if fending off Lythos' comment. 'I believe there is something seriously amiss, and we need to get to the bottom of it.'

'We?'

'Yes, Lythos. Why else would I come to you? I was Atreu's sage – so I have a strong interest. From what I've uncovered, this whole matter is a mystery that needs to be investigated thoroughly. I suspect a crime has been committed, and I'm asking for your help.'

Lythos looked straight at Micah for the first time in the conversation. 'You want my help?'

'Of course. We need to uncover what has happened and present it to the Circle. We need to know whether an act of negligence by a sky-watcher has caused a possible catastrophe, or whether a crime has in fact been committed.'

'You suspect a sky-watcher?'

'Of course, who else could it be?' Micah tried to appear genuinely puzzled. 'That's why I chose to discuss this with you here. The sky-watchers never eat in the Great Dining Hall.'

'I did wonder why you were speaking to me here ...'

'These sky-watchers – they keep to themselves. Who knows what they are planning?'

'They never nominate for the Circle,' said Lythos. 'That has always concerned me, but –'

'Look, I'm not making any accusations. I may be wrong, but we must uncover the truth.'

Lythos nodded and then stood up. 'I am glad you've come to me with this,' he said. 'I will try to uncover what I can.'

'Thank you, Lythos. That's what I was hoping to hear.'

Lythos turned to go when Micah held up the frost-apple for him. 'Here,' he said, 'don't forget your fruit.'

*

It had been three days since they had left Hellespont, and they had seen no sign of any pursuit. The sky was a frosty blue and the air rarely lost its chill. Apart from trimming and hauling in the sails, there was little else to do. Aeshya often latched the tiller in position because the current was keeping them mid-river. The terrain on either side of the Maelstrom was barren and largely snow-covered. Occasionally they saw clusters of bushes huddled together on mounds jutting out from the snow, but the only animal life were the occasional charcoal-coloured birds with dull red beaks and cries like a rasping cough, which Aeshya called shrakes.

The wind cutting across the starboard bow had not been particularly strong, but the *Perisher* had, to Atreu's inexperienced view, been moving at quite a considerable speed. Aeshya spent most mornings instructing them on how to enact the various commands that she would give as they went through the helles. Verlinden's efforts, although somewhat half-hearted, were competent, and the tension between the two women stayed just below the surface. Riell managed particularly well, but Atreu wasn't surprised that the windrider's skills should somehow carry over. While Riell wasn't as elegant or composed as he appeared in the air, he certainly had skills when it came to capturing the wind in the sails. Aeshya even began allowing him to take the tiller.

None of them had relaxed, however, despite the relative monotony of the journey so far. Aeshya's drills and constant warning of the imminent rapids kept them all on edge. When the call finally came just before midday, it was almost a relief.

'Helles ho!' Aeshya gave out the cry as she stood on the forecastle of the boat and peered ahead.

Atreu, Verlinden and Riell immediately climbed the masts and harnessed themselves in position, ready to trim the sails according to Aeshya's orders. Aeshya herself walked calmly to the secured tiller, unhitched the catch and took it firmly in both hands.

Atreu shielded his eyes as he peered into the riverscape ahead. At first all he could see was the blue-grey water of the Maelstrom turning white. Next, he became aware of a rushing sound that reached his ears through the sharp wind gusts which swirled around the mast. Soon he sensed that the *Perisher* had started to relentlessly gather speed, and he felt a side-to-side sway that he hadn't noticed before.

There was a sudden lurch and he lost his grip. If it weren't for the harness, he would have been flung to the deck. When he recovered, he heard Aeshya yelling at him.

'Trim the sails!'

He shook his head to regain his composure, annoyed with himself that he had missed the hand signal telling him to haul in the sails. He braced his feet in the mast struts and tensed as he started to turn the winch.

'Secure mainsail!' was the next command, and Atreu quickly tied the rope. He watched as Aeshya's gaze shifted from the flags above him, which indicated the wind direction, to the ever-approaching white water ahead.

The next command was one he hadn't heard during their training sessions. 'Hold on!'

Almost immediately, the *Perisher* lurched as if it had run into a hole in the river. Atreu's head jerked back as the ship climbed out the other side. The water was now churning around them, and the boat bounced in the waves that were slapping against the hull with great force. Atreu's harness creaked around him, but after a while he managed to move with the rolls and jerks. Then they hit the true whitewater and the *Perisher* surged like a geyer diving on prey. Atreu felt as if his breath had been swept from his mouth and left upriver. It took him a while to realise that Aeshya was calling them back down to the deck.

Although the *Perisher* was moving faster all the time, the lurches had, for the moment, disappeared. Atreu clambered down the mast carefully, holding tightly to the rope ladder. Once on deck, he joined the others at the tiller.

'That wasn't as bad as I expected,' said Atreu.

'It would have been easier if you weren't daydreaming,' said Aeshya, turning the tiller slightly as she watched the mast flags. 'The conditions will get much worse soon.'

'Worse?'

Aeshya smiled grimly. 'This is a child's game – this stretch of white water here. Wait till we reach the heart of the helles, where the ill-wind blows.'

'The ill-wind? You've never spoken of that.'

'It brings ill-fortune to speak of it on land.'

'What nonsense superstition is this?' said Verlinden.

Aeshya looked at Riell. 'You must know of this. Tell your friends that I speak the truth.'

Atreu looked at Riell, who had noticeably paled. 'There are stories of ill-winds amongst the windriders, but I don't know how true they are – no windrider in my memory has flown this stretch of the Maelstrom.'

'What stories?' asked Verlinden.

'The winds drive you to the brink of madness,' said Riell.

'Sailors dive into raging torrents, and windriders plummet earth-ward like rocks.'

'Aeshya, you claim this happens?' said Atreu.

'Yes. When the ill-wind blows along the Maelstrom, madness follows.'

'And it will be blowing today?'

'Winter is the worst time, and we know that season is upon us.'

'What have you done to us, Aeshya?' Atreu felt a chill shoot through him.

'You needed to go downriver, didn't you? You needed to go quickly. I've given you the quickest possible passage. The longer you waited, the worse the danger would have been. I've given you the best possible chance.'

'So what do we do?' asked Verlinden.

'You follow orders, and we stand some chance of keeping our minds.'

'I want to know now what we need to do.' Verlinden's jaw was firmly set.

'I'm going to be the one in the greatest danger,' said Aeshya. 'I have to man the tiller as we go through. If you three can trim the sails when I tell you and get into the cabins quickly enough with your heads under the blankets, you will survive.'

'How will you save your sanity?' asked Atreu.

'You will need to tie me here to the tillpost with knots that I can't untie, but with my hands free so that I can still turn the tiller.'

'You're going to fight the mind-ghosts of the ill-wind,' said Riell, 'and continue to steer the *Perisher*? How can you do that?'

'It has to be done. The rapids are at their most treacherous through the gap where the ill-wind blows. We cannot leave the *Perisher* at the mercy of the current.'

'Have you steered through the ill-wind before?' asked Atreu.

'Yes, but not on a ship this size, and not this close to winter, when it is raging towards a crescendo.'

'But you made it through successfully?'

'That depends what you mean by that. I went close to losing my mind. I still can't remember it too clearly. The second helmsman completed the crossing.'

'What? You had two helmsmen?' said Atreu.

'Yes, it's the way ships usually deal with the ill-wind. The second helmsman tries to block out what they can, while the first mans the tiller until they lose consciousness. The second then takes over.'

'This is sounding worse and worse,' said Atreu. 'How are we going to make it through with only you at the tiller?'

'I told you, I am an experienced river captain.'

'It's what you haven't told us that worries me,' said Riell. 'According to you, the helles were supposed to be just rapids. Are there any more surprises in store for us?'

Aeshya stared at him. 'It was best that you didn't know what was in store for you. What difference would it have made, except to strike fear into your hearts? You were obviously determined to get to Farepont. Would full knowledge of the helles have stopped you?'

'No,' said Riell, 'but it may have made us proceed more cautiously.'

'That's exactly what we couldn't afford to do. With every day closer to winter, the danger grows.'

'That's why we couldn't gain passage downriver, wasn't it?' said Atreu. 'No one was going to risk running the ill-wind.'

'Yes, that's right – you had no hope of finding anyone. Except me.'

'And that's why the *Perisher* was so poorly guarded,' said Verlinden. 'The captain and crew had no intention of returning downriver until after winter.'

'It all makes sense now, doesn't it?' said Aeshya, almost smiling. 'On the other hand, there is no danger of anyone chasing us from now on. No one in Hellespont will be mad enough to risk the ill-wind.'

'Except you,' said Atreu.

'Except us,' she said.

Atreu stared at the foaming path of the river ahead. He could see the embankments in the distance rising gradually on either side. High above them, clouds streaked across the sky.

'Tell me this,' said Atreu. 'If you had a full experienced crew on board, would you attempt to sail through the ill-wind as the sole helmsman?'

'No. I've heard that it has been done, but I've never spoken to anyone who has done it.'

'We have our own reasons for taking the risk,' said Atreu. 'Why are you doing this?'

The ship rolled suddenly, and Aeshya adjusted the tiller.

'This boat could bring my father back to life. What challenge would you avoid if you wanted to achieve that?'

Before Atreu could answer, the *Perisher* rolled again.

'The answer seems obvious to me,' said Riell, after they had all regained their balance. 'I'll be the second helmsman.'

'Some of the most experienced river captains on the Maelstrom would lose several nights' sleep before making that offer,' said Aeshya.

'We don't have several nights, do we?' said Riell.

'No,' said Aeshya, 'and you don't have the experience.'

'I've experienced every wind the Mountain can offer, and I can't see too much difference between sails and a windrider's wings.'

'You've shown some skill, but –'

'I don't want to waste time arguing with you. You say the second helmsman only takes over after the first has lost consciousness. What difference does it make to you if I'm here with you? If you make it through yourself, then you lose nothing.'

'You may lose your mind, though, Riell.'

'Let that be my concern.'

'I'm afraid it's not just your concern. You could endanger me if you sink into madness.'

'I have skill flying at high altitude,' said Riell, 'where there are always threats to your mind.'

'The ill-wind is different.'

'How do you know?'

Aeshya's eyes locked on the windrider's, and they stared at each other, unblinking. 'All right,' she said finally. 'Here, take the tiller – I don't have long to show you what to do.'

'What do Verlinden and I do?' asked Atreu.

'If you want me to start ordering you about outside of sailing instructions, I can do that.'

'I meant when the ill-wind blows.'

'You will have to keep all your wits about you, even if you are buried under a dozen blankets. As I said, I will need you to trim the sails further and to tie me to the tillpost just as we encounter the first gusts.' She grabbed Riell's hand and guided it to where he should turn the tiller. 'Until then, I'd suggest the two of you have a rest, and get something to eat. It will be a long night.'

'And how will we know when the ill-wind is blowing?' asked Atreu.

Aeshya gave a grim smile. 'You won't need me to tell you that.'

*

Leyvin and Lythos were walking along one of the gossamer-thin bridges of the Keep, the wind gusts causing it to sway unpredictably underfoot. The sun had barely emerged, and the spires lacked their usual glint, shining instead with a dull, tarnished glow.

'The skies look empty without the windriders,' said Leyvin.

Lythos was growing impatient with his brother. 'I am trying to discuss something of crucial importance here, Leyvin, and all you can give me are pointless observations.'

'Dear, dear brother,' said Leyvin. 'Look around – not only are there no longer any Faemir at the Keep, the windriders are also gone for now, fulfilling their duties. The Keep is as it should be.

You have accused me of giving away too much power in the past – look at us now. We're on our way to convene the Circle, and everything has fallen into place for us.'

'I don't care for your tone, *dear brother*,' said Lythos, mocking Leyvin's voice. 'All is not as it should be.'

'No? The Faemir are fighting our war for us. We all know they are more efficient soldiers than the Maelir. The windriders are leaderless. From the reports we have, no new Ascender will make it through to Zenith this year – so there won't be any more surprises like Atreu. How could things be better?'

'Your arrogance never ceases to astonish me, Leyvin. You haven't even bothered to respond to my news about Micah's questions.'

'I don't care about what Micah says or does. Perhaps he thinks that because he filled Praether's place in the Circle, he can somehow assume his authority. You and I know that is not true. He is nothing. He has been a figure of either mirth or disgust among the Inner Sanctum for so long – what is he going to achieve?'

'All he has to do is find evidence, and he won't need to do anything. The Circle will do the rest.'

'Evidence of what, dear brother?'

The bridge swayed suddenly under a strong gust of wind. 'We know what we're talking about.'

'No, we don't,' said Leyvin. 'At least, *you* don't know what you're talking about.'

'Micah wants me to investigate the missing sky-watch charts.'

'That shows how stupid he is.'

'I had the feeling, though, that he was subtly trying to entrap me.'

Leyvin sneered at his brother. 'Micah isn't capable of anything as sophisticated as that. If he is asking you, then that is probably a good sign.'

'Are you sure you're not underestimating him as you did Praether?'

'Let's not invoke the ghost of the arch-librer,' said Leyvin, scowling. 'Praether died after a lifetime's belief in the three Books, and he still had no proof. His last act within the Circle caused him to be expelled. Is it possible to underestimate that?'

'Old Praether still wears away at you, doesn't he?'

'We're dealing with Micah here, not Praether. He knows nothing and is capable of nothing.'

'So what do I tell him?'

'You say that you haven't found anything yet, but that the two of you should keep each other informed about who you are speaking to about the matter, and what they have said.'

'Do I tell him I've been speaking to you?'

'Lythos, sometimes I'm amazed that you are my twin. How can we look so much alike and yet be so different?'

'Enough of the arrogance. You're getting worse, you know – if that's possible. Just tell me whether I should reveal to Micah that I spoke to you about the missing sky-charts.'

'Of course you do, you fool. He would know you were lying if you didn't. Tell him that I had heard some rumours too, and was most concerned. Tell him that I will also look into the matter, if he thinks it warrants it.'

The two walked through an archway and into a tower. Lythos dropped his voice. 'It worries me that you won't tell me exactly what you've done. You usually gloat over every detail in your plans.'

'It's best this time that you don't know, dear brother. There's too much at stake.'

'But if the sky-watchers –'

'Don't worry about the sky-watchers. They believe themselves above the workings of the Circle and the rest of the Keep. They care about the stars and clouds. They won't want to grubby their hands with earthly matters.'

'I know I've said this many times before, Leyvin, but I truly hope you are fully aware of what you are doing.'

'I always am, dear brother. I always am.'

*

Verlinden stoked the hearth fire and watched the broth simmer. 'I'm finding this difficult,' she said.

'We're all learning,' said Atreu. 'Aeshya knows what she is doing, but I'm not sure if I like the way this voyage is going.'

'That's not what I meant,' said Verlinden.

Atreu handed her the two bowls in silence. Verlinden ladled the broth, accidentally spilling some on her hand as the ship pitched. 'Damn!' she cried as she dropped the bowl.

'I have some salve in my pack.'

'Don't worry, Atreu. I'll live.' She took a gourd of cold water and poured it over the burn. 'Look at me,' she said, half laughing. 'I used to be part of the fiercest army the Mountain has ever seen, and now I'm scalding myself on hot broth.'

Atreu finished ladling the broth, then they sat down at the table and started to eat.

'I'm not sure about Aeshya,' said Atreu. 'The more I see of her, the less she appears to be what she first led us to believe.'

'I suppose we're getting where we want to go, aren't we?' said Verlinden. 'Isn't that the main thing?'

'Is it? A cause can be tainted by the way you go about it.'

'That sounds a lot like the view of someone who has never done anything.'

Atreu stopped spooning his soup and glared at her. 'I think it does matter how you go about things.'

'Does it? Now this sounds like an argument against the Faemir,' said Verlinden.

'Do we have to bring the Faemir into this again? Why bring up old wounds?'

'Because we're deliberately not talking about new ones.'

Atreu looked into his broth.

'The world is changing,' said Verlinden. 'Perhaps we both need to reassess some decisions we've made.'

Atreu said, 'I wasn't arguing for or against anyone – we both have worked so hard for peace between the Maelir and Faemir.'

'Yes, and look at the two of us. We barely speak to each other.'

'I ... I don't know what to say to you, Verlinden.'

'Atreu, my belly will start swelling soon. Please tell me if you want the child.'

It seemed to Atreu as if the cabin was suddenly swirling. He grabbed hold of the table to steady himself. 'I have a choice?' he asked, fighting the vertigo.

'There are ways that the Faemir use.'

'I know nothing of women being with child, and I know nothing of the ways of being without a child.'

'Does it matter how it's done? What matters is what we do. If I were still in the Faemir army, there would be no choice. A Faemir cannot be with child in a war. The situation we are in is not as clear. We must talk about this because soon it will be too late, and we won't have a choice.'

'You keep saying we, Verlinden.'

'Of course I do, Atreu. This is your child that I am with.'

Atreu buried his head in his hands. 'I don't know. I don't know what to say. I don't know what to do. I have been confused many times since I left Valesend, but this ...' He trailed off, and a silence hung in the cabin.

Verlinden got up and stood next to where he was sitting. She reached down, took his hand and placed it on her belly.

'There is something in there that is part of both of us. We have a choice. No one can tell us what to do. Not the Faemir army and not the Holy Orders.'

Atreu slowly stood up, keeping his hand on Verlinden's belly. 'Will you be able to complete our quest?'

'By my count, I have three or four moons before travelling will become difficult.'

'That means we may have enough time.'

'So you want the child?'

Atreu nodded, and Verlinden drew him tightly to her. They were about to kiss when the ship lurched violently.

Atreu drew back and saw his fear mirrored in Verlinden's eyes. They ran to the cabin door and raced outside. Atreu felt a difference the moment he stepped onto the deck. The wind had shifted so that they were now heading straight into it.

Aeshya's command rang loud and clear. 'Trim the sails. An ill-wind is blowing.'

Riell was already up the main mast and drawing in the mainsail. Atreu and Verlinden clambered up the other masts and did the same. From his vantage point, Atreu could see the wild waters ahead. Spray from monstrous waves shot up to sail height, and on either side of the Maelstrom, giant cliffs with sharp, serrated surfaces sloped in on them.

Atreu quickly secured the sail and climbed back down. As he headed towards the tiller, where Aeshya stood, the *Perisher* pitched and lurched under his feet like the worst impermanence. Before he had reached the others, he heaved, emptying his stomach out onto the deck.

'Don't worry about that,' said Aeshya. 'You'll see far worse things than a stained deck before all this is over. Now, Riell, come here, and we'll tie you to the tillpost.'

She locked the tiller and showed Atreu and Verlinden how to make the knots she wanted. 'See, the harder he tries to pull at it, the tighter the knot will become. That's what we're going to need.'

The spray shot into Atreu's face as he concentrated on Aeshya's instructions. The wind was battering him, and he was suddenly aware of a sharp pain in the front of his head.

Aeshya then indicated another rope. 'Now tether me to the tillpost as well, and do this right – my life will depend on it.'

With her help, Atreu repeated the system of knots she had secured Riell with.

'Quickly,' she said, 'the ill-wind is gathering force. Get that blanket in the tillerbox and cover Riell with it.'

'What?' protested Riell. 'How will I know what is happening with a blanket over my head?'

'Look out as often as you dare,' said Aeshya. 'Believe me, you will be wishing you were covered with a hundred blankets before this is over.'

As Atreu unfolded the blanket, Riell said, 'When will I know to take the tiller?'

'That I don't know,' said Aeshya. 'How do you judge when someone has lost their mind?'

The wind was now threatening to blow the blanket out of Atreu's hands as he threw it over Riell, who was now sitting on the deck. The windrider tucked it firmly under his body, leaving a small gap for air to come in.

The boat was lurching more violently now, and wave after wave crashed against the hull. Atreu felt the wind hit his face and enter his head to feed the stabbing pain that was growing there. For a moment he thought he could see dark figures emerging from the white water ahead.

'What are they?' he cried.

'Rocks,' said Aeshya, spinning the tiller to the right, 'but you can never be sure when the ill-wind is blowing. Now get down below, you two. Bury yourselves as deep under blankets as you can.'

Atreu felt sick in the pit of his stomach as he and Verlinden made their way into the aft cabin where they slept. The boat was rolling so much now that it was as if they were walking upslope one moment and then downslope the next. By the time they reached the cabin door the stabbing pain in Atreu's head had grown into a shrieking noise in his ears. He took a last glimpse at Aeshya before he stepped inside. Her black hair was flying wildly in the spray-soaked wind.

When Verlinden closed the door behind them, the shrieking eased. 'That's better,' she said.

'I thought that noise was inside my head,' said Atreu. 'How are Aeshya and Riell going to stand it out there?'

'I don't know, Atreu,' said Verlinden, pushing the blanket back on her bunk, 'but let's make certain we follow Aeshya's instructions.' She beckoned him to join her. 'Come on, let's watch each other go mad.'

Atreu gave a wry smile, and climbed in next to her. They moved so that they lay entwined, and then pulled the blankets over their heads, making a fold so that they could breathe.

'Do you remember that night in the storm in the Upper Reaches when I held you?' asked Atreu.

'I remember,' she said.

'We spoke then, didn't we?'

'Yes, we did.' Verlinden pressed herself closer and Atreu felt her warmth. They lay there in silence as the wind blew outside with ever-increasing fury. After a while it seemed as if someone was just on the other side of the door, pounding at it to get in.

'That could be Riell,' said Atreu.

'It can't be,' said Verlinden. 'It's the ill-wind. Riell is tied to the tillpost.'

The shrieking sound was again inside Atreu's head and was growing rapidly. 'But it could be Riell. We can't just leave him out there.'

'Stop it, Atreu, stop it. It's not Riell. He would be calling to us if it was.'

'But what if he's so terrified he can't speak.' Atreu's head was aching unbearably now.

'You're not thinking clearly, Atreu. If it is him, he could go to another cabin, couldn't he?'

The pounding grew increasingly frantic. 'Did you hear that?' cried Atreu. 'He shouted at us to help him.'

'I didn't hear anything, Atreu. I've got this pain, this pain in my head. I can't stand it.'

The ship pitched violently and flung them out of the bunk and onto the floorboards. Now that they were free of the blankets, the shrieking penetrated even further into their heads.

Verlinden jumped back onto the bunk. 'Come on, quickly Atreu. The blanket helps.'

'No, I have to help Riell.' Atreu headed towards the door, but Verlinden grabbed him.

'There's no one there,' she said. 'Don't open that door.'

'If it's him I couldn't live with myself.'

'Don't open the door, Atreu.'

Atreu pushed her back to the floor, but before he could reach the door, she had grabbed him again. The pounding had reached a crescendo.

'Did you hear that?' cried Atreu. 'That was Riell's voice.'

'I can't hear anything above the shrieking.'

'It's Riell I tell you.' He swung around and knocked her to the ground. Before she could grab him again, he reached the door and opened it.

The wind hit him like a wave of raw fear. Before him stood a pale man with shredded clothes flailing wildly behind him. The left side of his face had been clawed away. 'Help me,' the man cried in a voice that no human lungs could produce.

As the man reached out for him with knotted fingers, the shrieking filled Atreu's head and he froze, unable to move even the smallest muscle. He felt himself being pulled back into the cabin, and before he knew it, he was lying on the floorboards and Verlinden had closed and bolted the cabin door again.

'Did you see him?' cried Atreu.

'You're still trying to tell me Riell was out there?'

'No, the man with half a face.'

'I saw nothing, Atreu. There was no one there.'

Atreu started trembling uncontrollably.

Verlinden led him back to the bunk and pulled the blanket over them.

Atreu immediately felt the pain in his head ease. 'You didn't see anyone, Verlinden?'

'No.'

'Then I am going mad.'

'You can't be if you think you are – hold on to that.'

Slowly, Atreu's tremors subsided. 'I'm sorry, Verlinden. How could I have endangered you like that?'

'Don't concern yourself, Atreu. Let's just see if we can survive this.'

Atreu fought the painful shriek still keening inside his head. He closed his eyes and searched for the coloured threads he usually saw there, but all he could see was a pale, throbbing dot, which grew larger with every pulse.

He felt Verlinden pulling him closer so that her face touched his. He reached up to stroke her other cheek. With a shock he realised it had the pits and troughs of a furrowed field. He screamed and jumped back to see he had been embracing the half-faced man. He scrambled to the bunk on the other side of the cabin and felt someone jump on top of him with a blanket, pinning him to the bunk.

'Atreu, stay calm. Just stay under the blanket.' Verlinden's voice cut through the maddening shriek.

Atreu's breaths gradually eased. 'Did you see him?'

'No, there is no one here but the two of us.'

'Can I see your face?'

'Please, Atreu, I don't want to lose you.'

Atreu tried to shake her off, but couldn't. 'I need to see your face.'

'All right, Atreu. I have a blanket over me as well, so I'll have to lift it off. Let's do this quickly.'

Atreu felt the weight shift from him, and he raised a corner of his blanket. Verlinden's eyes were wild and her expression grim, but it was her. As the shriek inside him started to grow again he pulled the blanket back over his head.

'Verlinden, please keep talking to me. It helps,' he said, taking comfort from the weight of her body on his.

There was no response.

'Verlinden, did you hear me?'

Nothing – except she seemed to shift subtly.

'Please ...' his plea trailed away as a chill shuddered through him.

When Verlinden finally spoke, he lost consciousness before she finished the last word.

'Atreu, there's someone on top of me.'

Chapter Seventeen

River-shrakes cawed forlornly in the grey skies overhead as the *Perisher* ploughed downstream at the mercy of the current. Atreu struggled with the tiller, aware that he had little control, and anxiously watched the Maelstrom in front of him widen into a vast, lake-like expanse of water. The wind blew sharply into his ears, and the horrors of the helles still reverberated in his skull. It had been several days since he had regained consciousness, and the daemons that the ill-wind had swept into his head still came back to him in staccato snatches. A pall of unreality hung over the boat as the broken main mast, propped up by sail-ropes, dominated the deck like a giant crooked finger.

So lost in his disjointed thoughts was Atreu that he only became aware of the footsteps on the creaking deckboards when they were almost upon him. He glanced over his shoulder to see Verlinden helping Riell shuffle across the deck.

'Riell, you shouldn't be out here,' said Atreu. 'You should be resting.'

'I've grown tired of lying in a bunk and sipping broth, Atreu.' Riell tried to give a weak smile.

'You must be on the mend,' said Atreu. 'You at least remember who I am now. How are you feeling?'

'I'm not sure if I can honestly say better. It could be that I've simply grown used to the confusion in my head. The bruises are at least healing.'

'Still no idea where they came from?' asked Verlinden.

'No – every time I try to recall what happened, the shrieking seems to start again.'

'Any sign that Aeshya will regain consciousness?'

Verlinden shrugged. 'She still occasionally says some words in a strange tongue, but she hasn't moved or opened her eyes.'

'If we can't get her to eat or drink anything, she will perish,' said Atreu.

'She must have borne the full brunt of it,' said Riell. 'I just wish I could have been more help out here instead of cowering under a blanket.'

'Don't be too hard on yourself,' said Atreu. 'If you can't remember what happened, you can't be certain that you weren't some help at the height of the helles.'

'Here, Atreu, let me take the tiller. I need to feel like I'm actually doing something. Everything seems so ... so grey somehow, grey to touch, grey to taste – does that make any sense?'

Atreu helped to prop the windrider up as he took hold of the wooden spokes. 'It's a good way of putting it,' he said. 'Here, I hope you can do better than I am. With the main mast broken, we have almost no control.'

'Any plans about what we do now?' asked Riell.

'Unless we can get some sort of help for Aeshya,' said Verlinden, 'I don't think we'll go much further.'

'You're right,' said Atreu, 'but I haven't seen any signs of life apart from those damned shrakes.' He shook his fist at the dark, red-beaked birds as they continued to caw relentlessly above their heads.

'Riell, do you know where the next rivertown is?' asked Verlinden.

'I'm afraid my knowledge of this part of the Mountain is

sparse. Windriders don't fly anywhere near this part of the Maelstrom.'

'At least the waters have smoothed,' said Verlinden.

'I can barely see the riverbanks now,' said Atreu. 'How wide can the Maelstrom get?'

'What's that out there?' said Riell, pointing at several dark points in the distance, which were rapidly growing.

'If they are river pirates,' said Verlinden, 'I don't think we're in a fit state to put up much of a fight.'

Atreu continued to stare at the points until he could make out six boats, with six oarsmen in each, furiously rowing against the current towards them.

'I don't think river pirates would use rowboats, would they?' said Atreu.

'Who knows?' said Riell. 'They're moving incredibly fast, considering they're rowing upstream.'

Atreu watched the boats fan out in a V-shape as they approached. The oarsmen had the look of people who had weathered a hundred storms – their faces were raw and cracked, and their dark brown hair tangled mops. Despite attempts by Atreu and Riell to signal to them, they continued to surround the *Perisher* with a grim determination, almost totally oblivious to the fact that there was anyone on board.

Verlinden drew her knife when the oarsmen started throwing weighted ropes, which curled themselves around the *Perisher*'s railing, but Atreu gestured for her to put it away.

'Are you simply going to let them climb aboard?' asked Verlinden.

'They may not mean us harm,' said Atreu.

'No? Well, I would feel more confident in believing that if they at least acknowledged we were here.'

The men made no attempt to climb onto the *Perisher*. Instead, once all the ropes were secured, they started rowing furiously downstream in the direction they had come from, dragging the *Perisher* with them.

'Hey,' shouted Verlinden. 'Where are you taking us?'

One of the men briefly looked at her, and Atreu could only read his expression as one of utter fear. The others kept their heads down as if their lives depended on it.

It was some time before Atreu realised they were rowing in the direction of the middle of three islands which loomed out at them in the greyness ahead. Soon, he could make out some of the details of the shore, and as they drew closer, his despair grew. The island was little more than a large, almost treeless outcrop of rocks with what appeared to be a small cluster of rude stone houses. The shore was strewn with what Atreu could only guess were the skeletons of dozens of huge river beasts.

'I don't like the look of this at all,' said Verlinden. 'Atreu, I think it would be a good idea if you went to get your knife.'

'I'll get my sword,' said Riell, but stumbled as he took a step in the direction of the aft cabin.

'Let's not be foolish here,' said Atreu. 'Do you really think we could somehow fight our way out of this if they are hostile?'

'Do you have a better plan?' said Verlinden.

'They haven't threatened us yet,' said Atreu.

'You can say that right up until someone lunges at you with a weapon,' said Verlinden, 'but by that time, it's too late.'

'These are Maelir,' said Atreu. 'I just don't feel that we have to assume Maelir are hostile.'

'That's what I've always had to do.'

They became aware that one oarsman from each of the six boats was now climbing up the ropes onto the *Perisher*.

'Here they come,' said Verlinden. 'You still think they bear us no ill?'

The oarsmen continued to act as if no one was on board. They quickly used the fore and aft winches to drop anchor. Once the anchors had been secured, their demeanor changed, however, and one of the men approached Riell and Atreu.

'You've been blown by the ills – I can see.'

'Yes,' said Atreu. 'Our captain is below. She bore the brunt of it. Can you help her?'

'She? Her?' He shuddered as if touched by a spectre. 'She'll be no captain, her.' He gave Verlinden a side glance. 'Is she fire hair like this one?'

'No, she has dark hair,' said Atreu.

The oarsman seemed to be a little relieved.

'My name is –' Atreu had his sentence cut short by a sharp blow to the head.

Verlinden drew her knife and was almost at the oarsman's throat when he quickly backed away with his palms up. 'No names on board,' he said. 'Names are for the shore. Please come with us.'

'You want us to come with you?' asked Riell.

'Yes, we can cure the ill-wind.'

'I'm not sure if I can make it into your boats,' said Riell, as he watched the other oarsmen lower the *Perisher*'s ladders.

'They're not boats – they're currachs. We will help you.'

'And Aeshya, our captain?'

'Yes – the captain as well.'

Atreu and Verlinden grabbed their packs and climbed down the rope ladder into one of the waiting currachs. Atreu was amazed at how fragile the oarsmen's boats were. With their thin ribbing of wood and high prow, they were unlike any boat he had seen. It seemed impossible that any less than three dozen of them could have combined to tow a ship the size of the *Perisher*, but he had seen it with his own eyes.

The oarsmen helped Riell into the currach and lifted down the still-unconscious Aeshya as they had said they would, then they rowed to shore in silence. The thin hull of the currachs enabled them to glide almost onto the stony beach. Atreu was relieved to find that what he had thought were huge riverbeast bones were merely the skeletal remains of the ribbing of boats.

Once the oarsmen's feet touched shore, their demeanor softened still further. The one who had hit Atreu approached him and said, 'The name is Inish – welcome to the Bleak Isles. I'm most sorry for blocking your name, but names are not for boats.'

'I see,' said Atreu. 'Is it all right if we tell you ours now?'

Inish nodded, and Atreu quickly introduced himself and the others. The oarsman still seemed to find it difficult to look Verlinden in the eye.

'There is a truce, you know,' said Atreu, 'between Maelir and Faemir.'

'A truce – what is that?' asked Inish, as he and the others locked their oars into place.

Atreu scratched his head. 'When two sides in a war decide together to end the fighting.'

'A war?'

'You ... you don't know of the war that has ravaged the Mountain?'

'There's been no war on the Bleak Isles. We have no time for such things.'

Atreu looked at him in amazement. How isolated were these people, here in the middle of the Maelstrom? 'You must know of the war, and that the Mountain is now under dire threat from the Nazir?'

'The who?'

'The Dusk People,' said Atreu. 'We know very little of them, but they emerge only at night and are gaining control all over the Mountain.'

'The currachsmen have control of the Bleak Isles,' said Inish. 'That's all that matters. All those who step on our shores have our goodwill and hospitality. We live in the wake of the ill-wind and we have n'er met an enemy that can cause us more grief.'

A low, moaning wind blew across the rock-strewn island as the currachsmen led them towards a cluster of stone houses set back from the shore. Riell was propped up by one of the men as he walked, and two others carried Aeshya.

'This is my hame,' said Inish, quickly unstacking a loosely

packed pile of rocks which obviously functioned as a door to his house.

Atreu noticed that Riell and Aeshya were being taken further.

'My son, Tharan, will shelter them,' said Inish. 'He has this year come of age and has taken a hame and a weer. He is known among us for his healing.'

Atreu and Verlinden were welcomed inside by a woman with a weather-worn face who introduced herself as Inishweer. A low, strange-smelling fire burnt in one corner, and once Inish had replaced the door-rocks, the two-roomed house warmed slightly.

'We have food with us,' said Atreu, when it became clear that Inishweer was about to serve them stew from the pot that hung over the fire.

Inish glared at him. 'I don't want to strike you twice today,' he said, his voice a growl.

'He did not mean to offend,' said Verlinden quickly. 'It's just that you appear to have so little.'

Inish did not look at Verlinden, and instead took a step towards Atreu.

'I mean no offence,' said Atreu quickly. 'I would be honoured to share your meal with you.'

The words seemed to appease Inish, and he nodded slowly while Inishweer passed the plates of stew. Atreu and Verlinden followed the currachsman's lead and sat down on the floor to eat, with the plates in their laps.

Verlinden spooned her stew half-heartedly for a while, and then said, 'I realise we are your guests, and are most grateful for this ...' She waited for Inish to acknowledge her, but when he didn't, she continued, '... and we have no wish to offend your customs ... but I believe you also have a duty not to offend your guests.'

Inishweer nearly choked on her stew.

The room was silent as Inish placed his spoon on his plate and swallowed his mouthful. 'Currachsweers do not speak in such ways,' he said, still not looking at Verlinden.

'I am not a currachsweer. I am a Faemir.'

Inish took some time to respond. 'I see – you are the ones we now have a truce with.' He put another spoonful of stew into his mouth, then asked, 'How does a Faemir hame compare to a currach's hame?'

'We have no home,' said Verlinden.

Inish looked at her for the first time. 'You know, sailors who we rescue and bring ashore always hold pity for us. They can have the wind raging in their heads with a fury that barely lets them think, but they always hold pity for the currachsmen.'

'I hold no pity,' said Verlinden.

'Ar, I see. You have less than I, so how can you pity?' He took several more spoonfuls before he spoke again. 'You have the fire hair – it is an ill-omen.'

'It is my hair that offends you?'

'Not offends.' His voice regained its gruff edge. 'It is an ill-omen. We fight the winds in many ways on the Bleak Isles. An ill-omen gives the wind power against us.'

'So you think red hair gives the ill-wind strength?' asked Atreu.

'First they pity, then they disbelieve,' said Inish. 'It is always the same. You'll see soon enough – like all the others.'

'What do you mean?' asked Atreu.

'You will learn.'

Inishweer offered them all watery tea.

'Do your women speak?' asked Verlinden.

'Ar, we do,' said Inishweer. She shot a glance at Inish. 'But with a currachsman like mine, it is not always easy to find the time to squeeze in my own words.'

'It sounds to me like you're fortunate not to have red hair,' said Verlinden.

A faint smile almost passed onto Inishweer's lips. 'This tea will help you clear your mind of the ill-wind.'

'Thank you,' said Verlinden, taking a sip. Immediately, she felt as if her nostrils had widened and she was taking in air that cleared her head of the echoes that had been troubling her for the last few days.

'My man believes in all the omens,' said Inishweer, ignoring Inish, who was glaring at her as he drank tea from his mug. 'Weers on boats do not please him. Think yourself fortunate that you were not bare-footed as well – that would have brought all manner of calamity down upon us.'

'You know it is foolish to even speak of such things,' said Inish.

Inishweer continued addressing Verlinden. 'It is ill to speak in a currach – you would have noticed that –'

'Enough!' Inish slapped his hand on his knee. 'My weer's tongue is foolish.'

Atreu and Verlinden finished their tea, and Inishweer indicated the blankets in one corner of the room for them to sleep on. Inish and Inishweer bade them good night and disappeared into the back room. As he held Verlinden closely for warmth, Atreu thought for a moment that he heard muffled laughter, but soon the only sound was soft snoring coming through the wall.

'What strange people these currachs are,' whispered Atreu. 'And to live in a place that is so untouched by what is happening on the Mountain – I can barely understand their lives and how they think.'

'Are the Bleak Isles any stranger or more isolated than the Keep?' said Verlinden.

'But these people have no idea who the Faemir are. I suspect if I told them I was an Ascender, it would be meaningless to them.'

'It's what's in their hearts that matters,' said Verlinden.

'And what is that?' asked Atreu. 'What do these people want from us?'

'I don't know. Do you know what sort of tea that was?'

'No, but my head feels clearer than any time since we emerged from the ill-wind.'

'Do you trust these people?' asked Verlinden.

Atreu shifted slightly. 'I would like to, but nothing since I started my Ascent has been what it seems, and I no longer feel sure that anyone acts except for their own good.'

'Don't you find that sad?'

'Perhaps the truth is sad.'

Verlinden yawned and buried her head further in Atreu's chest. 'I'm not going to concern myself with the world's problems tonight. We're warm, and we're together – does much else matter just now?'

Atreu stroked her neck in response. Soon he was aware of Verlinden's rhythmic breathing. The fire was still burning low, but showed no signs of dying. In the red-tinged light his gaze wandered from the wild jumble of bare dry-stone that formed the walls of the currach's house to the crude rye-thatching in the roof. What if the truth he sought was a sad one? They were the last words he had shared with Verlinden before she had fallen asleep. But did he believe them? What if he did finally come to the ultimate Truth of his Ascent, and it revealed nothing but sadness? The thought struck home for the first time. He had always assumed that while the path to the Truth was an ordeal, achieving it would be a joyous thing. Was that the last piece of naïvety in him that had to be discarded? Would he have to accept that the Mountain was a place where no one acted out of good-heartedness, that any kindness or nobility was merely an appearance, masking selfish drives?

Was he thinking more clearly now than he ever had? Or were the vestiges of the ill-wind still gusting around his thoughts? Was the ultimate Truth worth finding, or would it have been better for him to have kept the naïve delusions of Atreu from Valesend who had just set out on his Ascent?

He reached across into his pack, taking care not to disturb Verlinden, and pulled out first his Book and then the Book of Maelur. Turning to the first page of the Book of Maelur, he read the opening words in the dull firelight:

I write this for the generations to come so that they may learn of the great Mountain which is the axis of the universe, its spirit the heart of the world. And as with any heart, when it is broken it cries in pain for what has been lost, and when it is mended it cries in joy for what has been regained.

The opening words were still there in the changed form that he and Praether had uncovered. The Book spoke to all the generations to come, not just future Maelir. Atreu knew his Truth: for the heart to be mended and the joy to be regained, the rift between the Maelir and Faemir had to be healed. That was happening slowly, but he sensed now that it wasn't enough. Maelur's opening words had still more meaning to be revealed. He reread them to be certain nothing had changed. No, every word was as it had been since he and Praether had opened both Books together for the first time. Their meaning nagged at him now, though. Was there something else that was there for him?

He opened his own Book and riffled through the pages of incomprehensible words until his eye was caught by his uncle's name ...

*

Micah could almost feel the stars glinting overhead as he climbed the last steps onto the Sky-reach platform. Collapsing into a sitting position, he heaved in deep breaths as Sethor concentrated on the reflections in the water and furiously worked on a chart. By the time the sky-watcher had finished, Micah's breathing had eased enough that he could speak.

'Well, I can't say I thank you for drawing me into this, Micah,' said Sethor, 'but I think I have uncovered something far more dire than you ever suspected.'

'So a crime has been committed?'

'I believe so – but this is something far more monstrous than you could imagine.'

'I must have evidence if I am to bring allegations against Leyvin,' said Micah. 'I want the Circle to be told the full truth.'

'Ah, the full truth, Micah. You think you are talking about the full truth, but you don't even begin to comprehend what I have uncovered.'

'If the First Speaker plotting to endanger the only two remaining Ascenders and the leader of the windriders isn't a sufficiently monstrous act for you, then I'm not sure what could be.'

Sethor shook his head. 'I'm not surprised that you can't conceive of anything worse. You low-Liche are so caught up in entanglements of your own making that you can't see the truth in the heavens.'

'Sethor, I have heard your thoughts on our activities before.' Micah stood up and walked towards the chart table. 'If you think all this is beneath you, then I won't argue the point. As you know, Atreu is my nephew, and I was his sage during his Ascent. This is more to me than a blind search for truth. I have disappointed many people in the past, but I feel I have disappointed Atreu most of all. He is more dear to me than anyone, yet I have lied and misled him. This betrayal strikes at my heart.' He leant across the chart table. 'Sethor, I need to know what has happened.'

'All right, Micah, I will tell you what I have uncovered, but there is far more to these missing charts than either of us could have guessed.'

'So, is there a forgery on the sky-watcher's log?'

'No, I believe the signature is Leylan's.'

'So Leylan was here at the start of his watch?'

'I'm almost certain of it.'

'So Leyvin climbed up the Sky-reach tower to persuade Leylan to carry Verlinden to the Source?'

'No, he was flown up by someone.'

'Leylan?'

'No, Leylan was already here drawing charts.'

'Then who? If we knew who it was, we would have evidence against Leyvin.' Micah tapped his hands on the chart table. 'The windriders should be returning from their mission with the Faemir in a few days. Then we'll know.'

'No – we won't.'

Micah stopped tapping. 'What do you mean, we won't. There will be a few windriders staying with the Faemir for the attack from the Maelstrom, but most will be returning to the Keep. Who was the windrider who carried Leyvin up to the sky-tower that night?'

'Riell.'

'What?'

'I can't be absolutely certain, but all the evidence points to Riell carrying Leyvin up very early that eve.'

'How, then, could Leyvin have persuaded both Leylan and Riell to carry the Ascenders when the evidence indicating that a dangerous storm was imminent was right in front of them?'

'I don't think he could have done that.'

Micah frowned. 'You're not making any sense.'

'I think I am,' said Sethor, smiling. 'I have reflected on Leylan's performance as a novice sky-watcher and have studied the charts that Leylan had worked on in the past, and there is an important clue there.'

'And?'

'I've actually already given you a clue about what I'm going to say.'

'If you have, I've missed it.'

Sethor was still smiling at Micah's exasperation. 'All right, since you can't work it out for yourself – Leylan was prone, particularly under stress or time pressure, to making the classic error of novice sky-watchers. As you know, the charts are not made directly from the skies but from their reflection in the water. Everything is in *mirror image* of reality, and it takes a great deal of experience to be fully aware of the implications of this. Leylan made the mistake that novices often make – it appeared to him as if the storm front was moving rapidly *away* from the Keep, rather than towards it. He saw no danger.'

'But how did Leyvin know that Leylan's interpretation of the charts was incorrect?'

'The evidence of the brewing storm was present in the previous two shifts. The timing of its movement was still unclear at that stage, but there was at least a possibility that it would move through quickly. Aremin remembers Leyvin questioning him about it after his watch, but he says it all seemed innocent at the time.'

Micah stroked his beard. 'Leyvin didn't know that Leylan would misread the skies, but he knew there was some chance that he would. He had nothing to lose. The subtlety is beyond anything I've ever come across.'

'Nothing surprises me about the low-Liche.'

'So it was easy for Leyvin to persuade him and Riell to carry the Ascenders,' said Micah. 'Without talking to Riell or Leylan, though, we won't be able to prove that Leyvin was at fault. Do you have anything you can offer me as proof?'

The sky-watcher looked at the reflection of the starscape in the pool of water. 'I'm going to have to begin the next chart soon.'

Micah bit his top lip in an attempt to maintain his control. 'Don't make me beg, Sethor. I need your help.'

'I've done what I can. The crime is in Leyvin's persuasive powers – those sorts of things are considered a virtue in the Circle, aren't they? Perhaps his intention originally was to simply persuade Riell that the windrider to carry the Faemir Ascender should be Leylan. Leyvin knew Leylan was unhappy as a windrider and that some would even say Leylan was disturbed. He certainly knew that Leylan was probably the least skilled of any windriders with full rank. He didn't want to give the Faemir much chance of making it to the Source.'

'And the storm was an extra opportunity that presented itself, and which he exploited,' said Micah. 'That's the way he has always worked.'

Sethor began unrolling another scroll.

'I thank you for your help,' said Micah. 'From what you have told me, I believe a crime has been committed, albeit far more devious than I had anticipated. And I shouldn't have expected anything so crude from Leyvin. I can assure you that I will do what I can to hold Leyvin to account for his actions.'

'You know, Micah, I have said from the start that it doesn't concern me. I suppose I should be the one thanking you.'

'Why? Is this more sarcasm?'

'No, Micah. I understand our motivations are divergent, but your request has led me to a close examination of all the recent charts, and as I said to you before, I believe something far more sinister than you would ever be able to conceive of has occurred.'

'Well, are you going to tell me, Sethor?'

The sky-watcher dipped his quill in the ink and started working on his next chart. 'I will need two more nights to confirm it without a shadow of a doubt.'

'Confirm what?'

'Ah, Micah, I see you are suddenly interested in my charts again.' He made several more marks before looking up. 'I will reveal all once I am certain. I cannot afford to make a mistake.'

'Does it concern Leyvin?'

Sethor laughed. 'How narrow your focus is. The answer is yes, it will concern Leyvin – it will concern all of us.' His eyes widened. 'In fact, it could destroy all of us.'

'I think you overestimate your work a little, Sethor.'

Sethor almost choked.

Micah went to go.

'I'll give you a clue,' said Sethor.

'No games for me now, please. I have a long descent ahead of me.'

'Tomorrow is the winter solstice, the longest night and the shortest day. There's your clue. You missed my clue about the reflection – try to work this one out.'

'I'm sure I have greater things to exercise my mind than grappling with obscure clues to matters which may be of great import to you, but which probably mean nothing to me. I bid you farewell, Sethor, and leave you to your charts.'

'Ah, Micah, you are not nearly as clever as you believe you are.

You are trying to goad me into telling you by feigning lack of interest.'

'You're right,' Micah said, and disappeared down the ladder.

*

Atreu let his Talisman drop down on his chest. His eyes were heavy from reading in the low firelight. So things were afoot at the Keep, and Micah was at the centre of it. Atreu knew Micah would do what he could, but he suspected that only when Riell returned to the Keep would the case against Leyvin have a chance of standing. For some reason, though, it was the impending doom that Sethor was predicting that struck a chord with Atreu. Somehow, Sethor had come across something of significance. If only Atreu could find out what that was.

He went to pick up his Book again, but felt a weariness overwhelm him. Solstice, it had something to do with the winter solstice. Was that really tomorrow? Where had all the days since Equinox disappeared to? He fell into a half sleep to the sound of the wind whistling across the bare rocks of the Bleak Isles.

For a moment, he felt the sun of Zenith on his face. He sat perched high atop a pillar with his eyes wide open, staring straight into the sun. Although he saw clearly at first and the rays warmed him, before long he could feel the light burning into his eyes. Yet he couldn't look away – it was as if his muscles had turned to rock. Finally, his vision started to darken. Was he going blind? What do you sacrifice when you stare too long into the clarity of the sun? Slowly, the black spot before him started to grow. He strained to turn away, but couldn't. He tried to close his eyes, but it was as if he had no eyelids. His final instinct was to scream, but that too was taken by the dark.

Just as his vision was about to plunge into total blackness, he became aware of Verlinden's soft breathing. He held himself closely into her warmth, and finally fell into a dreamless sleep, barely aware of the tremor that shook the rocks beneath him.

Chapter Eighteen

On the third afternoon on the Bleak Isles, Aeshya regained her sanity. Riell had watched Tharan and Tharansweer wrap bandages soaked in currachs-tea three times every day and three times every night. When Aeshya's eyes had opened on the second day, Tharansweer had propped her up so that she could sip the brew – at first so tentatively that it barely wet her lips. After a time, as the ill-wind faded, her mind narrowed sharply into focus.

'Where is the *Perisher*?' was her first question.

'It lives,' said Tharan.

Aeshya recoiled from the currachsman as if he were some phantom from the helles.

Riell tried to calm her. 'We are safe in the home of Tharan, on the Bleak Isles.'

'Here, the tea will help,' said Tharansweer, offering a steaming mug.

Aeshya lashed out in an attempt to knock the mug out of Tharansweer's hand, but only succeeded in spilling some of it.

Riell tried to calm her. 'Please, Aeshya, these people have rescued us.'

'I don't want any of their poison,' she said sharply.

Riell turned to Tharan. 'I'm sorry for –'

'No matter,' said Tharan. 'The ill-wind blows minds in ways that are hard to fathom.'

'I want the *Perisher* back,' said Aeshya.

'We cannot return what we haven't taken,' said Tharan.

'The currachsmen have been repairing our main mast,' said Riell. 'It didn't survive the ill-wind.'

Aeshya seemed taken aback. 'You're repairing it?'

'Ar, it won't last another trip through the helles,' said Tharan, 'but it may make do until Farepont.'

There was a whistle outside and Riell could see the rocks that formed the entrance to Tharanshame being removed. Inish entered, followed by Atreu and Verlinden.

Atreu nodded at Aeshya. 'Inish said you would be well this morning. He had a lot of faith in Tharan's healing powers.'

'What have you promised to trade these people for my mind?' asked Aeshya.

'Nothing,' said Atreu. 'Inish has just told me that the *Perisher* will be ready for us to sail out tomorrow.'

Aeshya eyed Inish suspiciously. 'What sort of people are you?'

'Currachsmen,' said Inish.

'What do you want of us?' asked Aeshya.

Inish and Tharan exchanged a glance. 'That question we are asked by every sailor we save from the ills,' said Inish. 'We can never answer it.'

'Well, I want to see my boat,' said Aeshya, standing up suddenly, then feeling a weakness in her thighs. Riell reached out to steady her, and although she made a half-hearted attempt at brushing away his help, she let him hold her.

'Take her to the boat,' said Tharan. 'Movement helps clear away the ills.'

'The fishers will be returning soon,' said Inish, glancing from Aeshya to Verlinden, and then addressing Atreu. 'Keep these two away when the currachs come in.'

'We would bring them ill-fortune if we went near their precious boats,' explained Verlinden, when she saw Aeshya's confusion. 'Just be thankful your hair is black.'

*

Riell, Atreu and Verlinden took it in turns to help Aeshya as they made their way to a rocky outcrop that jutted out into the water in the direction of the *Perisher*. The wind gusted around them, and the air was grey with low, swirling clouds. Now and then Atreu felt what he thought was a tremor beneath him, but each time, he convinced himself it was a trick of the waves on the rocks.

'I can't see what they've done to the *Perisher* from here,' said Aeshya as she strained to look at the main mast.

'They say they've bound the mast,' said Atreu.

'Why should we accept what they tell us is true?' asked Aeshya.

'Why should we assume it is a lie?' asked Riell. 'These people have not only done us no harm, they have given us everything they have to offer – and it's not as if they have an overabundance of anything here.'

'I think you've been in the clouds too often, Riell,' said Aeshya. 'In my experience on the river, no one just gives you help without wanting something in return.'

'I think that applies in most places I've seen,' said Atreu, 'but give these currachsmen a chance. Speak to them. You may find yourself changing your mind.'

'I'll keep my mind my own, thank you,' said Aeshya. 'I'm too grateful to have it back for me to think about changing it.'

'Here come the fishers,' said Atreu, pointing to some black points emerging from the grey, just to the right of where the *Perisher* was anchored.

The currachs, with their high, curved prows, seemed to slide from the grip of the waves rather than challenge them head-on, the slender oars in each boat gliding together in one smooth action.

'So you really believe these people will simply bid us farewell tomorrow?' asked Aeshya.

'I would like to believe that they can be trusted,' said Atreu.

Aeshya gave a derisive laugh. 'There are many things I would wish to be true. That wish can be the most dangerous of all. Look at the way they live – they have no sails in their boats, and there doesn't even appear to be enough wood on the isle to build doors for their houses. The *Perisher* would be a great prize for them.'

'They have rescued us,' said Riell, 'given us shelter, food and healing – and you don't trust them?'

'No,' said Aeshya. 'They want something from us – mark my words. Don't be surprised if they drug us all tonight.'

'You can't possibly think there is a real danger,' said Riell. 'I've seen Tharan and his wife change your bandages day and night since we arrived on their shores.'

Aeshya's jaw was firmly set. 'I for one won't be eating or drinking anything tonight – and I'll be lying awake with my knife at my side until morning.'

'I have little cause to trust any Maelir,' said Verlinden, 'but why would the currachsmen heal you in order to kill you?'

'I don't pretend to understand them,' said Aeshya, 'but I've heard stories of strange isle-dwellers who are so superstitious they sacrifice people to the Maelstrom.'

'I think your mind is still a little addled,' said Atreu.

'Perhaps,' said Aeshya, 'but in my experience, no one helps you unless they have something to gain from it. The only way to deal with people is to know what they want.'

Their attention was taken by the currachs as they glided onto the rocky beach. Atreu sensed immediately that something was not quite right. The steady rhythm of the oars was quickly replaced by a disorderly disembarkation. The currachsmen clustered into a large group and, no longer held by the silence of their currachs, immediately began an animated discussion. Inish, Tharan and several of the other currachsmen who had remained on the isle soon joined the fishers on the beach. Occasionally, several faces would turn to the rocky outcrop where Atreu and the others sat, and fingers would be pointed.

'I don't like the look of this,' said Aeshya. 'We need to find out what they are talking about.' She went to get up, but Atreu held her back.

'Wait,' he said. 'You and Verlinden stay here. We don't want to offend them.'

Verlinden got up. 'I'm going with you. If my presence near their precious boats offends them, then that's not my concern.'

Aeshya nodded and pulled Atreu's hand away from her.

The four of them got up and made their way to where the fishers were still engaged in discussion.

As they approached, there were a series of cries.

''Tis the fire-hair.'

'Take the weers away.'

'More ill-omens.'

Atreu singled out Inish. 'What has happened?' he asked.

Inish glared at Verlinden and Aeshya. 'The weers must go,' he said. 'Take them.'

Verlinden met his gaze. 'No one takes me anywhere against my will.'

Several currachsmen muttered under their breath, but made no move towards Verlinden.

Atreu could feel the tension build in the silence.

Inish, Tharan and two other currachsmen broke away from the cluster and walked slowly towards where Atreu and the others stood.

'We truly don't mean to offend –' began Atreu, but before he could finish his sentence, the men had surrounded them and had locked their hands behind them in a vice-like grip.

Atreu struggled, but the currachsmen's arms were as hard as rocks.

'Never trust anyone who appears to help you for no reason,' said Aeshya bitterly as they were marched to an empty outer building of the village.

Once inside, their hands and feet were tied and they were left. Atreu could soon feel his hands numbing from the growing cold and the constriction of the restraints.

'Aren't you Faemir meant to be great warriors?' said Aeshya. 'I've barely recovered from the ill-wind, but I would have expected you to put up more of a fight.'

'It was so unexpected,' said Verlinden. 'And that grip – I've never experienced anything like it.'

'Perhaps we've all learnt our lesson now?' said Aeshya.

'I'm not sure about that,' said Riell. 'They still haven't actually harmed us.'

Aeshya laughed hollowly. 'You don't call imprisonment harming us?'

It had grown so dark that they couldn't see each other's faces anymore when the sound of approaching footsteps could be heard. A figure carrying a torch entered the building – it was Inish. The currachsman held all their packs in his other hand. He threw them on the ground next to Atreu, then commenced lighting a fire.

'There may be food in our packs,' said Atreu, 'but we can't eat it with our hands tied.'

Inish grunted a reply.

'All right,' said Verlinden. 'I am sorry I didn't stay away from your currachs.'

'It is too late now,' said Inish.

'What do you mean, too late?' asked Atreu.

'Fire-hair on the water, weers captaining ships – there were too many ill omens.'

'What has happened?' asked Atreu.

Inish didn't answer for some time. Finally, he said, 'Two fishers have fallen into the water today.'

'And?' Atreu left the question hanging.

'Did you not hear me? The Maelstrom has taken two currachsmen.'

'You said they fell into the water,' said Atreu. 'Could they not have been rescued?'

Atreu could see genuine puzzlement on Inish's face. 'There are no rescues for currachsmen in the water,' he said.

'What are you saying?' said Riell. 'The other fishers let them drown?'

'Ar – the Maelstrom takes its own.'

'What nonsense are you talking?' said Aeshya. 'I've seen many men drown, but how can you ignore someone desperately trying to keep their head above water?'

'There is no desperation,' said Inish. 'Currachsmen know to let the Maelstrom take them.'

Aeshya said, 'Are you saying that your people would not swim to save their lives?'

Inish's brow was furrowed in the torchlight. 'Currachsmen cannot swim,' he said. 'It is the Maelstrom's right to take us.'

'My mind may have been addled by the ill-wind,' said Aeshya, 'but your people must permanently border on madness.'

'It is our way,' said Inish calmly. 'Our currachs don't challenge the waves, and we do not challenge the Maelstrom. We almost n'er lose a currachsman, but today we lost two.'

'And you think it is because of me?' said Verlinden.

'You are an ill-omen – ar.'

'You can't blame me for that,' said Verlinden. 'The waters of the Maelstrom can be unpredictable, can't they?'

Inish could barely bring himself to look at her. 'Two currachsmen. Did you not hear me? We have never lost two in the one day. The fishers tell me there were unnatural waves.'

'Unnatural waves?' said Aeshya.

'Ar – we know the Maelstrom, and these were waves of the like we have n'er seen.'

'I can't see how I could –' Verlinden was interrupted by Atreu.

'Has anyone felt any impermanence since we arrived on the Bleak Isles?' he asked.

'I can't be certain,' said Riell, 'but, yes, I think I have.'

'Impermanence?' said Inish, as he took out blankets for each of them. 'What is this?'

It was Atreu's turn to look bewildered. 'Are you saying you have had no shaking of the ground here? No chasms forming? No pillars coming out of the ground?'

'No, these things don't happen on the Bleak Isles.'

'This must be one of the few places on the Mountain where there is no instability,' said Riell. 'Everywhere else, things are being torn apart.'

'But I've been feeling something,' said Atreu. 'That could explain the unnatural waves. Couldn't it?'

Inish nodded. 'Perhaps shaking ground under the river could cause them, ar.'

'Then that's your explanation,' said Atreu. 'It's the instability – it has nothing to do with Verlinden.'

Inish thought about it for a moment. 'Even if this is true, the others will say you have brought it with you. It is the same in the end.'

'Do you think it's the same?' asked Atreu.

'N'er in one day has the Maelstrom taken two currachsmen. N'er has a flame-haired weer been carried by a currach. The ill-omen is clear.'

'You really believe that?' Verlinden spat out the words.

'I believe what I see.'

'But you didn't see the unnatural waves,' said Atreu. 'You didn't see what happened to the two currachsmen, did you?'

'No, 'tis true.'

'So you're accepting the word of the fishers.'

'What do you say? Currachsmen are true.'

'I don't doubt that they tell the truth,' said Atreu, 'but could they have been mistaken in what they saw?'

'A currachsman knows riverwaves. They are our lives.'

'But you didn't *see* them,' said Atreu. 'You said you believe what you see.'

Inish hesitated.

'What have you seen of the Mountain outside the Bleak Isles?' asked Verlinden.

'The Bleak Isles are our hame.'

'But what else have you seen?'

'I can see the riverbanks and beyond.'

'Have you never stood on the bank and wondered what there was past the horizon?'

'Currachsmen n'er stand on the bank.'

'Are you telling me you don't leave the Maelstrom?' asked Verlinden.

'What about Hellespont upstream or Farepont downstream?' asked Atreu.

'The Bleak Isles are our hame.'

'So the Maelstrom around the Bleak Isles is all you've seen?' said Atreu.

'Ar.'

'It takes a year to travel the Mountain from the Base to the Summit,' said Atreu. 'There are countless villages and towns on it, and cities a hundredfold, some one hundred times the size of this isle.'

'I have heard tales, but n'er believed them.'

'Because you haven't seen them – right?'

'Ar.'

'But I have seen these towns and cities,' said Atreu. 'At least some of them – because I don't think there is a Maelir alive who has seen one hundredth of what the Mountain is. But I have seen many things. I have seen what the instability can do. I've seen the pillars coming out of the ground in front of me as I walk. I've seen huge holes opening up and giant beasts climbing out into the night.' He looked intently at Inish. 'Do you say I'm not true?'

Inish's weatherworn face was impassive, but Atreu could see something in his eyes.

'Do you say I'm not true?' repeated Atreu.

'Two currachsmen were taken by the Maelstrom in one day.' Inish wasn't blinking. 'Currachsmen know the Maelstrom and they know waves. These were waves the likes of which were n'er seen.'

'I believe your words are true,' said Atreu, 'but you must believe mine – there is instability all over the Mountain. The few places that have remained untouched, like the Bleak Isles, are eventually all affected. The Nazir have been tunnelling up through the Mountain for generations. They are trying to claim it through a terrible war, and no part of the Mountain is beyond their grasp.'

'Currachsmen will fight to the death anyone who tries to take our hames.'

'The Nazir use beasts and wraiths to fight for them. It will not be a fight where your strength and determination will be enough.' Atreu drew a breath. 'Those deaths today had nothing to do with Verlinden's red hair, or with the *Perisher* having a woman for a river captain, or with any of us. That's the war coming to your isle.'

'This is your war, and you have brought it with you.'

Atreu strained at the cords that bound him in exasperation.

'Forget it,' said Aeshya. 'Riverdwellers are known for their stubbornness, but these currachsmen must be the worst of them all.'

Inish rummaged through the packs for some food. He fed them each dried oatcakes and gave them sips of water from the gourds. Atreu chewed and watched the low, strange-smelling fire the currachsman had lit for them.

Aeshya kept tugging angrily at her cords. 'So,' she said, 'what are you fine currachsmen going to do with us, now that we have caused you so much misfortune?'

'We will decide tonight.'

'You are going to drown us and take our boat, aren't you?' said Aeshya.

'We will decide tonight.'

'Just let us go,' said Riell. 'We will take the *Perisher* and leave your isle tomorrow, just as we had planned to do.'

'The taking of the two currachsmen requires the ill-omens to be put to rest.'

Inish stoked the fire in silence and then got up, as if to go.

'Wait,' said Atreu. Inish cocked his head in his direction as he continued. 'There are some things in my pack that I would like you to get out. Please, two books and a small glimmerstone.'

'Why do you want these things?'

'You say that you believe what you see. I want to show you something.'

'I must return.'

'No, please. You don't realise how important our journey is. We are far from the cause of those deaths today – we are the only ones who can stop them from happening again and again and again.'

'These books and this stone – what are they?'

'Please get them out, and I will tell you.'

'I must return.'

'Wait – please. I'm an Ascender, so is Verlinden. One of the Books is our Talisman.'

'I know nothing of Ascenders or Talismans.'

Atreu was taken aback. 'But you must know something of these things. You must know of the Ascent, and the Holy Orders – the Liche and the Felsen. Riell is a member of the new Order of the Wynde.'

'I know the Bleak Isles. I know the Maelstrom. I know fish, water and waves.'

'But what of Zenith. How do you celebrate it?'

'For the nine days of Zenith, all the currachs battle the helles to show the river our strength. It is the only time when we can defy the Maelstrom.'

'So you recognise Zenith? What happens when twins are born?'

Inish's face dropped in the firelight. He took several deep breaths. 'The twice-born are an ill-omen.'

'What?' said Atreu.

'They are ill – how can the second be fed?'

Atreu felt an icy shiver along his back. He didn't want to hear the answer to the next question, but he knew he had to ask it. 'What happens to the second twin?'

'It is put to rest.' Inish's lip was trembling.

Atreu and Verlinden looked at each other, unable to speak.

'The whole system of the Ascent is based on twins,' said Riell. 'Twins are the basis of the Holy Orders. The Mountain is ruled by twins – are you saying that you kill any second-born twin here on the Bleak Isles?'

Inish looked at the ground.

'Verlinden and I are both identical twins,' said Atreu, trying to regain his composure. 'I was born second to my brother Teyth. Are you saying that your beliefs tell you that if I had been born here, I would have been killed as a baby?'

Inish shook his head impulsively, as if trying to ward off a thought. Finally, he looked up at Verlinden. 'Were you second born?' It was the first time he had addressed her directly.

'I don't know. My sister was taken by Faemir during a raid, and I was somehow saved and taken away to another Maelir village. I have no mother, father or mid-wife who knows of my birth.'

'And you have no hame?'

Verlinden shook her head.

'And what of you?' he asked Riell. 'You are a Holy Man – are you also a twin?'

'Yes.'

'And were you also second born?'

'No,' said Riell flatly, and refused to say anymore.

'Well,' said Aeshya, 'it looks like I'm the only one here who isn't a twin. And the way things appear, there won't even be one of me tomorrow.' She nodded in the direction of the leftover oat-cakes. 'Can I have some more of those before you go?'

Inish fed her another cake. 'I am not a twice born,' he said, 'but Tharan was.'

'You killed your own child for your superstitious beliefs?'

asked Verlinden, suddenly painfully aware of what was growing in her belly.

'It is the currachsmen's way.'

'You are fools,' said Verlinden.

'We are currachsmen.' Inish straightened up and looked at the entrance.

'Don't go yet,' said Atreu. 'I haven't shown you what I wanted to show you. Open the book with the letter A on it.'

'I know nothing of letters.'

'The one on the right, then.'

Inish reached down and opened Atreu's Talisman. As he did, the glimmerstone started glowing. The currachsman stared open-mouthed.

'You see it, don't you?' said Atreu.

'Ar, I see it.'

'Then you believe it? My hands and feet are tied. I can't be playing some trick on you.'

'I have n'er seen the like, but what does this show?'

'I haven't finished,' said Atreu. 'Now open the second Book.'

Inish's hand faltered slightly as he opened the Book of Maelur. He jumped back in shock as the entire room was suddenly bathed in a bright light emanating from the glimmerstone.

'What omen is this?' The currachsman was blinking furiously.

'No omen, Inish,' said Atreu. 'Do you see the power of the two Books compared to one?'

'Ar.'

'The whole Mountain outside the Bleak Isles believes that the twins of life must be brought together. Your beliefs are wrong.'

'Currachsmen's beliefs are true.'

Aeshya grunted in exasperation. 'Give up with this stubborn fool. Let him go back to the others so they can decide our fate. You're wasting your time.'

Atreu said, 'Inish, listen to me. These Books are the truth. We are on a quest for the third Book which matches these. Imagine what the third Book will do. I believe it will bring peace to the Mountain.'

'A thrice-born Book?'

'Yes, if you want to think of it that way. Twins are special, but the thrice born, the third way, is the ultimate truth.'

'I have spent too much time here.' Inish made sure they all had blankets wrapped around them. 'The fire will help keep you warm until the morn.'

'Keep us warm tonight so that we can die tomorrow,' said Aeshya. 'Could you close one of those books – the light is hurting my eyes.'

As Inish closed the Book of Maelur, and the light dimmed, a thought struck Atreu. 'How old is Tharan?' he asked.

'My son has come of age – he is eighteen years.'

'And you said that he has special healing powers?'

'Yes, he can ward away the ill-winds unlike anyone on the Bleak Isles.'

Atreu nodded. 'He's a twin in his eighteenth year. He should be on his Ascent.'

'You're right,' said Riell. 'Tharan should be climbing to the Summit as an Ascender.'

'Currachsmen do not climb Mountains,' said Inish. 'They row currachs.'

'At least tell him what I have told you tonight,' said Atreu.

Inish nodded imperceptibly. Without turning around, he said, 'Until the morn,' and then he was gone.

After a moment, Riell said, 'These people are so set in their ways – I can't believe what I heard tonight.'

'Are the currachsmen the only ones set?' asked Atreu.

'That's a strange thing to say. These people are so superstitious they kill every second-born twin.'

Atreu shifted uncomfortably. 'Is what we do so different? Of all the Maelir twins born the same year as me, I am the only one alive. If the Ascenders had never left their towns and villages, at least some of them would still be alive.'

'Atreu, I am used to you thinking some strange thoughts, but what you are saying is outrageous.'

'Is it?'

'The twins died in the pursuit of truth. How can you compare that to the currachsmen's talk of ill-omens?'

'They believe their way is true.'

'That doesn't make it so.'

'Nor does our belief.'

'What are you saying, Atreu – that you place our Holy Orders on the same level with these omen-fearers?'

'No, Riell – but I am questioning whether it is all as clear as it seems. These currachsmen are decent people. You have to see that.'

'Decent people who are going to kill us in the morning because I have red hair,' said Verlinden.

'I don't think they will,' said Atreu.

'You believe that little show with the Books and the glimmerstone will work?' asked Riell.

'That, and a few of the things I said.'

'Have you three finished with your little discussion now?' asked Aeshya.

Atreu looked at her. 'You've been quiet. Don't you care what happens to us?'

'Of course, I do. I care enough to do something about it.' Aeshya pulled her hands from behind her back to show that she had managed to free herself of the cords.

'How did you manage that?' asked Atreu, open-mouthed.

'No knots are tight enough to bind me. If you had let him go earlier, we would already be safely downriver.' She was now working at the ropes on her feet.

'I wish you had told us you were good with knots,' said Verlinden.

'It's better that you didn't know – that way you couldn't give me away.' Aeshya stood up and started untying Verlinden's cords.

'You think we can get away from the Bleak Isles the way we did from Hellespont?' said Atreu.

'Of course. The *Perisher* is a fast ship, and from what I've seen of the repair work on the mast, it will hold.'

'These currachs are very fast,' said Atreu, as she started on his cords. 'And we won't be escaping from drunken sailors this time.'

'It sounds to me like you want to take your chances with this meeting they are having.'

'I don't know,' said Atreu. 'I don't think their decision is obvious.'

Aeshya had now untied all of them and was putting her blanket in her pack. 'You suit yourself. Do what you want – I'm sailing the *Perisher* to Farepont, with or without you.'

Riell and Verlinden got up. 'Come on, Atreu,' said Riell, 'these are twin killers. No matter what you see in them, their lives are ruled by blind superstition.'

'The Faemir were twin killers not so long ago,' said Atreu, 'but things change.' He got up and started filling his pack. When he closed his Book, the glow from the glimmerstone faded immediately.

The four of them stepped outside into the frigid night. Above them, the stars sparkled in a cold brightness, and Atreu felt the air sting his nostrils as they made their way cautiously down to the shore, taking care to avoid the dull lights of the currachsmen's hames.

Aeshya indicated one of the dozen or so currachs which now sat on the rocky beach.

'Are we just going to take it?' asked Atreu.

'We could swim,' said Aeshya, sarcasm dripping from her tongue, 'but this is a little cold, even for me.'

They lifted the currach. Atreu found it surprisingly light. Once the boat was in the water, they all jumped in, took position on one of the cross benches and started rowing.

'This is the thinnest wood I've ever seen on a boat,' said

Aeshya. 'It's a wonder the Maelstrom doesn't claim more of these currachsmen.'

Once they found their rhythm with the oars, the advantage of the currach became clear as it sped through the water towards the *Perisher*.

Before they were halfway, Atreu became aware of lights moving back on the shore. 'I fear we've been discovered,' he said.

'We need to row faster,' said Aeshya, and they picked up the pace.

Atreu could see that one currach with its full complement of six oarsmen was now in rapid pursuit. The *Perisher* was just in front of them, but the currachsmen were quickly closing the gap.

Aeshya let out a groan and slumped forward.

'What's wrong?' cried Atreu.

'That damned ill-wind,' she uttered between ragged breaths. 'I thought I had recovered.'

'I'm surprised you've made it this far,' said Riell.

Aeshya grunted. 'It always pays to let others think you are in worse condition than you are.' She had somehow managed to find her knife, and the blade shone in the starlight as she held it in her hand.

'You think we're going to fight off six currachsmen?' asked Atreu.

Before anyone could reply, there was a volley of whistling sounds, and Atreu felt a circle of rope suddenly tightening around his chest and pinning his arms to his sides.

'Damn,' cried Aeshya as her knife fell out of her hand and clattered onto the thin wooden bottom of the currach.

Atreu saw that with uncanny accuracy, the currachsmen had thrown nooses around each of them, as well as one around the high prow of the boat. The oarsmen were now doggedly rowing them back to the shore.

Aeshya strained at the cords in an effort to pick up her knife, finally managing to get hold of it again. She leant against the pull of the rope towards Verlinden, who was sitting next to her, and started cutting at her cords. The currachsmen had towed them much of the way back to the Bleak Isles shore when Aeshya finally managed to cut Verlinden free. Verlinden then quickly cut the rope attached to the others, and the one on the prow.

The four of them immediately took position, swung the currach around and started rowing back out to the *Perisher*.

'Here they come again,' cried Atreu. The currachsmen had turned around and were once more in pursuit.

There was another volley of whistles, but this time Aeshya launched her oar into the air just in time for the oncoming ropes to entangle themselves along the long slender handle, rather than hitting their desired targets. The oar bounced against the side of the currach and fell into the water behind them.

Two ropes hit their mark – one on the prow and one around Riell – but Aeshya quickly cut them before they had any effect.

'Let's hope they run out of ropes now,' said Atreu.

He had barely finished his sentence when the whistles shot again through the night air. Aeshya was ready, and flung another oar up to meet them.

Only one rope made it, pinning Verlinden's hands to her chest for a moment before Aeshya cut her free.

'They still haven't given up,' cried Atreu.

The oarsmen were now throwing everything into their rowing, and Atreu could see that two more currachs had been launched. The *Perisher* loomed close, but the currachsmen were bearing down on them. As the lead pursuit boat veered starboard to come up beside them, Aeshya openly brandished her knife in defiance. Atreu could see four of the currachsmen had stood up in anticipation of boarding, each one carrying what looked like a weapon. He thought for a desperate moment to swing an oar at them, but before he could do anything, everything suddenly turned upside down as he was hit by a wall of icy water.

He emerged coughing to see that Aeshya and the four currachsmen had been thrown overboard into the Maelstrom. Both currachs, though oarless and filled with water, amazingly, were still afloat, and Riell, Verlinden and the remaining two currachsmen were soaked, but safe.

Aeshya was swimming towards the *Perisher*, but to Atreu's horror, the four currachsmen in the water, though clearly alive, were making no attempt to stay afloat. One of them was so close to his currach that he could easily have grabbed hold of it – yet he didn't. Atreu desperately searched for a floating oar or piece of rope that he could use to help them, but there was nothing. And by the time he turned back, the men had all disappeared.

'You superstitious fools,' he cried at the remaining two men, who were standing deathly still in their currach. He could see now that they were Inish and Tharan.

The water was calm again after the giant wave, and Atreu, Riell and Verlinden stood in waist-high water in their currach, staring at the two currachsmen. Around them, a hollow silence reigned.

Atreu gestured palm upwards at the waters between them, where the men had drowned. 'Why?' he said softly.

Inish met his gaze with a deep sadness in his eyes. He opened his mouth as if he was about to speak, then changed his mind.

Atreu nodded slowly. 'I know the answer, my friend,' he said. 'You are currachsmen.'

There was a shout from the deck of the *Perisher*, and Atreu looked up to see that Aeshya had climbed up and was now casting a rope in their direction. Riell secured it to the prow of the currach, and Aeshya started winching the boat towards the *Perisher*.

Once they were against the hull, Atreu and the others climbed the rope ladders up onto the deck. Aeshya fired orders to set sail immediately. When he had finished his tasks, Atreu stared down at the water and saw that Inish and Tharan were now being towed back to shore by the two other currachs.

The repaired mast withstood the first gust of wind, and the *Perisher* was on its way downriver. When the tiny torch lights on the shore finally disappeared and the Bleak Isles greyed into the night, Atreu trembled and turned away.

Chapter Nineteen

The Maelstrom narrowed sharply two days downriver of the Bleak Isles. Jagged rocks jutted out of the water midstream and Aeshya had to use all her ability as a river captain to avoid them. She was getting almost no sleep, as Riell was the only one who had acquired enough skills to relieve her for any length of time, and there were large stretches which only Aeshya could navigate. Her task was made worse by strange waves which seemed to come from unexpected angles at unpredictable times. Atreu now had no doubt that these were caused by instability under the river bed. Throughout the short days, he could see evidence of a landscape beyond the Maelstrom ravaged by the most horrific instability. As he stared aghast at the endless leagues of cracked and pitted sur-face, strewn with monstrous corrugated pillars leaning at insane angles, he could only be grateful that it appeared uninhabited – although he could never be certain that it had always been so.

Dusk was gathering as Atreu brought some food and water to Aeshya at the tiller. The air was already frosting around him and the boards of the deck creaked under his feet as he walked.

'Can I take over for a while?' he asked.

Aeshya nodded wearily, her face drawn and her body visibly feeling the strain. 'Just hold her mid-river. We won't come across any rocks for some time. It would be a lot easier if the days weren't quite so short.'

'We're just past the solstice, aren't we? Things should be starting to get better.'

'I don't know, Atreu. I'm too weary to know if it's day or night most of the time. The ill-wind could still be having a lingering effect on us.'

'I can't see how you can just keep going like this,' said Atreu. 'I've already thanked you for everything, but –'

'No more gratitude, please. I was saving my own skin too. Don't worry, I'll find some way you can repay me. I'll make do with this food and water just now.'

She started eating as Atreu took the tiller.

'Are you sure you don't want to take that into the cabin?'

'No, I'll only get warm and fall asleep and possibly never wake up.'

'You know, Aeshya, I am still getting an echo of that horrific shriek in my head from the ill-wind just as I'm falling asleep. It must be worse for you.'

Aeshya nodded. 'I try not to think about it. No wonder those currachsmen were so mad, living the way they do in the wake of that wind.'

Atreu chewed his bottom lip. 'Tell me, what was it like on deck that night? Riell has either blanked it out or simply won't tell me.'

'To be at the brink of madness. How can you put it into words?'

'You knew what it was going to be like, Aeshya. How could you have willingly faced it again?'

Aeshya continued to chew for a while and then swallowed. 'It was much stronger than I remembered it, and far worse than I could have imagined it.'

'We *are* into winter now.'

'Even so – there was a power there that was beyond anything I thought was possible. It's as if something was feeding it.'

Atreu shuddered. 'Did you ... did you see anything?'

Aeshya gave a hollow laugh. 'The helles-phantoms? Yes, I saw them all that night. I heard them all, and I felt them all.'

'What sort of phantoms are they that you can feel them?'

Aeshya threw her head back and closed her eyes for a moment. 'I can hear them again.'

'I'm sorry.'

'No, it's probably better to talk about them – bring them out so that they don't lie so deeply buried inside my head.'

Atreu stared at the waters ahead. 'Did ... did you see the one with only half a face?' His voice sounded tremulous to his own ears.

'You saw half-face?' Aeshya was clearly surprised.

Atreu nodded.

'How? Were you on deck?'

'No – he was at the cabin door ... I thought it was Riell ... and then he was inside –'

'Inside the cabin? I've never heard of the helles-phantoms doing that. They are becoming bold.'

'You speak of them as if they are real.'

'You know the difference between what is real and what isn't?'

'I used to.'

'They say the helles-phantoms are the spirits of crewmen whose minds have been lost to the ill-winds, that the wind itself thrives on madness. Half-face and all the others are pieces of insanity blowing around forever, seeking their soul-brothers to ease their loneliness.'

'That sounds like stories I used to make up for my brother Teyth when ...' A shudder crept through Atreu.

'What's wrong?' asked Aeshya. 'If there's something ahead, I can't see it.'

Atreu drew several deep, steady breaths to try to quell the germ of fear that was multiplying inside him.

'I have enough trouble battling the phantoms inside my own head,' said Aeshya. 'Don't give me more to fear. What's wrong?'

'I ... I just had an insane thought. I ...' Atreu trailed off.

'What is it? It's probably better if you put it into words.'

'Perhaps that's exactly what I can't do.'

'You're not making much sense, Atreu.'

'As I said, it's an insane thought. Completely, totally insane.' He drew several more breaths. 'For some reason, when you were talking about the helles-phantoms, I thought of all the stories I used to tell my brother when we were young.'

'What sort of stories?'

Atreu gulped. 'About the Nazir. Stories that turned out to be true.'

'What?'

'I know ... it makes no sense to think about that.'

'It sounds to me like the ill-wind is still blowing a gale in your head.'

'Perhaps the winds have just blown some phantoms to the surface that were already in there.'

'Who knows how they work?'

'*What was that?*'

'What is the matter with you, Atreu? I think you'd better return the tiller to me.'

Atreu pointed to the right riverbank with a shaking hand, and Aeshya followed the direction of his finger.

On the bank, deep shadows appeared to be forming and reforming in the darkness. Suspended within them were bright eyes the colour of fresh blood.

'Please say they are in my mind,' said Atreu.

'If they are in your mind,' said Aeshya, 'then they are in mine also. What are they? I've never seen their like.'

'I can't be certain,' said Atreu, 'but I believe they are Dusk-wraiths. They are the spawn of the Nazir that have been terrorising the Mountain.'

'Can they get to us?'

'I'm not certain.'

They watched as the shadows seemed to darken and congeal.

To Atreu's horror, a tendril started to snake out from the mass towards them.

'Here – give this to me,' cried Aeshya and grabbed the tiller from him. She swung the *Perisher* away from the oncoming shadow.

'Look out,' cried Atreu, 'there's another one coming from the other side.'

Aeshya compensated, and she and Atreu watched the two tendrils coil their way closer, thinning as they approached. Before they reached the bow of the *Perisher*, the tendrils collapsed and dissipated.

Atreu drew a breath of relief. 'It looks like they can't reach us.'

'Not if we stay mid-river,' said Aeshya, 'but that won't always be possible with some of the rocks we'll encounter soon.'

Trembling, Atreu peered into the darkness as several more tendrils came out from the wraiths on both sides of the river, each of them collapsing and falling well short of the ship.

'You look white,' said Aeshya. 'Go back below deck – I'll keep the tiller.'

'But –'

'Look – I'm the captain here. There's no sense in you being up here. Tell Riell to come up in a few hours. I may need some help by then.'

'You don't know anything about these Dusk-wraiths.'

'I've seen enough to know I just have to keep away from the banks,' she said. 'Just go below – I don't need you talking to me about stories coming true.'

When Atreu returned to the aft cabin, Verlinden and Riell were lying on their bunks with their eyes open. A candle burnt on the small table.

'Something has happened, hasn't it?' asked Verlinden.

'How can you tell?'

'It's in your face.'

'The Dusk-wraiths are out there.'

'What?' Verlinden and Riell both sat up.

Atreu gestured for them to lie down again. 'I think we're safe mid-river. Their reach is limited across the water.'

'And Aeshya can keep us mid-river?' asked Riell.

'Yes – but she wants your help in a few hours. She's exhausted. I think the main danger will be if she falls asleep at the tiller.' Atreu sat down and buried his face in his hands.

'There's more, isn't there?' asked Verlinden.

Atreu nodded into his hands.

'What is it?'

Atreu looked up. 'I have to tell both of you this. It sounds like I'm losing my mind, but I have to tell you.'

Verlinden and Riell waited, the silence punctured only by the creaking of planks.

Atreu finally continued. 'When I was a boy, I used to tell Teyth stories.'

'Stories of what?' asked Verlinden.

'The ones Teyth always wanted to hear were about the Dusk People.'

'So what are you saying?' asked Riell.

'As Aeshya was speaking to me about the helles-phantoms, I suddenly had this thought. It was something in the way that she described them that made me realise I'd been pushing back this idea deep into my mind for a long time. Perhaps it's the ill-wind still at work, but the thought is out now.'

'Atreu, what is it?' asked Verlinden.

'Those stories – I was making them up, or at least I thought I was.' He drew a breath. 'And yet, they've all come true.'

'That's impossible,' said Riell. 'Are you sure you can remember the details of these stories well? This must have been many years ago. Your mind could be playing tricks on you.'

'No – I can remember them as clearly as I can remember what just happened on deck. It's the same with my dreams. I could never remember them before my Ascent, but now I can recall every detail clearly.'

'But how could you know about the Nazir attack?' asked Verlinden. 'You told me your father was the only village leader at the Base to maintain patrols against them. These stories must have come from him.'

'Partly, perhaps – but the really frightening thing is that I know I was making up the stories at the time.'

'What are you saying, Atreu?'

Atreu ran his fingers through his hair. 'I know I was pretending. I know I was playing a game to try to frighten Teyth.'

Riell started to protest, but Atreu interrupted.

'Now, listen to me – how well-kept a secret is the Keep?'

Riell looked at him curiously. 'No one outside the Holy Orders and the windriders has in the past known anything of its existence. You know that.'

'I know what I've been told about it. Failed Ascenders would have no idea of its existence – am I right?'

'Yes – Ascenders would normally be kept at the Hold between Zenith and their judgement at Equinox. They would be flown blindfolded to the Circle for their audience, and they would be flown back blindfolded. The procedures are most strict.'

'Is there any chance any of them could have seen the Keep?'

'Not apart from the inside of the Areol – and they would have no idea where they were.' Riell frowned. 'Believe me, Atreu, the secrecy of the Keep is paramount. I've seen the process as an Ascender and I've commanded the windriders who fly up the Ascenders. A failed Ascender couldn't possibly know of the Keep or have seen it. Our whole system has depended on it in the past.'

'So my father couldn't have known about it?'

'No.'

'Micah wouldn't have told him?'

'No. It is forbidden. Why these questions, Atreu? You know the answers already.'

Atreu chewed his bottom lip. 'I'm trying to avoid a conclusion I don't want to reach.'

'What is it?'

'How could I know what the Keep would look like before I was flown there by you?'

'The question makes no sense. You couldn't have known.'

'But I did.'

'What?'

'When you first carried me over the edge of the Keep and I saw the spires – I knew I had seen them before. It was a game Teyth and I played as children. We would each try to convince the other that we could see the Summit. To sound convincing I almost forced myself to believe what I was telling him – and eventually there was no difference whether I was really seeing the Summit or whether I was making it up.'

'That doesn't prove anything, Atreu. I'm sorry, but –'

'No listen, Riell. After a while all I saw up there were the silver spires and towers. Over time they became more and more clear, and more and more detailed.'

'I see – but ...'

'Riell – when I finally saw the Keep, it was exactly as I had pictured it when I was a boy. *Exactly*. Don't you see what this means? You've already said Father couldn't have known of its existence, let alone been able to describe it to me. No one told me about it, yet I knew ... I knew ...'

Atreu was shaking, and Verlinden got up and put her arms around him. 'Stop doing this to yourself,' she said. 'There must be an explanation.'

'How is this possible?' asked Riell.

Atreu looked into the windrider's eyes. 'The stories of the Dusk People, the Keep ... everything ... I made them all up ... like the words in my Book. Don't you see?'

'No,' said Riell.

Atreu shivered violently and Verlinden held him more tightly. His face convulsed. 'What if I have ... somehow ... created these things ... with my words?'

Riell got up out of his bunk and started pacing from one side of the cabin to the other. 'That is insane. That is insane.'

'I could see the Keep when I was a boy.' Atreu's voice was thin and strained. 'I didn't just describe it. I could actually see it. How is that possible? From the Base of the Mountain – I was as far away as I could be. How is that possible?'

Riell's head jerked back and forth. 'This ill-wind – it has driven you to the brink. Your mind is twisted. You could not have seen it, and you didn't see it.'

'But I did.'

'You think you did, Atreu. And you have only thought that you did since we passed through the helles.'

'The Nazir – how could I have known they were going to attack?'

'Did you? You said your father believed they were still a threat. He must have told you these stories since you were very young. They became a part of you before you were even aware of it. There are other explanations, Atreu.'

'I don't know what's real anymore.' Atreu closed his eyes.

'Where does it stop, Atreu?' Riell knelt down in front of him. 'This is the hubris I was talking about at the Source. You don't have this power. I didn't have the power I thought I had – and I learnt that lesson. You have to learn it too. How could you have created any of these things? Words don't work that way. If you say they do, then you're saying you created me or Verlinden. Can't you feel Verlinden holding you as you sit there?'

Riell reached out and put a hand on his shoulder. 'Can't you feel me right now?'

'I could feel the helles-phantom in that very bunk over there,' said Atreu. 'Was that real or not?'

The windrider staggered back. 'Please, don't talk of that night.'

Atreu opened his eyes again to look at Riell. 'There are so many things you don't talk about. Do they make you think too much? Is it safer to keep them hidden?'

'Please, Atreu, I can't –'

'You push too much under the surface, Riell. Let them out.' Atreu's tone was becoming increasingly strident. 'Could you feel the phantoms? Like you can feel me? Is that the test if something's real?'

'No!' cried Riell, pushing away at invisible assailants.

'Please stop it – both of you,' said Verlinden. 'There is madness in the air tonight. Let's not feed it anymore.'

Atreu slumped back into her arms and Riell walked slowly towards the door.

'There *is* madness in the air tonight,' said the windrider. 'I'm going to see these Dusk-wraiths for myself.'

With that, he headed out onto the deck.

Verlinden helped Atreu into his bunk, curled down beside him and pulled the blanket up.

When his breathing steadied into a rhythm, she spoke softly to him. 'You are not responsible for what is happening on the Mountain,' she said. 'The killing, the deaths – you haven't created them. I know that within my heart, and you must know it too.'

'I don't know what I know any more, Verlinden.'

'I think you do.'

Atreu found the softness in her voice soothing.

'There are strange things happening,' said Verlinden, 'but you are the one who can stop the Nazir. You haven't created them, but you can stop them. We need to keep our focus on the quest for the third Book. The truth will be there – you know that in your heart.'

'How is it you know my heart so well, Verlinden?'

'Because it is my own,' she said.

'What makes you certain?'

'Because we share a child, Atreu. Because we share a child.'

Atreu pressed his lips against hers and felt her warm breath pass into him. They made love with a tenderness Atreu thought he no longer had within him. For the most exquisite of moments his mind cleared and he saw the indescribably bright sun of Zenith once more.

As they lay exhausted in each other's arms, the brightness faded slowly, but the clarity remained.

Atreu reached down to pick up his Book. He opened it, and they both began to read ...

*

Lythos stared anxiously through the window and braced himself as the room shook under his feet. Outside, a tower of lights crumbled and crashed to the ground. The noise of tumbling buildings continued across the Keep after the instability had stopped, and it took some time for the silence to return. When the door creaked, the Holy Man jerked his head in its direction.

'Where have you been, Leyvin?' he said as his brother stepped into the room.

'Several bridges have snapped,' said Leyvin. 'Come on, I've called a special session of the Circle.'

'You've called a what?'

'You heard what I said, Lythos. Now just stay calm.'

'I thought you would be organising an evacuation.'

The ground started trembling again.

Lythos almost lost his footing before he managed to grab hold of the table.

When the shaking stopped, Leyvin said, 'We can't afford to panic. Now think about this –'

'I don't want to think about anything,' said Lythos. 'The Keep is falling down around our ears, and you've convened the Circle.'

'Yes – we need to decide what to do as calmly as possible.'

'Calmly?' Lythos could feel the blood rising in his face. 'Calmly?'

'Yes. Think about it – most of the windriders are still downslope with the Faemir. We can't go anywhere in a hurry, can we? Most of the damage is occurring in the buildings near the eastern monasts. The instability hasn't reached the heart of the Keep. Just stay calm. Blind panic in this situation is the worst thing we could do.'

Lythos took a deep breath. 'All right. All right. I see what you are saying. What do we do?'

'I believe I have a plan. While you and so many others have been panicking, I've been gathering information.'

'And?'

'Trust me, dear brother, as always,' said Leyvin. 'Now, let's get to the Areol.'

*

By the time Leyvin and Lythos took their place in the Circle, all the other members had arrived. The chairs shook slightly as Leyvin spoke.

'I believe we are all aware of the reasons for convening the Circle tonight.'

There were several impatient mutters.

Micah cleared his throat and asked, 'How many windriders are there currently in the Keep?'

'Let us deal with some other issues first,' said Leyvin.

'I would suggest,' said Micah, 'that the number is exactly the first thing we need to address.'

Micah met Leyvin's icy stare. He knew he was challenging the First Speaker's authority by not using the correct formal address, but he had calculated that Leyvin wouldn't want to risk challenging him under the circumstances.

'I tend to agree with Liche Micah,' said Second Speaker Holthim. 'We need to know at what rate we can be evacuated from the Keep if necessary.'

There were loud exclamations from around the Circle.

'Please,' said Leyvin, 'this is exactly what I wanted to avoid. Our procedure has always been to look at all issues calmly and closely. That's how we make the best decisions – not through disorder and panic.'

'If you had answered the question the first time I asked it,' said Micah, 'we could have moved on already.'

Leyvin was clearly agitated. 'Why is it, Liche Micah, that we should begin with the extreme consideration of some sort of evacuation of the Keep? Where do you propose we evacuate to? The Keep is the safest place on the Mountain. It has always been the most stable. Where would the windriders take us?'

'The Source,' said Micah calmly. 'It has always been as stable as the Keep, and there is no chance of buildings crashing down around our heads.'

Murmurs of assent quickly filled the room.

Leyvin's eyes swept along the faces of the Holy Men. He could see he had lost control of proceedings.

Holthim's voice rang above the others. 'Please, Leyvin, how many windriders are there currently in the Keep?'

'Two dozen,' said Leyvin flatly.

The Circle erupted. Several Holy Men got up out of their chairs.

'How can this be?' asked Third Speaker Baelren when the tumult had died down.

'Please, all of you resume your seats,' said Leyvin. 'We were all aware of the War Council's decision for the windriders to carry the Faemir soldiers downslope into battle.'

'We didn't know the detail,' said Holthim. 'I had no idea we would be left so few windriders to serve the Keep for so long.'

'We are in times of war,' said Leyvin. 'The Keep is well stocked with food and it was under no direct threat. There was no reason to keep any number of windriders here but the bare minimum.'

'Shouldn't the windriders have returned by now?' asked Micah. It was a calculated question. He had no knowledge of how long their mission was to take, but he was hoping Leyvin didn't know that.

Leyvin's eyes were burning in Micah's direction. It was clear he was weighing his options. 'Yes,' he said finally, 'they should be back by now.'

'What news then do we have of this campaign?' asked Baelren.

'We have had no news,' said Leyvin.

'No news?' said Holthim, his voice laced with an edge of panic.

'So,' said Micah, 'what you really meant to say is that we shouldn't consider evacuation because that is not an option open to us?'

A rumbling sound echoed through the Areol.

When it had finished, Leyvin said, 'Please, all of you, if some of our decisions in the past don't appear appropriate, we can only try to make the right ones now, given our circumstances.'

'So, outline our options as you see them,' said Holthim.

Leyvin regained some composure. 'That is what I was attempting to do from the beginning, Second Speaker Holthim.'

'And the Circle would like all the information you possess,' said Micah. He knew his words carried a subtle implication that Leyvin had misled the Circle over the windrider issue. Normally the First Speaker would make an issue of it, but Micah hoped that, given the urgent circumstances, he would consider it a safer course not to.

Leyvin hesitated and then said, 'From what we can tell, the instability is centred on the monasts on the eastern edge of the Keep. As you can see, the heart of the Keep here in the Areol is barely affected.'

'How long will that be the case?' asked Baelren.

'No one has any idea. Impermanence is unpredictable. It has been known to be dormant for long periods of time.'

'It has also been known to escalate quickly,' said Micah.

'True,' said Leyvin. 'We have little knowledge of instability – but we do understand the construction of our buildings. From what I've been told, the instability we are currently having is not great. The problem is that the Liche towers and bridge were not built to withstand these tremors.'

'So the danger is the towers collapsing on us?' asked a large Felsen monk.

'Exactly.'

'So how does that help us?' asked Holthim. 'There are no large areas devoid of buildings within the Keep. Where do we escape to?'

Leyvin had the hint of a smile on his lips. 'The Felsen monasts are low, solid constructions. We have many on the western edge of the Keep, which is as far away as possible from the centre of the instability.'

Micah felt the Circle relax. Leyvin had managed to regain control, and the implied accusations that Micah had been able to direct towards him would now carry little weight. Perhaps the First Speaker was too clever for him after all.

Lythos now spoke for the first time. Micah noticed that his restlessness had disappeared, and he appeared calm and in control. That was never a good sign. 'If we are in agreement, I will organise for the message to reach all members of the Inner Sanctum. All those save the monks in the deepest librum ante-chambers could be safely ensconced in the western monasts by morning.'

There were several nods of approval, then Leyvin started to speak. 'I move, therefore –'

Micah interrupted. 'I feel we need to address one other issue first.'

'Please, Liche Micah,' said Leyvin. 'I am all for calm, rational discussion, but there is some urgency here.'

'This does concern our immediate position, First Speaker.'

Micah and Leyvin stared at each other in silence as the Areol shook again. The painted stars on the domed ceiling overhead trembled.

Micah knew that Leyvin was assuming he was about to bring up the disappearance of Atreu and the others. His mind raced to find a way to use that.

'Speak now, Liche Micah,' said Leyvin when the tremor stopped, 'but I will be obliged to cut you short if it doesn't pertain to our immediate situation.'

'Thank you, First Speaker,' said Micah. 'I will be brief. It is my understanding from Ascender Atreu that –'

'I will have to end your hearing there, Liche Micah. Ascender Atreu cannot have any relevance to our evacuation.' He drew a breath to continue.

'If you let me finish, you will see that he does,' said Micah quickly.

'Please,' said Second Speaker Holthim, 'I can see that a naming is imminent. I would respectfully say that we do not have the time for challenges and deliberations right now. May I suggest Liche Micah be given a brief time to complete his statement?'

'These are not our procedures,' said Leyvin.

'Not unless we all agree,' said Holthim. 'Are there any objections?'

Leyvin bit his lip as he waited, but no one protested. Micah could see the perspiration beading on the First Speaker's brow. Leyvin was obviously convinced that Micah had found some evidence against him regarding the missing Ascender.

Micah spoke slowly, his eyes locked on Leyvin's. 'As there is no protest, I will –'

'I name you, Liche Micah.' Leyvin's voice was strained.

The Circle was now in uproar.

'This is madness,' said Baelren. 'Are we going to sit here until the Areol crashes down on our heads?'

'The Rituals and procedures of the Circle must be followed under all circumstances,' said Leyvin, but his voice could be barely heard above the commotion.

Lythos jumped on his chair and started shouting. 'All of you, sit down please!'

The sight of a Holy Man standing on his chair in the most formal of rooms shocked the Circle into calm.

When everyone had resumed their seats, Micah said calmly and steadily. 'I challenge your naming.'

'Second Speaker Holthim, you are first,' said Leyvin.

Holthim gave a frustrated sigh. 'We will try to make our deliberations swiftly.'

The Areol trembled again as Micah and Leyvin filed out of the double carved doors into the hall outside.

'My only regret,' said Micah, once the doors were shut behind them, 'is that Praether isn't alive to see you finally fall.'

He could see the blood rush into Leyvin's face. 'If you think they will rule against me, knowing that doing so will cause me to lose the First Speaker's position, you are a fool.'

'We will see,' said Micah. 'Why would I risk my own safety as well as everyone else's if this wasn't of prime importance? They know the Circle may not convene again for some time – and who knows if the Areol will survive the instability.' Micah smiled. 'No, Leyvin, they will want to hear what I have to say at all costs. Praether successfully challenged you twice – the pleasure of the final challenge is mine.'

Leyvin sneered at him. 'You haven't been in the Circle long enough to know how they think. If they rule against me, they have lost me as their First Speaker; if they rule against you, you may have lost one of your lives, but nothing else. Believe me, when faced with a choice, they will always opt for the least change, regardless of the merits of the two options. You are a fool, Micah. You've always been a fool.'

Micah gritted his teeth. 'Atreu will be the one to bring you down in the end, even if it is from his grave. They will rule in my favour because I have invoked his name.'

'What nonsense are the two of you talking about?' The voice came from their left.

Micah looked across to see Sethor standing there, listening to their exchange.

'I sometimes feel that perhaps I've been a little hard on the low-Liche and the Circle,' said Sethor, 'that perhaps things have improved. But then I hear something like this, and I know nothing has changed.'

'What are you doing here, Sethor?' asked Micah.

'There was a matter I spoke to you about, remember? I promised I would provide the Circle with my conclusions once

I had the evidence. Well, as you can see, here I am – waiting patiently to have my audience with the all-important members of the Circle. I was told I had to wait until you had finished your earth-shattering deliberations, so of course that's what I have been doing.'

Leyvin had paled at the sight of Sethor. 'We ... we won't have time for your evidence.'

'I'm afraid you will have to make time,' he said.

Just then, Micah and Leyvin were recalled into the Areol. When they resumed their seats, Holthim said, 'We have made our decision. We rule against Liche Micah.'

A smile crept onto Leyvin's lips. 'Thank you, Second Speaker Holthim. We will now –'

'Please, First Speaker Leyvin, I haven't finished giving our ruling.'

Leyvin was taken aback.

'We rule against Liche Micah,' said Holthim, 'but we also rule that Liche Micah's statement be heard.'

'But that's impossible,' said Leyvin. 'Rulings must be one way or the other. This makes a mockery of our procedures.'

'It is possible to vary the procedures,' said Holthim, 'if the Circle is in full agreement.'

Leyvin stared angrily at Lythos, who wouldn't meet his gaze.

'Please, Liche Micah,' said Holthim. 'Finish your statement and be brief.'

Micah cleared his throat. 'As I was going to say, it is my understanding from Ascender Atreu that our instability has been caused by the tunnelling of the Nazir for generations through the Mountain towards the Summit. While the Keep has been free of instability, it has been free of the Nazir.'

The Circle was in confusion again as they all digested the implications of what Micah was saying.

'You believe,' said Holthim, 'that an attack on the Keep itself by the Nazir is imminent?'

'I would say there is strong evidence that they are on their way.

Of course, the Nazir themselves still haven't shown themselves to us, but none of us would stand a chance against the Dusk-spawn that they send out to fight their battles.'

'So the danger for us now is not so much the instability, but what may follow,' said Holthim.

'*Exactly.*'

The members of the Circle turned towards the open door to see who had spoken.

Sethor stood there with a large roll of charts under his arm. 'I have given up waiting for leave to speak to all of you, and I gather all of us have a sense of urgency, so I thought it best to interrupt your proceedings.'

'Please remove him,' ordered First Speaker Leyvin. 'We don't have time.'

'I believe sky-watcher Sethor has some information that is of utmost importance to the Circle,' said Micah.

Leyvin was now extremely agitated as he eyed the charts. He had escaped expulsion from the Speaker's chair once again, but he obviously feared Sethor's evidence. When he spoke, his voice had a shrill tone. 'We must commence the evacuation now. I thank Liche Micah for his observations. I support any preparations we can make for a future Dusk-spawn attack. Whatever sky-watcher Sethor has to say to us will have to wait.'

'No, it won't, you pompous fool, Leyvin.' Sethor leaned against the doorframe with one hand in a gesture of utter disdain for the Circle. 'I care nothing for the Circle and its empty procedures and convoluted words. I am going to tell you what I have discovered because I care for the Keep and I care for the Mountain.'

'It is customary to address the Circle from the centre,' said Holthim.

'I will speak from here. You are not the centre of our world as you all think. Most of you have no idea what it is I and the other sky-watchers do, besides provide you with weather predictions, but here, in these sky charts, is the most important evidence you will ever see.' He brandished the roll in the Circle's direction.

'What is it, Sethor?' said Micah.

'You speak of preparations for an imminent attack. You had better prepare for far more.'

'You said it had something to do with solstice,' said Micah.

'Yes – and if it wasn't for the accuracy of the sky-watcher charts, you would have remained blissfully unaware. What is it that gives us our power, what is it that the Dusk-spawn fear most?'

'The sun,' said Micah, with a terrifying inkling of what Sethor was about to say.

'Exactly,' said Sethor. 'And that is what is being taken away from us.'

'You are a madman,' said Leyvin, regaining some composure. 'Let us disperse the Circle – he can rant into an empty room.'

Sethor laughed. 'This is your First Speaker. Remember what he is saying now. Anyone is free to leave, of course. Stay only if you wish to hear what I say.'

No one moved. Leyvin frowned, but remained seated.

'These charts here and my calculations prove without a doubt,' said Sethor, 'that since winter solstice, the days have continued to become shorter and the nights longer.'

The Circle fell into a deathly silence.

'You are absolutely certain of this?' asked Holthim.

'There is no mistake.'

'The Nazir will overrun us,' said Micah. 'There will be no hope. This must have been their plan from the beginning.'

'I don't know about Nazir plans,' said Sethor, 'and I don't know why it is happening – but it is happening. The darkness is growing.'

'By your calculations,' said Micah, 'if it continues unabated, how long will it be before the sun fails to rise?'

'I can predict that to the day.' He paused as the eyes of the Circle watched him. 'We will lose the sun entirely by next Zenith.'

*

Atreu let the Book fall back onto the bed and looked at Verlinden, unable to find any words. Outside, he could hear the drone of the Dusk-wraiths on the riverbank.

Chapter Twenty

Now that the *Perisher* was sailing through parts of the Mountain that had once been inhabited, Atreu didn't know whether the days or nights were worse. The ever-decreasing daylight hours saw a passing parade of charred and deserted villages on both riverbanks. The few Mid-Reachers who had somehow survived the ravages of both Faemir and Nazir attacks now eked out a miserable existence, spending the nights in anchored boats midstream and the days foraging for food in what remained of the riverbank settlements.

The lengthening nights at least protected Atreu and the others from witnessing the unrelenting evidence of a devastating war, but the darkness held its own dangers. The Dusk-wraiths now descended at sunset and covered both riverbanks like a thick, undulating fog until daybreak. On starless nights, when clouds bore down on the Maelstrom from above, it was as if the *Perisher* was trapped inside an oppressive tunnel. Tentacles would snake out constantly over the river towards them, increasing in length as the night wore on. Usually they would fall well short of the ship's deck, but sometimes, when the river had narrowed and Aeshya had to steer closer to a bank to avoid a moored boat, the tentacles managed to get uncomfortably close.

Although other boats often approached the *Perisher* during the day, and imploring faces stared up at Atreu and the others, Aeshya insisted that they make no contact, and that under no circumstances should they allow anyone on board. She claimed that such approaches were a common river-pirate ploy, and that a ship the size of the *Perisher* would be a great prize. The tension between Aeshya and the others over this policy grew with every passing day. Finally, when a boatload of children rowed in their direction one morning, Atreu could contain himself no longer.

'We can't just sail past,' he cried. 'They're only children. They must be starving. We have enough food that we can give them some.'

Aeshya's lips were thin and her jaw set. 'I haven't come this far to endanger us now.'

'Aeshya, we have food we can give them,' said Atreu.

'Look at those faces,' said Verlinden. 'How can they be river-pirates?'

'What do you know of river-pirates,' said Aeshya angrily. 'None of you know anything about the river that I haven't told you. I've already explained that pirates will do anything to gain possession of a ship like the *Perisher*. We don't have the numbers to fight off any attack once they're on board. I am not taking the risk.'

'I can't in my heart keep going like this,' said Atreu, 'and I know the others feel the same.'

'I think we should take the risk,' said Riell.

Aeshya's lips thinned further. 'As far as I'm aware, I'm the captain here.'

'We have followed all your orders,' said Atreu.

'And we'll reach Farepont in a few days if you continue to follow them,' said Aeshya.

Atreu glanced down at the boat, which was still approaching them from the starboard side. Several boys, who could not have been older than ten, were rowing towards them, their faces grimy and hopeful.

'Can't we just throw them some food?' asked Atreu.

'We would have to tie their boat to ours to do that in this current,' said Aeshya. 'That would be the same as opening a door and inviting them in.'

'Why don't you look at them?' asked Verlinden.

Aeshya continued to stare straight ahead. 'I have a ship to steer.'

'You're afraid to look at them, aren't you?' said Verlinden.

'I faced the helles-phantoms – why would I be afraid to look at some children?'

'You're afraid you might weaken,' said Verlinden. 'Isn't that right?'

'We have an agreement,' said Aeshya. 'I'll get you to Farepont as your river-captain, and you are my crew.'

'I've had enough of this,' said Atreu, as the boys swung their boat parallel to the *Perisher*. He stepped over to the rail and began to untie one of the ropes.

'You're a fool,' cried Aeshya, locking the tiller into place and heading in Atreu's direction.

Verlinden and Riell grabbed her and held her back. She struggled for a moment, until Verlinden said, 'Look at them.'

Aeshya looked down and saw five young, exhausted faces looking up at them. A sixth boy was busy securing their boat to the *Perisher*.

'Could we please have some food?' asked one of the boys.

'All right,' said Aeshya, turning away, 'give them something. Let's just be as quick as possible.'

Riell and Verlinden headed below deck.

Atreu noticed the pile of blankets at the rear of the boy's boat. 'Don't tell me you all sleep in this boat?' he asked.

The boy who had spoken glanced around nervously.

There was something in the boy's look that suddenly put Atreu on edge.

'Aeshya –' Before Atreu could finish, the blankets in the boat had been thrown off to reveal three men brandishing knives. The first was already using the rope to scale up the side of the ship before Atreu even registered what was happening. He was almost at the deck level when Aeshya leaned over and cut the rope with her knife. The man tumbled back onto the others, who had also commenced climbing, and all three now lay sprawled in the boat.

'You were right,' said Atreu, shaking his head. 'I'm sorry.'

'Never mind sorry,' she said. 'Let's hoist the sails – looks like this is a trap. Look over there.'

Atreu could see boats of various sizes approaching from all sides.

'Over here.' Verlinden's voice rang from the port-side of the *Perisher*.

Atreu could see smoke billowing from the aft-cabin as he and Aeshya raced across.

'Damn,' cried Aeshya. 'They're using flame arrows.'

As she spoke, a volley of fire-tipped arrows arced through the sky towards them and landed on the foredeck.

'I'll get some blankets from the other cabin,' said Riell.

'No,' said Aeshya. 'Now listen to me. This is a tactic I've seen before. The crew ends up frantically trying to put out the fire while the pirates board the ship. Our only hope is to hoist the sails first to try to outrun them.'

'What? And let the *Perisher* burn?' said Riell.

'Yes – this time I don't want any questions. Let's go.'

Aeshya raced back to the tiller and Atreu, Riell and Verlinden scaled the three masts. When Aeshya gave the signal, Atreu released and secured his sail and then clambered back down.

'Now do what you can to put out those fires,' said Aeshya.

'If they put one of those flame arrows through the sails,' said Atreu, 'that will be the end of us.'

'You don't know river pirates very well,' said Aeshya. 'The *Perisher* would be useless to them without the sails. They won't try to damage them. Hopefully we'll soon be out of range anyway. Now get going with those fires.'

It took some time to quell the flames with the available blankets and water. Atreu was exhausted by the time he and the others returned to Aeshya at the tiller platform.

The *Perisher* had outdistanced the river-pirate boats, and the Maelstrom stretched out before them.

'We should have listened to you,' said Verlinden. 'That was so close to being a disaster.'

'I don't want to hear any apologies,' said Aeshya. 'Just learn a lesson from it.'

'Who would have thought those young boys –'

'Never trust anyone – that's the way I've survived on the river.'

'But not every boat that approaches us can be filled with river-pirates,' said Atreu. 'How could we have had the misfortune to decide to help the one that was?'

Aeshya frowned. 'We're not out of this yet – so don't even think about helping anyone else. What's our food and water situation after that fire in the aft-cabin?'

'Not good, I'm afraid,' said Riell. 'We had all of our provisions stored there. Nothing has survived.'

'How many days sailing is it to Farepont?' asked Atreu.

'Three or four,' said Aeshya.

'So what do we do?' said Verlinden. 'Starve until then?'

The sun was starting to dip below the horizon again, and a bitter chill gripped the air.

'Do any of us know what state Farepont is in?' asked Aeshya. 'With these Dusk-wraiths crowding the river every night, who knows if we will be able to get any food there. It is largely a floating town, but the parts of it on or near the riverbank won't be safe.'

'All right,' said Atreu, 'we can all see the problem now – you must have some ideas.'

'Yes, I do,' said Aeshya, 'but you won't like any of them.'

'Tell us,' said Atreu.

'If we come across any boats, we can relieve them of any provisions they have.'

'You mean steal?' said Atreu.

'I told you that you wouldn't like it.'

'But whoever we took the food from then themselves would starve.'

'Unless they manage to steal from someone else.'

Atreu shook his head. 'We can't do that.' Riell and Verlinden nodded in agreement.

'So if you were starving, you wouldn't fight someone for a scrap of food?' said Aeshya.

'Not if it was theirs.'

'How do you know whose it is? How do you know they didn't steal it? What if they've done some terrible thing to get it?'

'But you don't know that,' said Atreu. 'You have to assume it was theirs.'

'Do you? In my experience it probably isn't rightfully theirs anyway.'

'Obviously your experiences are different to mine,' said Atreu.

'Are they? Whose experience told them to be suspicious about those boys? I don't think the differences are in our experiences – you just haven't faced what yours tell you.'

'Look,' said Atreu, 'I am not going to steal food from anyone.'

Aeshya looked at him and then at Riell and Verlinden.

'All right,' she said, 'we have one other option.'

'What's that?' asked Atreu.

'We go ashore and see what we can find.'

Out of the corner of his eye, Atreu could see that the Dusk-wraiths were gathering again, now that the sun had set.

'It should be safe to do that during daylight, shouldn't it?' asked Atreu.

'I don't know enough about these wraiths,' said Aeshya. 'We can only assume they won't be a danger during the day. The problem will be desperate Mid-Reachers looking for food in the deserted villages and towns.'

'Do we have to go into the towns?' asked Verlinden. 'Can't we find something to eat in the countryside?'

'At this time of the year? Perhaps some winter berries, but with the reduced sunlight, I wouldn't expect to find too many of those, either. We need more than a few berries. You three will also need provisions for your journey after Farepont – where do you think they will come from?'

'I see we have little choice,' said Atreu. 'Let's go ashore the first chance we get in the morning.'

'We'll pass several towns and villages tomorrow,' said Aeshya. 'I think the largest one is Midfell – that would probably be the best one to try.' She looked at the three of them in turn. 'So are we agreed, or do you want to question my judgement again?'

Atreu nodded as he stared into the darkness ahead. 'Let's just hope dawn breaks and we get the chance.'

*

The cobbled stones under Micah's feet shook as he made his way to the outer monasts. Slung over his back were the few belongings he had hastily decided to take with him. Behind him he could hear the beautiful silver spires of the Keep crashing to the ground, but he could no longer bear to look at the sparkling lights descending like clusters of shooting starts. How long would it be before the Sky-reach tower itself fell?

Around him were other Holy Men, each stooped under a weight they were unused to carrying, each with a grim look that Micah had rarely seen. The saddest sights were the scribes and librers, struggling with large loads of books. Their expressions were ones of hopelessness – they each knew that what they were carrying was just a tiny fraction of the knowledge stored in the various Keep librums.

In the skies above the Keep, Micah caught the occasional glimpse of a windrider carrying a load to the western monasts. He hoped desperately that the next time he looked up, he would see the sky filled with the returning squadrons of windriders. Without them, the Keep that had been so impregnable was looking more and more like a trap. He knew the Holy Men were totally defenceless, devoid of any combat skills. In the event of an attack by any Dusk-spawn, there would be the most horrific carnage.

Micah entered the low, squat monast that he had been assigned to. He placed his bundle of belongings against the bare stone wall. Once his eyes had adjusted, he noticed Lythos sitting with his back propped up against the opposite wall.

'So this is it,' said Micah. 'We just sit here and wait?'

Lythos shifted as if suddenly aware that his back was aching. 'If you can suggest something I can do that will make a difference, Micah, I'll consider it.'

'The Circle will meet again,' said Micah. 'Don't give up hope on that.'

'Will it?' He seemed to be nodding slowly. 'Does it matter?'

'What has happened to you, Lythos? You used to be the one with all the fire. Where's your anger? You barely spoke at the last meeting.'

Lythos made a sound that almost sounded like a laugh. 'My brother doesn't do so well without me to balance him, does he?'

'I know that's what Praether used to say – and he was a wise old arch-librer.'

'Leyvin hasn't listened to me for some time. He expects me to trust his judgement.'

'Do you?'

Lythos didn't reply.

'Tell me something, Lythos, why did you –'

'I know what you're going to ask me, Micah. You want me to tell you why I voted to allow you to continue your address, when I could have easily vetoed it with just my vote.'

'Yes, that's exactly what I was going to ask.'

'I'm not certain that I understand myself. I think I wanted to give Leyvin an indication that he could no longer assume my unquestioning support.'

'Why? You didn't know what I was going to say. We both know that I have suspicions concerning his actions with the two

Ascenders. How did you know I wasn't going to present evidence that would destroy him?'

'I didn't. I can only suspect what he did, because he no longer confides in me. I ... I suppose I wanted the truth to come out.'

There were several shouts from outside. A Liche Holy Man rushed through the doorway. 'The windriders are returning,' he cried.

Micah and Lythos ran outside into the narrow cobbled street and peered into the star-filled sky.

'Where are they?' Micah asked the Liche who had called them.

'The news I have is that they are almost at the lip of the Keep.'

Micah could see Holy Men everywhere climbing onto the flat monast roofs to get a better view. All around him, monks were spilling out into the narrow streets.

And they all waited. It was as if the entire Keep was holding its breath.

There was a gasp as the first windriders appeared. They arched up past the Keep's edge into the sky above the monasts. Micah felt his heart race as, one by one, they emerged from below the Keep horizon.

Then they stopped coming.

Micah blinked, as if his vision was failing him. Where were all the others? They must be still coming. He stared at the empty sky, which was now lengthening behind the final windrider, until the realisation hit.

That was it. There were no more returning windriders. A mere hundred at the most – that was all.

Most of the Holy Men had climbed down wearily from the rooftops and shuffled back into the monasts when Micah finally looked down.

It was then that he realised that Lythos, too, had only just given up.

Micah put his arm around the Liche Holy Man and they walked inside.

*

The sun was already well past its high point as Atreu and Verlinden weaved their way through the deserted streets of Midfell. The houses stood like charred skeletons, and the wind whistled through the gaps in the walls. Atreu could see what had happened in the town from the evidence before him. Barricade fires had been erected around several large buildings to ward off the Duskwraiths, and in many cases the fires had flamed inwards, onto the buildings they were supposed to be protecting.

'We should be heading back to the *Perisher* soon,' said Atreu. 'The sun has been setting so quickly I don't want to take any risks.'

'We can't go back empty-handed,' said Verlinden. 'There must be some food somewhere in this town.'

'We tried the marketplace and couldn't find anything. What else can we do? It will be pure luck if we happen onto a building that has something. It looks like looters have already been through.'

Verlinden stepped into a house which seemed to be intact, and looked around. A moment later she stepped out, her face white.

'What's wrong?' asked Atreu.

Verlinden suddenly bent double and threw up. 'Don't go in there,' she said as she wiped her mouth.

'We need to get back to the Maelstrom,' said Atreu. 'Aeshya will want to weigh anchor and get away from the bank before there is any chance that the wraiths will descend. We can last another day without food.'

'You know we still have a little time,' said Verlinden. 'Let's make use of it. Who knows if we will get another chance like this – Aeshya says this is the largest town before Farepont.'

Atreu reached out to help support her, but Verlinden shrugged him off.

'Please don't treat me as if I am ill,' said Verlinden.

'But you are with child – that must make a difference.'

Verlinden drew a deep breath. 'Yes it does, Atreu. My body hasn't quite felt my own for some time. I can't do what I was once able, but then, I don't think any of us are planning a pitched battle with the Nazir.'

They stepped around a small chasm and continued.

'You must know more about Maelir towns than I do,' said Verlinden. 'Where, apart from the marketplace, would we find food? Somewhere that looters wouldn't immediately think of.'

Atreu frowned. 'We could try some inns,' he said finally. 'They usually have a reasonably large supply of food.'

'Those inns we saw at the riverfront appeared as if the looters had well and truly combed through them.'

'But there could be inns on the outskirts of the town. Cluric's inn in Teuron was a long way from the centre. It was a place where farmers and herdsmen met, rather than town merchants.'

'That sounds like our best chance then, Atreu.'

'Have we got enough time to go so far from the riverbank?'

'Come on, Atreu, let's hurry.'

As they approached the outskirts of Midfell, more of the buildings lay untouched by fires. The streets, however, were torn by large chasms, and several houses had been impaled by giant pillars. It was clear that the attack had come from the west and that the inhabitants had fled towards the Maelstrom. The final stand for those who were unable to get onto boats would have been on the riverbank. Atreu shuddered at the thought of how many bodies lay at the bottom of the Maelstrom.

'That's an inn, isn't it?' said Verlinden, pointing to a building that appeared fully intact.

As they approached, they could hear the sign declaring it to be The Leeward creaking in the wind. Atreu and Verlinden exchanged a glance and then pushed the door open.

Atreu half-expected to see the pallid bodies of farmers still sitting at their tables. The inn, though, was totally deserted. In the strange silence, it seemed to Atreu like a painting of a crowd scene where all the people had been erased. Glasses of ale sat half-full on tables, and plates with partly consumed meals dotted the room. In one corner, a fiddle and bow lay propped against the wall, as if waiting to be picked up at any moment.

'The kitchen would be through here, wouldn't it?' said Verlinden.

Atreu nodded, and followed her.

The stench of rotting vegetables hit him immediately, and he reeled back.

Verlinden had already opened several cupboards. 'I think we've found what we want,' she said. 'Look, corn, rice and oats. These potatoes and onions should still be edible, too.'

'Let's take what we can carry, then,' said Atreu as he opened the drawstring on the sack he had brought, 'and get back to the *Perisher*.'

They found a section with various kinds of cured meats and a cupboard full of pickled vegetables, and they quickly filled their sacks.

'I've never seen so much food in an inn,' said Atreu. 'This must have been a wealthy town.'

'There's not much left of all that Maelir wealth now, is there?' said Verlinden.

Atreu shook his head as he drew the string and tested the weight of the sack over his shoulder. 'I think this is about my limit if we are going to travel back quickly.'

Verlinden slung her sack over and they headed back outside.

Atreu surveyed the injured landscape just beyond the town. As far as the eye could see was a chaotic jumble of pillars and chasms. Trees and bushes grew on bizarre angles where the ground had lifted beneath them. Was this what the Mountain was becoming?

The wind stung the backs of their necks and behind their ears as they made their way through the streets of Midfell. The sun was now low on the horizon, casting elongated shadows across their path. Atreu knew Verlinden was struggling under the load. They had stopped several times, and the rest periods were lengthening.

Verlinden was looking increasingly pale and would close her eyes during these periods and hold one hand across her stomach.

Each time they rested, Atreu suggested that she lighten her load, but each time, Verlinden would shake her head and sling the full sack onto her back once more. When her gait became unsteady, Atreu flung his load down and said, 'Just leave yours behind. You're not going to make it back to the *Perisher* at this rate.'

Verlinden stopped walking. 'If I just have a little rest.' Her face suddenly went deathly white and Atreu raced over to her. She half-collapsed into his arms, but somehow managed to stay on her feet.

'That's it,' said Atreu. 'We need to get you back now. Forget the food.'

Verlinden drew a deep breath and then pushed Atreu away. 'I am not becoming a weak Faelen,' she said. 'This load is the same weight as yours – I can carry it.'

'But you're with child,' said Atreu.

Verlinden glared at him. '*I have not become a Faelen.*' She grabbed the sack, slung it over her shoulder and, despite Atreu's protests, proceeded with a grim determination.

They made good progress until they reached the market square, where she collapsed and rolled onto the cobblestones.

Atreu rushed over and tried to revive her, but her breathing remained shallow, and her eyes didn't seem to register his presence. He looked to the horizon in a panic. With the sun already partially consumed by the silhouettes of the damaged Midfell buildings, he knew he didn't have time to return with Riell so he could help carry Verlinden back.

Atreu lifted her onto his shoulders and tried to make some progress, but his legs buckled under him.

Damn. What was he going to do? He scanned the market square for somewhere to hide. The temperature had dropped and the cold now bit into his bones.

'I won't let them get us,' he whispered to Verlinden. 'I won't let them get us.'

Finally, he dragged Verlinden through the door of a building which seemed undamaged. Inside was evidence of a wild panic, with clothes strewn everywhere and furniture upturned. He found a bed in the corner and lifted Verlinden into it, carefully covering her with blankets. He then went back outside and retrieved the two food-laden sacks. Then he bolted the door and fastened the locks on the windows, aware how futile the actions would be against the wraiths. He toyed briefly with the idea of starting a fire, but decided their only hope was if they gave no indication they were there.

He looked out of the window as the darkness folded down over Midfell. Perhaps the miraculous would happen and they would come through the night unscathed. He shivered and turned towards Verlinden. *If only I was a great warrior like Teyth instead of what I am.*

He walked over and felt her forehead. Her skin felt as cold as the ice of the Upper Reaches. He watched her for a moment, her hair bright red flames against pale skin. Then he got into the bed next to her and held her in his arms. Drawing on all the power he had, he surged the heat of the R'angkur through his body and into hers. He felt the sun of forgotten summers and took her with him. And as their bodies melded in the heat, he could feel her heartbeat strengthening. He breathed with her soft, shallow breaths until they deepened. And at the point where Verlinden's body was coaxed back to recognition, Atreu became aware of another heartbeat, faint, yet steady, which had been touched by the R'angkur.

As he lay there, lost in the warmth, his perception blurred. At some indefinable time, voices wafted in through the open window, and he had the sense that he was experiencing something he had experienced before. Gradually, the voices registered inside his head. He got up slowly, so as not to disturb Verlinden, and walked over to the window. Outside, the night had a sharp-edged clarity. It was as if the stars had somehow been lowered, and now hovered close to the ground.

In the middle of the square Atreu could see where the voices were coming from. A large screen attached to two poles stood dead centre, and behind the screen, dark shadows played. Atreu watched, entranced, as the story unfolded ...

A large Mountain erupted in the middle of the screen. Behind it sat a large sun, dominating the action around it. A wave of angular-limbed people with sharp faces came from the east, scaled the Mountain and stayed. The silhouettes of the people spread across the slopes from the Base to the Summit and merged with the land. The Mountain and the sun pulsed gently with the rhythm of a heartbeat and seemed to grow, imperceptibly at first, like a living being.

Then another wave of people came from the west in boats – people with round faces and contoured limbs. They, too, scaled the Mountain, clambering over the slopes, which now had merged to the edges of the angular people. The rounded people couldn't fit comfortably into the edges that now existed on the surface of the Mountain. They pulled out picks and shovels and started to hack away at the slopes. Cries of pain echoed through the air, and the Mountain trembled, but the rounded people continued, and, piece by piece, the edges and corners were removed and cast down to the flat area beyond the Mountain. They hacked and cut until the surface was a smooth line, and only stopped when the cries of pain were a faint echo from beyond the Base.

The rounded people then cheered and danced, and eventually no cries of pain could be heard at all. They then set about trying to merge with the slope as the angular people had done, but they always remained distinct and never *became* the surface. Yet they persisted. But despite their persistence, the Mountain and its sun pulsed like a heartbeat and never grew.

Atreu felt the pull of the scene being acted out in front of him. Without being fully aware of his actions, he walked to the door, unbolted it, and stepped outside into the market square. He moved towards the screen without ever taking his eyes from the shadows. When he came to a halt in front of it, he was momentarily aware of a familiar bittersweet smell, but then lost himself in the play again.

Atreu noticed that while the rounded people continued in vain to try and merge with the slope, the discarded angles beyond the Base started to move. They re-formed into the angular people, but somehow they were not quite the same as they had been. The pieces were joined in twisted, misshapen ways, and when they walked, they moved with a clumsy, grotesque gait.

The Mountain drew them, as it had done before, but this time they didn't walk on the surface, because the rounded people now guarded the Base. Instead, they disappeared into the darkness of the Mountain's very heart, and merged with it.

At first this seemed to make no difference to the rounded people, but eventually the Mountain started trembling and the sun shrank. Then sharp angles and tears began appearing on the surface of the Mountain, and new cries of pain could be heard. The new sharp angles that tore through the rounded people re-formed into the misshapen figures which had disappeared into the Mountain. Gradually, all the round curves were being replaced by ugly edges, and the Mountain looked like a grotesque version of what it had once been.

And as the Mountain transformed, the sun shrank further still. With every sharp edge that ripped through the round people like a knife, the sun diminished just a little bit more. Finally, just as the Mountain lost its final curve, the sun vanished altogether.

And after the sun disappeared, the Mountain's trembling became more violent, until large fissures appeared through its length and breadth. These fissures widened and stretched until the Mountain appeared as a series of pieces, rather than a whole.

Finally, the Mountain fractured into a thousand pieces and shattered, like a rock hit by a hammer.

Atreu stepped even closer to the screen, now hoping desperately that the pieces would somehow move and re-form, but they lay lifeless. He stood there, waiting for something to happen. Was that it? Was that the end of the play?

He looked around and saw through the darkness that the rooftops of all the buildings surrounding the marketplace were crowded with angular-limbed, sharp-faced figures with pale eyes. Thousands upon thousands of them had massed in every available space, and they sat absolutely still, so that they appeared like grotesque extensions of the buildings themselves.

Atreu was again aware of the bittersweet smell that seemed to be wafting from behind the screen. He stepped towards it and drew a deep breath before pulling it down. Behind it was a small, thin, orange-haired man sitting motionless in front of a fire and holding a small model of the shattered pieces of the Mountain.

'Belzalel told you never to look,' he said, with a tone that was both sad and joyous.

'The truth was always in the shadows, wasn't it Belzalel?' said Atreu.

The little man put down the model he was holding. 'The puppets. They don't know. But Belzalel knows. Yes, poor Belzalel knows. Two are missing. Find the one who is two.'

Atreu felt an ice shiver down his back. 'Have I been one of your puppets, Belazalel? Have you been telling my story?'

The little man stared at the shattered pieces and started trembling.

Atreu moved closer to the dying fire. 'It's r'lung, isn't it? You're burning it all. You will finally be free of it.'

Their eyes met and the truth passed between them.

Then Belzalel closed his eyes.

Atreu knew there was nothing else to be said. He turned and walked back through the marketplace to the house where Verlinden still lay. He closed the door and stood again at the window.

Belzalel remained sitting, motionless as the r'lung fire died behind him. When the last glow finally faded into the darkness, it was as if the enchantment had broken. Atreu watched the mass of angular figures on the rooftops come to life. As one, they swarmed in towards the motionless little man in the centre of the square, and he disappeared under the seething mass. The only words Atreu thought he heard were, 'just my luck'.

Atreu turned away, unable to watch.

Verlinden still lay on the bed, sleeping peacefully. He walked slowly towards her and got in beside her again, feeling her warmth and the strong steadiness of her breathing.

*

When Atreu awoke to a voice calling his name, the sunlight was streaming in through the window. He looked around, not believing for a moment that he and Verlinden had somehow survived the night. He got up, suddenly remembering the strange dream he had dreamt.

He opened the door and rushed outside to see that it was Riell calling out.

'We're here,' he shouted. 'We're both alive.'

Riell ran to him and embraced him. 'I can't believe it, Atreu. I can't believe it.' Tears ran down his cheeks as he spoke.

'I've had a strange night, Riell, but I feel I am close to understanding now.' Atreu could feel the tears welling up in his own eyes.

Riell pulled back and they turned to go into the house together, when the windrider stopped.

'Who is that?' he said, pointing to a small figure lying in the centre of the square.

'A master puppeteer,' said Atreu. 'He was closer to the truth than any of us.'

They walked towards the motionless form. Atreu could see Riell's face crumple as he bent down towards the limp body of the little man and cradled him in his arms.

'Did you know Belzalel?' said Atreu.

Riell's voice was soft and trembling. 'He was my brother.'

Chapter Twenty-one

Atreu was surrounded by darkness. There were no threads, no dreams. Not even thoughts of threads and dreams entered his mind, just blackness, stretching upwards and outwards, blanketing his vision like a shroud.

He opened his eyes slowly. A figure tended a fire in front of him.

'Where … am I?' asked Atreu. He had to dredge the words from the back of his throat.

The features of a vaguely familiar face flashed across his vision, and the dizziness returned.

'Just wait a moment,' said the voice. 'It will come back to you, Atreu.'

'Atreu?' Yes, that was his name.

The darkness slowly cleared and he saw Verlinden looking at him.

'You're lost again, aren't you?' she said.

Atreu looked down at the table and saw the two Books open at what looked like identical pages.

'This has happened before,' he said.

'Yes, you have been poring through the Books since we returned to the *Perisher*.'

'The *Perisher*?'

'Yes. It's been three days now and you've had almost no sleep. I don't understand why you are pushing yourself. We've almost reached Farepont and from there we have to continue on foot. How can you do that if you are exhausted?'

Atreu frowned and said again, 'This has happened before.'

'You keep saying that. Every time you come back out of those Books. You've been going through them page by page, Atreu. Why?'

Atreu glanced around the cabin as if seeing it for the first time. 'We both survived the night in Midfell.'

'Yes,' said Verlinden, smiling, 'we both survived.'

'Have I told you what I saw that night?'

'Yes,' said Verlinden, 'several times now. Your story hasn't changed, so I'm beginning to believe it really happened.'

'You saw the body, though, didn't you? You saw Belzalel. That must be proof.'

'Perhaps. There was no screen, though, or any evidence that anyone else besides that little man was there in the square that night. I'm not sure what a body proves. A frail Maelir died in the Midfell market square – can we say anything else with certainty?'

'Have I told you before what I think the shadow play means?'

'Yes, you think the Mountain may collapse and the sun will die. That conclusion fits in with what Sethor told the Circle, but how and why it is happening is not as clear to me. And what was that you saw? A dream? A vision? A piece of the future? A warning?'

'I felt it was the truth. And if it was, then it must somehow be connected with the Books.'

'I know you're looking for confirmation of your interpretation, Atreu, but you are being worn down by your search, and you can't keep going without sleep.'

'But it's more than confirmation I'm looking for. I want to make some connection with the Nazir through the Books. I feel that's the key now, and if I don't find that connection, the Mountain is doomed.' He looked directly into Verlinden's eyes. 'But we've spoken about this before, haven't we?'

'Yes. It's frightening – you become so absorbed in the Books that it's as if you disappear into them. Then when you come out, you can barely focus on where you are now.'

'But I feel I'm getting closer each time, you know. I tell you a little bit more each time I come out, don't I?'

'Yes, a little. I barely noticed it at first, but yes, you do.'

'Have I told you anything new this time?'

'No, not that I can tell.'

'You know my Talisman is retelling the story of my Ascent.'

'Yes, and the Book of Maelur is now telling you the full story between Zenith and Equinox.'

'That's right – and I know there is something I must find when comparing the two. I know there is a clue there somewhere.' Atreu ran his fingers through his hair, closed his eyes and drew a long breath.

'You might be able to find it more easily if you had some sleep,' said Verlinden.

'There's something in the comparison between the two Books. I just know it.' He beckoned her over. 'Here, please try again.'

'I've tried so many times, Atreu. You know I can't seem to read either Book when they are both open at the same time. You ask me this each time.'

'Please try again. Look, here, I'm up to chapter twenty-one in both books. You haven't looked at these pages yet.'

Verlinden shook her head. 'This is very frustrating, Atreu. I can't –'

'Please, Verlinden, try one more time. The Books are erratic, remember. Who knows?'

'All right, Atreu.' She leant over Atreu's shoulder and looked at the two sets of pages. 'Hey, I can read them,' she said.

'See – this could be the breakthrough. Keep going and tell me if you notice anything.'

'Atreu – have you read this chapter yet?'

'No, why?'

'Have a look at them. You'll notice it straight away.'

Atreu looked at the first paragraph of the chapter in his Talisman:

Atreu was surrounded by darkness. There were no threads, no dreams. Not even thoughts of threads and dreams entered his mind, just blackness, stretching upwards and outwards, blanketing his vision like a shroud.

He then glanced across at the first paragraph of the equivalent chapter in the Book of Maelur. His head jerked back with a start. The two paragraphs were identical.

He read them both through again carefully, word by word, and there was no doubt about it. They were identical.

'How can they be the same?' he asked. 'The stories are completely different.'

'If you read a bit further, you would find out,' said Verlinden. 'Look here.' She pointed further down the page in Atreu's Book. 'You were obviously travelling with Micah here.'

Atreu scanned the page, then turned his attention back to the Book of Maelur. He flicked over to the next page. 'This was before my address to the Circle, when I was reading my Talisman to try to find some meaning.'

'So what you're doing now is reading about reading your Book, which is telling your own story.'

Atreu grabbed hold of the table with both hands for support. 'Either we've hit some unusual waves or my head is spinning,' he said.

'I'm afraid it's all in your head, Atreu.'

'But you can read it too, can't you?'

'Yes.'

'So what is this telling me?' said Atreu. 'I think this is the clue I've been looking for.'

'I don't know, but one of the first things you said when you came out of the Books this time was that you felt this had happened before.'

'But you said yourself that it *had* – I've been reading these Books since we left Midfell.'

'I think you may have meant it in a different way.'

'This repetition here between the two Books – that's what I could have been talking about, isn't it?'

'Perhaps.'

'How can each Book tell a different story yet have this repetition?'

'I don't know, Atreu, but the answer to that question might be the key we are looking for.'

Atreu turned back to the Books and compared the opening pages of each chapter again. When he looked up at Verlinden, the blood had drained from his face.

'What's wrong?' asked Verlinden.

'I've just had a thought,' he said. 'What will happen when I get to read chapter twenty-one in the third Book?'

He closed his eyes and tried to fight his way through the swirling darkness.

*

It should have been morning when Aeshya called them all on deck, but it wasn't. Atreu had finished reading the two Books and was desperately tired when he felt the cold river wind on his face for the first time since leaving Midfell. He could see that the Dusk-wraiths had continued to mass on both banks, and they now towered almost at mast height, cold, blood-red eyes staring down at them. Some of the snake-like tentacles that reached out for the *Perisher* were now all but touching the deck before they disintegrated.

'It's hard to judge anymore,' said Aeshya, 'but I think we will reach Farepont just after sunrise.'

'Those Dusk-wraiths are getting very close,' said Atreu. 'How do we know Farepont is still inhabited?'

'Farepont is a floating town, and the Maelstrom is very wide there. The danger to the Fareponters will be other Maelir trying to find a safe haven, rather than the wraiths.'

'Will they let us enter the town?' asked Verlinden.

Aeshya smiled. 'The *Perisher* is all we need to gain entry. A three-master will always be welcome in Farepont.'

'And that means your father is going to be very happy, doesn't it?' said Riell.

Aeshya narrowed her eyes at Riell. 'You don't believe me, do you?'

Riell shrugged his shoulders. 'It's not our concern what you do once we get to Farepont. Our arrangement is over and you've kept your side of the bargain.'

'But you don't believe that I'm returning the *Perisher* to my father, do you? After all we've been through, you don't trust me. I could have left all of you in Midfell, couldn't I?' Her face was flushed.

'Yes, you could have,' said Atreu. 'Now let's discuss what happens when we get to Farepont. The safest and quickest path is to enter the Rimforest at Treyheim, right?'

'Why ask me a question if you don't trust me to answer truthfully?' Aeshya stared ahead with her hands on the tiller.

'Please,' said Riell, 'there's no need to discuss this now, is there?'

'All of you make me sick,' said Aeshya. 'I'll be well rid of you. You all think you're better than me.'

'No, we don't,' said Riell, trying to appease her.

'And you're the worst, Riell. I'm certainly not good enough for you, am I?'

Riell's face reddened. 'I –'

'Don't try to deny anything. Just stick to your purity. It's easy if you let someone else dirty themselves for you.'

Atreu and Verlinden exchanged a glance.

'You know we are all grateful to you,' said Atreu. 'If the Mountain is to be saved, then it couldn't have been done without you.'

'Don't give me a place in any of your grand plans,' said Aeshya. 'I'm not worthy of it.'

'I think you're there whether you want to be or not,' said Atreu.

Aeshya's lips thinned as she pressed them together. 'Let's not get too far ahead of ourselves,' she said. 'Dawn still hasn't broken, and we haven't reached Farepont yet.'

'But we are almost there, aren't we?' asked Atreu.

'Yes, but the Maelstrom narrows just before we reach it – and those wraiths are getting close. Don't think we're safe yet.'

'Can't we just lower the anchor and wait for sunrise?' asked Verlinden.

'Not mid-river here. It's much too deep. And I don't think we want to go any closer to the shore, do we?'

'What about turning around and using our sails to maintain our position against the current until dawn?' said Riell.

Aeshya looked at him. 'I may make a sailor out of you yet – that's an alternative worth considering. It could work, but there are risks in a current this strong. And we would also need to turn towards one of the banks to do it – the wraiths would love that.'

'All right,' said Riell. 'What are you saying we should do?'

Aeshya looked at him with a curious mixture of emotions in her eyes. 'So I'm showing you what to do to the bitter end, am I?' She released her grip of the tiller. 'You take the tiller, Riell. You should have the skill to keep us mid-river.'

She pulled out a knife from under her tunic and, looking at Atreu and Verlinden, said, 'I'd suggest you get your knives – we're about to join the war.'

*

When it became obvious that the Maelstrom was narrowing, Atreu felt his body tense as he brandished his knife. What would

Teyth do if he was alive and with them on the *Perisher*? Would his baresark rage have helped against the Dusk-wraiths?

A tentacle came towards Atreu and he drew a breath. He watched as it reached towards the bow, collapsing just short. He realised he had been gripping his knife so hard that his knuckles were hurting.

He stared ahead – the banks seemed to be encroaching further on the Maelstrom, but it was impossible to tell whether this was real or an illusion. He imagined the sky above them was lightening and the stars fading – how long was it until dawn?

He heard a shout from Aeshya. Turning his head, he saw her slash at a tentacle that had reached over the bow of the ship. The tentacle evaporated, but Aeshya was left holding her wrist in pain.

'Damn,' she cried, 'I didn't think it touched me. It's as if the pain has come up through my knife.'

Atreu's attention was caught by two wraith tendrils coming towards him. He tensed, ready to strike. They probed forward, towards his neck, and instinctively he jumped back. The wraith arm reached forward a short distance, and then collapsed.

Atreu was shivering with relief when he heard Verlinden cry out, and the sound of her knife clattering on the wooden deck.

She was holding her forearm when Atreu raced over to her. 'I've lost sensation,' she said.

'This is madness,' said Atreu. 'We can't fight them like this.'

'I'll do it on my own,' shouted Aeshya as she stabbed at another tentacle that had made it over the deckline. She screamed in pain as she cut through it and watched it dissipate.

'These wraiths have defeated whole battalions,' said Atreu. 'What are we trying to do here?'

Aeshya glared at him, her face twisted in pain and frustration. 'I should never have sailed downriver with a crew of cowards.'

Atreu walked towards her. 'I'm not a coward.'

'Anyone who feels they have to say that usually is, in my experience,' said Aeshya.

'You have no experience in fighting these wraiths,' said Atreu, 'so I think you should listen to me.'

'What experience do you have?' She almost spat the words in disgust.

'I've seen what happens when a battalion is under siege by them. I know what it's like.'

'How do you know? You're not a soldier – you wouldn't have survived the blink of an eye in a siege.'

'The Books have shown me. This is a fight we cannot win with weapons.'

'No? What do we use then – our bare hands?'

'I'm going to use my head,' said Atreu. 'Why fight these Dusk-wraiths if we don't have to?'

'What are you saying?'

'You're thinking of them as river-pirates breaching our deck.'

'Here comes another one,' cried Aeshya, brandishing her knife.

'Just step back,' said Atreu.

Aeshya hesitated and then took a step away. The wraith collapsed before it reached her.

'See, it doesn't matter if they cross the deckline, does it?' said Atreu. 'They aren't river-pirates.'

'So you're saying we just stay here, mid-deck?'

'Yes. The river is still narrowing, but we may be safe until dawn. Why fight the wraiths before we really have to? We're just trying to get to Farepont, remember.'

Aeshya fell silent. The only indication that she had accepted Atreu's strategy was when she moved to join Atreu and Verlinden mid-ship, near where Riell manned the tiller.

The wraiths' arms were now regularly breaching the deck, but were collapsing far short of Atreu and the others.

'You were right,' said Aeshya after some time.

'We're not quite safe yet,' said Atreu. 'They're still getting closer.'

'It's almost dawn. It looks like we'll make it to Farepont. You know, the three of you have never told me where you are going after Treyheim and the Rimforest.'

'We will be travelling from Treyfell to Teuron and then on to the Plains of Vygird,' said Atreu. 'The reason I haven't told you is because you haven't asked.'

'A person's business is their own,' said Aeshya.

'Then why ask now?'

Aeshya shrugged. 'Who knows? Maybe after what we've been through I care about what happens to the three of you.'

Just then, the first rays of the sun rose above the eastern horizon.

'We've done it,' cried Riell.

The Dusk-wraiths groaned and pulsed on the riverbanks and started receding, their eyes paling as dawn broke.

Aeshya visibly relaxed. 'I think this calls for a celebration. Where's that ale?'

'I'm afraid our ale didn't survive the fire,' said Riell, 'and Atreu and Verlinden didn't bring any back from Midfell.'

'But you found the supplies in an inn, didn't you?' Aeshya's mouth fell open. 'How could you not find some ale?'

'We didn't think to bring any,' said Atreu.

Aeshya shook her head. 'I don't know how I made it with a crew like you.' The tone in her voice, though, had changed back to what it had been like at the start of the voyage.

She disappeared aft. The sky was lightening when she returned carrying four tankards and a small barrel under her arm.

'Where did you find those?' asked Riell.

Aeshya smiled. 'You have some mysteries you're keeping from me – let me keep one or two from you.'

She started pouring ale into the tankards. 'And I don't want anyone saying it's too early in the morning for this. If the sun was rising when it was supposed to, it would be close to midday by now anyway.'

'Faemir don't drink ale,' said Verlinden, waving away the offer.

Aeshya shrugged and then held her tankard high in the air.

'To the *Perisher*. Neither helles nor ill-wind could beat her. Neither pirates nor Dusk-wraiths could stop her.'

Atreu and Riell drank from the tankards as the sun appeared and the thin, dark green line of the Rimforest's edge came into view in the far distance.

Riell raised his tankard again, as Aeshya had done. 'To the best river captain on the Maelstrom.'

She looked at the windrider with a softness in her eyes. 'What a shame about that covenant,' she said, and took a deep draught.

*

The *Perisher* sailed into Farepont just as the sun reached its highest point for the day. Atreu stood on the forecastle and watched the myriad of anchored boats and floating dwellings glide past, each one sporting a uniquely patterned coloured flag. He gasped at the sheer number of the vessels as the Maelstrom widened dramatically. Even with the dwellings on the banks clearly damaged by the ravages of war, Farepont was an impressive sight.

The river current had become barely perceptible, and the blue waters of the Maelstrom shone in the pale mid-winter sunlight. Atreu became aware, as they sailed further in, that the town was alive with activity. All around, people were traversing floating walkways between various buildings or rowing between dwellings. There was good-natured shouting to be heard from merchants bartering with each other, the excited calls of children emerging from their homes, and the constant lapping of a thousand oars as they sliced through the water. And as sails of every imaginable colour were being unfurled before him, Atreu could pretend, just for a moment, that the war didn't exist.

But as his eyes darted from one part of the scene to another, his thoughts darkened. Such magnificence existed on the Mountain, yet now places like Farepont were islands in the river of war that was flooding his world. How long would these last remaining places survive?

Aeshya was standing on the tiller platform and steering the *Perisher* through the clear river-corridors between the anchored boats and floating houses. She stood there erect, almost willing the Fareponters to notice her ship and hold it in awe despite its patched-up main mast and burnt-out aft deck.

'Your father will be pleased to see you, won't he?' said Atreu.

'It will be the *Perisher* that will bring him the most joy,' said Aeshya.

'Are you sailing to his house now?'

Aeshya slumped a little, as if suddenly hit by an unwelcome thought. 'We'll find him at one of the floating inns. I know which ones are his favourites – he has quite a few, so it may take a while.'

Atreu noticed two sleek sailboats rapidly approaching them, each containing several uniformed men. 'Who are they?' he asked.

Aeshya eyed them curiously. 'They're Farepont river shyreffs. They would usually register new boats coming in, but I don't know why there are so many of them.'

The sailboats were quickly manoeuvred so that they were parallel with the *Perisher*'s hull and almost touching.

'Permission to come aboard,' shouted the large river shyreff in the lead boat.

'What are we going to do?' asked Atreu, addressing Aeshya.

'I don't think we have much choice.' Aeshya signalled to Verlinden and Riell to lower the hull ladders and ropes, and then shouted, 'Permission granted.'

Two dozen shyreffs soon stood on deck.

'What is the problem?' asked Aeshya.

The head-shyreff slowly looked Aeshya up and down. He then turned his attention to Verlinden. 'You're Faemir,' he said to her, and then, turning back to Aeshya, 'You, I'm not sure about.'

'What difference does it make?' said Aeshya. 'You must know there's a truce.'

'A truce?' The shyreff laughed grimly and looked around at the others behind him. 'That truce was made a long way from Farepont.'

'Who's threatening you?' asked Verlinden. 'The Faemir or the Dusk-spawn? As far as I know, the Faemir didn't attack Farepont even when we were at war with you.'

'Sometimes the real dangers lie in a false peace,' said the shyreff.

'What are you talking about?' said Riell. 'That sort of talk is going to cost us the war. The Faemir are now our allies. I'll vouch for Verlinden. What is it you want of us?'

'I used to respect the word of windriders,' said the shyreff, 'but I doubt any of us can be certain who to trust anymore.'

'I will ask the question again,' said Aeshya. 'What is it you want? I've always found Farepont to be a welcoming place – what has changed?'

The shyreff ignored her question and looked over the deck carefully. 'Where is your captain?' he asked.

'I'm the captain.' Aeshya's voice was steady and deliberate.

The shyreff raised his eyebrows slightly. 'I suppose you are now going to tell me that this ship is yours.'

'It belongs to my father. I am returning it to him from Hellespont.'

The shyreff was taken aback. 'You've battled the ill-winds in mid-winter? Is that how you lost the rest of your crew?'

'No,' said Aeshya. 'These three have been my only crew since Hellespont.'

The shyreff looked at the other three again. 'A Faemir, a windrider and ... and an Ascender, if I recognise the garb under that dirt.' He addressed Atreu. 'Aren't you going the wrong way? The Summit is upriver.'

'I completed my Ascent last year.' Atreu pointed to Verlinden. 'We are the only two surviving Ascenders who made it to Zenith.'

The shyreff raised his eyebrows again. 'Now you're telling me a Faemir can ascend. I'd heard rumours, but this is more than a truce if that is true.' He nodded to the other shyreffs. 'All right, let's take them until we can sort this out.'

Aeshya had already drawn her knife. 'You were not given permission to board the *Perisher* so that you could take her away from me.'

'We're not pirates,' said the shyreff. 'We need to make sure of certain things.'

'Since when are ship captains treated this way in Farepont?' said Aeshya.

The shyreff glared at her. 'Since we were forced to give our best ships and crews to the Faemir.'

'What has happened?' asked Riell.

'You should know. It was the windriders who carried the Faemir here.'

'My wings were damaged in a storm in the Upper Reaches. I've been travelling the Maelstrom ever since. I have no news of what the windriders have been undertaking.'

'So you know nothing of the new battle plan?' said the shyreff. 'Fight the Nazir from the Maelstrom?'

'No,' said Riell. 'But surely your ships weren't simply taken from you for the campaign?'

The shyreff smiled grimly. 'With an army of Faemir and windriders in our midst, what choice did we have?'

'So you wouldn't have willingly given those ships?' asked Atreu.

'With our best ships and crew gone, we are defenceless. The wraiths seem to creep closer every night, and pirates are a problem all the time. Any ship and crew coming through has to be checked.'

'You won't take the *Perisher* from me,' Aeshya repeated, brandishing her knife defiantly.

'Aeshya, let them do their checking,' said Atreu. 'They will find the *Perisher* belongs to your father.'

'Who is your father?' asked the shyreff.

Aeshya stood motionless. 'I am going to ask you only once more – leave my ship.'

The shyreffs now drew their swords.

'Aeshya –' Atreu began, before she interrupted.

'Don't think I don't know what's happening here, Atreu. You are where you wanted to be, so I'm no use to you anymore. I'll fight for the *Perisher* alone then.'

'You are mad,' said the shyreff. 'How do you think you will stop us?' He gestured to the others to capture her.

'Wait,' said Verlinden. The shyreff hesitated. 'I'd better warn you – she *is* a Faemir warrior, and unfortunately for all of you, she's a baresark.'

'What?' The head shyreff glanced around nervously at the others, who were now deadly still.

'How do you think we managed the voyage from Hellespont mid-winter with a crew this size?'

'A baresark.' The shyreff repeated the word to himself.

'You must have heard of the Faemir baresark warrior.'

'Of course I have. You're telling me this is her?'

'Look at her,' said Verlinden. 'Who else would face a dozen shyreffs with only a knife in her hand? Has she flinched? Is there anything about her that suggests she thinks she won't be able to fight you off?'

'I don't believe you,' said the shyreff, but there was a hint of doubt in his voice.

'Do you really know the true nature of a baresark?' asked Verlinden. 'The more threatened they are, the stronger and more dangerous they become. The greater the numbers against them, the more vicious they will be.'

The head-shyreff was now clearly nervous.

'I've seen what a baresark can do,' continued Verlinden. 'They can mutilate whole battalions with their bare hands. It makes you sick, watching them in full fury.'

She stepped closer to the head-shyreff. 'And do you want to know the most horrific thing about a baresark? They have no control once they start. You can't appeal to their mercy, you can't reason with them. They are possessed with a fury that only death and carnage can quench.'

The head-shyreff swallowed and his Adam's apple bobbed up and down. He couldn't bring himself to look at Aeshya anymore. 'Is it too late?' His voice faltered.

'Just back away from her slowly,' said Verlinden. 'Look at the ground. Keep your head low. And whatever you do, don't make any sudden movements.'

All the shyreffs were now backing towards the deck rails. One of them fell, tumbling over a coiled rope, and the others froze.

'One more of those stumbles and you might start the fury,' said Verlinden. 'Just move steadily, and leave the ship without looking at her.'

The shyreff who had fallen picked himself up, and was the last to climb over the rails, onto the rope ladders and back down to the shyreff-boats.

Atreu leant over the rails and watched them sail rapidly away. He turned to see Aeshya was still standing as she had been, a look of menace on her face and still brandishing her knife.

'They're gone,' said Atreu.

Aeshya didn't move for a moment. It was as if she was in a trance. Then she suddenly burst out laughing. The others quickly joined her, and the noise got so loud that Atreu worried that the shyreffs might hear, even across the distance they had travelled.

'A baresark?' said Aeshya. 'What made you think of that?'

Verlinden stopped laughing. 'My sister was one, and I think the way you stood there so defiantly – it was exactly what she would have done.'

'Your sister was a baresark?' Aeshya's laughter faltered a little.

'Yes, she was the Faemir leader Valkyra. You remind me of her in some way.'

'Valkyra? Your sister was the dreaded Valkyra?'

'Yes.'

'And you say I remind you of her?'

'In some ways – some of the better ways.'

Aeshya stared straight ahead, past the forecastle.

Atreu followed her line of sight and saw a group of buildings which looked like floating inns. 'Should we see if we can find your father now?' he said.

'You three should prepare for your journey to Treyheim.'

'We have a long night to get ready, haven't we?' said Atreu. 'Isn't it only a day's travelling to the Rimforest? It wouldn't make sense heading off before daybreak.'

Aeshya nodded.

'Well, we can help search for your father then, can't we?' said Atreu.

'Our agreement is over,' said Aeshya. 'Don't feel you owe me anything.'

'But if –'

'Look.' Aeshya was suddenly angry. 'Nothing I did on our voyage was in anything but my own interest. If I saved you, I was saving myself. Forget any feelings of gratitude – I don't deserve them.'

'Just because you *think* you don't deserve them, doesn't mean you don't actually deserve them,' said Atreu, 'but we'll respect your wishes. Just take us somewhere we can stay the night and we'll work out where to go in the morning.'

Aeshya groaned. 'All of you are so frustrating.' She looked at Atreu, then Verlinden and then Riell. 'Spend the night on the *Perisher* – you probably won't find anywhere else to sleep with the way the war is going.'

She turned the tiller towards the floating inn on her right. 'Come on, perhaps we'll be in luck and you'll meet my father.'

They descended the rope ladders, stepped onto the creaking platform in front of the inn, and followed Aeshya inside. It took a moment for Atreu's eyes to adjust. The thought struck him that it was strange that inns, no matter where they were on the Mountain, rarely had large windows.

This inn was gloomier than most. Several old sailors sat along benches, looking like they hadn't moved in years. Aeshya had already sat down near them and was glancing around with a strange look on her face. The walls were decorated, if that was the word, with old ropes, nets and pieces of broken mast.

Atreu noticed that Riell was standing in a corner looking at a large wooden object that had been mounted on the wall.

'What is it?' asked Atreu.

Riell gestured him over. 'Can't you see?'

Atreu stepped closer and squinted through the gloom. 'They're part of a set of windrider wings,' he said.

The innkeeper appeared from a rear door. 'Will it be ales for all of you?'

'Where did you get this from?' asked Riell.

'The wings?' The innkeeper snorted. 'There were quite a few of those floating around a few weeks ago.'

'What do you mean?'

The innkeeper looked him up and down, obviously realising that Riell wore the garb of a windrider. 'I didn't think you lot had much to do with inns.'

'You said there were wings floating about? What are you talking about? The windriders who carried the Faemir to Farepont – what happened to them?'

'A sad business,' said the innkeeper. 'You can't blame me for taking the wings, though. It's river law. Flotsam. They were just floating around. That makes them mine – so don't start telling me I've stolen them. Don't tell me that.'

'No, no,' said Riell. 'I'm not accusing you of anything. I just want to know what happened.'

The innkeeper started to get agitated and began talking more quickly. 'I'm not a thief. They were just floating around. Who's going to make use of broken windrider wings? Who's going to do that? It's the river law. Ask anyone.'

'Look, I just want –'

The innkeeper threw up his hands in a flurry. 'All right, take them back then. I don't want any trouble with windriders. As if we don't have enough trouble around here. Take them if they're yours. Just take them.' He turned around and quickly disappeared into the back again.

'You've put the wind in Barlyon's sails,' said one of the old men, a tankard of ale in front of him.

'We've only just arrived in Farepont from upriver,' said Riell. 'Could you tell us what has happened here?'

The old man nodded into his half-empty ale. 'Keep buying me ales and I'll talk for as long as you want.'

'I can afford to buy you *one*,' said Riell.

'It all happened about two weeks ago,' said the old man, coughing into his hand. 'We got up one morning and the sky was filled with windriders as far as the eye could see. I thought I was dreaming at first. I didn't even know there were that many of you. We only ever see one or two at a time here, but this must have been thousands of them.'

'And each one was carrying a Faemir, right?' asked Verlinden.

He looked at her like he had just noticed she was there. 'That's right. That was more Faemir than I'd ever seen in my life. Farepont's always been a safe sort of place.'

'So what happened?' asked Verlinden.

'A new battle strategy, from what I was told,' said the old man. 'The Faemir were going to launch a campaign against the Nazir along the river from here to Stromspont. It made sense to me, but then, I'm an old man who spends his days talking and drinking ales, not a soldier.'

'So the Faemir found enough ships and crew to take them?'

'Yes. No one here is too keen on fighting, but the Maelstrom is still safe from those wraiths, and it was the Faemir who were going to do the actual fighting.'

'Did any of the windriders go with them?' asked Riell.

'Some. I don't know for certain how many.'

Riell looked at the broken wings. 'Then what happened?'

The old man started coughing. He reached out for his tankard of ale and took a deep draught. 'No one knows exactly, but most of the windriders were here for a few days, waiting for the right winds to head back wherever they came from. It's often calm around here mid-winter ...'

'And?'

'I believe I'm ready for my next ale.'

Atreu grabbed his tankard and headed through to the back. 'I'll get you your ale.'

'Please,' said Riell. 'I need to know what befell the windriders.'

'The winds finally arrived late one day.'

'They didn't fly out at dusk, did they?'

'In case you haven't noticed, the days are getting shorter and shorter. It's dusk before you know it. It's not natural anymore.'

'They wouldn't have been so foolish as to fly out at dusk,' said Riell.

Atreu had returned by this time with a full tankard, and he placed it in front of the old man.

'Thank you – there's nothing like an ale when you're telling a story.' He took a draught. 'Now, where was I?'

'You were saying the windriders flew out of Farepont at dusk,' said Riell.

'No, I don't think I said that. They may have misjudged dusk a little, but I don't think that was the problem. People have made some guesses at what happened. I think you can't underestimate those Dusk-wraiths. They've been growing every night – you can see it. There've been times when they've blotted out the stars. I heard tell that the windriders thought they would be safe once they were flying, but they must have picked one of the nights when the wraiths were airborne to leave Farepont.'

'The windriders were attacked mid-air by the wraiths?'

'No one could tell too clearly from down here, but that's what probably happened. It was raining windriders that night, though, that's for sure.'

Riell buried his face in his hands. 'How many survived?'

'Only a dozen or so of the ones who fell. Who knows how many escaped the wraiths altogether.'

'And the survivors are still in Farepont?'

'Most of them needed to recover, and they've been trying to repair their wings.'

'Where are they?' asked Riell. 'Could you take me to them?'

The old man smiled. 'I could probably find out – but I don't like leaving tankards half drunk.'

'That's the best you've been for a long time,' said Aeshya. 'Only half drunk.'

'There's only one thing that will make me better than that.'

'She's moored outside,' said Aeshya.

'Don't torment an old man.'

'I would never do that.'

His eyes narrowed. 'You're serious, aren't you?'

Aeshya nodded. 'Come and see for yourself.'

The old man got up. 'Oh,' said Aeshya, glancing at the others. 'This is my father, Jethrah.'

Chapter Twenty-two

As the first wave crashed through Farepont in the small hours of the morning, Atreu was flipped out of his bunk and onto the floor.

'What was that?' asked Verlinden, pulling her blankets away and jumping out of her bunk.

Still half-groggy with sleep, they climbed out onto the deck just as another giant wave pounded the *Perisher*, and they lost their footing.

Atreu got to his feet and looked around. Only a fraction of the many lights that had been shining in Farepont when they had gone to bed were still alight. The sounds of confused voices poured into the air, followed by the ominous clang of bells ringing from the darkness. Upriver, a dark shadow of water loomed up at them like a moving hillside. Atreu braced himself as the wave crashed against the *Perisher*'s hull, but was still unable to keep his balance.

By the time he had recovered, more Farepont lights had been

extinguished, and the clangour of bells, which had faded as the wave had moved through the town, was now back at full strength.

Atreu reached for Verlinden's hand as they stared into the darkness upriver, waiting for the next wall of water to bear down on them. It was some time before he could allow himself to relax.

'Hopefully that's the last of them,' said Atreu.

'They were far bigger than anything I remember seeing in the helles,' said Verlinden. 'Were they more unnatural waves, like the ones the currachsmen were talking about?'

'How can Farepont be a safe-haven for so long, and then be engulfed by instability just after I arrive?'

'Don't start thinking you're responsible again, Atreu. The safe havens on the Mountain are all disappearing, but it's got nothing to do with you. The Nazir are winning – that's all there is to it.'

'If we don't get to the Caves of Arach soon, there will be nothing left of the Mountain to save.'

'*Perisher* ho!' came a cry from the waters below.

Atreu leant over the rail to see Aeshya help her father from a rowboat tied to the hull below, and up the rope ladder.

As Aeshya and Jethrah climbed onto the deck, Atreu could smell ale on their breaths.

'We need to get away from here,' said Aeshya.

'You think there are more waves to come?' asked Verlinden.

'Yes – I can feel it. And from what I can see, they are peaking just as they hit Farepont.'

'How can you feel anything with all that ale in your stomach?' asked Atreu.

Aeshya glared at him. 'Don't worry about how much ale I've had. You should take the time to enjoy yourself, too, while you've got the chance. It might do you some good.'

'Our journey isn't over,' said Atreu. He turned to Jethrah. 'Do you think there's more to come?'

'We've never had anything like this before,' said Jethrah, slurring slightly. 'A few waves have moved through recently and given us a bit of a ride – but nothing more.'

Atreu drew a sharp breath. 'Where's Riell?'

Aeshya shrugged.

'I said, where's Riell?'

'I don't know. We took him to where the surviving windriders are, on the outskirts of downriver Farepont.'

'You didn't try to find him after the waves hit?'

'It's in the opposite direction to the *Perisher*,' said Aeshya.

'You and this damn boat,' said Atreu.

'Look, Atreu, how safe do you think a rowboat is in these giant waves? I had to get us back here as quickly as possible.'

'Will Riell be safe where he is?' asked Verlinden.

'Are any of us?'

'So you just left him to drown?' Atreu felt blood rushing to his face.

'The waves may have eased by the time they reached the downriver outskirts,' said Jethrah. His eyes ran across the deck of the *Perisher* from one end to the other.

'I told you,' said Aeshya, 'I didn't have time.'

'Didn't have time?' Atreu clenched his teeth. 'You've got what you want, and now we don't matter anymore.'

Aeshya took a step towards him. 'Don't try to make me feel guilty. I'm not your protector. We had an agreement, and it's over now that we're in Farepont. We're all responsible for ourselves. Don't try to make me responsible for Riell or any of you.'

Atreu looked at Jethrah. 'I hope you enjoy the *Perisher* – if it is yours to enjoy.'

'What are you talking about?' said Aeshya.

'All right,' said Atreu, still addressing Jethrah. 'Is this precious boat really yours, or have we helped your daughter steal it from its rightful owner?'

Jethrah looked away and there was a deep silence for a moment. 'She was mine once,' he said slowly, his ale-soaked breath frosting in front of his face, 'but I had to sell her.'

Aeshya put her arm around her father as he started shaking. 'There, Atreu, you have your truth. That's what you wanted, isn't it? That's all that matters to you. He sold it – that's the truth.' She looked up at Atreu with tears welling in her eyes. 'But if you're going to fish for the truth, then make sure you know all of it – not just the part that agrees with what you already believe.'

Atreu couldn't meet her eyes.

'My father was forced to sell the *Perisher*,' said Aeshya. 'There were always merchants who wanted to take her from him. They could have given him the chance to make one more voyage. He would have been able to sell the cargo and get the money. Just one more voyage and he could have paid his debts.'

'Aeshya, they don't want to hear this.' Jethrah's voice was broken.

Aeshya shook her head. 'They didn't give him a chance. They were in the right. Of course they were. That's how things work on the Mountain. They had the money so they were in the right. We're the thieves. We should be ashamed of ourselves. Is that what you wanted to hear? Does that bring joy to your heart?'

'I didn't mean to call you a thief,' said Atreu.

'What else could you have meant by your question? You, who think you are so virtuous, who think you stand above everything – you're not even being honest with yourself.'

'I –'

'Don't even try to defend yourself. I know what you think of me. I've known it from the start.' She gestured back down to the rowboat. 'There are provisions there for you. I don't know why I bothered.'

'I truly am sorry,' said Atreu. 'The thought of Riell ... it just ...'

'Of course, Atreu, you're the only one who feels anything.' She wiped the tears from her face. 'Do you know that the *Perisher* is the name the new owners gave her? Do you want to know what her real name is?'

Atreu tried to turn away from her gaze, but couldn't.

'She's called the *Aeshya*.'

Just then another wave hit and water flooded across the deck, knocking everyone off balance.

Aeshya was the first to scramble back onto her feet. 'Unfurl the sails,' she cried as she raced to the main mast.

Atreu and Verlinden sprang into action, and by the time they had climbed back down after unfurling the fore and aft sails, Aeshya had already winched in the anchor and had her hands on the tiller.

When the next wave crashed into them, the *Perisher* had already gained some forward momentum and rode along with the swell, rather than being overwhelmed by it.

Atreu could see other captains around them who had had the same idea, and were now racing in the eye of the wave. Aeshya spun the tiller starboard and then port in a desperate attempt to try to avoid the floating buildings that lay ahead.

The *Perisher* hit the corner of a platform and the ship lurched violently to the side.

'Trim the aft sail,' cried Aeshya. 'If we go side-on to the wave, we'll go down.'

Atreu took a step towards the aft mast, but saw that Jethrah had already scaled it and was pulling in the sail ropes.

'Strap yourself into the harness,' shouted Atreu.

'No time,' called Jethrah, as he worked the ropes and shortened the sails.

The *Perisher* lurched again as it clipped a small boat and Jethrah lost his grip. He was left swinging in mid-air, one hand clutching the leather harness.

Atreu scrambled up the mast and threw out a rope for him to grab hold of. Jethrah pulled himself back towards the mast and hung on grimly.

As Aeshya worked the tiller, the *Perisher* swung back so that its aft was again face-on to the wave. They were now out of the most heavily populated parts of Farepont, making navigation easier. Then the wave started to lose its power, until finally it no longer had the force to carry them, and the water washed through the hull, leaving the ship in calm water.

Atreu and the others joined Aeshya at the tiller platform. Sunrise had finally come, and the light revealed the carnage around them. Boats floated upside down in the water, and the Maelstrom was filled with Fareponters, all swimming to the nearest floating platform.

'What now?' asked Atreu.

'One thing we *don't* do is start hauling people up into the *Perisher*,' said Aeshya. 'We need to get as far downriver as we can – Farepont is obviously no longer safe.'

Atreu was about to speak, but Aeshya continued. 'I don't want another argument. While you're still on the *Perisher*, I'm the captain. The Fareponters are all strong swimmers, and it looks like most of the buildings are still afloat. I think we will have a hard enough time finding Riell and the other windriders. They are the ones you should be worrying about.'

She saw Atreu staring at her. 'Don't look at me like that,' she said. 'Did you expect that I would leave him behind? I haven't put those vows of celibacy to the test yet.'

*

The *Perisher* had reached the outer edge of Farepont when Atreu spotted Riell standing on a platform, waving at them with both hands. Around him were the bedraggled figures of a dozen windriders.

Aeshya saw them too, and steered the ship alongside the platform. She gave the orders for the others to lower the rope ladders so that Riell could board.

Atreu embraced the windrider as he stepped onto the deck.

'See what happens when you leave us?' said Atreu, smiling.

'Those waves *were* a bit of a surprise,' said Riell.

'Aeshya wants to head downriver,' said Atreu. 'She thinks there are more on the way.'

'There are many ways into the Rimforest apart from Treyheim,' said Aeshya. 'You need to travel east anyway if you want to reach Treyfell. The Maelstrom runs almost parallel to the Rim for several days. Sailing east for a day or two may even save you some time. You just have to make sure you find the Treyfell path once you enter the forest.'

Riell shifted awkwardly on the spot and looked down at the other windriders back on the platform.

'What's wrong?' asked Atreu.

'For all we know,' he said, 'the Keep may be completely cut off and unprotected.'

'What are you saying?'

'The windriders have a covenant which did not change when we became the Order of the Wynde. All of us have to try to return – it's our duty.'

Atreu nodded slowly. 'I see.'

'How will you return?' asked Verlinden.

'The others have been collecting damaged wings and have started repairing them. They believe they have enough wooden struts to put together a set of wings for each of us, and there is enough sail material in Farepont to finish the task.'

'You're going to stay here?' asked Atreu.

'Only for as long as it takes to complete the repairs. Those waves have set us back a little, but we should be able to get airborne in a week or so.'

'I see.'

'Atreu, I'm a windrider.'

'I know, Riell, I know.' Atreu sighed. 'I've kept you away from your duties and your own kind for far too long.'

'I have my doubts about your safety in Farepont,' said Aeshya. 'You only felt the tail end of the waves here at this end. It's chaos upriver – and I'm convinced not only that we haven't seen the last of the waves, but that they are going to be peaking further and further downriver.'

'So what are you going to do?' asked Riell. 'Try to outrun the waves?'

'I don't see a better option. I can't see the point in just sitting here and waiting for them to hit again.'

Riell looked across at the other windriders. 'We don't have a choice.'

'You always have a choice,' said Aeshya. 'You just have to know how to look at things.'

'Well, what choice do we have?'

'Come with my father and I downriver. The *Perisher* is a big ship – we can carry your wings until you repair them. I need a crew that I can trust won't steal the *Perisher* from us – and I know how hard that can be to find.'

'What will you do when we have completed our repairs and return to the Keep?'

'I'm just trying to survive the next few days – I'll worry about that problem when it is upon me.'

Riell glanced back down at the other windriders. 'How much time do we have to decide?'

'I want to leave Farepont as far behind as possible before nightfall. The way the days are shortening, that doesn't leave us much time at all, particularly if you want to load the wings on board.'

Riell nodded and headed back down the rope ladder to where the other windriders were still standing.

*

Micah sensed the discomfort around the room – it seemed to him that they were all competing for the same stale air. The fifty-nine members of the Circle were crowded into the largest chamber they could find in the monasts. There was no room for any chairs, even if they could be found among the Felsen, so the Holy Men stood shoulder to shoulder in a series of concentric circles, in an attempt to mirror as closely as possible the customary formation.

In the centre of the crowded circles stood the windrider Theander. The floor shook intermittently as he spoke.

'The wraiths are increasingly airborne – that was a lesson we learnt,' he said. 'They can't go far above the ground, but they make it difficult for us to see what is happening on the surface on the Mountain.'

'But you must have landed during daylight,' said Leyvin.

Theander shook his head. 'The air currents outside the Upper Reaches are unpredictable. If we landed, there was always the danger that we wouldn't have the updraughts to ascend again. We avoided landing at all costs. The winds in the Mid-Reaches are more predictable at altitude, so we rarely got close enough to the ground to really see what was happening.'

'But what did you see?' said Leyvin. 'Yours is the only information we have about what is happening.'

Theander drew a deep breath. 'I'm afraid I don't have any good news. I saw no part of the Mountain that was untouched by instability or the Dusk-spawn attack.'

'No part?'

'As I said, we didn't get a chance to survey a great deal, but what we saw was complete devastation. Towns and cities deserted or aflame. Masses of Maelir moving aimlessly across the Mountain by day, and countless fire circles to ward off the wraiths at night.'

'It was my understanding,' said Holthim, 'that the Maelstrom and the Rimforest were safe.'

'The Rim's canopy still appears to offer protection. The Maelstrom was safe from direct attack, but that is only of consolation to those who live mid-river, like the Fareponters, or who spend the nights in boats. From what I could see, the Dusk-wraiths take possession of both banks soon after dusk and have been encroaching on the water a little further every night.'

'So what hope is there, Theander?' asked Micah. 'You must give us some hope.'

Theander's shoulders slumped noticeably. 'In truth, I don't know what I can say. The windriders' numbers were decimated when we took off from Farepont. I've never seen anything like it — we had no defence against the Dusk-wraiths. The one advantage we have always had is that we were airborne. Against the wraiths, it's almost a disadvantage.'

'What of the Faemir battalions across the Mountain?' asked Baelren. 'How are they faring against the wraiths?'

'From the altitude we were flying it was impossible to tell Maelir from Faemir. I saw no evidence of the Faemir battalions holding their ground anywhere. Rhea and the others we carried from the Keep had set off on their campaign downriver with a few riders, but I have no news of how they are faring.'

'It appears our slim hopes rest with them,' said Holthim.

'There is another hope,' said Micah, 'and that rests with the Ascenders Atreu and Verlinden. Do you have any news of their fortunes?'

'No,' said Theander. 'I understand their destination after the Source was Farepont, but I could find no evidence that they had been there.'

'When would they have been expected to arrive?' asked one of the other Liche.

'Impossible to say,' said Holthim. 'It depends how long they spent at the Source.'

'It also depends if they made it to the Source in the first place,' said Micah, 'and whether Riell and Leylan were in a fit state to carry them on to Farepont after the storm.' He made it obvious to the other Circle members that he was staring at Leyvin. He then turned to Lythos. 'Do you have nothing to add to what is being discussed? This is not like you.'

'I don't believe in saying anything if there is nothing to achieve,' said Lythos. 'Look at us in here – this is not the Circle, so why are we pretending that it is, and why are we pretending that what we decide here can influence anything?'

'But the Areol is only a shell,' said Holthim. 'It is the members who are the heart of the Circle. We are all still here, and I don't think our minds or our judgement are diminished.'

'No, but our means of implementing our carefully thought-out judgements have diminished to almost nothing. I believe we are fooling ourselves if we think any decision we make here can make a difference.'

'We have to find some hope,' said Micah.

'We have little more than a hundred windriders in the Keep. With every moment that passes, another of our beautiful buildings crashes to the ground. It is only a matter of time before even these monasts crumble. We have nowhere to go, and without the windriders, we have no means of getting there.'

'I believe there is a chance of evacuation to the Source,' said Theander. 'It would take many weeks to carry all the Holy Men there with the few windriders now in the Keep, but at least we have some hope.'

'Do we know whether the Source is untouched by instability?' asked Micah. 'It would be pointless evacuating otherwise.'

'I believe Micah has a good argument,' said Holthim. 'The Source has always been stable, but then, so had the Keep until recently. Theander, can you send a windrider to the Source to see what state it is in?'

'I've already done that under First Speaker Leyvin's instructions,' said Theander.

Holthim appeared a little taken aback. 'That was a sound strategy, First Speaker Leyvin, but why had you not informed us, and why have you not offered evacuation to the Source as an option during this session?'

'Second Speaker Holthim, I hope you are not suggesting anything untoward. I believed it was Theander's place to report the strategy to the Circle. I discussed it with him shortly after the windriders returned, and we agreed that evacuation to the Source was our only hope. I believe we have no option but to pursue it as quickly as possible.'

'This seems a contravention of our procedures, doesn't it?' said Holthim.

Leyvin stared at the Second Speaker. 'Then challenge me.'

There was a tense silence before Lythos spoke. 'So we have a remote chance of evacuation,' he said, frowning at Leyvin. 'But that will only stave off the inevitable, unless we can somehow defeat the Nazir.' He took his eyes off his brother and addressed

Theander. 'I need to ask the question that all of us have been avoiding. The nights continue to grow and the days shrink. Is there anything you have seen, Theander, that could give us a chance of staving off the Mountain's fall into dusk?'

The room fell into a silent tension. It was as if everyone wanted to hear the answer to the question, and yet also wanted to shield themselves from the words.

Theander finally answered. 'I have seen no evidence that anything can be done to defeat the Dusk-spawn and save our world from darkness.'

No one spoke for a long time. All eyes eventually turned to Leyvin, in the hope that he would offer some response.

'I believe this session is over,' he said finally.

There was an awkward pause, and then the Holy Men started to file out of the chamber.

*

As a pallid dawn broke and the Dusk-wraiths started receding from the riverbank, Atreu and Verlinden made a final check of their provisions. Atreu knew they would have very little daylight to make it to the safety of the Rimforest. If they were out in the open when the sun set again, there would be no escape from the wraiths. Aeshya had assured them that this was as close as the Maelstrom would get to the Rim's edge for many days, so this was their best chance.

The rope ladders had already been lowered in anticipation. Riell had offered to row them ashore and was already waiting, oars in hand.

Atreu turned to say farewell to Aeshya. 'I know you don't want me to thank you,' he said, 'but I will anyway. If someone told me there was a river captain on the Maelstrom with more courage, I would not believe them.'

'That makes a change,' said Aeshya, smiling. 'Normally you are too trusting.'

Verlinden embraced her and said, 'You could have been a fine Faemir.'

Aeshya laughed. 'Perhaps, if you enjoyed yourselves a little more, you might have had a chance of converting me. Good fortune to both of you.'

Atreu and Verlinden bade farewell to Jethrah and the windriders and climbed down the ladder into the boat.

Riell started rowing, and Atreu scanned the shore for any Dusk-wraith remnants. He saw no signs, but the light this morning seemed to have a grey hue. Riell fought his way through the tangle of riverweeds near the shore and the rowboat touched bottom.

'It looks like you two are going to get your feet wet,' said Riell.

Atreu and Verlinden finished tying their packs onto their backs.

'We had better get moving,' said Atreu.

Riell nodded. 'I can't believe that our paths are finally parting. I have faith in you, Atreu. The fate of the Mountain rests with you both.'

'I should never have asked you to come on the voyage,' said Atreu. 'I had no right.'

Riell shook his head. 'This is not the time to discuss what we've done right or wrong. Let us keep that for when we are both old and grey, and can spend our days remembering, rather than doing.'

Atreu and Riell embraced, and Atreu clasped his hand, and raised it into the air in the manner of his people. It was a gesture he had almost forgotten since leaving Valesend. With sadness, he realised that the last person he had embraced in this way had been Teyth.

'We will both miss you,' said Verlinden, after Riell had pulled back. 'If it wasn't for your actions there would have been no truce between the Maelir and Faemir.'

Riell took the oars in his hands. 'Now go, both of you. Time is disappearing for all of us.'

Atreu and Verlinden stepped out into the water and waded through the thick riverweeds to shore. By the time they had reached dry land, Riell was already halfway back to the *Perisher*.

Atreu gave a last wave in his friend's direction, and then he and Verlinden headed away from the river.

*

Micah sat on the edge of the Keep and looked down at the dark swirling clouds below. The ground shuddered intermittently – the frequency of the waves of instability was increasing. Micah had tuned out the sound of crashing buildings in the distance, and could no longer bear to look at the dark, empty spaces between the sparkling towers, which grew with each tremor.

With a start, he realised someone had sat down beside him. It took him a moment to register that it was Lythos. They exchanged a glance and then both stared down past their feet at the grey swirls.

'Is this how it ends?' asked Lythos finally. 'Will this great pillar we are on shatter and everything we have up here simply crash to the ground?'

'It makes so many of the things we have spent time arguing about seem a little petty,' said Micah.

'You know, Leyvin is still hatching further plans. He never stops.'

'What plans are there left to hatch?'

'I suspect he's making certain that he will be one of the first to leave for the Source if we receive reports that it is still stable.'

'Did he tell you that?'

'Not directly. I don't think I'm part of his plans anymore – but I know him well enough to work out what he is doing.'

'Are you not going to try to be among the first group?'

Lythos shrugged. 'I don't know. I'm not sure I see the point, if everything is going to be destroyed anyway.'

'I'm going to move that as many books as we can salvage are taken first,' said Micah.

'That sounds like old Praether's last wish.'

Micah ran his fingers through his beard. 'I'm glad he didn't live to see this. He loved books, but he always loved the Keep, too. What is happening here would have destroyed him.'

'It's destroying all of us,' said Lythos.

The clouds above their heads parted for a moment and the sun shone through with pale, sickly rays.

'The sun is dying,' said Micah. 'Can you feel it?'

'Yes, I've sensed it for some time.' Lythos' voice was soft, as if he was afraid of being overheard.

'Do you remember Praether's last session in the Circle?' asked Micah.

'Yes, very clearly.'

'He knew he was finished, didn't he?'

'He did – there was no way he was going to avoid being expelled. And yet, he left with a parting argument that changed everything. It was something the likes of which only Leyvin could have even come close to.'

'You know, that's how I think we should all go when our time is nigh.'

Lythos looked at Micah. 'You are right.' He stood up. 'What would Praether have done if he was still alive?'

Micah stopped stroking his beard. 'I don't know, but he wouldn't have given up hope, and he would have continued to believe what he had always believed. He would have faith that a book would provide the answer.'

'I would like to believe that the answers are somewhere.'

Micah got up and the two walked away from the edge together.

*

The sun was already dipping dangerously close to the horizon when the dark green fringe of the Rimforest beckoned at a tantalising distance. The terrain had been flat and treeless, with few obstacles other than the occasional boulder or small chasm. Atreu's breaths were ragged and his legs were aching with each step that they took, but he was more worried about Verlinden, whose face was showing the strain of the pace they had set.

'We should rest for a short while,' said Atreu in a breathless voice.

'You know we don't have the time,' said Verlinden. 'I don't know how I'll be able to get moving again if we stop.'

'The Rimforest is just ahead.'

'Yes, Atreu, I can see.' She increased her pace for a few steps, but then dropped back again.

'Steady, Verlinden, just keep ... damn.'

A long, narrow chasm suddenly yawned in front of them, and they came to an abrupt stop.

'What do we do now?' asked Atreu, scanning left and right, but unable to see where the chasm ended.

Verlinden was doubled over, raking in breaths. Atreu tried to put his arm around her, but she shook herself free. When her breathing eased, she straightened up and pointed to the chasm. 'Can you see a boulder or tree stump on the other side that we can loop a rope around?'

'Nothing,' said Atreu. 'And there's nothing anywhere near the lip of the chasm on this side that we could tie the other end of the rope to, either.'

Verlinden scanned the terrain, desperately looking for something that would help. 'You know,' she said, 'I think we could possibly jump it.'

Atreu looked dubiously at the yawning gap in front of them. 'Perhaps if we weren't carrying packs and we were both fully fit we could.'

'Are you saying I wouldn't make it?'

'Look at you, Verlinden, you're exhausted. I know how my legs are feeling right now – yours must be far worse.'

'Do you have a better idea?'

'This chasm can't go on forever,' said Atreu. 'Let's at least see if we can find the end of it.'

'Don't be foolish, Atreu. Look where the sun is. I feel more confident about tackling this chasm than battling Dusk-wraiths.'

'I'm not confident about either.'

'Wait – what is the matter with me? I think I've spent too much time with Maelir. Only one of us has to be able to jump the chasm – and we can haul the packs over separately. We can then use the rope to get the other one across.'

Atreu chewed his bottom lip. 'I don't want any argument. With you in your current state, I will be the one to jump across.'

Verlinden started to protest, but he stopped her. 'You are with child,' he said. 'I know you pretend it doesn't make a difference – but it does. Don't think I don't notice the bulge in your belly. I don't want to lose two of you.'

Atreu placed his pack on the ground.

'Look, there's a ledge jutting out slightly here,' said Verlinden, putting her weight on it to test it. 'Here's where to launch your jump. A few short spans like this could make all the difference.'

Atreu started walking back for a run-up.

'You should pace out your run first,' said Verlinden. 'Like this.'

She started from the ledge and ran with several large steps towards Atreu. 'Are you sure you know what you are doing?' she said.

Atreu ignored her and instead followed her lead in stepping out his run-up. When he felt the distance was right, he stopped and turned around to face the chasm. The sun was low, and the light slanted in at his eyes.

He took a deep breath, swivelled back on his heel with his lead foot, and then ran, faster than he had ever run. His legs pumped up and down, his feet pounded the ground, and the chill air whipped past his ears.

The chasm seemed to open up in front of him like a ravenous mouth. Then he lifted his right leg for the final step. With an almighty yell, he pushed his foot onto the jutting ledge and jumped with every muscle he could muster.

Atreu felt an updraught of warm air as the chasm yawned below. *Fly*, he thought, *fly without wings ... Riell, it can be done.* For an instant it was as if the scene around him petrified – a myriad of lights shone from deep in the rock below and the darkening sky hovered above, and he hung between them, as if he were inside a painting. Then came the descent, and he watched the other side of the chasm approaching.

Before he had time to realise he wasn't going to make it, the tip of his foot touched the edge and it crumbled away any support. He felt himself sinking into the crevasse and reached out instinctively to grab hold of the lip of the chasm. The muscles in his arms cramped with shock, but he hung on, and slowly pulled himself up.

As soon as he had got to his feet, Verlinden threw him the end of the rope. He quickly pulled across the two packs Verlinden had tied to the other end. After untying them, he threw one end of the rope back to her.

Verlinden tied it securely around her chest. 'Now, you've done something like this before,' she said, 'so don't doubt that you can bear my weight – even if there is a little extra now.'

Atreu thought of the time, which now seemed so long ago, on the edge of the Maelstrom when their eyes had first met. He wrapped the rope around both wrists so that it wouldn't slip, then spread his legs and bent his knees in anticipation of the sudden jolt.

'No,' cried Verlinden, 'take it off your wrists. If you can't hold my weight, you'll fall too.'

'Then we fall together,' said Atreu.

Verlinden knew she didn't have time to argue. She turned her back towards Atreu and started lowering herself over the edge. The further down she could climb, the less the jolt that Atreu would feel when he had to bear her weight. She didn't get very far until her feet slipped and she hung almost weightless in midair.

Then the cord around her chest suddenly bit into her, and she felt herself swaying towards the other side, as if on the end of a pendulum.

She reached out with her right hand to soften the impact as she crashed into the jagged surface of the chasm wall. For a moment she thought she was going to fall, but the rope remained taut.

'Are you all right?' cried Atreu between clenched teeth.

'Yes – start pulling me up.'

'I'm trying.' Atreu planted one foot, and then the other, as he backed away from the chasm in small steps.

The rope was biting into his wrists, and his legs were screaming for release, but he kept going. He had almost lost the sensation in his hands when Verlinden finally scrambled over the edge of the chasm.

They embraced, but Verlinden quickly pulled away and started untying the rope. 'Come on,' she said. 'It's almost dusk.'

The air around them seemed to change palpably as they broke into a run towards the Rimforest, thickening and becoming more substantial with every step they took.

'I can feel them,' said Atreu, gasping for air. 'The wraiths are gathering.'

He pushed his tired legs even faster and Verlinden matched him stride for stride. Up ahead, he could now make out individual trees, and the forest was no longer just an amorphous mass of green.

A gut-wrenching drone started up behind them. Atreu glanced over his shoulder. 'Don't look,' he cried.

Dense, pulsing clouds with monstrous red eyes were now emerging from the chasm they had just crossed. They spread low across the flat landscape like a flood of shadows moving relentlessly towards the Rimforest.

'They're coming, aren't they?' shouted Verlinden, a look of wild panic on her face.

Atreu's lungs desperately sucked in air. He looked around to see that the wraith flood was bearing down on them from horizon to horizon.

The forest was now so close he could smell the florid vegetation.

Verlinden stumbled, and for a moment Atreu's heart sank, but she regained her footing and they continued their charge. The wraiths were almost at their heels when the line of trees stretched out just in front of them.

'We're almost there,' cried Atreu.

He felt the cold sting of death on one foot.

'Dive,' he shouted, and they both leapt forward into the thick undergrowth.

Atreu glanced back to see that the wraith flood had stopped short just before the Rimforest canopy. His head was spinning and he was unable to move for a long time. When he regained the use of his limbs, he pulled Verlinden towards him and held her as they lay among the soft leaves.

'We're safe for another night,' he said, 'and that's all we can hope for just now.'

Verlinden reached into her pack for a blanket and wrapped it around them as they lay listening to the welcome rustle of leaves in the night breeze.

Chapter Twenty-three

Alone windrider soared through the still, bitter air over the snowscape of the Upper Reaches. The normally strong updraughts for once had waned, and the rider was forced to fly at a lower altitude than he was comfortable with, cursing the unpredictable weather patterns that had beset the Mountain in recent times. His eyes constantly scanned the pale forest of ice below for signs of Dusk-spawn. He knew that the fortunes of the Keep rested on the outcome of his mission. If only the Source was untouched by the horrors that racked the Mountain, the most holy of places could provide a refuge for the Inner Sanctum. The Source seemed the last chance for the Holy Men to salvage something from the carnage around them.

To his surprise, the windrider's eyes caught a skerrick of movement in the frozen terrain below. He angled his wings to descend until he could make out the dark-hooded figure that was moving steadily, head down, across the snow. The windrider hovered for a while, trying to convince himself that it was safe to land. Subtly, he shifted his weight so that he touched the ground just in front of the hooded figure.

The figure stopped, but the shadows under his hood gave no indication of where he was looking. The windrider could now see that he wore the cowl of a Felsen.

'What is your destination?' asked the windrider.

The monk didn't answer at first, as the silence of the Upper Reaches framed the two facing figures.

Finally, the monk replied. 'I seek the Keep.'

'Are you from the Source?' asked the windrider.

'Yes.'

'The Source is my destination. Tell me, is it safe from the impermanence that besets the Mountain?'

The monk's silence echoed back at the windrider.

The windrider swallowed, his stomach muscles clenching in anticipation of the answer to his question. When he gained some control over his fear, he repeated, 'Is the Source safe from the impermanence which besets the Mountain?'

The monk made several rasping noises in the back of his throat, as if he was trying to force out an answer that didn't want to come. 'The Source is not safe,' he said.

The windrider shuddered as he heard the words. Swallowing again, he said, 'The Inner Sanctum needs to find a place to evacuate to. Instability is destroying the Keep. Is there no part of the Source that can provide sanctuary?'

'The Source is not safe.' The words came a little easier the second time.

The windrider nodded in acknowledgment. 'What is your destination?' he asked.

'The Keep. I come to tell the Circle what I know.'

The windrider looked at the steam billowing out from under the monk's hood. 'You are still several days' march from the Keep,' he said. 'I can carry you there. It appears that there is no point in completing my mission.'

The monk looked up at the sky, and for a moment the windrider thought he saw a flash of eyes in the darkness under the hood.

'I will come with you,' said the monk.

The windrider strapped him into his harness and tested the wind direction with his hand. 'This will be a little more difficult than usual,' he said. 'For some reason the updraughts are weaker than is normal. We won't be able to fly very high – but it shouldn't matter.'

The monk remained impassive.

'You will have to run with me,' said the rider, 'so that we can get airborne.'

Although there was no indication that the monk had heard, the windrider started running and the monk matched his pace. The rider tilted his wings and their feet left the icy snow.

*

It was starting to grow dark when their lack of altitude began to concern the windrider. Indeterminate shadows had begun moving across the snow, shadows not cast by sunlight.

'Try to push down on the stirrups,' said the windrider.

Whether the monk did so or not was hard to tell, but what was obvious was that they weren't ascending.

Suddenly a dark, snake-like shadow uncoiled in their direction. The windrider swerved left and managed to avoid it.

'Push down hard,' said the rider, 'and lean back.'

He sensed a shift in weight, but the updraughts didn't have enough force to lift them any higher.

Another thin tendril lashed up at them, but again the windrider managed to arc away.

The shadows were now massing below them as dusk descended towards night. The windrider saw the wraiths billowing as far as the eye could see, and he knew that he and the Holy Man would not survive until morning.

He swerved right and then left in a frantic attempt to evade the probing tendrils, desperately drawing on all the skills he had, but knew he would eventually tire.

The thought passed fleetingly across his mind that if he unstrapped the monk, he would be able to ascend out of the Dusk-wraiths' reach, but even as the thought touched his consciousness, he cast it aside, ashamed at its very existence. There was no question. He was ruled by the covenant and had no choice.

As the shadows reached out for them with greater and greater ferocity, the windrider's movement became increasingly frantic. Left. Right. Right. Right. Left. Until finally, the sky, the shadows and the air became a blur.

And then, it was as if it all receded far below. Was this what death was like? How beautiful that while his body plummeted, part of him was reaching skyward.

And yet, and yet. Was that what was happening? He looked around. Far below, the dark shadows reigned, but he had somehow mysteriously gained altitude. There was something very strange, of that there was no doubt. The air around him was not as it should be. Then he realised what it was – there was no wind at all. And still he was gaining altitude. A windless flight.

He looked down at the monk strapped to the frame.

'Are you doing this?' he whispered to the silent air.

The monk didn't answer.

'You are,' said the rider softly. 'I can feel it. I know you are.'

When they reached a cross-draught, the reality of what was happening hit him, and he tilted his wings, suddenly aware that he still had control of the direction they were going.

Higher and higher they went. And the windrider didn't fight the ascent. His muscles relaxed, and he loosened his grip on the crossbar.

Through the clouds they flew. On the other side the stars shone with a fierce intensity in the ink-black night sky.

The windrider lost any sensation of a dream as his senses honed to a sharp-etched clarity. He looked down, suddenly aware that his eyesight had become acutely focused.

To his amazement, he saw to the edge of the Rimforest where, on a bed of soft spongy leaves, an Ascender was reading a book by candlelight. The Ascender looked up, and their eyes locked.

'I see you,' said the Ascender in a soft, knowing voice.

The windrider spoke his reply with a sound as insubstantial as a wisp of cloud. 'I see you too.'

'I am Atreu.'

The windrider felt as if he had just started to breathe again after lying dormant, and the air coursed through his body. 'I will tell them there is still hope.'

The Ascender's gaze shifted subtly, and the rider knew he was indicating the monk strapped to his wings. 'The Felsen, he will show you the third way,' said Atreu.

The windrider looked down at the motionless monk. 'I will carry him safely to the Keep.' When he refocused his eyes, the Ascender in the Rimforest was lost behind a curtain of night sky. 'Good fortune, Atreu,' he said.

*

Atreu lay there, feeling the softness of Verlinden's body and listening to her steady breathing. Night birds called to them from further inside the forest, and an infinity of leaves rustled in a soft breeze.

The sun should have long since risen when Verlinden awoke, but the air was still dark when she opened her eyes.

'I have seen something I haven't seen before,' said Atreu. 'The power is growing.'

Verlinden looked down at the still-open Talisman and the words leapt into her consciousness.

The windrider lost any sensation of a dream as his senses honed to a sharp-etched clarity. He looked down, suddenly aware that his eyesight had become acutely focused.

To his amazement, he saw to the edge of the Rimforest where, on a bed of spongy leaves, an Ascender was reading a book by candlelight. The Ascender looked up, and their eyes locked.

'Who is this windrider?' asked Verlinden, drawing away from the words.

'I don't know him,' said Atreu. 'That's one thing that has changed this time. I know his thoughts. I know his fear. I know how the windrider's covenant binds him. I am inside his head and his emotions. But I don't know him.'

'Is this what you've been waiting for?'

'I'm getting closer. I can feel it. This isn't just my story anymore, nor is it just the story of those I know well, like Teyth and Cluric. This is the story of people on the Mountain who I have no knowledge of. The power is growing. Read further.'

Verlinden's eyes refocused on the open page where she left off.

'I see you,' said the Ascender in a soft, knowing voice.

The windrider spoke his reply with a sound as insubstantial as a wisp of cloud. 'I see you too.'

'I am Atreu.'

The windrider felt as if he had just started to breathe again after lying dormant, and the air coursed through his body. And as his body sprang to life, he noticed the sleeping form of a woman next to Atreu. 'I will tell them there is still hope.'

'This is strange,' said Verlinden. 'Just as I read these words saying that he has seen me, I suddenly remembered that I dreamt exactly that during the night.'

Atreu furrowed his brow. 'What are you saying?'

'I dreamt that –'

'No – about the words that told you he saw you.'

'Here,' said Verlinden, reading the last two sentences aloud. 'And as his body sprang to life, he noticed the sleeping form of a woman next to Atreu. "I will tell them there is still hope."'

Atreu leant across and squinted at his Book. 'I don't remember reading that.'

'Here,' said Verlinden, pointing to the words.

'You're right – how could I have missed it?'

'Your Talisman has strange powers and gives you information in strange ways.'

Atreu looked at Verlinden. 'Our Talisman, remember. It has reminded us of that just now.' He pointed to the page again. 'Read the next sentence aloud.'

Verlinden continued. 'The Ascender's gaze shifted subtly, and the rider knew he was indicating the monk strapped to his wings. "The Felsen, he will show you the third way," said Atreu. The windrider looked down at the motionless monk. "I will carry him safely to the Keep." When he refocused his eyes, the Ascenders in the Rimforest were lost behind a curtain of night sky. "Good fortune to you both," he said.'

Atreu nodded. '*Both* of us again. We are enmeshed in this together, Verlinden. The story is yours as well.'

Verlinden smiled. 'This is a strange and wondrous Book that we have. I can't even begin to understand what has just happened.' She stared at Atreu. 'You may not know the windrider, but you know who the Felsen is, don't you?'

'Yes,' said Atreu. 'I do.'

They got up and strapped their packs onto their backs. There was still no sign of the sun as they headed off into the forest. Atreu glanced back at the dark, wraith-infested terrain which abutted the Rim. He sensed a brooding tension there, eager for release, and wondered with a slow shiver how long the ancient trees would remain safe from the Dusk-spawn.

As Atreu and Verlinden pushed their way through the undergrowth, parting the dark fronds and clambering over large, twisted roots, Atreu became increasingly aware of his pack pulling down on his shoulders. He thought at first that it was his body, unused to marching, reacting to the exertions of the day before. But the longer they continued, the more convinced he became that his Books were in some strange way weighing him down.

Eventually they entered a small glade and he stopped and

swung his pack from his back. He immediately felt relieved of a burden.

'What's wrong?' asked Verlinden. 'We have covered very little ground.' She was looking remarkably refreshed after a good night's sleep.

'I think it's the Books, Verlinden.'

'The Books?'

'I ... feel they have somehow suddenly increased their weight.'

Verlinden eyed him curiously as he opened his pack and reached in for his Talisman.

'Here, feel this,' he said as he handed her the Book.

Verlinden at first reached out with one hand, but then grabbed hold with the other as well. 'You're right, Atreu. This feels like ledstones.'

Atreu pulled out the Book of Maelur. 'And this one is the same.'

'What does this mean?' asked Verlinden.

'It's going to make things harder for us,' said Atreu. 'That's one thing we can be reasonably certain of.'

'But it has to mean something, doesn't it? Everything to do with the Books means something. Is this a good sign or a bad sign?'

Atreu frowned as he looked from one Book to the other. 'Praether would have had some idea. He had a way of interpreting things like this.'

'How would he have interpreted this?'

'I don't know.' Atreu chewed his bottom lip, deep in thought. 'He may have said it was a bad sign. If the Books are getting heavier, that could mean they are telling us to stay where we are, or at least not to move as quickly.'

Verlinden lifted the Talisman, testing its weight. 'But the Books have never directed us in that way, have they?'

'No.'

'Can you think of anything more subtle?'

'The Books could be increasing in meaning as we approach the end of the quest. That could be why they are getting heavier.'

'Heavier with meaning? That sounds like something Praether could have said.'

'That doesn't make it right, unfortunately,' said Atreu.

'What if the two Books increase in weight as we get closer to the third Book?'

'Perhaps you're right, Verlinden, but the Caves of Arach are still many days' travelling. If this is what is happening, then the two Books could weigh more than a hundred Maelir by the time we reach the Plains of Vygird.'

'So what do we do?'

Atreu looked around as the forest subtly changed to a lighter green hue. The leaves trembled in the soft breeze as if they were waking from a slumber. A lone whip-bird rang its beautiful call somewhere ahead of them.

'I don't think we can let this rule our direction,' said Atreu. 'We need to find the path to Treyfell, whatever the interpretation, or we will never make it to Vygird.'

Verlinden looked at the Talisman in her hands. 'We have a practical problem, though, don't we? You can't keep carrying both Books. I'll take one.'

'I don't want you burdened in your condition,' said Atreu quickly.

'I feel fine today, Atreu. I'll give the Book back to you if I start to struggle.' She started to put the Talisman in her pack.

'Wait!' said Atreu.

Verlinden eyed him curiously. 'What's wrong?'

'I ... I don't know.'

'You still think of this Book as yours, don't you?' She felt her face flush. 'Despite everything you've said, you don't really accept my joint ownership, do you?'

'Of course I do, Verlinden, of course I do.'

'Do you?' She tapped the Talisman. 'You said yourself that

in your version of the story, the windrider didn't even see me. I wasn't even there.'

'You ... you were there.'

'After I had read that I was there, yes.' Verlinden glared at him. 'You try to reassure me, don't you? You try to reassure yourself. The quest is ours. The Book is ours. But is it?'

'Of course –'

'Don't lie to me, Atreu. I've seen this from the beginning. I've tried to push it aside, to ignore the signs. I let you reassure me, but I don't think that deep down you have accepted that this is my quest as well.'

'I –'

'I don't want to hear a lie, Atreu. I know you want to believe that we are equal. Part of you does believe it. The part on the surface. The part that you let yourself think about. But in your heart of hearts, you have never really accepted it.'

Atreu stood limply in an open-mouthed protest.

'All right,' said Verlinden. 'I will make it easier for you. Here, you take your Talisman, and I'll take the Book of Maelur.'

They swapped the Books they were holding and put them into their packs.

The forest was awash with a suffused green light as they continued their journey. Atreu made better progress now that his burden had been eased, but he felt an awkwardness that stopped him from broaching the subject with Verlinden. His eyes followed the line of the ancient, twisted trees reaching up to the forest canopy. Perhaps she was right. Did he truly believe that Verlinden's claim on the Book was equal to his? Perhaps he didn't. The Talisman never lied. Yet ... Verlinden wasn't there with him in the version that he first read – even as she was sleeping next to him. There was no escaping the implications of that. Perhaps he was just like all those Holy Men who gave the Faemir equal status, but in truth didn't believe it.

With the moist forest floor underfoot and the thick lichen-encrusted vines hanging from above, he thought of his first experience of the Rim. How different was he now? This was the first time his Descent had taken him somewhere familiar. He half expected to see a slightly younger Ascender Atreu coming up towards him from downslope. He knew he had changed, but there was still something of the younger Atreu that he had to let go of. Perhaps he had to give up this last hold on the Talisman that he was claiming for himself. Was that the last barrier to the truth? If it was, then it was going to be a hard final hurdle. He couldn't do it by simply claiming that Verlinden shared the Book and the quest equally. He had already done that. He had to feel it – to really feel it. And that was something he couldn't control.

His thoughts were taken by several shouts as they pushed their way through several thick fronds into a small grove. In front of them stood a gaunt woman with moist, tangled hair, brandishing a knife. Behind her huddled three children with frightened voices.

'We have nothing,' said the woman, her voice trembling slightly. 'Just leave us. Don't send us back out.'

Verlinden held her hands up. 'We mean you no harm,' she said.

'Just leave us, please,' said the woman.

'We're not bandits,' said Atreu. 'We are seeking the Treyfell path.'

'I don't know anything about Treyfell.' The woman's hand was now trembling so much she could barely hold the knife.

'We have some food,' said Atreu. 'Please share a meal with us.'

The woman's face changed as if she had been slapped in the face. When Verlinden pulled out some dried meat and biscuits for her, the woman wiped away several tears before accepting them and passing them on to her children.

'Where are you from?' asked Atreu, chewing on a piece of meat himself.

'We used to live in Ariathe before it was burnt to the ground by the Faemir,' she said.

Verlinden looked away.

'Then they put us in camps near Peleusar, but we were driven from there by the Faemir.'

'There is a truce now,' said Atreu.

'So I've heard – not that it makes much difference to me. I've lost my home and I've lost my husband.'

Atreu continued to chew in a self-conscious silence. 'You and your children have survived the Nazir, that couldn't have been easy.'

The woman's eyes started to get a strange look in them. 'We're alive, that's all I can say. It was luck at first. I think that's all it was – fool's luck.'

'But you're safe here in the forest,' said Verlinden.

The woman's face twisted into an ugly grimace. 'I haven't escaped, you know. None of us have.' She held her forefinger against her temple and turned it. 'They're in here, and once they get inside you, they never leave.'

'The Dusk-wraiths,' said Atreu. 'Did they get you?'

'They get us all, don't they?'

Atreu shifted uncomfortably. 'Tell us, please, tell us what it's like. We've been sailing the Maelstrom for a long time.'

The woman's head shook uncontrollably from one side to the other. 'You want me to tell you what it is like? To tell you. I wish someone could have told me and spared me the horrors of experiencing it. In the end, you just lie there when the sun goes down, as close to the fire as you dare, and hope that they will overlook you this time.' Tears formed in the corners of her eyes again. 'And you know what? Sometimes they come and sometimes they don't, but you never can predict it. So even if you survive another night untouched, you know it doesn't mean anything.'

'You should be able to find enough food here in the Rimforest,' said Verlinden. 'You can sleep in peace here.'

The woman backed away from her. 'Why do you want us to sleep?'

'I just said –'

'You keep telling me I'm safe. I know that's not true. The forest has never been safe. Yet you want me to sleep – you want me off my guard, don't you?'

The sounds of several people making their way through the undergrowth could be heard behind her. She dropped the last morsel of food and grabbed her knife.

'This is an ambush, isn't it?' she cried, her eyes cold with fear.

'No,' Atreu protested.

'An ambush!' she cried again, signalling to her three children. 'Come on – it's time again.'

By the time three men entered the grove, the woman and her children had disappeared into the dark green vegetation.

'Ah, I thought we'd find some trespassers,' said the stocky man in front.

'Trespassers?' Atreu raised his eyebrows. 'Since when is the Rimforest owned by anyone?'

'No arguments, now. We'll just have a quick look in your packs and then escort you back out.'

'Are you mad?' asked Verlinden. 'You're not going to look in our packs, and there is no way we're going back the way we came.'

'We're heading to Treyfell,' said Atreu. 'So if you would kindly set us in the right direction, we will be on our way.'

The stocky man eyed him up and down. 'You look like a Lower Reacher to me. Although I don't think too much of someone who has stolen an Ascender's garb – that's even below something I would do.'

'I *am* an Ascender. Ascender Atreu from Valesend.'

'I see. I see. And this is your little Faemir princess.' He leered at Verlinden. 'A nice touch with the tattered pieces, but I think you haven't quite got the colour right.'

He went to feel the material on Verlinden's tunic, but she backed away and swiftly pulled out her knife. 'If you touch me or my clothes again, I'll cut your throat.'

The man went white.

'Now, we're going to continue our journey to Treyfell,' said

Atreu, pointing in the direction the men had come. 'Is this the right way?'

The other two men were eyeing Atreu and Verlinden cautiously.

'You can never be too certain these days,' said the stocky man. 'Too many people are losing their fear of the Rim. We can't just let anyone in, can we?' He smiled, showing an array of rotting teeth.

'So you just steal what you can from them and then send them back out to the mercy of the Dusk-wraiths, do you?'

Verlinden spat at the feet of the leader.

'Now, now, let's not –'

'Get out of our way,' said Verlinden, 'and just be thankful that you've all survived with your throats intact.'

'Come on, let's leave them,' said another of the men. 'Why get involved in a fight if we don't have to?'

'Yes, why not stick to women with children,' said Verlinden, glaring at them. 'I've seen some sorry sights since this war began, but you must be the sorriest.'

She stepped up to the stocky man and raised her knife towards his throat. 'You are nothing but a coward.'

'Verlinden – don't!' cried Atreu.

The other men hadn't moved.

A breeze riffled through the leaves around them, and a flock of birds cawed from a nearby tree.

'Now, now,' said the stocky man. 'We're not looking for any trouble. The Treyfell path is through there.' He pointed over his right shoulder. 'Once you reach it, turn left.'

'Verlinden?'

Verlinden slowly lowered her knife and she and Atreu packed up and started to go.

'We are sorry for the misunderstanding,' said the leader.

'Don't apologise to me,' said Verlinden. 'Just be aware that Faemir soldiers are starting to move through the forest. The next woman you meet might not be as forgiving.'

The men exchanged nervous glances as Atreu and Verlinden continued through the forest.

When they were out of earshot, Atreu said, 'I haven't seen you like that before.'

'I suppose I have some bad memories of the Rimforest.'

'Would you really have slit his throat?'

'I don't know. These Maelir bandits are the worst kinds of cowards. How many helpless women do you think they've stolen from and then hounded back out into the Mid-Reaches to be at the mercy of the Dusk-wraiths?'

'You're right. It looks like war brings out the best and worst in people.'

They pushed their way through the dense foliage until they hit a path, where they turned left.

As the day progressed, it became obvious that many people were overcoming the age-old fear of the Rimforest and seeking refuge under its high canopy. Most of the people they came across were ex-soldiers who had grown weary of battle and had found in the Rimforest some respite from the relentless war. Now and then they happened upon groups of people who said they were the only survivors of whole villages. Although bands of bandits preyed on lone travellers and small groups, as Atreu and Verlinden had discovered, by and large, it appeared that these larger groups were left alone.

Atreu became increasingly aware that this experience of the forest was totally different to his Ascent. Although the Rim had not been physically changed by the war as had the other parts of the Mountain, it seemed to have had much of the spirit sucked out of it. It was no longer the magical place Atreu had previously encountered. The forest no longer breathed with the strong, steady rhythm of a living being, and the ancient trees struck him more as empty shells than the virile custodians they had once seemed to be. He knew it was their deep roots that held the ground together against the ravages of the Mountain's instability, and he could only pray that they weren't tiring of the battle.

And how long could the forest cope with the influx of people? How long would it be before the refugees shook off their fear of the Rim in large numbers, and word filtered through that it was the last safe haven? How long would it take for the vegetation to be trampled under countless feet and the delicate balance between the plants to be destroyed?

Atreu shuddered at his thoughts as the short day again turned into night. Even without the Dusk-wraiths claiming the space around him, Atreu felt a black mood come over him. What joy was left for him if this most ancient place, too, was succumbing to the horrors of the Nazir?

Time lost its meaning as they trudged on through the night. Atreu's pack now pulled on his shoulders as it had done earlier, and he felt the strain in his neck and back. It worried him that it had reached the point where one Book now weighed what two Books had weighed not so long ago. Whatever was happening, it was increasing. Verlinden's face showed the strain of the weight of the Book of Maelur, but her pace never slackened.

It was well into the night when Atreu suggested that they have a short rest before continuing. Verlinden protested at first, but he insisted, and after they made themselves comfortable in a nest of foliage, she was sound asleep within moments.

Atreu's thoughts still roiled bleakly inside his head as he lay there watching the patterns of dark fronds meshing overhead in the breeze. He took out the glimmerstone and lifted out his Book with both hands. As he turned the pages, he had a sense that he was searching for something. His Talisman had often been frustrating, but ultimately it had always yielded answers and provided him with hope. This time, however, the pages themselves seemed to be resisting him. They grew heavier and harder to turn as he approached the end of the Book.

Finally he reached a point where he simply couldn't turn to the next page. He looked down in the pale glimmerstone light and started to read ...

*

The sixty members of the Circle had again crowded into the chamber of the monast. Micah eyed the hooded Felsen monk in the centre with an intensity matched by the others. News had filtered out that this was a Source Holy Man who had been found trekking towards the Keep. That in itself was sensational news, but there were other rumours about him which Micah had heard, and if true, this monk was a strange man indeed.

'It would be some time since you've had any experience of the Circle,' said Leyvin. 'As you can see, our conditions are not what they once were, but I trust you are aware that we are eager for any news that you might bring.'

'You speak a great deal without meaning,' said the monk in a voice that resonated through the chamber.

Leyvin frowned at the response. 'Tell us, then, is the Source safe from the Mountain's instability?'

'The Source will not survive intact.'

There was a collective gasp around the tightly packed room. Hope of escape had, with those words, been sucked out of the dank air around them.

'Did you manage to escape to warn us?' asked Holthim.

'No, I came for a different reason.'

'Who are you?' asked Leyvin, narrowing his eyes. 'It is customary for Felsen to fold back their hoods when addressing the Circle.'

'It should not matter who I am,' said the monk.

'Please,' said Micah, 'it is most unusual that one from the Source travels to the Keep. There must be an extraordinary reason to take you away from your meditations.'

The monk appeared to take a deep breath. 'There is such a reason. I have to tell you that the war against the Nazir is not what it seems.'

'And what does it seem to be?' asked Leyvin.

'It seems that we have justice on our side.'

Murmurs suddenly filled the room.

'I think most of us,' said Micah, 'are now convinced that justice was not fully on our side in our war against the Faemir. I can't see how we are once again in the same position.'

'Our position is worse,' said the monk. 'In this conflict we have *no* justice on our side.'

'This is absurd.' Leyvin's voice rang above the commotion. 'What does a monk from the Source know of the conflict on the Mountain? I think we've heard enough.'

'I believe we should hear him out before we dismiss him,' said Holthim.

As the tumult increased, Leyvin was forced to shout. 'Silence, please. Silence! This is a Circle in session, despite our surroundings.'

When a tense silence had been restored, Leyvin addressed the monk again. 'We are the victim of a totally unprovoked attack, and the Mountain lies in ruins. Tell me how we are at fault.'

The monk coughed several times before replying. 'The Mountain was not uninhabited when Maelur and his followers arrived here. We took homes away from an innocent people.'

'This is madness,' said Leyvin. 'There are no stories of people on the Mountain before we came.'

'All records and evidence were suppressed by our Maelir forebears.'

'Nonsense,' said Leyvin. 'We see it as our duty to record everything that happens. Our librums are filled with books, and scribes devote lifetimes to their tasks. How is it possible that such a fact could somehow disappear?'

The monk didn't reply.

'I asked you how it is possible that such a fact could somehow disappear.'

'I cannot answer that,' said the monk. 'I can only tell you what I know.'

'How do you know this?' asked Holthim.

'The knowledge is stored in a book.'

'There are no books at the Source,' said Leyvin. 'There never have been. What nonsense are you talking now?'

The monk repeated, 'The knowledge is stored in a book.'

'Is it the Book of Atreu?' asked Micah quickly, 'or the Book of Maelur?'

'No,' said the monk.

Micah felt his hopes subside again.

'What book are you referring to?' asked Holthim.

'This one,' said the monk, and he pulled out a large brown leather-clad book from beneath his cloak.

Leyvin stepped forward and took the book from the monk. Micah watched the First Speaker go white as he examined the cover and the opening pages.

'Please pass it on so that the rest of us can examine it,' said Holthim.

*

Atreu tugged at the next page of his Talisman, but it wouldn't turn. What was happening here? He had to know what Book was about to be revealed to the Circle.

Come on, damn you, he mouthed silently to himself. How could his Talisman be doing this to him?

He tried several more times to turn the page, but it wouldn't yield. Tears of frustration started forming in his eyes. He wiped them away and looked around, first at the night-shrouded forest vegetation and then at the sleeping form of Verlinden.

'Verlinden, I need your help,' he whispered.

He gently shook her until she opened her eyes. 'Is it time to move on?' she asked wearily.

'No, Verlinden. There is something very important happening in the Keep.' He pointed to his Talisman. 'There is a book which confirms what I thought was the meaning of Belzalel's shadow play. The monk has just presented it to the Circle. I sense it is of crucial importance.'

'What book? Where does it come from?'

'I don't know. I can't turn the page to find out. Please, Verlinden, you try. We have to find out what this book is.'

Verlinden reached down, grabbed the page in the top right-hand corner with her thumb and middle finger, and in a swift motion turned the page.

Atreu's eyes hungrily sought the next words, and Verlinden read with him …

*

When Leyvin didn't move, Holthim took the book out of his hands and started examining it closely.

'What is it?' asked Micah. 'We can't afford to wait until each one of us has studied it.'

Holthim stared at Leyvin, open-mouthed. 'You know what this is, don't you?'

Leyvin didn't respond.

'I'm going to look at this for myself,' said Lythos, pushing his way through the throng. 'Give it here.' He took the book and started flicking through it.

'What is it?' asked Micah again.

Lythos held the book out towards the monk. 'Is this what it appears to be?'

'Yes,' said the monk. 'It is the Book of Metheus.'

A collective gasp filled the room.

'And who are you?' demanded Lythos as he approached the monk.

Before the Felsen had time to answer, Lythos had pulled back his hood and then staggered back.

Cries of 'Praether!' immediately rang through the air.

'No, not Praether, you fools,' said Leyvin. 'Arch-librer Praether is dead.'

The monk stood silently and met the gaze of every Holy Man

in the chamber. 'I am not Praether,' he said, raising his ancient head. 'I am Metheus.'

With that, the Circle fell into a deep silence.

'It was our understanding, Liche Metheus,' said Holthim, finally cutting through the vacuum, 'that you were on the Plains of Vygird.'

'I was in that place a long time,' said Metheus.

'And you travelled to the Source from Vygird?' asked Holthim.

'I did, and not for the first time.'

'How is that possible for an old man in times of war?' asked Lythos.

'Ah, a *how* question. Perhaps the least important, but I will tell you. The first tunnel the Nazir built under the Mountain leads directly to the Source.'

'What? The Nazir know where the Source of the Maelstrom is?' asked Lythos.

'They have always known,' said Metheus. 'They were the ones who showed the Maelir where it was.'

'We thank you for your efforts,' said Leyvin, who had regained some of his composure. 'We will consider carefully what you have told us here.'

'No, wait,' said Lythos. 'I want to know why Metheus has come to the Keep.'

Leyvin glared at his brother. 'I think we understand Metheus' message. We can examine the Talisman and make our judgements.'

'I will answer the why question because such questions usually go to the heart,' said Metheus. 'I saw in Ascender Atreu when he was in the Caves of Arach the way forward for our people, which had been lost to me. I believe we still have a chance towards true Ascent.'

'You're here because of Atreu?' said Micah.

'Yes.'

'Then we have a tragedy of the worst kind,' said Micah. 'He

undertook a quest for you and the third book. The Circle sanc-
tioned it.'

'There is no tragedy. I have spoken to him.'

'What?' Micah's heart raced. 'He's alive?'

'He left the Source with two others and has descended the
Maelstrom with them. The windrider who carried me can confirm
that the two Ascenders are now in the Rimforest.'

'This is insane,' said Leyvin.

'Metheus, how do you know this?' asked Micah.

'My Book has told me.'

'And who was the third to leave the Source?' asked Micah.
'Riell?'

'Yes. He is also still alive, as far as I know. The other windrider
perished, and if there is a tragedy, it is his.'

'But if the three Books were brought together and the quest
fulfilled, why did Atreu and Verlinden continue their Descent?'

Metheus hesitated. 'I kept my Talisman hidden. And I did not
reveal myself to Ascender Atreu at the Source.'

'What?' Micah looked at him incredulously. 'Did Atreu not
speak of his quest?'

'Yes, but this is not the Book you seek, Atreu. Find your origin. Complete your Descent to the beginning. We must all return
to our source.'

There was an awkward silence.

'Who are you addressing?' asked Leyvin.

'I addressed Ascender Atreu.'

'Are you mad?'

'I have been accused of that many times, but if I am mad then
the truth is an insanity.'

'I think we should discuss these revelations now,' said Leyvin.
'I would ask you to leave, Metheus, so that we can deliberate.'

'There are some related matters that need to be resolved first,'
said Micah calmly, aware suddenly of an opportunity.

'We have some major revelations to deal with,' said Leyvin.

'Perhaps,' said Micah, 'but this is a matter of procedure. I believe Metheus has a place in the Circle.'

Leyvin glared at Micah. 'What are you suggesting?'

'You know very well what I'm suggesting, Leyvin, although you pretend that you don't for your own purposes.' Micah sensed his words striking Leyvin like blows. 'As I understand it, Metheus left the Circle and the Keep of his own free will – he was never ejected. I believe he still has a place here.'

'You cannot seriously be suggesting that after all these years, Metheus can claim a place in the Circle.'

'This *is* a matter which must be considered rather than dismissed,' said Holthim.

Leyvin was now flushed, and Micah could sense that he almost had him where he wanted him. 'This is outrageous,' said Leyvin. 'A Holy Man who leaves the Circle cannot simply return and displace a member to reclaim his seat.'

'With Riell absent, there is a vacancy,' said Micah, nodding slowly at Leyvin. Finally, finally, he had the First Speaker. 'There is no issue of displacement to consider. Isn't this a matter of a vote?'

Holthim turned to Metheus. 'Do you wish this vote?'

'I have returned for the Circle,' said Metheus.

'A vote, then,' said Leyvin, his shoulders slumping. 'Metheus to sit in Riell's seat until he returns.'

All the hands were raised, and Leyvin joined them in resignation.

'Metheus,' said Holthim, 'you have returned.'

The ancient Liche remained impassive.

Micah glared at Leyvin. *Now for the final strike.* 'I believe we must consider one last procedural issue resulting from Metheus' return.' *Leyvin knows it's coming.* 'From my understanding, Metheus held the position of First Speaker when he left the Circle. Am I correct?'

'It is true,' said Metheus.

'I would submit to the Circle,' said Micah, 'that as we have accepted that Metheus can reclaim his place in the Circle despite his long absence, we must also accept that he can reclaim his position as First Speaker.' There, he had said it – there could be no faulting the logic, and Leyvin knew it.

All eyes were turned towards Leyvin, as the Circle awaited a response. It was Holthim who finally spoke. 'First Speaker Leyvin, have you nothing to say?'

Leyvin stared blankly at Micah, and then at Metheus. When he spoke, his words were tinged with exhaustion. 'I offer no counter argument.'

*

Atreu watched the branches of the forest canopy weave and inter-mesh like a shadow play above him. The words he had just read were still ringing inside his head as he tried to make sense of them.

'You said yourself,' said Verlinden, 'that nothing has turned out the way you expected since you left Valesend.'

'You're right, Verlinden,' said Atreu. 'Of course it would never have been as simple as finding Metheus in the Caves of Arach. How could it have been?' He drew a deep breath. 'I ... I ... need to somehow change my whole thinking.'

'You had to change your thinking about the Faemir – it's possible to do.'

'How could I not have seen it was Metheus? I was too caught up in my own belief that I was finding a third way. I was foolish. There were no triplets. Riell was right, I was caught up in my hubris.'

'Atreu, Metheus' book was not the third book. He spoke directly to you through the words on the page. You read what he said: you must seek your origin. You know what he means, don't you?'

'I no longer have faith in my judgement, Verlinden. Metheus said to complete my Descent to the beginning. How can I be certain what that means?'

'You can't, but it surely must mean that you must return to Valesend. That was the beginning of your Ascent.'

Atreu chewed his bottom lip. 'The third Book – it must be my father's. That's the only explanation possible. Our quest has always been for the Book of Tyr.'

A gust of wind blew through the canopy, and for a moment the dark pattern of interlocking branches reconfigured above Atreu's head.

Chapter Twenty-four

Night seemed to reign now, and the thin daylight hours dissipated all too quickly into the ever-encroaching darkness. Atreu knew that the forest canopy muted the effect, and shuddered every time he pictured the starkness of night's domination beyond the Rim's edge. What lay ahead for him, now that the very foundation of his quest had changed? What other clues had he missed along the way? He realised now that the thought of seeing his father and his village had been in the back of his mind since he had undertaken his Descent, but the pull, which had once been an undercurrent, was now coming to the surface. In hindsight, it seemed natural somehow that the truth for him lay at the very beginning.

He tried not to envisage what was ahead. Was it possible that Valesend had somehow been spared from the wraiths? Was his father safe? His quest was suddenly more immediate than it had ever been. It was no longer a search for an old man in a remote cave – he was now searching for his home and for the truth about his father and his father's Ascent. Atreu felt an increasing burden with every short day, and the exotic Rim plants that had so fascinated him on his Ascent became little more than a blur on the sides of his vision. He lost track of time and was surprised when one morning, as the sunlight started to filter through the leaves, he saw that the forest was thinning just up ahead. Soon, the canopy broke up to reveal pieces of pale blue sky. Unlike the Mid-Reaches, there was no sharp line where the Rim ended. At first, tree stumps were interspersed with fully grown trees, until finally the stumps dominated the terrain, and the overhead branches no longer interlocked.

'How far is it to Treyfell?' asked Verlinden.

'We'll make it well before the sun sets again,' said Atreu, 'if that's what you're asking. Hopefully, there will still be enough trees around the village for us to be safe there.'

The path was now wider and less-defined than it had been in the Rim, but Atreu remembered it clearly from the morning long ago when he had been walking in the other direction with another flame-haired girl. The strangeness of traversing familiar paths was still growing with every step. He had become so used to new experiences that familiarity was something he was struggling to cope with. He felt himself being drawn to Hrulth's inn, but an anxiousness about what he would find there gnawed at him.

The sun had reached its peak for the day when Treyfell came into view. At first Atreu was relieved that the village still seemed to be intact. The homes were all there, looking like house-shaped trees growing out of the ground, and tiers of smoke puffed out of the chimneys into the still air. But as they got closer, Atreu could see things weren't exactly as he remembered them. All around the village in the downslope direction were the dormant remains of a barricade fire.

Atreu felt a sharp arrow of anticipation as they entered Treyfell and made their way through the all-but-deserted streets to Hrulth's inn. Once they reached the door, he rang the bell and waited, a knot gradually tightening in his stomach.

'I told you, no ale while –' The large imposing figure of Estla opened the door and looked at him with her mouth hanging open mid-sentence. 'Well, will surprises never cease? Ascender Atreu has returned to us.'

'You never expected to see me again, did you?' asked Atreu.

'I don't believe in never, my boy.' She looked across at Verlinden and her jaw dropped once more.

'There is a truce, you know,' said Atreu.

'I don't know much about truces,' said Estla, still gaping at Verlinden, 'but it appears there are more surprises in store for us.'

'This is Ascender Verlinden,' said Atreu.

'Of course she is. Of course she is. But I'm forgetting myself here. Please, come in, where is my hospitality?' She waved them in and they walked through the doorway into the warm room.

'You remember my daughters, of course,' said Estla, pointing to the three girls sitting by the open fire. 'Audum, Silth and Fiala. I would normally add that they are all still to be betrothed, but I see there is not much point now.'

Atreu felt blood rush to his face as he and Verlinden sat down near the fire. His eyes met Audum's and she smiled at him, her dark red hair glinting in the flame light. So his memory wasn't playing tricks on him – she did have a resemblance to Verlinden.

'Well, I have to say that your choice in travelling companion has improved,' said Estla, handing Atreu and Verlinden each a mug of steaming tea. Staring directly at Verlinden, she said, 'So, you say you are a Faemir ... Verlinden?'

'I didn't actually say that, but that's right.'

'I've often wondered how a *race* of women is possible. You know, I think I'm starting to get an idea.' Estla slapped her knee and let out a raucous laugh.

Verlinden looked into her tea, suddenly acutely aware of her growing belly.

'I am perhaps not a true Faemir,' said Verlinden. 'I lived for nine years with a family in a Maelir village before it was attacked by a coveyn and I was taken.'

'I see, I see,' said Estla. 'There is obviously more to you than ravaging and pillaging.' Her chest heaved with laughter, but even as she laughed, she didn't take her eyes from Verlinden. 'So, not a true Faemir, but an Ascender. Was your twin sister taken as well?'

'Valkyra was a Faemir her whole life. I ... I don't know how we were separated, or how I ended up in that village.'

'You say *was* a Faemir?'

Verlinden frowned. 'She didn't survive the war.'

'What is all this noise down here?' said a voice from the top of the stairs.

Atreu looked up to see Hrulth standing there in his night-gown. 'You made it home,' said Atreu.

'Yes, I ...' Hrulth squinted. 'I can't believe this. Is that you, Ascender Atreu?' He made his way down the stairs, holding onto the rail.

'Careful, Hrulth,' said Estla. 'You should still be in bed.'

'Nonsense,' said Hrulth. 'Who knows with these short days and long nights when I'm supposed to be sleeping?'

When he reached the bottom of the stairs, Atreu rushed over to embrace him. 'Come, I want to hear your story,' said the innkeeper. 'You must have so much to tell, and I suspect Estla hasn't given you a chance to even begin.'

'I'm afraid I never became a soldier,' said Atreu as he helped Hrulth to a chair.

'A vastly overrated calling,' said Hrulth as he sat down and began stroking his bushy red beard. 'Estla, I think this warrants some ale.'

'You'll have tea,' said Estla, 'and if you don't watch your tongue, it will be over your head.' She handed him a mug of steaming brew. 'I've given him some liberties since he came back,' she said to Atreu, 'but the time will soon be nigh when being a returned, injured soldier won't protect him anymore.' She laughed as she returned to speak to Verlinden.

'So, Hrulth, you survived the journey from Peleusar,' said Atreu.

'Yes – has Estla already told you of my entire campaign?'

'No,' said Atreu. 'I know much of what happened in Peleusar, though.'

'How is that possible?'

'It's a long story, which I'll save for later.' Atreu leant forward. 'There's also much that I don't know. Do you know what has befallen Cluric?'

Hrulth lowered his mug of tea. 'The finest soldier I saw in all my time – and I don't say that just because he is my nephew.'

'Is he still alive? Did he make it home?'

'I'm not sure how to answer either of those questions, Atreu.'

'I would like to know the truth.'

'Ah, Ascenders and their truth.' Hrulth put his mug down on the floor and slowly pushed himself up out of the chair. 'All right, Ascender Atreu, come with me and I will show you the truth.'

'Where are you going?' asked Estla, looking up from her conversation with Verlinden.

'I'm going to take Atreu to see Cluric,' said Hrulth.

'Is he here?' said Atreu.

'Don't get too excited,' said Hrulth, taking Atreu's arm and directing him back up the stairs.

The two of them walked up to the second storey, and Hrulth led him through one of the doors along the corridor. The shutters on the window were firmly shut and the only light in the room came from a candle whose single flame was burning low.

Once Atreu's eyes adjusted, he could see two immobile figures. One was lying in the bed, eyes open, unblinking, staring at the ceiling. The other sat on a chair next to the bed and was hunched over, elbows resting on the blankets.

Atreu approached them slowly. 'You must be Jenethelen,' he said to the hunched figure.

The woman's head turned slightly in his direction and she nodded.

'I didn't tell you her name,' said Hrulth.

'I told you, I know much of what happened in Peleusar,' said Atreu.

'What do you know of Peleusar?' asked Jenethelen, her head not moving as she spoke.

'I know what it was like when the Dusk-wraiths attacked you. I know the fear you felt. I know that you saved Cluric during the first battle.'

Jenethelen looked up at Atreu, and he could see shadows in her eyes. 'How can it be that you know these things?'

'I ... I have a Book which tells me.'

His revelation barely registered on Jenethelen's face. It was as if she was beyond being surprised by anything. 'Do you know what it was like, night after night, waiting for them, sensing in your bones they would come? Do you know what it is like to, little by little, have your reason eaten away?'

Atreu stood silently.

'Do you know how it feels when death bores into your skull like a cold worm and claims you?'

Atreu took a deep breath. 'I feel things that I read, and I have read some of these things. Is it the same as actually experiencing them? That is something I don't know. I've never read and experienced two identical things so that I could compare.' He looked down at the unmoving form on the bed. 'Is Cluric alive?'

'He breathes – ever so faintly,' she said. 'If that means he lives, then he lives. If you judge life any other way, then he doesn't.'

'How long has he been like this?'

'The wraiths massed as we approached the Rimforest,' said Hrulth. 'The darkness had grown towards the end, so that we had no choice but to travel at night. They would have overwhelmed us as we made our final dash for the Rim, but Cluric fought them off so that we could make it into the forest.'

'We went back to get him at daybreak,' said Jenethelen. 'He started breathing once we got him into the forest, but that was as far as he recovered. He's been like this ever since. The wraiths must have wormed their way into his mind once too often.'

Atreu reached down to touch Cluric's face. It felt as cold as the ice of the Upper Reaches. 'Cluric of Teuron,' he said, 'this is Atreu. We have found each other.'

He stood there, unable to speak for some time, until he became aware that someone was in the doorway. He glanced up to see Estla and Verlinden standing there.

'Hrulth, I need to speak with you,' said Estla. 'Let's leave the young ones for a moment.'

Hrulth left as Verlinden entered.

'You're Jenethelen, aren't you?' said Verlinden.

The two Faemir exchanged a long look. 'You must be the twin of Valkyra that I have heard has become an Ascender,' asked Jenethelen.

'My name is Verlinden.'

Atreu turned his attention to Cluric. 'My friend, there is so much I want to tell you. Our paths forked that night on the Mid-Reaches, but somehow I feel they have been in parallel for at least part of our journeys.'

'I've brought the Book,' said Verlinden, holding it out. 'I thought it might help.'

Atreu took it and riffled through the pages. 'It's here,' he said. 'The story you have with Jenethelen. This is the part where you and Jenethelen met in Peleusar.' And with that, he began to read out loud.

Jenethelen was mesmerised by the words, and after he had finished, Atreu could see that some of the light had been rekindled in her eyes. He searched the pages again. 'Here the two of you are digging for brimstones.' And as he read, Jenethelen started straightening up in her chair.

'And here,' he said, after locating a third place in the Book, 'is when the two of you first kissed.'

When he had finished, Jenethelen's face was flushed and it was as if she had sprung back to life. 'What is this wondrous book you have here?'

'It is the Talisman of our Ascent,' said Atreu.

'So it had some value after all.'

Atreu opened his mouth in amazement when he realised it was Cluric who had spoken.

'Yes, my friend,' said Atreu, 'the Book had some value after all.' He reached down to touch Cluric's hand and then stepped back and watched Jenethelen embrace him with tears running down her cheeks.

When she had pulled back and Cluric had propped himself up in the bed, Atreu grabbed Verlinden's hand. 'And this is Verlinden,' he said.

'Another Faemir Watcher?' said Cluric. 'It looks like your story will be at least as interesting as mine.'

'Atreu will tell you all about it later,' said Verlinden. 'I think we'll leave the two of you just now.'

Atreu was about to protest when he recognised the look in her eyes. 'Of course ... we'll ... come back up later.'

Atreu and Verlinden walked back downstairs to join Hrulth, Estla and their three daughters. Hrulth seemed to be unable to take his eyes from Verlinden. Even when Atreu told him that Cluric had regained consciousness, it took a moment for the news to register. 'Cluric is with us again?' said Hrulth. 'Is that what you're telling me?'

'Yes,' said Atreu. 'Are you all right? You seem distracted.'

'This is truly a wonderful day then,' said Hrulth, clapping his hands and rubbing them together. 'A wonderful day indeed.'

'The sun's already setting outside,' said Estla, 'so let's hope our good fortune carries over into night.'

'I think this warrants an ale, don't you?' said Hrulth, looking hopefully at his wife. 'I haven't felt this good in a long time.'

'Fiala, Silth,' said Estla, 'fetch us some ale. This is a time to celebrate many things. One tankard for your father will be enough.'

As the night progressed, however, Hrulth drank more than one tankard, and with each one, his mood became merrier. At one point when Silth was playing the lyre, and his singing was becoming louder and more ribald with every song, Estla took away his half-full tankard and refused to give it back. All through the evening, however, he rarely took his eyes from Verlinden. Only when Cluric came down the stairs with Jenethelen was his attention taken momentarily.

'What a day and what a night it's been,' he cried. 'This calls for another ale, woman. Where's my tankard?'

'Don't you woman me, Hrulth. You've had enough ale for one evening.' Estla had a smile on her face, but there was no doubt she would stand her ground.

'Cluric, Cluric, you're with us again,' said Hrulth. 'This is a miracle. I can feel it. Things have turned. I know there's a horrible war still raging past Treyfell's borders, but we've all truly come home tonight.'

'Hrulth, will you hold your tongue just for a moment and let the rest of us speak?' Estla offered Cluric and Jenethelen chairs by the slow-burning mirwood fire. 'Cluric, my dear boy, it is good to have you back. How do you feel?'

'I ... I feel healed, Aunt Estla. Do you know how often I thought of this warm hearth while I faced battle?'

'Thank you,' said Cluric to Atreu and Verlinden. 'Thank you to both of you. I don't understand what has happened here since you came, but I know it's all changed now.'

'Home, home,' said Hrulth, staring at Verlinden again with a wide grin across his face. 'How wonderful it is.'

'Hrulth, I think we don't want to hear your continual ranting,' said Estla. Perhaps it's time you went to bed.'

'To bed? To bed? What are you talking about, woman? Let's have another song. Silth, another tune –'

'Enough, Hrulth,' said Estla. 'We've listened to enough of your singing for one evening. The family may put up with it, but you can't expect others to do so.'

'Family, ah, family.' He winked clumsily at Estla. 'Yes, well there *are* one or two non-family members here.'

'What are you ranting about, Uncle Hrulth?' asked Cluric.

'Never mind your uncle,' said Estla. 'He's had far too many ales tonight for someone who hasn't drunk any in a long time.'

'Ah, family.' Hrulth was still staring at Verlinden when Estla started helping him out of his chair.

'Time for bed.'

'Get your hands off me, woman.'

'I said not to woman me. Next time you say it, I'll ram it down your throat. Just because you've been giving orders to soldiers for the last year doesn't mean you're going to get away with ordering me about.'

'See what happens when you get married?' said Hrulth, addressing Atreu and Cluric. 'And my wife isn't even a Faemir.'

'Now, come on,' said Estla. 'I think you had better get to bed before you say something you'll regret.'

'Come here,' said Hrulth, gesturing to Verlinden.

'Don't be a fool,' said Estla.

'No, Estla, this is not a night for secrets or hidden thoughts.'

'Hrulth, don't. I'm not certain ...'

'Let's all decide for ourselves here, Estla.' He gestured to Audum to come to him. 'Look at the two of them together. I don't need any more evidence than that.'

Atreu looked at Audum and Verlinden standing next to each other. From their dark red ringlets down, there was a striking resemblance. 'What are you saying, Hrulth?' he asked.

Hrulth nodded in Cluric's direction. 'You know what I'm about to say, don't you?'

Cluric didn't answer.

Hrulth settled back down in the chair, and Estla stepped away. 'Cluric's father – my brother – and his young family were staying with us the night of the Faemir raid on Treyfell many years ago. Who knows why the Faemir chose that night of all nights to attack our village? It was the first and only time it happened. It was the night Cluric and Edric's father was killed. It was also the night we lost our beautiful twin baby daughters.'

Atreu gasped. 'You're saying you believe Verlinden and Valkyra are your daughters?'

'So that's why you were asking me so much about myself,' said Verlinden.

Estla nodded. 'There was something in your face when I first saw you at the door. And your hair – it's a very unusual shade of red. I've only ever seen one person with hair that colour – and that's Audum.'

'But how can you be certain?' said Atreu. 'Verlinden ... you ...'

'I can't be, but ... twin girls with flame-coloured hair,' said Estla. 'It all fits with what Verlinden knows of her origins. How many twin girls would there be with such hair who were taken by Faemir?'

'You *are* certain, though, aren't you Estla?' said Hrulth. 'You just don't want to admit it to yourself.'

Estla's chest began to heave as tears rolled down her cheeks. 'Yes, I know it. A mother knows.' She held out her arms for Verlinden.

There was an awkward moment when Verlinden looked at Atreu, totally bewildered. Then she felt overwhelmed with emotions she didn't remember feeling before, and she embraced the big woman and allowed herself to be encircled in her arms.

*

Much later that long night, after many more ales had been drunk and stories told, Atreu and Verlinden lay together in a soft bed and listened to the sound of the trees outside their shuttered window.

Two are missing.

Atreu shivered. Was that the trees whispering?

Two are missing. Find the one who is two.

Of course. Belzalel's words – spoken the last time Atreu lay in this same bed. It was impossible, but there was no doubt the little puppeteer had somehow sensed the truth about Verlinden and Valkyra. He had raced out into the forest, knowing that Verlinden, the one who was both Faelen and Faemir, was to be found in the Rim.

'Has this all been a dream?' asked Verlinden, still finding more tears despite the many she had already shed.

'Not unless everything from the very beginning has been a dream.'

'Could this really be real? I have a mother and father. I have three sisters. Cluric is my cousin. I ... I can't grasp that this is possible. How can any of us be certain? We can't be, can we? All this could be taken away from me in the morning.'

'I don't know how we can be certain of anything anymore,' said Atreu. 'That is one lesson my Ascent has taught me all too well. But don't concern yourself about certainty. If you believe it, and all the others do – does anything else matter?'

Verlinden started stroking Atreu's hair. 'What happens now? I've found something that has been lost to me, yet the Mountain is still lost. It doesn't seem like that could be possible. What do we do?'

'Just enjoy the moment, Verlinden. Let's do what Aeshya always did. We'll worry about tomorrow when we wake.'

Atreu let his mind drift to all the joyous events he had experienced since commencing his Ascent. The girl in Heimfell who led him in a giddy dance on a starry night. The part of the journey he had shared with Cluric. The strange beauty of the Rimforest, still untouched by war. The bustling colours of the market at Peleusar. On and on his thoughts drifted until he felt the joy of Zenith again, with Verlinden by his side, and then ...

Atreu held his Book lightly under his arm as he walked along the corridors. He stopped in front of an open doorway and stared in. The cave shone with a thousand glimmerstone clusters; they glistened with fires of jade and amber and crimson. And from the ceiling, the lights of the ancient stones hung in a pale webbing.

Like threads, thought Atreu as he searched deep in the pockets of his broadcloth. Finally, his hand hit upon something hard. He took it out and held it in front of his eyes. It was the glimmerstone he had taken so long ago. It was now cold and dull, and looked like any other stone.

The voice of an old man sounded in his head, a voice speaking to him from a cave under a sandy plain.

'Take what the Mountain offers you,' it said, 'and create, so that it belongs to both of you.'

'Your Book,' said Atreu, 'why didn't you tell me about your Book?'

'I told you – you must find your origin, Atreu, and the Book you seek is much closer to your heart. My time has passed. It has come upon me swiftly in the end, but I feel I have done more than I could have hoped. The Circle now has the knowledge and it will never be the same again.'

'Wait, Metheus, don't leave.'

'My time has passed.' With the last word, Metheus' voice started failing.

'No, Metheus, please, before you go, tell me what I must do.'

'A *what* question. They usually hide something else.'

'Please, Metheus, an answer.'

'You must find the answers to your own questions. It has always been so. Look to your heart.'

The final word trailed off into a wisp of steam. Atreu watched it hover just in front of his face. Taking a deep breath, he drew the vapour into his lungs and it seeped into every fibre of his being. In one fluid motion he began to exhale and the cloud reformed. He watched as images took shape within it, each one dissolving to be replaced by another: a blighted sun, a shattered Mountain, a black river, three cloaked figures sitting in the shadowy recesses of a cave, and finally, the face of a man.

When Atreu recognised who it was, the cloud faded into the air, and he was lost in a confusion of dreams and half-thoughts until just before dawn.

With daybreak, the sharp light of clarity hardened his resolve, and he knew what he had to do.

*

Estla had protested loudly when Atreu and Verlinden announced their plans to continue their Descent to Valesend immediately, saying that she wanted all her daughters with her. When Cluric and Jenethelen said they would join them as far as Teuron, she became even more irate. Treyfell had been reduced by the war to a village of mainly women and children, and she didn't want to see the four of them risk their lives needlessly. And yet, neither Atreu nor Cluric felt they had any choice.

The sun was barely above the horizon when Atreu and the others skirted around the Treyfell barricade fires and headed downslope.

'You could have waited a few more days,' said Atreu.

'I've been lying in that bed for too long,' said Cluric. 'I don't think I need any more rest. I need to find Edric. And I need to go home – whatever is waiting for me there.'

'I know the feeling,' said Atreu.

According to Estla, the last news that had reached Treyfell about Teuron was that it had escaped relatively unscathed, but it had been a long time since anyone had ventured upslope – and that wasn't a good sign. There had been no news at all from Valesend since the Faemir war had begun.

A sharp wind had sprung up just after dawn and it battered at their backs as they headed downslope, almost as if it was pushing them along. The terrain bore the scars of months of incessant instability. Large pillars angled up from the ground, crowding in at them and blocking their view. Cluric had tried to ease the oppressive atmosphere earlier with some banter, but he soon gave up. No one could pretend this was a light-hearted journey. Atreu tried to convince himself that the fact that no news had filtered upslope for some time was not necessarily a bad sign. Communications were never as strong in this sparsely populated region as they were in the Mid-Reaches. Yet it was hard for him not to let black thoughts enter his mind.

Atreu was constantly aware of how heavy his Book had become. Whatever the significance of the weight increase, entering the Lower Reaches proper hadn't changed anything. Cluric's experience with the Dusk-wraiths gave Atreu some confidence that the four of them would survive the several nights they were exposed before they reached Teuron. According to Cluric, there was no doubt fire kept them at bay unless they massed in large numbers – and even when they did, the flames weakened them considerably.

But when the sun started dipping all too soon, Atreu's doubts started to grow.

Cluric pulled out a torch from his pack, and the others followed suit. As Atreu began to get out his flint, Cluric said, 'No, we shouldn't light any fires unless we have to. Fire attracts them.'

'It attracts the wraiths, yet weakens them?' asked Verlinden.

'Yes – it took me some time to work that out. The bigger the fire, the more wraiths it attracts.'

'So that's why Peleusar was attacked by such huge numbers?' said Atreu.

'Yes, although I don't think eliminating the barrier fires would have been any help. The wraiths are an impossible assailant to deal with. There are problems whatever you do.'

'What should we do now, then?' asked Atreu.

'If we are fortunate, we can move through the night undetected by them. Try to keep as silent as possible. Noise seems to attract the wraiths as well. I think that's one reason why the Faemir, with their battle cries, sustained far more devastating attacks.'

'And if we are not fortunate?' said Verlinden.

'We light these torches as quickly as we can. If we only have to deal with a small number, the torches could be enough to fend them off.'

'We've only ever seen wraiths in large numbers,' said Atreu. 'What happens if they are swarming around us?'

'Then we resort to a barricade fire. It's a last resort because you draw the wraiths to you, and then it's a matter of praying for dawn.'

Atreu and Verlinden exchanged a glance. 'That doesn't seem like much of an option with the nights lengthening all the time,' said Verlinden.

'No.' Cluric smiled grimly. 'Our best chance is if we keep moving as swiftly as we can. Hopefully this wind will aid us. The wraiths find it harder to form when there's a strong wind blowing.'

Atreu felt a sickening twist in his stomach when the last rays of sunlight vanished into the ether. His eyes darted in all directions as they continued downslope. He expected every pillar to conceal wraiths eager to seek them out with their cold, probing fingers. Throughout his Descent he had been protected from their attack – by the Maelstrom, by sunlight and by the Rimforest – but now he was, for the first time, totally exposed. The thought terrified him.

'Is there anything else, anything at all, we can do?' he asked Cluric.

'Ssh.' Cluric put his finger to his lips. 'We'll have to whisper now.'

Atreu lowered his voice. 'Is there anything else you've come across that may help us?'

'There was a Mid-Reacher we came across upslope of the Rimforest who said he had found that covering yourself with thick blankets somehow helped.'

'Thick blankets?' said Verlinden. 'Are you sure?'

'That's what he said – I never had the chance to try it, but he was still alive, so perhaps there was something to it.'

Atreu looked at Verlinden. 'That seems a strange coincidence, doesn't it?'

'It does.'

'What coincidence?' asked Cluric.

'There's a section of the Maelstrom called the helles,' said Atreu, 'and when a certain wind blows, the only way to stave off madness is by covering yourself with blankets.'

'And this had nothing to do with Dusk-wraiths?'

'Not as far as I know,' said Atreu. 'I gathered the helles and the ill-wind had always been there. We certainly didn't see any wraiths until much further downstream.'

'The blankets work against the wraiths,' said Jenethelen softly.

The other three looked at her –she had hardly spoken that day.

'How do you know?' said Cluric. 'We never tried it.'

'I've been thinking about it since we met that Mid-Reacher,' said Jenethelen. 'I'm sure now that the blanket was how I escaped the Dusk-wraiths when they first attacked the Faemir at Peleusar.'

'You've never told me that,' said Cluric.

'I told you I hid when they attacked. Did I have to tell you I cowered under a blanket like a little girl while my sisters died horrible deaths? Did you have to know how much of a coward I was?'

'You're still alive and they're not,' said Verlinden. 'It's not as if you could have done anything to help our sisters.'

Jenethelen drew a deep breath. 'It helps to hear another Faemir say that.'

They continued in silence through the darkness. The wind gained force as the night lengthened, and Atreu felt it sting the exposed skin on the back of his neck. He had to take care with his footing, as small chasms constantly appeared in their path. Nightmare images of Midfell kept forming in his mind. He knew he still hadn't quite come to terms with what happened that night, but the swarm of Nazir that had descended on Belzalel in the end was tearing into his consciousness now that he was out in the open and vulnerable again.

'Cluric, have you actually seen a Nazir?' he asked, ensuring his voice was low.

'It's hard to tell. Sometimes, at night, when we were lying somewhere, trying to get to sleep, I thought I saw something – but I was never sure if I was dreaming.'

'What did they look like to you?' asked Atreu.

'They were ... different. I only really saw – or thought I saw – a silhouette in the darkness. They always stood differently to the way a Maelir or a Faemir stand. It's hard to describe. It was like their bodies had been broken and reset in the wrong way.'

'They're not … round, like us, are they?' said Atreu.

'You've seen them?' asked Cluric.

'Yes.'

'You would think that they would be sighted more often now,' said Jenethelen. 'The people of the Mountain are on their knees. Surely they could just walk in now and finish us off?'

'They possibly could,' said Atreu, 'but unless we really know how they think, we can't judge their actions properly.'

'Damn!' Cluric stopped suddenly and started lighting his torch.

Atreu peered through the dense night air and saw a dark shadow emerging from behind a pillar towards them. He managed to light his torch after several attempts in the blustering wind. By the time the flame was burning, Cluric had already thrust his torch like a sword into the shadow. Atreu joined the others in attacking the wraith, and it faded into the night like a dark cloud of steam.

When it was clear that no other wraith attack was imminent, Atreu breathed a sigh of relief. 'That was easier than I thought it would be.'

'Don't get too confident,' said Cluric. 'That was a very small wraith, and there were four of us. Let's extinguish our torches and get moving. Our best hope is that there are no other wraiths in the vicinity.'

The second attack came from behind. A tendril had started to wrap itself around Atreu's torch before Cluric managed to cut it off from the wraith mass with his flame. Verlinden and Jenethelen destroyed what was left just as Atreu had lit his torch.

The wind battered their backs with increasing ferocity as they continued, and Cluric glanced nervously over his shoulder every few steps.

'What's wrong?' asked Atreu.

'Can you hear it?' said Cluric.

Atreu strained to capture any sound above the rushing of the wind. After a while he became aware of a droning sound in the distance. 'Is that what I think it is?'

Cluric nodded. 'It's hard to tell, but it sounds like a huge wraith mass behind us.'

'What do we do?'

Verlinden started to relight her torch.

'No,' said Cluric. 'That won't help if there are as many back there as it appears.'

'Could it be a trick of the wind?' said Atreu hopefully. 'Perhaps they are a lot further away than they seem.'

'Perhaps, but somehow I doubt it,' said Cluric. 'Remember, Dusk-wraiths are partly wind driven. They can't fight against the wind like we do.'

'That means the wind is blowing them towards us,' said Verlinden.

'Yes,' said Cluric, 'and at a furious pace, judging by this gale.'

'It will be pointless trying to outrun them,' said Jenethelen.

'So there's no escape?' asked Atreu.

Cluric shot another glance over his shoulder. 'They'll get us – make no mistake. You'd better brace yourselves.'

'Brace ourselves for what?' asked Atreu, swallowing with a throat that was suddenly dry.

The droning noise had increased so that it was now unmistakable above the fury of the wind.

'You're going to feel what it's like to die,' said Cluric. 'Hopefully the wind will push them over us so that we're not in contact for too long. That's our only chance.'

'And if it does?' said Verlinden.

'We'll gain consciousness sometime after dawn.'

Atreu felt his heart pounding against his chest wall. 'So we'll survive?'

Cluric's expression didn't appear very confident. 'The wraiths won't be able to linger over us. The problem will be if this is a huge wraith mass. Even if each part whips over us with lightning speed, we could be in contact with the mass for some time.'

'Does it sound like a huge mass to you?' asked Atreu.

Cluric didn't answer.

'Cluric?'

'It's hard to tell in this wind, but my guess from the volume of that drone is that there are about as many wraiths back there as there were in Peleusar.'

'We have to start a fire,' said Atreu, as the drone started vibrating in his skull. 'We have to do something. We can't just hope that they'll pass over us quickly.'

'A fire won't stay alight in this gale,' said Cluric.

'We could try the brimstones,' said Jenethelen.

'All right,' said Cluric. 'Let's stop and do what we can here. We won't be able to outrun them, so let's make a stand.'

Jenethelen opened a drawstring bag and started carefully placing a series of fire-red brimstones in a large circle around them.

'What about the blankets?' said Verlinden.

'All right, let's try them,' said Cluric. 'Perhaps they will make a difference.'

As Atreu pulled out his blanket, the drone was now so powerful, he was finding it hard to think straight. 'Try not to let any air in,' he yelled, unsure whether his voice had travelled to Cluric and Jenethelen.

He curled up with Verlinden under the two blankets they had between them and tucked the ends under their bodies so that their weight anchored them to the ground.

It was pitch black in the cocoon they had created for themselves.

'We're going to survive,' he said. 'We're going to survive.'

'Let's try to save our breath,' said Verlinden. 'There's not much air in here.'

Atreu lay there for a time, trying to picture Verlinden as she lay in his embrace, listening to the drone burgeoning to greater intensity, and waiting for the Dusk-wraiths to descend.

And then a cold wave of ice coursed the length of Atreu's body, and his thoughts froze. He could still hear the wind-driven wraiths rage to a fever pitch around them, but his mind had locked. The image of Verlinden was there, like a static painting, but nothing else.

The image started fading, but he fought for it as the wraiths howled their inhuman cry through the blankets.

Verlinden. He strained to hold on to the image despite the drone, which threatened to fill every space inside his head.

Verlinden.

Verlind

Ver

And with an act of will from a vestige of consciousness that remained his own, he pulled her back to him.

Verlinden.

*

It was still dark when Atreu pulled away the blanket, and the wind still beat at him incessantly, but the wraiths were gone.

Chapter
Twenty-five

The sun barely rose above the horizon anymore, and when it did, grotesquely elongated shadows traversed the landscape, leaving nothing untouched by their dark stain. It was as if sunlight was an aberration and darkness the natural state. Fresh instability racked the terrain, as new chasms tore open in the travellers' path, and pillars cracked, shattered and then fell, to be reclaimed by the earth.

Atreu and the others had been subject to further sporadic Dusk-wraith attacks on the road to Teuron, but they had been able to fend them off successfully. There had been no sign of a repeat of the massed attack they had experienced, and Cluric could only put that down to the gale force wind, which had not eased since they left Treyfell.

As they neared Teuron, Atreu sensed Cluric was becoming increasingly apprehensive.

'I'm sure Edric will be all right,' said Atreu.

'Does your Book tell you that he is?' asked Cluric.

'No.'

'I have to know his fate, and that of the town I deserted.'

'You didn't desert anyone, Cluric. The war you left to fight was a Mid-Reach war – Teuron was never going to be threatened by the Faemir.'

'The war, even the war against the Faemir, was nothing I expected it to be. You know, I really don't know now why I left Teuron.'

'Don't torture yourself, Cluric. If there's one thing I've found on Ascent, it's that nothing is what you expect it to be. You can't regret. All you can do is deal the best way you can with the decisions you made.'

Cluric and Atreu strode pace for pace in the dark silence for some time. 'You know,' said Cluric after a while, 'there have been some strange parallels in our experiences since we left Teuron.'

Atreu nodded as he glanced up ahead at Verlinden and Jenethelen, who were deep in conversation.

'Tell me again how your brother died, Atreu.'

'You are torturing yourself, Cluric. Edric will be alive, I just know it. We'll be in Teuron soon, and you'll see.'

'I hope you're right, Atreu.'

The stars shone brightly in the sky when they finally left the forest of pillars behind them. Downslope, through the clear night air, they could see a tall, raging fire.

'Does Teuron burn?' said Jenethelen.

'It looks like a barricade fire,' said Cluric.

A wall of heat hit them as they approached the barricade. Atreu stared into the wild flames that flailed furiously in the wind. Blinded by the light, he couldn't be sure that there was anything on the other side.

'The townspeople aren't taking any chances with a fire this size,' said Atreu.

'I don't know where they are going to find the wood to keep it going for very long,' said Cluric.

They walked parallel to the barricade, as far away from the heat as was comfortable, looking for a break.

'How are we going to get in?' asked Verlinden.

Cluric put his hand to his mouth and shouted through the flames, 'Can anyone hear us?', but his voice couldn't compete with the howling wind and the sharp cracking sounds of wood being consumed by fire.

Atreu could see that Cluric was growing increasingly frustrated as they continued.

'We're so close,' said Cluric, shaking his head.

'At least we'll be able to get in at dawn when they douse the flames,' said Atreu.

'Who knows when that will be?'

'The Teuroners are obviously determined to ward off the Dusk-wraiths – do you really expect there to be a break in the barricade somewhere?'

'So you're saying we have no choice but to sit here until the sun rises?'

'I don't know. It looks like it.'

Cluric stared morosely into the flames. 'Wait,' he said suddenly. 'The lake – we could get into the town through the lake.'

'Of course,' said Atreu. 'If the Teuroners know that wraiths don't come across water, they will use the lake as part of their barricade.'

'Let's hope they know wraiths can't cross water,' said Verlinden.

They made their way downslope, skirting around the town, until the Teuron lake came into view.

'You were right, Cluric,' said Atreu.

The fire stopped just on the shore of the lake and recommenced on the other side.

'The lake bottom slopes very gently,' said Cluric. 'We should be able to wade across.'

They entered the shimmering water and walked thigh-deep around the end of the fire and onto the shore on the town side of the lake.

The moment they stepped out of the water, several torch-carrying townspeople came towards them. As they came closer, Atreu was surprised to see they had drawn their swords.

'Please come with us,' said the one in front.

'Do we look like wraiths?' said Atreu.

'Please come with us.'

Cluric took a step forward. 'Larath, it's me – Cluric. I've returned.'

Larath's mouth opened. 'Cluric – you made it back to Teuron.'

'How about putting those swords down? This is not much of a welcome.'

'Sorry, Cluric, our orders are to bring anyone who breaches the barricades to Wothan.'

'Wothan? So he survived the Faemir campaign?'

'The Teuron battalion covered itself in glory.'

'Did it? It would have been the only one on either side that did. Strange that I didn't hear any news of its victories.'

'Perhaps if you had taken part in the war, you would have heard.'

'He was in the war,' said Atreu, 'as part of the Treyfell battalion. They were in the heart of the fighting defending Peleusar. Where was the Teuron battalion?'

Larath frowned. 'I'll let Wothan answer your questions.'

'Since when is Wothan in charge of Teuron?' asked Cluric. 'Where are the councillors? What about Delian?'

'Things have changed since you left,' said Larath.

'Of course they've changed,' said Cluric, 'but you still haven't told –'

'Come on, this way,' said one of the other Teuroners, brandishing his sword in Cluric's direction. 'We can't afford to spend all this time talking.'

Cluric glared at him. 'Do I know you?'

'Does it matter?' said the Teuroner.

'Listen to me,' said Cluric. 'I'll come with you to see Wothan – we all will. I want to know what is happening here. But I didn't come back from war to have one of my own people threaten me with a sword. If you wave that thing in my direction again, you won't have a hand to hold it.'

The Teuroner made a noticeable sound with his throat and lowered his sword.

'All right,' said Cluric. 'Now let's go.'

As they walked towards the town centre, Atreu could barely believe how much Teuron had changed. All around them people were busy pulling their houses down, cutting the pieces up and creating giant piles of wood. What had once been a town of wide streets and neat houses now looked like a place that had been mortally wounded.

'What is happening to my beloved Teuron?' said Cluric, barely able to choke out the words.

'The barricade fires are hungry,' said Larath. 'We have to keep feeding them.'

'Damn these Nazir,' said Cluric. 'One way or the other, they get us to destroy ourselves. Without staining their hands, they make us drain our own blood away, little by little.'

As they entered the town square, Cluric saw several Teuroners he knew, but they were all so busy cutting wood that they didn't even look up when he shouted a greeting.

'In here,' said Larath, pointing to the town hall.

'So Wothan thinks he's chief councillor now, does he?' said Cluric.

They were led into the large forechambers, and Atreu could see Wothan sitting behind a table in the far corner. Above him, mounted on the wall, were two giant grale's heads, eyes afire, tongues hanging out from between rows of sharp-edged teeth, the vague smell of burning dung still emanating from them. Wothan was shouting to a group of people in front of him and gesticulating wildly. Finally, he waved them away, and looked up at those who had entered the chamber.

'Don't tell me we have even more Lower Reachers seeking refuge?'

'Not quite,' said Cluric, stepping forward.

Wothan squinted at him in the torchlight and a look of recognition crossed his face. 'Well, well ... Cluric has returned. How quickly they skulk back when Teuron is the only safe town in the Lower Reaches.'

'From what I can remember,' said Cluric, 'you were the one known for your skulking.'

Even in the low light, Cluric could see Wothan's face reddening.

'You won't last long in Teuron with that sort of talk,' said Wothan. 'And who else do we have here?' His eyes locked on Atreu. 'Don't tell me the Ascender has returned a failure?'

Atreu took several steps forward so that he was standing next to Cluric. 'Let's not be too hasty about who we declare failures,' he said.

Wothan looked past him at Verlinden and Jenethelen. 'Ah, two Faemir. Welcome to Teuron, both of you. If you behave yourselves, we might let you stay and make good Teuron women of you.'

Both Verlinden and Jenethelen went for their knives, but Cluric gestured for them to stay calm.

'Where is Delian?' he asked.

'This is not a time for councillors and failed Ascenders to be in charge.'

'You can't usurp the rightful leadership of Teuron,' said Cluric.

'Leadership in war goes to those who have the power to exercise it.'

'Where is Delian?' asked Cluric again, his voice steady and clear.

'He was one of the first casualties when the war reached Teuron.' Wothan waved his hand dismissively. 'Now, let's determine what we are here to determine.'

'And what's that?'

'Whether we can allow you to stay.'

'What?'

'We're getting refugees from all over the Lower Reaches. We can't let everyone stay.'

'I've had enough of this,' said Cluric. 'This is my town, and these people are my guests. You won't sit in judgement of any of us.'

'I'll sit in judgement of anyone within the barricades,' he said.

'We'll see about that,' said Cluric, drawing his sword.

'Get that weapon off him,' yelled Wothan. 'Why is he still in possession of it?'

Two Teuroners drew their swords and stepped towards him. Cluric thrust his sword at them, knocking their weapons out of their hands so that they clattered on the floor. Jenethelen had also drawn her sword and was in battle stance, pointing it at the other Teuroners.

Wothan jumped out of his chair and made a lunge for his sword, which was leaning against the wall next to the table. But Cluric was too quick for him, and had flicked Wothan's weapon away with his own before he could reach it.

Wothan backed away from Cluric, glaring at him with an edge of fear on his face.

'So you've come back a soldier, have you?' he said.

'No,' said Cluric. 'I've just come back.'

'You won't live for long if you threaten me,' said Wothan. 'Teuron belongs to me.'

'No, Wothan, it belongs to all of us. What's left of it.' He sheathed his sword and Wothan relaxed visibly.

'I'm glad you've come to your senses, Cluric.'

'After what I've seen since I left Teuron, I don't know if I will ever come to my senses.' He pointed to Wothan's upturned chair. 'Why don't you sit back down and play whatever games you want to play – I want to see my brother just now.' Cluric looked up at the heads mounted on the wall. 'Still killing defenceless beasts?'

'I kill anything or anyone it suits me to kill. Do you know how many Maelir there are in Teuron who would strike you down on my order?' A sneer crept onto Wothan's face. 'I don't think you have any idea who you're dealing with.'

'You seem to be the same person who used to try to impress the townspeople by hunting sleeping grale.'

A flash of anger crossed Wothan's face, but he quickly regained control. 'You will change your view. Go and speak to Edric – he'll tell you how things are now. Ask him what the Teuron army will be doing at dawn. You may want to join us to see how things have changed – I guarantee you will see some killing you've never seen before.'

'I doubt if I will be impressed by any of your killing,' said Cluric, turning to go.

Atreu held out his arm to stop Cluric. 'Wothan,' he said, 'you said Teuron was the only safe place in the Lower Reaches. Do you have any news of Valesend?'

'Valesend?' Wothan gave a half-smile of disdain. 'A group of refugees from there tried to enter Teuron some time ago. We turned them away – there wasn't one soldier among them.'

Atreu's shoulders slumped.

'Come on,' said Cluric. 'I don't think I can stand the stench in here anymore.'

The four of them left and walked along the Teuron streets towards Cluric's inn.

'Wothan's never been anything but a bully and a coward,' said Cluric, fingering the hilt of his sword.

'He thinks you backed down,' said Jenethelen. 'That's never a good tactic.'

'I'll deal with him later,' said Cluric. 'I don't know enough of what's happening here, and he certainly wasn't going to do much more than boast and brag.'

'What do you think the killing at dawn he spoke of is?' said Atreu.

'I have no idea. Whatever it is, though, I'll warrant it won't be something where he puts himself in too much danger.'

The roar of the barricade fire reached their ears again as they walked through the outskirts of Teuron. Cluric felt a sickening mixture of dread and anticipation – akin to the one he had felt when Hrulth was about to pull the Faemir arrow through his arm.

Just ahead was the inn. To Cluric's dismay, half of it had been demolished, and stood there like a skeleton. A Maelir was at work with an axe, hacking at pieces of wood and throwing them on a pile to one side.

Cluric called to him. 'Shouldn't you be serving ales?'

The Maelir looked up. There was a moment's confusion, then he said, 'I can't believe this. Cluric, is it really you?'

'Yes, Edric, it's me.'

The two brothers ran to each other and embraced for a long time, tears pouring down their faces.

Edric pulled back to look at his brother's face. 'You're back, Cluric, you're back.'

'Yes, I'm home.'

Edric looked across at the other three. 'Atreu, you brought him back.'

'I'm not sure that's quite the way it worked,' said Atreu.

Edric stared at the two Faemir, and then looked back at Cluric with raised eyebrows. 'It looks like you will have some stories to tell me. Come on, all of you, inside. I know the Mountain is falling apart, but there are still times when friends should share an ale.'

They entered the inn and sat down at one of the long tables while Edric filled the tankards. A low fire burnt in the hearth. Edric nodded in its direction. 'I know I shouldn't use precious wood on that, but it always seems so cold now. It also helps me pretend things aren't as bad as they really are.'

'What have you done with this wall?' asked Cluric, tapping some makeshift boards.

'I couldn't just leave what's left of the inn exposed to the elements. I was particularly glad of the wall when that gale started blowing.'

Cluric sat down on the bench and looked at his tankard of

ale. 'What's happening in Teuron?' he asked. 'Is Wothan really in charge?'

'I'm afraid so, Cluric. Delian was taken by the wraiths during the first attack, and the other councillors had no answers. Wothan offers simple answers, and the townspeople are clinging to them.'

'What are his answers?'

'Keep the barricade fires going, and keep them going high.'

'But we are dismantling our own town.'

'I know, Cluric, I know. Can you imagine how I've felt cutting up the inn that our father built?'

'Is there no other way?'

'Look, Cluric, Wothan and I don't exactly see eye to eye, but I can't really fight him if I don't have an alternative. We've all got quotas of wood we have to supply every day, and in exchange, we get food.'

'That's monstrous. Since when does he own the food?'

'I agree, but with so little sunlight, none of the winter crops have grown. It must be the same all over the Mountain. It's only with rationing that we can fend off starvation.'

Cluric put his head in his hands. 'This is worse than I could have imagined. We're all dying a slow death.'

'What else is Wothan doing?' asked Atreu.

'He's constantly turning away refugees from the other Lower Reach towns and villages.'

'How can you do that to your fellow Maelir?' said Atreu.

'Wothan argues that we have only limited resources. We would be punishing our own good planning if we let these people in.'

'You are telling me one horror after the other,' said Cluric, 'and I haven't heard you argue with any of Wothan's decisions.'

'I don't have an alternative, Cluric. I know what we are doing is despicable, but what else can we do? We let in only those refugees who are carrying either large supplies of food or wood.'

'How many of those are there, Edric?'

'Not too many.'

'How do they drive the refugees away?' asked Verlinden. 'Most of them must be desperate – there's not much left out there for them to go back to.'

'Well, that's the other sort of refugee we let in – soldiers, or Maelir who look like they can handle a sword. We need increasing numbers to hold back the refugees.'

'So fit Maelir can get in,' said Jenethelen, 'and women and children are nearly always turned away.'

Edric could barely meet her gaze. 'I ... I understand what we are doing is wrong – but if those barricade fires fail, we won't last one night. From what little news we have, Teuron is in much better shape than any other settlement in the Lower Reaches. For all we know, the Mountain's last stand could be here.'

Cluric looked at the makeshift wall and shivered as the howling wind snuck through the cracks and hit his face. 'Can it get any worse than this, Edric?'

Edric took a tentative sip of ale and then put his tankard down. 'Wothan will fight this to the bitter end.'

Verlinden shook her head. 'By sacrificing women and children.'

Edric looked at her and felt tears well up. 'Perhaps I'm a coward, I don't know.' He wiped the tears with the back of his hand. 'And there's even worse, from what I've heard. There's been talk of jettisoning the non-productive townspeople.'

'The what?' said Verlinden.

'I'm not sure exactly what they mean, but I think it's those who cannot chop wood or help defend the town.'

'The weak, the sick, the aged and the young,' said Verlinden. The words shot from her lips like arrows.

Cluric drew a deep breath. 'So it has come to this? We are no better than the inhuman Nazir that want to take the Mountain from us.' He looked slowly into the eyes of the others in the room. 'If we truly are no better than the Nazir, then I can't see any reason why we should prevail over them.'

'Surely we must strive to live,' said Edric.

'Should we? Why? So Wothan and his ilk can rule the Mountain?' He pushed his tankard away. 'I don't believe our people will follow him down this path. I can't bring myself to believe it.'

They sat there in silence for a moment, until Edric said, 'Wothan *has* made a breakthrough in the war.'

'What?' asked Cluric.

'He's captured a Nazir – as far as I know, no one else has done that.'

'He what?'

They stared at Edric open-mouthed.

'Have you seen it?' asked Atreu.

'Yes, they had it in a cage. It was bound by the hands and feet and paraded through the town square two nights ago.'

'That's incredible,' said Atreu. 'Do you know how hard it has been to sight Nazir even from a distance since the war started?'

'I suspect there was some luck involved,' said Edric. 'Then again, he and his band were successful grale hunters before the war. They would have known the chasms and crevices they hid in during daylight. He has certainly been determined enough to find a Nazir since he returned to Teuron – every available Maelir is sent out on patrol at daybreak.'

'So they've really got one?' asked Atreu. 'It's not a pretence he is putting forward to enhance his standing?'

'It looked real to me. It screamed very realistically when the townspeople fired rocks at it. And the blood looked the same colour as ours.'

'What did the people do?' shouted Atreu. 'They didn't kill it, did they?'

'It didn't look too good when we'd finished. Wothan's men took it away before we could do more damage.'

'We?' said Cluric. 'Don't tell me you were throwing stones at it too.'

Edric hung his head. 'One or two,' he said in a soft voice. 'I was just caught up in it all like the others. I know it wasn't right. It's just ... the built-up frustration ... I ... I'm ashamed of it now, but at the time ... can you honestly say you wouldn't have done the same, Cluric?'

'So it's still alive,' said Atreu. 'Has anyone tried to communicate with it?'

'No,' said Edric.

'What? But we could learn so much,' said Atreu. 'This is the opportunity we've been looking for. We broke the deadlock with the Faemir by speaking to them. This war has been so devastating because they've never shown themselves – if we could just communicate, there might be a chance.'

'I'm afraid Wothan has other plans for it,' said Edric.

'What are they?' asked Cluric.

'He's going to use this Nazir as bait for others. He plans to tie it to a stake near one of the large chasms just before dawn. When its kin come, the Teuron army will surround them and engage them in battle, keeping them above ground until daybreak.'

No one spoke as the enormity of the plan sunk in.

'So that's what Wothan was crowing about,' said Atreu. 'He even invited us to the killing.'

'I've been told I'm required for the slaughter,' said Edric softly.

'When does it end?' said Cluric.

Atreu drew a breath. 'I have a dark feeling about this. Is there any way I can talk to this Nazir before daybreak?'

'Not that I know of,' said Edric. 'It's very heavily guarded. You would only be able to do it with Wothan's permission.' He frowned. 'I know what he is planning is not pleasant, Atreu, but this is war. Why are you so sympathetic to the Nazir?'

'They were here first,' said Atreu. 'We've somehow managed to cover that up in our history. Our people were the ones who took the Mountain away from them. We banished them to the Steppes.'

'Are you certain?'

'Yes. I am filled with the same horror you are about what they are doing, but if they are only trying to get back what was stolen from them, can we truly see them as evil? Who has right on their side – the thief or the victim?'

'But this is our inn,' said Edric. 'Our father built it. Teuron is our town. I'm not a thief, none of us are.'

'I didn't say any of us were thieves. But our ancestors were – thieves and murderers. And we are the custodians of what they stole. We can't just ignore that.'

Before Atreu had finished his sentence, the ground started shaking so violently that the tankards tipped over and ale ran across the table and dripped onto the floor.

'This doesn't appear to be a time for ales,' said Cluric. 'Come on, let's see if we can get to see this Nazir.'

*

Wothan's face broke into a twisted smile when he saw Cluric and the others again. 'I wondered how long it would be before you came back. I suppose Edric told you about our little prisoner.'

'I want to speak with it,' said Atreu.

'You want to what?'

'Speak with it. Has anyone tried to do that?'

'Of course we have,' said Wothan. 'They either don't understand our language or can withstand a great deal of pain.'

'Pain? Were you speaking or torturing?'

'We wanted answers.'

'Have you informed any Maelir army commanders of what you have here?'

'What are you talking about? Commanders rarely bothered with the Lower Reaches even when communications were functioning effectively. We've sent many runners upslope since the siege of Teuron began, but none have ever returned.'

'So no one knows that you have it?'

'I sent a runner when we captured it. Who knows if he made it? I'm not going to send any more until we hear something.'

'Our commanders will want to deal with the Nazir,' said Atreu.

'Will they?' sneered Wothan. 'Well, as far as I can see, there's only one commander in Teuron, and you're looking at him. And it looks like we're the only ones who have captured a Nazir – perhaps your commanders can deal with the Nazir that they have had the skill to capture. For all we know, right now Teuron is the Mountain's last hope.'

Atreu chewed his bottom lip. 'I would still like to try to speak with it.'

Wothan looked over Atreu's shoulder and sneered at Cluric. 'And what about you? Are you begging me to see our prize as well?'

'I don't believe you actually have a Nazir,' said Cluric. 'You're not good enough a soldier to capture one.'

The blood started to rise in Wothan's face and Atreu could see him clenching his knuckles until they were white. 'All right,' said Wothan, 'I'll take you to our prisoner.'

Wothan and several armed Teuroners took the four of them to a small, heavily guarded building just behind the town square. The windows had been boarded across several times, and a large latch bolted the door from the outside.

'You won't have much time,' said Wothan. 'We have big plans, which mean moving before daybreak.'

'I know what you have planned,' said Cluric.

Wothan eyed Verlinden and Jenethelen from head to toe. 'I imagine you two would want to wait outside.'

'Then I think there's something wrong with your imagination,' said Verlinden.

Wothan gave the order to unbolt the door, and he and three of the guards drew their swords. After everyone had filed through the door, it was closed behind them. The torch flames carried by the guards shed a weak light onto the room.

Atreu was hit by a stench as his eyes immediately locked onto a figure crouched in the corner furthest from the door. He approached the figure slowly, his legs trembling in anticipation. It didn't move as he crouched down in front of it. He could see now its knees were pulled up tight towards its body and its head was buried in the sharp angle of its elbows. Pieces of dark clothing hung off its thin body in shreds.

'You must be cold,' said Atreu.

He thought there was a faint jerk in response, but couldn't be sure.

'Do you understand me?' said Atreu.

No response.

Atreu drew a deep breath, trying to form the right words in his head. 'I ... know the Mountain was yours,' he said. 'I know our people have done wrong.'

The Nazir's limbs untangled and it lifted its head. For the briefest of moments, their gazes locked and Atreu saw something in its pale, lidless eyes. Then, as if its head had grown too heavy for its thin neck to carry, it pulled its knees back up again and returned to the entangled position it was in when they had entered the room.

Wothan stepped up to where Atreu was crouched. 'I think we've overestimated these Dusk People,' he said. 'They don't look like they would last very long in battle.'

'I want to try some more,' said Atreu. 'I'm sure it understood me. Give me more time and I can find out some information that would help us all.'

Wothan laughed. 'I'll show you the only information I need. Watch.' He reached out with his sword and twisted the tip sharply against the Nazir's leg. There was a high-pitched wail of pain, although the Nazir didn't move, and deep red blood started to issue from the wound. 'See? They bleed. I've never come across anything that bleeds that I can't kill.'

Atreu looked at the bare, dark skin of the Nazir's arms and legs, and could see the evidence of a dozen such wounds.

He stood up and looked Wothan in the eye. 'This is not the way to end the war.'

'We'll see which one of us is right,' said Wothan. He turned to Cluric. 'Still doubt what we have here? Still doubt me?'

'No,' said Cluric. 'I know now exactly what sort of soldier you are.'

*

There was still no sign of the sun when the Teuron battalions stepped across the doused section of the barricade fire into the dark, shadow-infused landscape outside. Soldiers from all over the Lower Reaches had obviously swelled the numbers, creating an impressive army. The sick, heavy feeling in Atreu's stomach told him something horrific was about to happen, yet he knew this was where he had to be. He still had the faint hope that he could somehow change what was going to occur. His Book weighed heavily in his pack – so heavily now that every step was an effort. Verlinden matched him stride for stride, carrying the Book of Maelur. She had insisted that she, too, come on this gruesome mission. He had argued with her, but in the end recognised that her compulsion was as strong as his, and had to admit that he alone was not strong enough to carry both Books.

Atreu glanced at the heavily barred cage perched on the shoulders of several large Teuroners. The Nazir inside seemed even weaker than when he had seen it earlier, and the bars were at least twice as thick as its limbs. Since looking into the Nazir's eyes, Atreu couldn't help but think of it as a person – not a Maelir, something different, yet not so different.

The wind whipped around his ears as the march continued in the direction of the Plains of Vygird. There was a cockiness in the Teuroners that Atreu hadn't seen in Maelir soldiers since the very early days of the Faemir war. They marched with their heads high and a dark glint in their eyes that almost betrayed a smile threatening to escape.

'Verlinden, this is wrong,' said Atreu. 'I know these men have tasted little else but defeat, and now, finally, they are going to strike the enemy – but it's wrong.'

'I agree, Atreu – Maelir and Faemir have experienced unspeakable horrors, but I feel ...' she trailed off.

'I don't have the words for it either, Verlinden.'

As they marched through the barren, windswept terrain of bushes and trees stunted by preternatural darkness, the weight of Atreu's Book seemed to subtly increase with every step. The straps of his pack were now cutting into his shoulders. He tried to change his posture to ease the strain, but found no relief. Verlinden, too, was struggling with her load, sweat beading on her forehead, only to be swept away by the fierce gusts of wind that howled around them incessantly.

'I feel like we have the weight of the Mountain on our shoulders,' said Atreu.

'Perhaps we have,' said Verlinden. 'Perhaps that's what it means.'

As they entered the outer edge of Vygird, sands started whipping up into their faces. The few twisted trees that had dotted the landscape had disappeared, and ahead was a featureless undulation broken only by a series of gaping chasms.

Wothan gave the command to halt, and Atreu almost collapsed to the ground in relief. He carefully slid the pack off his shoulders and ran his fingers gingerly across the indentations in his skin.

The Teuroners had lowered the cage and surrounded it, swords poised, as one of them worked at the bolt. Once the cage was open, they lifted out the crumpled tangle of angular limbs that had lain there, inert, since they had left Teuron.

Atreu gritted his teeth as he watched the soldiers carry the Nazir to a raised area in the middle of a circle of large chasms. A large Teuroner had just finished hammering a giant stake deep into the sandy soil. Atreu could see that the Nazir's limbs had been bound tightly by a series of ropes. Wothan now walked along the line of soldiers with another rope in his hand. He tied one end to the stake, making the most of his audience with a series of flourishes. It then became clear that the other end of the rope was a noose. Wothan lifted the slumped Nazir's head with one hand and looped the noose around its long neck. Standing to the side so that as many soldiers as possible could see, he proceeded to tighten the noose.

When he had finished, he pulled the Nazir's chin up by the rope, and faced the Teuroners.

'This is where it ends,' he said loudly, his visage a grim, determined mask, and his hair flailing wildly behind him in the wind. 'This is where the Nazir will finally feel the sting of Maelir swords. This is the turning point in the war. Remember, all of you, that you were here and you played your part.'

He drew his sword and twisted its point into the Nazir's leg. A wail of pain sounded into the air. Wothan looked around at the chasms that encircled them. When it was obvious that nothing was emerging, he twisted his sword into the Nazir's leg again. Once more, a wail of pain came from the Nazir's lips.

Wothan again surveyed the scene, a grim smile on his face.

Again and again he twisted his sword into the Nazir's flesh, each time opening a new wound. And when blood streaked the Nazir's legs, Wothan started on its arms, and then its torso, and then its neck. Each time, a wail of pain filled the night sky, each wail louder and more penetrating than the one before, each one feeding into the next, building to an agonising crescendo.

'*Stop*,' cried Atreu when he could bear it no longer. '*Stop*. No living thing deserves this.'

Wothan glared at him, furious at the challenge. 'Silence the Ascender,' he cried.

Verlinden had already drawn her knife and she was joined by Cluric, Edric and Jenethelen, weapons in hand, as they stood between Atreu and the oncoming soldiers.

'There is no honour in this,' cried Atreu.

'I said, silence him,' ordered Wothan.

The soldiers came towards them, and Cluric lowered his

sword. 'So it has come to this,' he said, looking each of the Teu-roners in the eye in turn. 'You may be prepared to kill a fellow townsman, but I am not.' He turned to Atreu. 'I'm sorry, my friend, I can't do this.'

Edric and the others also lowered their weapons.

'You think this is right?' asked Atreu, as the Teuroners took their weapons from them and bound them.

'I want that one's mouth bound,' said Wothan, pointing to Atreu. 'I've heard enough of his voice.'

Atreu felt a cloth being tied around his mouth and secured at the back of his neck.

'Whatever you do, make sure he can't look away,' said Wothan. 'I want the Ascender to see what we're going to do here.'

With a determined smile on his lips, he returned to the Nazir, whose body was now punctured by innumerable wounds which wept blood across its dark skin.

'Now,' said Wothan. 'Let me hunt out the places where you are not yet bleeding.'

He pressed his sword into the shallow cheek of the Nazir and turned the tip sharply, boring a hole into its flesh. A wail deeper and more gut-wrenching than any before pierced the air.

'Ah,' said Wothan. 'I believe we are getting close to the mark.'

He pierced another part of the Nazir's cheek.

And then another.

And then another. And then another.

As the wails reached a pitch that pierced his soul, Atreu felt tears well up in his eyes.

'Stop it,' cried Verlinden.

'No,' came Cluric's protest, but all of them quickly had their mouths bound like Atreu.

And then Wothan started on the Nazir's other cheek.

Atreu struggled to look away, but a strong pair of hands held his head firmly in place. He tried to close his eyes, but a pair of thumbs pulled back his eyelids.

Wothan's sword was now poised over the Nazir's lidless eyes.

'They're coming,' he cried triumphantly as he squinted into the chasms. 'Get ready. We are all about to become the stuff of legend.'

With a sharp twist of his sword he pierced the Nazir's left eye, and Atreu's stomach rose to his mouth and he vomited on the sands of Vygird.

Chapter Twenty-six

Finally they emerged. A dark, sharp-angled mass issued from every chasm, a continuous wave of inhumanity. And with them flowed the final wail of pain, magnified a thousandfold, as if the one Nazir's agony was being felt by all of them. Out they poured, lidless eyes forming pale discs in the darkness, twisted limbs and torsos surging towards the Teuron army.

Atreu saw a flash of sheer panic cross Wothan's face before the Teuron leader turned to run back into the formation of soldiers. The Maelir all tensed, waiting for the moment to charge, the wind howling across Vygird and whipping the sand into an insane frenzy.

Then a strange thing happened.

Just as they reached the limp, bloodied figure slumped at the stake, the Nazir stopped. It was as if an invisible barricade blocked them, and they made no attempt to charge towards the Teuron soldiers. More Nazir continued to issue from the chasms, but they spread out to the left and right, widening the line of Dusk people, but not pushing them any closer.

The Teuroners stood and watched, unsure what to do as the mass of sharp-featured adversaries grew, but still did not attack. And still they poured out of the chasms, spreading across the sands until they had covered Vygird from horizon to horizon. On and on. And as they covered the surface of the Mountain, the wail of pain grew, filling the air until it seemed as if the wind itself had merged with it.

And then it all stopped.

The wail died into silence. The wind froze into stillness. And the wave of inhumanity was spent.

As far as the eye could see, Nazir covered the landscape.

The two adversaries faced each other in the deathly silence.

Atreu fought at his cords, but only succeeded in tightening the knot around his wrists. He sensed the tension among the Teuroners as they stared at the massive army in front of them. It seemed to him as if no one was breathing.

Atreu looked at Wothan. Sweat was beading on the big Maelir's forehead, and raw fear etched his face.

He won't give the order to attack, thought Atreu. *He can't.*

For an eternity the two peoples stood, facing each other, the Mountain frozen around them.

Then Atreu felt someone working the knot on the cloth in his mouth. He turned around when it was pulled away. 'Cluric,' he whispered. 'How did you get free?'

'Larath untied me,' he replied, working at the ropes that bound Atreu's hands and feet.

When Atreu was free, the two of them untied Edric, Verlinden and Jenethelen. The Teuroners stood mesmerised by the Nazir stand-off and barely noticed what was happening.

'That was the easy part,' said Cluric, his eye roving across the dark sea of Nazir stretched out before them. 'What do we do now?'

Atreu and Verlinden exchanged a glance and then went to their packs.

'What are you doing?' asked Cluric.

'The Books have always been the key,' said Atreu. 'Their time is now.'

He put his hands on his Talisman and tried to lift it out, but couldn't. It had grown too heavy. Looking across at Verlinden, he could see she was having the same problem with the Book of Maelur.

'Help me with this one first,' said Atreu.

Verlinden came across and helped Atreu try to lift his Book out of his pack. They both strained until their shoulders and arms ached, but they couldn't move it.

Atreu beckoned Edric, Cluric and Jenethelen over. 'We need your help. We can't do this alone.'

With considerable manoeuvring, each of them grabbed a part of the Book, and with an almighty heave, they managed to lift it out of Atreu's pack and put it on the sandy ground.

'Now this one,' said Verlinden, and they did the same with the Book of Maelur.

Atreu looked around. The adversaries still faced each other in a bizarre stand-off, neither daring to make the first offensive move. He positioned himself behind his Talisman and Verlinden mirrored his stance behind the Book of Maelur.

Atreu nodded to her and they both used all the strength they could muster to turn to the first page of their respective Books. The instant the Books were opened, a collective gasp seemed to issue from the Nazir army. Atreu looked around anxiously, praying that the Teuroners wouldn't respond and break the stand-off. There was a nervous shuffle among many of the Maelir soldiers, but otherwise nothing.

Returning to his Book, Atreu said, 'Verlinden, read me what it says on your first page.'

Verlinden's voice was soft and steady.

'When the Mountain becomes the Abyss
And what you breathe becomes what you expel
You will find what is hidden.
When the sun becomes night
And you become what you believe
You will find your heart.
When the Reader becomes the Teller

And the searcher is the one found
You will find the truth.
When you find what has been hidden
And one perishes at the other's hand
You will die the three deaths.'

Atreu turned away from his Talisman and stared at Verlinden as she read the last three lines. 'I think we are close to the answer, Verlinden. Read the last part again – it doesn't appear in my Book.'

Verlinden drew a breath and read again.

'When you find what has been hidden
And one perishes at the other's hand
You will die the three deaths.'

She looked up. 'I don't like the sound of that. Why is it only in this Book?'

'We are at a juncture, Verlinden. One way we find the truth. The other, we die the three deaths.'

'What three deaths – surely we can only die once?'

'It's the three races, Verlinden. The Maelir, Faemir and Nazir – we all die with the Mountain.'

'It can't be, Atreu. How can that happen?'

'It doesn't have to happen,' said Atreu. 'We can stop it – that's what the two Books are telling us. The paths are forking before us – we must choose the right one.'

Verlinden returned to the Book of Maelur. 'When you find what has been hidden, and one perishes at the other's hand.' She spoke the words softly to herself. 'I have it. I know what it means.' She raised her head and her eyes locked with Atreu's.

'Tell me ... please, Verlinden, tell me.'

'We have found what has been hidden. The Nazir – they have finally emerged.'

'But who is the one we don't want perishing at the other's hand?'

As Verlinden pointed to the mass of Nazir directly in front of him, it dawned on Atreu what she meant. 'You think that if that Nazir at the stake dies, we are all doomed?'

Verlinden nodded.

Then the full realisation hit Atreu. A sense of dread shuddered through him as he watched a tremor of movement across the Nazir front line. He fought the urge to turn away as the Dusk People lifted the dark, bloodied figure high above their heads. It was twitching uncontrollably, its one undamaged eye glinting dully through the darkness.

To the east, the first thin rays of daybreak crept over the Nazir-encrusted horizon. And as the sunlight travelled across the dark army, it was as if a wail of pain merged with it, growing and travelling with the rays until the entire Mountainside writhed in agony.

Yet the Nazir stood their ground against the sun.

And when the sunlight hit the injured Nazir, still hoisted high in the air, its wounds weeping a glistening red blood, it jerked violently ... once ... and then was still.

'No,' cried Atreu, his voice resounding above the dying wail. 'It can't die.'

It seemed to Atreu that there was a moment where everything stopped, and a thousand thousand eyes focused on him in an acrid silence.

And then the thin rays of sun which had emerged from the horizon seemed to be called back. The pale light that had infiltrated the dusk-scape leached back into the night sky. And when darkness had reclaimed the Mountain, the still, frozen air was again invaded by the howling winds.

Cries of despair filtered through the Maelir soldiers. The Teuroners' eyes all turned to Wothan in bewilderment, desperately seeking a command that they could hold onto.

Wothan remained paralysed in the same position he had held since the dark army had emerged from the chasms. Then, as if waking from a dream, he shook his head and gave the signal to retreat.

The Teuroners turned in unison, only to see that more Nazir had emerged from chasms and crevasses behind them, and that now they were completely surrounded.

'Put down all your weapons,' shouted Atreu.

'Keep your swords in hand,' cried Wothan, regaining the voice that had failed him. 'If we die, we die the stuff of legends.'

Atreu pushed his way through to the front of the soldiers. 'There will be no one left to record legends,' he cried. 'Put down your weapons. They won't attack us. They can't.'

Many of the soldiers started lowering their swords.

'Are you mad?' Wothan's voice now had a hysterical edge to it. 'Are we going to die like defenceless women?'

'They've never killed one of us,' said Atreu. 'Despite all the horrors, they've never killed a Maelir or a Faemir. And we've never killed one of them. We still have hope. Look.' He pointed to the injured Nazir, who was now being carefully placed in front of the Dusk army line, its faint movements indicating it was still hanging on to life by the thinnest of threads.

'Don't listen to him,' said Wothan. 'He's not a soldier.'

'They won't attack. Put your weapons down.'

'To glory,' cried Wothan, his hair flailing wildly across his face. 'To glory!' He raised his sword above his head.

'There is no glory here.' Atreu's words rang through the air.

None of the Teuroners raised their swords to match Wothan.

'Damn you. Then the glory will be mine alone.' Wothan ran, sword outstretched, towards the injured Nazir.

Atreu saw what he was about to do and dashed across to block him. With an almighty effort he flung himself at Wothan and they both hit the ground. It was only when Atreu tried to get to his feet that he realised his leg had been cut by the Teuroner's sword.

'I'll finish you first,' shouted Wothan, bearing down on Atreu now that he had regained his footing.

Atreu struggled to move, but a sharp pain tore down the length of his leg. 'Don't be a fool, Wothan,' he cried, looking into the Teuroner's wild eyes as Wothan charged at him, brandishing his weapon.

Then suddenly Wothan faltered, his eyes losing their fire, and he collapsed in front of Atreu with a sword embedded in his back.

Behind him stood the grim figure of Cluric. 'I never thought it would come to this,' he said. 'I have killed a Maelir.'

Atreu was about to answer when a shower of arrows hit the ground between him and the Nazir front line. He looked skyward and saw a squadron of windriders struggling to hold formation in the wild winds over the Plains. The sands of Vygird stained the air, obscuring his vision, but he could see that many of the riders were carrying Faemir warriors, who were busy taking aim with another set of arrows.

Again he tried to get to his feet, his arms flailing madly towards the Faemir. 'No,' he cried as he collapsed again, 'you don't know what you are doing.'

Another volley of arrows arced down, again hitting the ground between the two armies. Atreu knew he couldn't rely on the buffeting winds and poor visibility for much longer. Several of the riders carrying Faemir broke off from the others and swooped down closer to the Mountainside. To Atreu's horror, he could see that one of them was Riell, who was carrying Rhea, and the rider was using all his skill to steady himself in the buffeting gale so that the Faemir leader could take aim.

This one will hit its mark, thought Atreu.

'Riell!' he cried, but the wind whipped his voice away.

Atreu felt a hollow sickness in his stomach as the arrow flew through the air. He made one last futile attempt to somehow dive into its path, but it was to no avail. In the end, he could only watch as the arrow hit the injured Nazir who lay crumpled in front of him.

Atreu stared skyward to see more Faemir taking aim, suddenly aware that, one by one, the stars were fading, leaving an inky blackness where once a pinprick of light had burnt. Then the Mountain started to fall apart, the ground shaking as it never had before. Giant pillars burst from Vygird, taking Maelir and Nazir alike with them, all clinging desperately to the rock as they shot skyward. And giant new rifts appeared everywhere, sucking in those who had once stood on solid ground.

In the utter bedlam around him, Atreu became aware that Verlinden was now by his side, and she had the two Books under her arm.

'Come on, Atreu,' she shouted as the confusion swirled around their ears. She helped Atreu to his feet.

'The Books, Verlinden – how can you lift them?'

'I don't know, Atreu, but I *do* know now what we have to do.'

She supported Atreu with her free hand as they walked slowly towards the Nazir, who lay motionless on the ground. When they reached it, she bent down and carefully pulled the arrow out. A dull glint of light seemed to appear momentarily behind the Nazir's eyes, but then it disappeared without a trace.

'Is it truly dead?' asked Atreu.

'Yes,' said Verlinden.

She opened Atreu's Talisman. 'Here, you said the Books have given you the power over life and death. You claim you brought me back. You claim to have brought Cluric back. Now do it for this poor Nazir.'

'I ... I don't know ...'

'Do it, Atreu.'

The ground was now shaking maniacally under their feet. Atreu's thoughts swirled like the airborne Vygird sands. He opened his Book, flicking madly through the pages.

'I can't do this, Verlinden. I ... I don't have the control over our Talisman.'

'You do, Atreu, you do.' She opened the book of Maelur. 'Here, the two Books together – they give you the control.'

Atreu stared at the pages as he pored over both Books, but the words were a wild jumble, as if they too were falling apart.

'It must be at the end,' said Verlinden. 'Hurry. The answer must be at the end.'

Atreu turned towards the back of both Books. Finally the word *Verlinden* jumped out at him. 'I think I almost have it.'

He stared at the page and took short sharp breaths as he tried to exert his will onto the words. *You are mine.* He drew on everything he had learned and everything he had experienced since starting his Ascent. *You are mine. You will do as I want.*

For a moment the page turned as black as night and a riot of brightly coloured threads danced across the canvas. Amber and crimson. Jade and azure. He knew he could control them. It had always been about his will.

And gradually the threads turned into words, or the words turned into threads – he wasn't sure which. He felt himself being drawn into the page, and he read ...

And gradually the threads turned into words, or the words turned into threads – he wasn't sure which. He felt himself being drawn into the page and he ...

Then a chasm opened up under him and he felt himself slide into the Mountain, clutching the two Books as he descended. The red sand of Vygird enveloped him, pressing at his eyelids and threatening to fill his nose and throat. Down he slid, the noise of the tumult on the surface replaced with the all-encompassing sound of sand rushing past his ears.

Finally, the descent slowed and he felt himself come to a halt. He reached out and pushed sand away from his face, desperately hoping that he was digging in the right direction. He could feel his mind clouding as he made a desperate lunge to find air. *It can't end like this.* His fingers instinctively probed forward, until ... he shrank back at a pair of lidless eyes set deep in an angular face, staring at him.

'I ... mean you no harm,' said Atreu, raising his hand slowly.

The Nazir called out to someone behind it using a strange mixture of guttural and rhythmic sounds. Atreu was suddenly aware that he was in a large cavern filled with Dusk People. A Nazir paler than the others and wearing long, dark robes approached Atreu, and spoke a few words to him.

'I'm sorry,' said Atreu, his attention drawn by the shattered sun symbol he wore on his left shoulder, which seemed to ripple before his eyes. 'I don't understand.'

The pale Nazir repeated what he had said, and Atreu realised that the words, though infused with a strange rhythm and intonation, were familiar to him: 'You are fortunate to be alive.'

'There is not much point to being alive,' said Atreu, 'when the Mountain is dying.'

'What do you know of the Mountain?'

Atreu sensed they were each becoming attuned to the other's intonation. 'My name is Atreu. I have made an Ascent from the Base to the Summit. I have seen it slowly being destroyed,' he said.

'Slowly? How slowly? We have seen it dying over countless years.'

Atreu struggled to a sitting position. 'I know your people were here first. I know that we took the Mountain from you.'

'Who are you to know these things?' said the Nazir. 'Are you a Nevronim?'

'I don't know what a Nevronim is.'

The Nazir hesitated for a moment. 'Are you ... one who is higher than others.'

'A leader? You mean a leader of an army?'

The Nazir rotated his shoulders, which Atreu guessed meant he was thinking. 'Now you use a word *I* don't know. What is an army?'

Atreu leant back and chewed his bottom lip. 'When two peoples fight, the opposing sides are called armies.'

The Nazir's shoulders rotated again. 'I think I am starting to understand some things. Tell me, are you ... a leader of the ... the mind?'

'A Holy Man? No, I am not yet a Holy Man. I am Atreu, an Ascender who has chosen a different path. But I know our ancestors banished your ancestors from the Mountain.'

'You know this? Have you seen this?'

Atreu frowned. 'No, I haven't seen what happened. How could I have seen it? It happened so long ago.'

'You have no Telling.'

'Telling? I'm sorry, I don't understand.'

'No, you don't understand.'

Atreu glanced around at the giant, glimmerstone-lit cavern. Several injured Nazir were being attended to on the other side. His eyes locked on the prostrate form of Verlinden to his right.

He went to get up, but felt suddenly very dizzy. 'Is she alive?' he asked, pointing to her.

'Alive?'

'Is she breathing?'

'Yes, she is taking in breaths.'

'Then she's still alive.'

The Nazir started rotating his shoulders again. 'You use the word differently.'

'How is it you speak our language at all?'

'You know far less than you think of our past.'

'We took the Mountain from you. The Mountain was your world and we took it from you and made it ours.'

'But the Mountain was more than our physical world, it was our ... spirit, our heart. Your people took everything – our spirit, our heart, our language. I speak your language because you banished our own. You stole the words we created and you tried to destroy our memories of them.'

Atreu shook his head. 'We took your language away from you? How can this be?'

'Slowly, over the centuries, we have tried to get it back. Word by word we have added it to our Telling.'

'What is this Telling you speak of?'

The Nazir's mouth became a thin slit. Was this a grim smile? Or a frown? Or a grimace of pain?

'The Telling is our spirit. The Telling is our heart. The Telling is the Mountain. The Telling is the sun. The Na'zir are the Telling.'

'And the Telling is words?'

'Yes, the Telling is words – and your people took our words away from us.'

'I am sorry.'

'Are you?' A glint appeared in the Nazir's eyes.

'I know it may mean nothing coming from someone who is not a Maelir leader, but yes, I am truly sorry.'

'You are higher than others. I can sense it.'

'And you ... are you higher than others?'

'I am the Ur of the Na'zir.'

'The Ur?'

'The beginning, the origin.'

'Maelur led our people to the Mountain centuries ago. Are you to your people what he was to ours?'

The Ur's shoulders moved again. 'In our Telling, Mael'ur is Mael the Destroyer. He tried to take our beginning from us by taking the word for beginning, but gradually we have claimed it back.'

'I am sorry for what my people did to yours, but it was long ago. I am sorry for what Maelur did, but I live *now* – none of us alive now had any part in it.'

'What is long ago is *now* for us.'

'How can that be?'

'I cannot explain it in your language. We have barely regained the words in our own language to understand it ourselves.' He fell silent for a moment. 'I am the Ur. I ... I was born with a name which is part of my own spirit, but I am also the beginning. All Na'zir carry part of that beginning with their spirit, but I am its essence.'

'I have told you the name I was born with,' said Atreu. 'What was yours?'

'Lhycan.'

Atreu looked past Lhycan as he noticed a limp, blood-stained form being hoisted onto the sharp-edged shoulders of several Nazir.

'I tried to stop it happening,' said Atreu. 'They did not know what they were doing.'

'Your people have never known.'

'But you've killed so many of us. My people were only fighting back. Can you blame us for one death in return?'

'I don't understand.'

'Our peoples didn't understand each other from the beginning, did they? That's why it has come to this. The Mountain is tearing itself apart up there. Is it too late, Lhycan?'

'I don't know – her spirit echo may still linger, and sometimes a Teller can find a lost spirit and call it back into a body if death has not long overtaken it.'

'*Her* spirit echo? She is a ... a woman?'

'Why does that surprise you? It makes no difference, does it?'

'No, no of course not.' Atreu looked at the dark bloodstains that dotted her limp body. 'What is her name?'

'I will give you that word, Atreu, because you have so readily offered yours. Her name is Tashil. She is my mother.'

Atreu swallowed into a dry throat. 'Where are they taking her?'

'To a Telling. We will do what we can to find her spirit.'

'I may be able to help,' said Atreu. 'I ... I was holding two books when I fell into the chasm.'

'We have them.'

'You do? One of them is my – I don't know if you will understand the word – it is my Talisman.'

Lhycan's mouth lengthened into a thin slit. 'Your people took that word from us. I believe my understanding of that word is better than yours.'

'So you know how powerful my Book is?'

'*Your* Book?'

'I was given it after my ninth Zenith. Our Holy Orders give all twins a Talisman, which they carry with them on their Ascent –'

'Please,' Lhycan interrupted Atreu. 'You do not have to tell me all this. It was all ours before your people stole it from us.'

Atreu frowned. 'I have spent so long trying to find the truth, and I feel now I have been learning nothing.'

'The Maelir have always played around the edges. They stole our spirit and tried to make it theirs, but a stolen spirit can never have a heart.' Lhycan opened his robes to reveal that he was holding both Atreu's Book and the Book of Maelur. 'I have the Creator and the Destroyer here. Come with me. I sense that perhaps your presence will help us call the spirit back. You have been with the Creator a long time.' His mouth thinned again. 'At least you will see the truth – even if you die with it.'

Chapter Twenty-seven

Atreu got unsteadily to his feet and walked with Lhycan as they followed the procession of Nazir, with Tashil being carried at the head. The brilliantly coloured glimmerstone walls started shaking as they made their way through a wide passage, and one by one the lights in the stones winked out.

'We don't have much time, do we?' said Atreu.

'No, the Mountain's spirit is leaving and the Mountain is dying.'

Atreu looked at Tashil's body. 'One death makes so much difference – how can that be?'

'No Na'zir may deliberately kill. No Na'zir may deliberately be killed. This was the only way the Mountain would return to us. We had to remain true to our spirit. Any other way, and the spirit is lost and the Mountain dies.'

'But you have killed countless Maelir and Faemir.'

'You have killed yourselves. All that the Na'zir did was withdraw their protection.'

'What? You were protecting us against the Dusk-spawn – the wraiths, the grale, the Dusk-rats – for all those generations?'

Lhycan didn't reply.

'How could you be protecting us? Why would you protect us if we stole the Mountain from you?'

The procession of Nazir walked through a natural archway in the rock, but Lhycan held out his hand to stop Atreu before they entered the cavern. 'Atreu, your people have no spirit. They came to the Mountain a thousand generations ago searching for it, they have spent the endless years since trying to find it, but still they are empty shells. They stole our Holy Places and tried to make them their own. They built a giant city on the place you call the Keep, but beautiful spires do not give you spirit. They delve into their own minds with practiced arts at the place you call the Source, but playing games with your thoughts does not give you spirit.'

'So nothing is ours? We have created nothing?'

'It was all ours. The Ascent. The Talismans. Have you not wondered where the Talismans come from, where they gain their power?'

'I ... I thought the Holy Orders created them.'

'They were all ours, created by our Tellers, and the Maelir stole them from us.'

'So my Book ... the Book you are holding was never mine?' Atreu started to tremble. *Don't be a fool*, he thought to himself, *this is not a time for selfish tears.* He looked up to see Lhycan's lidless eyes staring at him intently.

'I sense something in you, Atreu. Yours is not the heart of a thief. Perhaps there are still things that I too must learn.'

Atreu became aware that the glimmerstones that studded the stone walls were now dying with increasing frequency.

'Eclipse is almost upon us,' said Lhycan. 'It is what many of us feared it would become.'

'I don't understand – I thought darkness is what your people wanted.'

Lhycan's shoulders moved from side to side. 'I see,' he said finally. 'You believe it was our doing. The sun dying.'

'Yes, wasn't it?'

'You truly do not understand. The power behind it was ours, but it was your theft that corrupted everything. When a spirit is harmed or stolen, it begins to feed upon itself and distorts into the opposite of what it once was. It is no longer whole, and spirit shards break away, losing their way in an eternal search for their origin. Since we were banished from the Mountain, these shards have sought places for their distortion to dwell.'

'Like in the ill-wind along the helles?'

'Yes.'

'And the Dusk-wraiths were the same. They were the stolen spirit shards returning to haunt us.'

'The wraiths were fed as our spirit grew through our Telling. We were feeding them, but not in the way you think. The spirit shards were twisted by the actions of your people. We were only striving to regain what we had lost. We had no control over the wraiths. We had no desire for eternal darkness.'

'But you are Dusk People – you cannot live in daylight.'

'We do not call ourselves Dusk People. That is one of your names for us. We are not creatures of the Steppes like the grale and the Dusk-rats. You have turned us into people of the Dusk.'

'But your eyes – how can you shield yourself from the rays of the sun?'

'Look at mine closely,' said Lhycan, leaning forward. 'All Na'zir have their eyelids removed at birth. That is the only way we can live in a world without sun.'

Atreu couldn't meet Lhycan's gaze. 'I'm sorry,' he said.

'Do you know,' said Lhycan, 'that one of the words your people took from us was our name for our own people. We had no choice but to call ourselves the Na'zir, the non-People.'

Atreu watched another glimmerstone wink out in front of him. 'There is so much more I want to ask you.'

'With our Ur-book, the Creator, returned to us, the Tellings will be strong. Who knows, there may still be a chance. Come, let us try.'

Lhycan led Atreu through the archway in front of them.

They stepped into a small cavern with three roughly hewn alcoves. In each alcove sat what looked like a Nazir Holy Man wearing dark robes and clasps similar to Lhycan's. In front of them lay the body of Tashil, and sitting silently in concentric semi-circles in front of her were the Nazir who had formed the procession.

'These are the Three Tellers,' said Lhycan. 'Our supreme Nevronim, Gyalsten, Gyalwa and Gedhun.' He turned to face the first Teller. 'Gyalsten, a spirit is lost and must be found.'

Atreu stared at the Nevronim in confusion for a while until he somehow tuned in to the sounds the first Teller was making. With a gasp, he realised that he could see them emerging from his thin lips as if they were written words.

As Atreu watched, the words wafted like leaves in a breeze, turning, twisting until they seemed to fold in on themselves. And as they folded, they transformed from words into a hazy image. A figure began to take shape, slowly solidifying into reality. Atreu narrowed his eyes when he realised it was a Maelir. The face ... it was so familiar. He shuddered – for a brief moment he thought he was looking at his reflection in the clear waters of a lake.

Then he realised it was Teyth.

'Little brother, we finally see each other again.'

Atreu felt a chill through every sinew. 'Teyth – it can't be you.'

'It *is* me.'

As Teyth started to walk through the Nazir seated on the cavern floor, Atreu noticed a dark shadow following just behind him, mimicking his movements, but not quite matching them perfectly.

'You are not my brother,' said Atreu. 'You are some apparition come to torture me.'

Teyth now stood immediately in front of him. 'It is me, Atreu. I am real.'

'I ... I can't believe it.'

'Prove it to yourself, little brother.' Teyth took another step towards him and they embraced. Atreu could feel the warmth of his brother's body. They clasped hands and raised them high in the Lower Reacher manner.

'How can you be alive?' asked Atreu.

'I said it was me, little brother. I didn't say I was alive.'

Atreu felt the cold sting of shadow on his hands and he pulled away. He looked at Lhycan. 'What is this Telling? Is Teyth here or not?'

'The Telling is always real, Atreu. Your brother is here with us.'

'So you didn't kill Teyth. Of course, Nazir don't kill. You couldn't have killed him.' Atreu glanced back at Teyth in confusion.

'The Nazir don't kill,' said Teyth, 'but the grale and Dusk-rats do. We didn't have a chance.'

'We?' asked Atreu. 'I know what that shadow is.'

As he watched, the darkness behind Teyth took on a life of its own. It stepped out as if from behind a screen of a shadow play, and Atreu saw who it was.

'Valkyra!' he said. 'So you torment my brother even now.'

'We have been one from the beginning,' said Valkyra. 'A bare-sark has no race.'

'Leave him now,' said Atreu. 'Give him peace.'

'It was not Valkyra's fault,' said Teyth. 'We were tied by a link which was too strong.'

'What happened to you, Teyth? You became something that was alien to me. The paths of our Ascents diverged, and you became … like her.'

'Forgive me,' said Valkyra.

'Forgive you?' said Atreu. 'Forgive you for slaughtering countless Maelir, for brutally butchering every Ascender bar me?'

'No,' she said hoarsely. 'Forgive me for taking your brother from you.'

Atreu turned away as he felt tears trickle down his face. By the time he had turned back, Teyth and Valkyra were gone.

He looked at Lhycan. 'The baresark rage,' he said, 'it, too, was the spirit we distorted coming back to consume us, wasn't it?'

'Yes,' said Lhycan. 'The distortion always finds a form.'

'Neither of them could help what they became. They had no control.'

'You speak as if the past and the now have no connection.'

'It was our ancestors' fault. Teyth and Valkyra – they as individuals had no control over it. The distorted spirit ... it had a hold of them in some way ...' Atreu's voice trailed off into silence.

'I don't think I have ever understood the Maelir word *individual*.'

Atreu shook his head. 'It doesn't matter ... I just wish they stayed long enough for me to tell them both that I forgive them.'

'They knew you had,' said Lhycan.

'How?'

'The words were in the air. They could see them.'

Atreu looked down at the body of Tashil. 'The wrong spirit returned, didn't it?'

'Yes,' said Lhycan. 'There are things happening here that I don't understand.' He looked around at the other Nazir who were seated, trance-like, oblivious to what was happening.

'You said we had no spirit,' said Atreu, 'yet a Maelir and Faemir returned. How can that be?'

Lhycan's shoulders dipped. 'They ... must have some of our spirit within them ... I don't know ... my understanding, like yours, is incomplete.' He looked down at where his mother lay, and then turned to face the second Teller. 'Gyalwa, a spirit is lost and must be found.'

Atreu was suddenly aware of a deep sound emanating from the second Teller. He looked around the cavern and saw the glimmerstones fading. Under his feet, the ground seemed to tremble with fear. *Please, this time find Tashil.*

Words began tumbling from Gyalwa's lips like a river torrent. Out they came, looping in waves towards the cavern floor and then shooting spray back up into the air. The words took shape and the stooped figure of an old man was suddenly walking towards Atreu, followed by several shadows not quite moving with the same rhythm.

'Praether,' said Atreu. 'You have returned to see my failure.'

'No, Atreu, we have returned for your apotheosis.'

'Apotheosis? I failed in the quest you foresaw. The Book of Metheus was so close, but I passed it by.'

'It is your quest which counts, Atreu, not ours.'

'What is my quest, Praether?'

'We don't have the answer to that question – only you do.'

Lhycan stepped forward. 'Who are you?'

'Ah, you finally acknowledge us, Ur.'

'I sense ... something strange from you.' Lhycan repeated his question, his lidless eyes reflecting the dying glimmerstones. 'Who are you?'

The old man smiled. 'We are the Reader.'

With that, the ancient figure of Metheus stepped out from the shadow. Then another emerged, who Atreu didn't recognise. The shadow still pulsed behind Praether, as if more threatened to come forth.

'I don't understand,' said Lhycan.

'You have flown close to the truth,' said Metheus, 'but you have failed to see what has been before you.'

'I am the Ur.'

'You believe the Maelir have no spirit, nothing that is eternal,' said the third Maelir. 'You claim that all we ever attained was through theft of yours. You are wrong. The Reader is the Maelir spirit. All the words we have written and read since we first stepped onto the Mountain. That is something we have created that was not taken from you. It is something we can now give you, freely, in return for what we have done to the Aevronim.'

'The Aevronim?'

'Yes, that is the true name of your people. The Aevronim – the people of the Sun.'

Lhycan's lidless eyes seemed to widen. He staggered, reaching out to Atreu to keep his balance. 'You have returned our name to us.'

'Return to the sunlight. The heart cries out and needs to be mended.'

Lhycan ran his fingers along one of the Books he was carrying. 'I know who you are,' he said. 'You are Mael the Destroyer.'

'I was,' he said. 'But I have changed. I am now Mael the Creator.'

'No,' said Lhycan, brandishing the Book of Maelur at the three old men in front of him. 'This cannot be. You cannot change. You cannot give back what you have destroyed.' He pointed at Tashil with the Book. 'Look. We call for her lost spirit, but she has not returned, and you stand here in her place, mocking us. You have now stolen even our Telling from us.'

'You can return your people to the sun,' said Maelur.

Lhycan's lips thinned. 'You try to deceive the Ur as you once did, Destroyer.' He flung the Book of Maelur at him, and the image of the three old Maelir wavered and then disintegrated into a confused flurry of words.

Lhycan walked towards his mother and bent over her, weeping. The entire rock face was now shaking violently around them, and glimmerstones fell from the cavern ceiling.

His voice took on the pitch of a small boy. 'Mother, I am so sorry. You were right – no good came of it.'

'There is one Teller left,' said Atreu. 'Surely there is still some hope.'

Lhycan looked up to stare directly at Atreu. 'The Telling is now yours, along with everything else. Here, take this.' He threw Atreu's Book back at him. 'You say this is yours. You are right. The Na'zir are nothing. The Na'zir have nothing.'

As glimmerstones started raining from the cavern ceiling, Atreu ran his fingers along the letter A embossed in the thick leather of the cover. 'I used to believe this letter stood for my name,' he said. 'We now know it stands for your people's true name.' Slowly, he began to walk towards the third Teller. Kneeling down in front of him, he said, 'Gedhun, an Aevronim spirit is lost and must be found.'

Gedhun was silent in response.

Atreu glanced around, alarmed. The remaining glimmerstones were rapidly extinguishing.

'Gedhun, an Aevronim spirit is lost and must be found.' The words strained at the edges this time.

Lhycan remained bent over Tashil.

'Help me,' said Atreu.

Just as Lhycan stirred, the last glimmerstone died and the cavern was plunged into darkness. Atreu lost all sense of orientation.

'Lhycan, where are you?'

'Don't open your eyes.'

'What ... what are you saying?'

'You promised you wouldn't look.'

'Teyth? Is that you?'

'I think I know.'

'What? Lhycan? Teyth?'

'You have to answer now.'

'What's happening ...'

Atreu was aware of a deep sonorous voice coming from somewhere. Then out of the blackness came a series of bright threads, twisting and dancing above him. He reached up to his eyelids, to be sure that his eyes were open. As the threads twirled, they grew and multiplied, emanating a soft light. He could see now that they were words of every imaginable hue, twining before him.

'Can you see them, Lhycan?' he called, and then gasped when he realised his own words had emerged as threads from his lips.

'Yes, Atreu, I can see them.' Lhycan's words also appeared as threads and began twining with all the others.

Then the threads took shape, weaving a bright figure before them that lit the cavern. Atreu was suddenly breathless. *It can't be,* he thought. *No, it can't be.*

'Father,' he said softly. 'So, you are a spirit? I have lost you too?'

Tyr looked at Atreu sadly, and the lines creasing his face turned down. 'I am sorry, Atreu.'

'Is everything lost?'

'You have failed in your Ascent because I failed in mine.'

'No, Father, you didn't fail.'

Atreu looked around at Lhycan, who had spoken the words. A chill shot through him. 'Are you stealing my words from me?'

Lhycan opened his mouth in confusion. 'No ... I don't know why I said ... I ...'

'I have failed both of you,' said Tyr.

Atreu's head spun. 'This is not Teyth here with us,' he said. 'Teyth is dead.'

'Then I have two sons still alive.'

Atreu felt the weight of the Mountain overwhelm him, and he staggered, collapsing to the ground. 'What are you saying, Father? Have I finally lost my mind?'

'No, Atreu. Lhycan is your brother. Look at the lightness of his skin. Look at his face.'

'How ...'

'Did you never wonder how I of all Maelir knew the Nazir were still a threat? No records of them remained anywhere on the Mountain, yet I knew.'

'I ... I ...'

'My Ascent gave me a truth that the Holy Orders didn't want to face,' said Tyr. 'I knew the Nazir had been tunnelling through the Mountain for generations. I knew they sought to return through Eclipse. After my truth was dismissed by the Circle, I travelled to the Steppes to prove to myself that I was right. I sought the truth, and found love.'

Atreu stared at Lhycan, whose lidless eyes bore back at him. 'You called him my brother – if there is any sense in what you say, you must mean half-brother.'

'I chose the correct word, Atreu.'

'You mean ... my mother was a Nazir?'

'Yes, Atreu. Her name is Tashil. She is lying in front of you.'

Atreu looked at the limp figure on the cavern floor, the dried blood of her wounds now a dull red, and tears poured down his face.

'How can this be?' he cried. 'How could she, of the countless Aevronim, be the one to be captured by Wothan?'

'She was looking for what I took away from her, Atreu. After all these years, she was still looking for her two lost sons. The only Aevronim that would ever wander the surface of the Mountain alone would be a mother looking for her children.'

Lhycan held out his arms to Tyr. 'Father, stay, please. Just a small while. I need to know you.'

'No, Lhycan, you know I can't. I am sorry I could not be a father to you. When Atreu and Teyth were born, and I saw their pure Maelir features, I knew I would have to leave you and Tashil, and return to the Mountain.'

'You chose them over me?'

'No, Lhycan. It was the only way we could all survive. I have failed in many things in my life, but in that decision I had no choice.'

Atreu wiped the tears from his eyes as Tyr's image started to darken. 'Wait, Father, your Book. I need the third Book to save the Mountain. The answers are there. You must give it to me.'

Tyr smiled and familiar creases danced around his eyes. 'I gave you my Book long ago,' he said.

For a moment Atreu was lost in a cloud of confusion, and then it was as if a shaft of light illuminated his understanding, and he grabbed hold of it. 'My Book was your Book.'

'Yes, Atreu. I gave you my Talisman for your Ascent. That is what has guided you. With each step, you have added to the understanding I had reached. You have the three Books. You have the three Books.'

Tyr's image continued to darken until it became a shadow surrounded by a band of bright illumination.

Atreu looked at Lhycan. 'Did you know?' he asked.

'I thought my father had died long ago. Mother never spoke of him.'

Atreu could see tears filling Lhycan's lidless eyes. 'We have lost our father,' he said, 'but there is still hope for our mother.'

'The Telling is all but exhausted,' said Lhycan. 'There are no words left.'

Find the one who is two.

Was that Belzalel? Was he still making the shadows come to life?

Find the one who is two.

Why are you still telling me this? I found Verlinden. I found the one who is . . .

A thought as clear as sunlight struck Atreu. 'Lhycan, there are still some words left. Can you hear them? *Find the one who is two.*'

'Yes, I can hear them.'

'It's *you*, Lhycan. You are half Aevronim and half Maelir. You are the one who is two and I've found you.'

Lhycan stared at him for a moment before speaking. 'There are many truths here. You are also half Aevronim and half Maelir. You too have found yourself.'

Atreu nodded slowly. 'And I believe there is yet another truth. Pick up the Book of Maelur. Quickly, before the light around Father's shadow disappears.'

'I don't want to touch that foul book again.'

'Quickly, Lhycan, pick it up and turn to the first page.'

Lhycan walked over to where he had flung the book and his lips thinned. As he opened it, Atreu opened his Talisman.

'Read what it says, Lhycan.'

Lhycan began reading, his voice becoming increasingly strained as he spoke the words: 'When the Mountain becomes the Abyss, and what you breathe becomes what you expel, you will find what is hidden. When the sun becomes night, and you become what you believe, you will find your heart. When the Reader becomes the Teller, and the searcher is the one found, you will find the truth.' He looked up at Atreu. 'Where are the words that speak of the one that perishes at the other's hands, of dying the three deaths? These are not the Destroyer's words.'

'No,' said Atreu. 'They have changed. And look.' He held his Book up for Lhycan to read.

Lhycan stood deathly still as he looked at the page. 'The words are identical,' he said.

'Yes – the Books have merged. They tell the same story. Now there is only one Book.'

'I understand, brother, I understand.'

Atreu and Lhycan embraced for a long time. When the brothers pulled away, to their surprise, they could see the glimmer-stones awakening, one by one.

They watched the shadow that was once their father slowly floating towards Tashil until it merged with her body and disappeared. With a gasp, they realised their mother was stirring.

Epilogue

'It's happening, isn't it?' asked Atreu.

Verlinden squeezed his hand more tightly. 'Hold on.'

A rushing sound raced around their ears as they pushed out.

'Don't let go,' said Verlinden, her voice straining at the edges.

Suddenly the release came and they were free of the pages. As they flew upwards, Atreu shot one final glance at the Book from which they had just emerged ...

*

'Don't open your eyes. You promised you wouldn't look.'

Atreu heard a squawk as he held the palms of his hands tightly against his eyelids.

'Keep them shut,' said Verlinden. 'Wait – just give me a moment ... all right, Atreu ... now.'

Atreu pulled his hands away and opened his eyes. Before him stood Verlinden, holding a swaddled newborn baby in each arm.

'They are beautiful,' he said.

Verlinden laughed. 'You probably can't even tell which one is the boy and which one is the girl.'

Atreu frowned, looking from one to the other. 'That's Teyth,' he said finally, 'and that one's Valkyra.'

'Wrong,' said Verlinden, smiling. 'Here, you carry Valkyra – let's take them to watch the sunrise.'

Atreu and Verlinden walked slowly through Valesend, each carrying a twin. The squat houses that had always seemed to grow out of the ground had fared better than the buildings in many other towns and villages in the Lower Reaches. The air was still and clear, and the stars on the edge of the Mountain were already fading in anticipation of the lightening sky. Soon, the Valesenders who had survived and returned would be rising, and another day of rebuilding would begin.

Despite the early promise of summer, a chill remained in the air as Atreu and Verlinden made their way to the glass-like waters of the lake and sat down on the sandy ground.

'You know,' said Verlinden. 'I had the strangest sensation just as these two were born.'

'Was it to do with the Book?'

'Yes,' said Verlinden. 'I saw the two of us breaking through the pages from within it and flying out into something beyond.'

'I had the same sensation, Verlinden.'

'What does it mean?'

'I don't know, Verlinden. I am content just now to sit here. Is it possible to know all the answers?'

Verlinden leant back into him. 'Will we show these two the Book when they are old enough?'

Atreu laughed. 'There may be some parts we don't want them to read.'

As he wrapped his free arm around her, the first rays of the sun filtered across the Mountain's edge.

Dear Reader

Thank you for reading *Eclipse* and joining me on the journey with Atreu, Verlinden and the others. I don't know about you, but I was sorry to say good-bye to them at the end. A special thanks to those of you who take the time to review my books for other readers. Whether you've written a review or not, if you enjoyed the Books of Ascension, *Zenith*, *Equinox* and *Eclipse*, I'd love to hear from you. I reply to everyone who drops in and leaves a comment. I like hear from readers, so please do. The easiest way to leave a comment or question is through the Contact Dirk form on my website (www.dirkstrasser.com/contact-dirk.html).

Looking forward to hearing from you.

Dirk Strasser

Stories of the Sand

Dirk Strasser

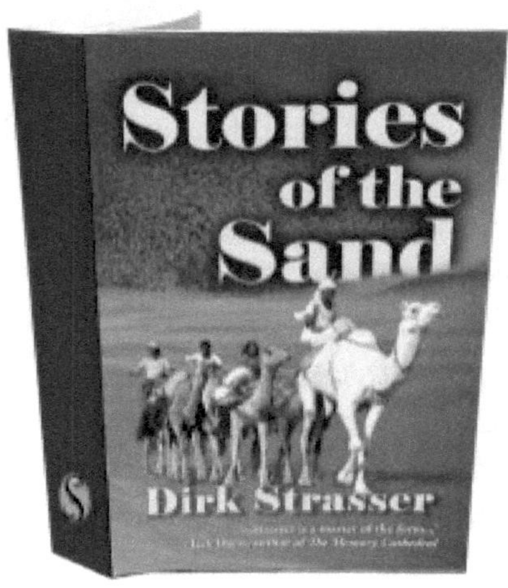

Watch as the sands take shape...

A desert wind whispers of memory and regret
An army marches high in the golden skies
A traveller grows tired of seeing the end of the world
A man no longer wants to be human
A people run eternally from the rising sun

'Dirk Strasser is a master practitioner of... the short story. This complex and intelligent collection... leaves an indelible after-image in the mind's eye.'
    –Isobelle Carmody, author of *The Obernewtyn Chronicles*

About Dirk Strasser

Dirk Strasser has won multiple Australian Publisher Association Awards and a Ditmar for Best Professional Achievement. His short story, 'The Doppelgänger Effect', appeared in the World Fantasy Award-winning anthology, *Dreaming Down Under*. His short fiction has been translated into a number of languages, and his acclaimed fantasy trilogy, The Books of Ascension – *Zenith*, *Equinox* and *Eclipse* – has also been published in German. His fantasy and science fiction short stories have been collected in *Stories of the Sand*. He founded the Aurealis Awards and has co-published and co-edited *Aurealis* magazine for over 25 years.

www.dirkstrasser.com

Twitter: @DirkStrasser

Join the conversation about The Books of Ascension with #booksofascension

Glossary

Aevronim – the people of the sun, the true name of the Nazir

Ascenders – those twins who, in their eighteenth year, make the Ascent to the Summit of the Mountain in order to gain entry into one of the Holy Orders

Ascent – the Ritual, formalised by the Holy Orders, of making the journey to the Summit of the Mountain for Zenith

Coveyn – a band of Faemir warriors

Crosanct – the monastery located at one of the few gaps in the continuous wall of cliffs that separate the Mid-Reaches from the Upper Reaches

Dusk People (Nazir) – the people who long ago had been banished from the Mountain by the Maelir to live on the Steppes, forever in the Mountain's shadow

Dusk-rat – a small, dangerous, light-sensitive rodent of the Steppes

Dusk-wraiths – insubstantial but deadly light-sensitive creatures released by the Nazir to gain final control of the Mountain

Eclipse – the phenomenon that occurs when after the winter solstice the nights keep getting longer until daylight disappears altogether

Equinox – the time of year when day and night are in perfect balance and when Ascenders are judged

Faelen – an insulting term used by Faemir to describe women who live with the Maelir

Faemir – the race of women who seek to destroy Maelir culture and civilisation

Felsen – the Holy Order of the Rock, characterised by austerity and powers of meditation

Grale – ferocious, light-sensitive beasts from the Steppes

Liche – the Holy Order of the Light, characterised by their use of astute arguments and clever word play

Lower Reacher – a Maelir from the Lower Reaches

Lower Reaches – the lower, sparsely populated region of the Mountain bordering on the Steppes

Maelir – the race of males who control and dominate all aspects of life on the Mountain

Maelstrom – the giant river which flows down the Mountain

Maelur – the leader who brought the Maelir to the Mountain and made the first Ascent

Mid-Reacher – a Maelir from the Mid-Reaches

Mid-Reaches – the densely populated middle region of the Mountain, separated from the Lower Reaches by the Rimforest

Nazir – the Dusk People

Nevronim – The Holy Order of the Nazir

Order of the Light – the Liche Holy Order

Order of the Rock – the Felsen Holy Order

Order of the Wynde – the Holy Order of the windriders

R'angkur – a meditative technique taught by the Felsen at Cro-sanct which allows people to spontaneously generate body heat and withstand extreme cold

Rimforest – the ring of forest which encircles the Mountain, sep-arating the Lower Reaches from the Mid-Reaches

Rituals – practices and techniques used by the Holy Orders as part of the Ascent

R'lung – the herb used by Liche Holy Men to enable them to travel long distances without rest

Sage – the title given to the Holy Man appointed to oversee an Ascent

Steppes – the flat region at the base of the Mountain which always lies in its shadow

Source – the holy lake which is the source of the Maelstrom and the destination of the pilgrimage that all successful Ascenders must make

Talisman – the object given to an Ascender by his sage which will determine the nature of his Ascent

Tellers – The three supreme Nevronim of the Nazir who choose the Ur and create the Talismans

Upper Reaches – the frozen upper region of the Mountain sepa-rated from the Mid-Reaches by a ring of cliffs

Ur – The title given to the spiritual leader of the Nazir chosen as a boy by the Tellers

Watcher – a Faemir whose task is to secretly observe Maelir in order to gain advantage in future battles

Windriders – the former Ascenders who ride the winds of the Upper Reaches with constructed wings and whose function is to aid and protect the Holy Orders

Zenith – the phenomenon which occurs during nine days in mid-summer where the sun passes directly over the highest point of the Mountain, the ultimate mystic power of which is experienced by twins at the Summit

www.ingramcontent.com/pod-product-compliance
Lightning Source LLC
Chambersburg PA
CBHW050948210726
48287CB00004B/1185